Go Away Zone

The Sunrise Trilogy book 2

Chris Towndrow

Valericain Press

Praise for Tow Away Zone (Sunrise Trilogy book 1)

"A gripping yarn - quirky characters, a pacy plot and a setting like you've never read before. A fun ol' read."
Paul Kerensa, Comedian & British Comedy Award-winning TV co-writer BBC's Miranda, Not Going Out, Top Gear

"Very enjoyable and easy to read with an unusual plot that keeps you guessing throughout. Highly recommended." ★★★★★
Amazon review

"This is a brilliant story. Clever, laugh-out-loud funny, and mysterious all at the same time. Heartily recommended." ★★★★★
Amazon review

"Really good fun to read with more than a touch of darkness, so much neon, a very odd pet and the best breakdown service on the planet. Very enjoyable and highly recommended!" ★★★★★
Amazon review

"An original, inventive storyline and a variety of three-dimensional characters that you will genuinely care about. Dialogue sharp enough to shave with, well-paced and bubbling with humour." ★★★★★
Amazon review

"In a surprising town a salesman finds everything he ever wanted. This is such an incredibly interesting story. I couldn't put it down. And I could never decide if the town was real or not. But the characters could have lived next door!" ★★★★★
Amazon review

"This is one of those books that will leave you with a smile on your face. Funny, relatable perfect characters, a story that kept me turning the pages and an ending that did not disappoint. This is a great book to take on holiday because it is light-hearted and fun." ★★★★★
Amazon review

"I struggle to compare this book with others. The words 'unique' and 'inventive' come to mind. The dialogue is well-crafted and funny, the characters are wonderfully individual, and the narrative is a kaleidoscope of colourful drama.
This book will stick with you." ★★★★★
Maddie – Professional editor

Valericain
Press

Valericain Press
Richmond, UK
www.christowndrow.co.uk

Go Away Zone / Chris Towndrow. -- 2021 ed.
978-1-9168916-2-3

If you read the first book, this is for you with gratitude.

If you haven't read the first book, you should.
It's awesome.

Chapter 1

'I thought it would have been shinier.'

'What?' Lolita raised a single eyebrow in the way that, weeks ago, Beckman felt only she could, before remembering all women had some form of "Really, dufus?" disguised as something less overtly condescending/challenging/disbelieving*. (* delete as applicable).

He pressed on regardless. 'I thought it would have been, you know, shinier. More metallic.'

'Is that really what you think?' An eyebrow remained buried in the tone.

'What do you want me to say?' (A good standby phrase, given no man on Earth ever fully knew what any woman was thinking, even one he might be betrothed to.)

'You could accuse me of joking. Teasing. Lying.'

'I may not know all your foibles, but it doesn't strike me as a joke, and it can't be a lie.'

'Why can't it be a lie?'

'Because we met after you called *me* dishonest.'

'I said you were *likely* to be.'

'Either way, you'd be a heel to lie to me. Plus, if we're getting married, we need a bedrock of honesty.'

'If you'd ever let me plan the date.' She rolled her eyes.

'Sure, hijack a discovery like this,' he waved a hand towards the space five yards in front of them, 'To kick my ass about your hot topic.'

'When a girl hears wedding bells, there *is* no other topic more important.'

'You might have warned me.'

'For a guy who's seen half the country and met like a million people, you don't know a hell of a lot.'

'Enough with the flattery.' He flashed a grin.

She poked her tongue out.

This was not an unfamiliar coda to their exchanges—and he loved her more for it. It kept him young and vibrant—although he'd hardly felt young and vibrant during the past decade. He'd been on a trundling treadmill until she'd veritably jabbed the Stop button and sent him careering backwards into her arms.

He returned his attention to the lack of a view they'd come to witness.

Only being honest—expected it to be shinier. Grander. Strangely alien.

Blame a guy for having unrealistic expectations based on a misspent youth in front of the TV?

He paced warily, taking extreme care not to get too close to something he couldn't see or touch. Or smell. Or hear. Or taste, even if he got close enough, which he was in no way tempted to do.

Are you tempted? Of course, you are. A tiny part. Come on—curiosity—it's how we're built. It's what drives innovation. An inquisitive mind is a great mind.

Except you're a lightbulb salesman in a small Arizona town. Edison, you are not. He used a brilliant scientific mind. You want to do the equivalent of poking a sleeping lion with a short stick.

Well, part of you does. A tiny, tiny, stupid part.

Plus, you poked a few lions already this year—and look how that turned out.

Kinda well, actually.

We only remember the good stuff—the happy days. Not the dumbass things we did along the way.

You got lucky.

Miss Lolita Milan was eyeing him with interest, love and almost maternal disbelief. The man-boy had a new toy.

Very lucky.

Except the man-boy wasn't sure how this new toy worked. Or what it was. Or where it was.

'How in hell have you all kept this a secret?'

'We don't want to be the new Area 51. I like a man in uniform as much as the next girl—'

'You never met my father,' he warned.

'—but a thousand of them turning the town into a circus is nobody's idea of fun. Come on, Beckman, you know Sunrise—'

'I thought I did.'

'—and we're a keep-ourselves-to-ourselves kinda place. Besides,' she said with a shrug, 'Maybe it's gone now.'

'Gone?! You brought me here to show me something you can't even see when it *is* there, and now say it may not be there anymore. And how would we know? Maybe it is a joke.' His eyes narrowed. 'Is that it, honey? Wanted to laugh at the new guy? Bring him to a dead-end road, spin an apocryphal tale and watch him skulk around like a curious cat, afraid of a mouse which may or may not be dead?'

He tried the single raised eyebrow thing but failed dismally. He always failed dismally, but it didn't stop him from trying—for one fundamental reason.

He was an idiot.

She didn't rise to it. She'd learned not to because (1) she knew he was joking, and (2) she also knew he was an idiot. One she dearly loved.

Instead, she put a hand on his upper arm. 'Beckman, I am deadly, deadly serious. For one, I thought you'd be interested, and for two, I don't want you absentmindedly wandering in there one day and *poof!*'

He gazed at where her eyes were habitually shielded by reaction sunglasses, well-used to the impression of being able to see beyond them, took her hand and held it tenderly.

'A guy knows it must be love when his girl doesn't want him to inexplicably vanish from the face of the Earth.'

'Certainly not while he has her car keys in his pocket.'

'Ah. The truest of true love.'

'And definitely not until he's changed his Will.' She fought a smirk.

'I have virtually nothing to my name, but it's all yours.'

'I believe that is the dictionary definition of marriage.'

'Ah. The hot topic. It's been at least two minutes. I was worried.'

'I'm pleased you're worried about me. I mean, I'm worried about you.'

'Going in there?' He jerked his head towards the thing neither of them could see and which may not be there in any case.

'Of course. Come on, you don't poke a sleeping lion with a short stick, do you?'

Absolutely not. Never crossed my mind.

'What about a long stick?'

She tilted her head down to reveal raised eyebrows over the rim of her glasses. After the Tongue Poke, the Disapproving Schoolmarm was her second favourite weapon. Perhaps it was the man-boy's fault for doing or saying so many things that warranted its use.

She was his own sleeping lioness, and he always had a proverbial short stick in his pocket. In the past weeks, he'd elicited many purrs, some growls, the occasional roar. Twice, he'd been clawed. Yet, he still carried a stick.

Because you're an idiot.

But at least you know you are, so that's all good.

Love will do that.

So, any time in the last romantically barren decade wouldn't have been disastrous to have diced with *poof!*, but right now was Dumb with a capital DUMB.

He kissed her to remind himself of those capitals.

And yet…

He turned to look at the Whatever It Was. She put hands on hips, indulging him, and they gazed towards the point in space where Strange Things Happened. Allegedly. He sought even a flicker of evidence to dispel any remaining notion that this represented one big hoax. Just a sign, a grain of truth. Sunrise's version of The Turin Shroud; something to give bedrock to belief.

After five minutes, the September sun climbing towards its warm zenith, he was turning away when something happened. Only a flicker, six feet above the ground. A pixelation. A glitch in The Matrix. As fast as it came, it went. The view of the scrub desert and distant mountains hazed oh so slightly. As if Whatever It Was winked at them.

Lolita's eyebrow rose in a "Didn't I Say?".

His mouth opened, and he pointed involuntarily.

Day One, when he'd met Saul Paul for the first time, the eye-patched tow-truck driver had quoted Shakespeare, as easily as putting on a hat, but as unexpected as if he'd been a frog uttering the words in Aramaic.

There are more things in heaven and earth, Horatio, than are dreamt of in your philosophy.

But this—the Whatever It Was? If poor Horatio had encountered this, he would have shat pineapples.

Lolita sashayed over.

'I know; "I told you so",' he offered.

'So, can we go? You look like you could use a root beer, and I sure do.'

'We simply get on with our lives?' There was childish disappointment in his voice.

'What else did you expect? *Play* with it?'

'It's just….' He didn't know what it was just, except that it was. It seemed a colossal anti-climax to walk away.

'Beckman. Darling. You're new around here. This is part of the tour, the full disclosure. In Sunrise, we *do* get on with our lives. What's the alternative?'

He opened his mouth to offer some alternatives that would (1) definitely be made up on the spot, (2) probably not be well received, and (3) likely have been ventured and rejected many times before by more qualified—or at least more longstanding—people than he.

He closed his mouth. She kissed it to mollify him, slipped a hand into his and led him back to the car. He glanced over his shoulder. The tarmac single track road petered out into the wilderness as if abandoned mid-construction. It served no purpose, led nowhere. Or nowhere that could be identified, quantified or any number of other -fieds.

'What do you call it?' He tried to sound disinterested.

'The Portal.'

Chapter 2

She piloted the Miata in a zigzagging route through the quiet street blocks.

Late Sunday morning was unseasonably quiet in Our Buck's. They tipped a nod to Buck at the counter-top brewing behemoth and took seats at a large table by the window. It wasn't quite Their Table but was nevertheless something of a custom, and in a friendly town, it had become common knowledge. Beckman, ever the creature of habit, found solace in the predictability. The long days, weeks, months and years of life on the road—which he'd imbued with routine—felt oddly long past, despite recent history, and this familiar café and its regular spot was the closest thing to a comfort blanket.

It wasn't the snuggest thing he liked being wrapped up with, however. That sat opposite, its waterfall of chocolate-coloured curls framing its picturesque vista. It had also just revealed a peculiar mix of the interior of Pandora's Box and the Emperor's New Clothes. Beckman's mind continued to perform a sterling impression of Disneyland's The Great Rocky Mountain Railroad. He wanted the attendant to shut the park or stop the ride long enough to let someone else have a turn.

An attendant did attend them. Buck set two tall glasses of America's Greatest Root Beer (trademark mark applied for, at least in Beckman's head) on the table.

The bear-sized proprietor almost heard the cogs inside his male customer's cranium, so he directed his remarks to the female one. 'He throw a rock at it?'

Lolita shook her head. 'I didn't let him get that far.'

'You wait. He'll go back. They all do. I did.'

'I can't think you'd ever listen to your parents' warnings, Buck. About anything, least of all that.'

'I'm still here, aren't I?'

'Large as life.'

'I'm not going anywhere. Still holding out hope for your big day.'

'I'm still waiting to find out when I get to *have* the big day.' Her right thumb and forefinger noodled with the modest diamond-encrusted ring on her left hand.

'And now you've given him something else to think about. Big mistake.'

'Don't think I don't hear every word.' Beckman licked his lips and set down the glass. 'It was there when you were a kid?'

'Sure,' Buck said.

'You don't reckon they'd put up a wall or a fence or whatever? Even a damn sign?'

'It's like this. If someone wants to get at something so bad, they will, whatever the obstacles. You need to make people *not* want to. The Bogeyman, whatever. Anyone wants to be dumb; that's their lookout.'

'Or brave,' Beckman suggested.

'Or dumb,' she insisted.

'Don't tell me you never threw a rock into it. Or worse,' he asked Buck, a wayward teen seeking precedence from a taller, older ringleader, one who's been around the block a few times, done the dares, owns the cool badge of being spoken to by the cops. Probably seen a real girl naked, maybe even made out with one too.

'Stoat Winterman. He was the one with balls.'

'I never considered you as deficient in the balls department.'

'Footballs.'

'Jeez, amazing, the guy walked straight.'

'No—footballs. He had footballs. And he could kick them too. Hankered after a kicker spot with the under-sixteens.'

'Okay.' Beckman didn't follow the drift and wondered why he never went to school with anyone called Stoat, although he was the Stoat of the class, name-wise anyhow.

'He said any pussy could throw a rock into The Portal. So he kicked a football in there. To show he had balls too, I guess.'

'And because he was also after a certain spot on the lower half of an under-sixteen girl who happened to be in attendance?'

'Over sixteen, actually. Stoat had some moral compass. But, yeah, Wynona Catskill was there.'

'What happened? To the ball. I mean, I can guess what happened to Stoat and Wynona, at least once, probably in the back seat of a car on the edge of town one night.'

'He gave the ball a low punt from about twenty yards. Keeping it low was important. We didn't know if this… thing had a height restriction—'

'We still don't,' Lolita added.

'—and in it sailed. Stoat could kick a ball.'

'Stoat was a legend, I get the picture. The ball!' Beckman begged.

'It was like….' Buck searched for an accurate description as if he'd never told this tale before—which was patently untrue. 'It was like a magic trick. Even Copperfield would have busted a retina. It simply vanished mid-flight. Like passing into another realm. Like it's falling beneath the surface of a vertical invisible lake.'

Lolita nodded. Beckman put two and two together and flashed an accusing look. Her hands came up defensively.

'Lolita Milan, you damn rascal! You've thrown a rock or seven in there too, haven't you?'

She held out her hands, wrists together as if waiting to be handcuffed.

Buck laid a hand on her shoulder. 'That's my girl.'

'You're both reprobates,' Beckman asserted.

'When some things get too much, when the world is weighing on your shoulders, when the messed-up parts of reality and people and behaviours get the better of you, it's a place to go. To stare into the abyss and muse, "I may not understand the real world, but this screwed-up spot really puts my actually pretty normal—and certainly dealable-with—life into perspective".'

'It's like throwing stones into a lake. Except we don't have a lot of lakes around here.' Lolita shrugged.

'It calms you down? Like it has a presence? It absorbs your negative thoughts?'

Buck laughed like thunder. 'Watch Star Trek much?'

Beckman opened his mouth to defend his geekery.

Lolita laid a soft hand on his. 'No. It makes you think, "Jeez, if I fell in there and was never seen again, my life would be a million times worse than whatever shit I'm facing now." It scares you into confronting your demons.'

'Like I said, it absorbs your negative thoughts.'

Buck patted Beckman's shoulder. 'Totally. But stay away, or you're grounded.'

In the past weeks, Buck had become the next best thing to a father figure—he already filled that role for Lolita—so Beckman played along. 'Yes, sir.'

Besides, you can't kick a football for shit, sunshine. Even the actual father figure knows that. And wasn't shy of saying it.

Ahhh, parental encouragement—there's nothing like it. And nothing like it is precisely what you got.

Buck winked and returned to his barista duties.

They drank for a minute, and she watched him ponder some more.

'Have any *people* gone in?' he asked.

'Not that anybody knows.'

'Hmm. Inconclusive.'

'Whatever you're thinking, remember Buck may not be able to technically ground you, but I can sure make the bedroom off-limits.'

'Baby, grounding or no, I'm curious. That's all.'

'I know.'

'So,' he gave the lioness the gentlest of prods, 'Has anyone fired a gun into it?'

'Beckman, you've had your gun moment. Dirty Harry, you ain't.'

'It's a thought experiment. Not violence.'

'You expect to tell the difference between a bullet vanishing from sight at a thousand miles an hour and one disappearing into thin air? Hell, you only started seeing in colour ten weeks ago.'

'Nine weeks, three days, nine hours.'

'Not that you're counting.'

He shrugged. 'It was a life-changing moment.'

'What was I, chopped liver?'

'Nine weeks, six days, two hours.'

'Jeez, Beckman, geek much?'

'I would have taken, "Aw, Beckman, that's so sweet, you're counting the actual time since our eyes met across a crowded room. What a dear romantic man you are, I'm so glad I get to marry you".'

You just raised the Hot Topic, dummy.

How to tell her what you think? She'll be crushed.

Not now, idiot. Not now.

Mercifully, she dropped it. 'How about you leave The Portal alone, my dear romantic man, like everyone in Sunrise who has an ounce of sense, and especially those with a girl they'd hate to lose.'

He swilled the last of his root beer. 'You can't blame a guy for wondering.'

'I absolutely don't. And I get the whole throwing stones thing.'

'Yeah, and not doing it when you're in your own glass house.'

'Busted, okay. End of. But there must be somebody in town who can give me the full nine yards. You understand—to quench my thirst for knowledge. Old guy, long straggly white beard? Lives in a mysterious tumbledown house. Wizened. Cackles. Might own weird things in jars. Tells tall tales about strange goings-on.'

'Ah.' Her eyes lit recognition. 'You mean Old Man Withers?'

'Yes! I knew it!'

'You want to go see him?'

'Sure.'

'So you'd better fire up the Mystery Machine and grab your talking dog, Shaggy.'

Just then, he could willingly have stepped into The Portal. Or been shot through it from an amusing clown cannon. It would have been marginally less painful than her corpsing at his expense.

She'll dine out for weeks on this. It's a good thing it's done out of love.

Or it had better be. Court Jesters are so passé.

He needed a distraction, a comeback. A fire alarm. An alien touchdown. Was that too much to ask?

His phone rang. He almost leapt out of his skin—something less potentially embarrassing than the duping he'd just received.

He tugged the trusty iPhone 6 from his pocket.

The display read, "TYLER QUITTLE".

He flashed it in front of her. In a nanosecond, her laughter ceased as if... well, as if it had passed through an invisible vertical barrier. In its place came an expression of equal parts distaste and disappointment. He'd had an idea that would happen. There was no point in seeking her approval for him to take the call, as it wouldn't be forthcoming.

But he answered anyway. If only to change the topic.

Chapter 3

She set the plates down in front of them. It was a balmy evening, and they were dining on the terrace. Whenever they did, he felt extraordinarily grown-up, which was odd, being already thirty-seven. Maybe it meant he was happy, like his life had arrived at the point it should be. The "pursuit of happiness" was over, and he'd managed to catch the elusive SOB.

Yet all was not rosy in the garden (the metaphorical version, not the one stretching out in parched greenery before them). The Hot Topic still rankled her, the revelation of The Portal scampered through his brain, and she hadn't even mentioned the call from Tyler. The man's form defined him—presumed guilty without trial.

A man can change—he himself bore living proof. Yet he was still a mere man, and what did mere men do when they wanted to know what was on a woman's mind?

They took pot luck and waded in, hoping to escape with at least their genitals intact, and on a good day, their dignity too.

He took a deep breath and pushed himself back off the boat's gunwale into shark-infested waters.

'Tyler has a proposition.'

She took her sweet time finishing the mouthful, keeping the idiot guessing whether the shark would bite or merely flash its dead eyes. 'I'm familiar with his *propositions*.'

'Proposition, singular,' he corrected daringly. He could poke sharks as well as lionesses.

Fortunately, she didn't rise to it. 'He still has a one hundred percent record of trying to entice you over to the dark side.'

'You make him sound like Palpatine.'

'Except with better skin.'

'He's not a bad guy,' Beckman supplicated.

'Not any more, you're suggesting.'

'You mean since his brush with death, brought on by a mystery assassin hired by a small-town dealer in Egyptian artefacts.'

'A small-town dealer in Egyptian artefacts, in whose house you are living. Rent-free.'

'Yes, the small-town dealer in Egyptian artefacts with the excellent tenancy terms and quite superb ass.'

'Since that brush with death, exactly. The one that's miraculously transformed him into the kind of guy you might want to give the time of day to.'

The sarcasm in her voice was a good sign because he needed to win her over. She'd nearly lost him to Tyler Quittle's charms once before, and in the back of their minds, the guy wasn't one to know a battle was over.

Except this time, it didn't sound like a battle. It sounded like a slam dunk money-spinner.

'When he has interesting propositions, yes.'

She set down her cutlery. 'Okay. Hit me with this proposition. Tenant, darling.'

'Short version, he wants me to take Sunrise as my own sales patch for Pegasus. On the side. In my spare time. No upfront investment.' He took another mouthful of the pork belly, gave her a querying expression with a splash of puppy dog eyes thrown in for good measure.

She'd have to be a monster to say No to this.

She didn't say no. She said, 'What's the catch?'

'Not one I can see. I know the town. I know the product. I have an excellent track record. Some extra cash, maybe for the *honeymoon*....'

'Excellent, Beckman. Like the patter. You'll do well. Except selling Milan's products, not Tyler's. You owe him, them, nothing. You did your time, and escaped. With your life—which was touch and go for a while.'

He waved it away. 'Ancient history.'

'I dine on ancient history. You may have noticed.' She gestured to the Egyptian vase on the table. 'So why go back?'

'I'm not going back. I'm doing a solid for a guy who tried to do me a solid.'

'Are you forgetting the week you have coming up? And the rather significant proposition of our own? Which will pay for more than a honeymoon?'

'Is this a "Please don't do it, Beckman"?'

'I don't see the value, is all.'

'Keep your friends close, but your enemies closer?'

'You said he wasn't your enemy.'

Oh, snap.

'Then I'm only keeping him close, not closer.'

'Nice escape, honey.'

'I've cheated an assassin's bullet. A hail of them, as I recall. Getting out of a verbal corner I've backed myself into is child's play.'

'As easy as selling Pegasus's little boxes in a town that laps them up?' she suggested.

'I've heard worse comparisons.'

'I'd only hold this against you if you did it behind my back. Which I know you wouldn't.'

'That sounds dangerously like a green light.'

'I'd rather you lock horns with Tyler in your spare time than hang around outside The Portal trying to find out what makes it tick.'

'Because I'm familiar with exactly what makes Tyler tick?'

'It was easy sales, easy women and unnecessary insults, if I heard your stories right.'

'It's only one of three now,' he asserted.

'I hope we're talking the same one.'

'With great power comes great responsibility.'

'Preaching to the choir, honey. You're not just dating a small-town dealer in Egyptian artefacts anymore—'

'With a great ass.'

'—with a great ass. You're dating the CEO of Milan Enterprises.'

'With a great ass.'

'And a dark cloud on the horizon. One which needs our focus. Having my Head of Sales distracted on a favour for an old buddy, enemy, enemy-turned-buddy, whatever, is not my ideal scenario.'

Beckman set down his cutlery, reached across the weathered oak table, and took her hands. 'Both the mergers we're working on, the stressful Milan EVI one and the much more pleasant Milan Spiers one, have my undivided attention. I, for one, know you have to put in the miles to get the reward.'

'Except last time you put in the miles and found out the reward was baloney.'

'Neither you, not even Walter Whack, are in the same ballpark—hell, not even the same sport—as Mr Malvolio.'

'The *late* Mr Malvolio.'

He shrugged. 'You play with fire; sometimes you get burned.'

'I've no intention of getting burned by this. Walter is a smart guy. He knows it's in all our best interests.'

'If only the same was true of Carlton.'

'I'm not having that asshole's name mentioned in this house. Especially by a tenant living rent-free,' she smirked.

'This tenant thing could wear pretty thin.'

'So get your ass moving and marry me.'

'You get *your* ass moving and have Walter sign the memorandum, so I'm marrying a financial solvent woman.'

'You get *your* ass moving and close the Coffee Planet contract, so we're bargaining from a financially solvent position.'

He sighed. 'Why did I think quitting real life for Sunrise was a downslope?'

'Because you're an idiot?'

'Yeah. But *your* idiot.'

'Not yet, Beckman, not yet. One more ring to go.'

'I had better move my ass about that too, huh?'

'You'll need a chiropractor pretty soon.'

'Or an ass transplant.'

Chapter 4

Monday morning.

Two words which, until recently, had regularly elicited the 8 a.m. sigh of the road warrior.

The only times the sigh was tempered were when Tyler woke up next to something soft, warm, and whose husband was out of town.

This morning, like each of the past nine Mondays, there was no sigh. Yet, not everything was one hundred percent perfect.

The floor-hinged gas pedal, for instance, was something of a downer. I mean, who the hell did Porsche think they were? Why couldn't they do it properly, like in his six-year-old black Chevy with two hundred thousand on the clock?

Downsides, he reminded himself. Gleaming, exquisitely manufactured, big bucks downsides.

Nine Mondays ago, the parsimonious headroom would have been an issue too. Not for him, at a pretty regular five-eleven, but for his companion. And not for her five-eight frame. Only for her ten-inch beehive.

However, nine Mondays ago was a different world.

Sixty-three days previously, they'd been on cordial co-worker speaking terms. He'd plummeted from the verge of all-conquering Salesman of the Year to merely-one-of-the-workforce Tyler Quittle in five minutes flat. Then some frankly strange shit happened at the office, and he'd grasped the nettle as opportunistically as if it was something soft, warm, and whose husband was out of town.

She'd had another regular Monday—the same as the previous fifteen years' worth of Mondays—until a certain Tyler Quittle (or Mr Quittle as she'd known him) had taken her for cocktails and dropped a bombshell worthy of the season-concluding episode of a Netflix drama.

Subsequently, he would have bought the Porsche anyway, even though she now recognised he had a Christian name. Regardless of her hair (in fact, regardless of the hairstyle of any woman he might be working with / courting / waking up beside on a typical Monday morning). He'd earned this car. Not admittedly through his deeds, good nature or pay packet. More through the litany of 8 a.m. sighs, dutiful subservience to Miss Broomhead's longtime boss, and last, if not least, because it was a handsome car and he was a handsome SOB, even if he did say so himself. Which he did.

It was simply meant to be.

Besides, the CEO of a multi-million dollar enterprise can't slouch about in anything with 204,873 on the odo. Especially when it doesn't have a head-up display, a panoramic glass roof and six hundred and some horses hidden in the trunk.

He hadn't *splurged*. He'd… upgraded.

'Tyler?' Something in her tone gave the impression she considered it a dirty word, or at least an overstepping of boundaries. A reticence. Maybe even her subservience to his wishes.

She'd put forward two valuable arguments for retaining formality :

(1) Mr Malvolio had always insisted she refer to him as such and to all employees by surname only.

(2) Even if Tyler / Mr Quittle had suggested it would engender more of a team spirit if everyone at The Pegasus

Corporation interacted more casually in future, surely she, as PA, must retain some semblance of dutiful service by referring to the new CEO as Mr? Otherwise it might smack too much of cosy familiarity, likely to raise eyebrows about potential *extra-curricular activity* goings-on between a boss and his secretary. Although none was.

Nevertheless, she'd seen good sense and used "Tyler", even if the intonation was "Mr Tyler" or "Can't you get the hint this is Uncomfortable for me, Mr Quittle".

'Yes, Amaryllis?'

He was unswerving in his mission to cure her of Surname Syndrome. Calling your PA "Miss Whatever-It-May-Be" was a relic of the 50s. It perpetuated a myth of overbearing and sexist C-Suiters— the last thing he wanted to be perceived as being, especially as it wouldn't be beyond the realm of possibility that it's exactly the kind of person he was.

Or at least, it had been. Before that fateful Monday.

He was already on the downslope from asshole to decent enough guy, but the power shift at HQ had accelerated the transition. He not only wanted to catch more flies with honey than vinegar, but he wanted to *actually do it,* because faking niceness was the easy way out.

It might lead to fewer soft, warm, available things happening, but that was the former life of Tyler Quittle, Travelling Salesman Extraordinaire, not new, improved, Tyler Quittle, Big Boss Man.

Ironically, although he'd gained the means to possess a vehicle not *un*known for its ability to attract what old Tyler Quittle called "chicks", he (1) was now primarily office-bound, (2) had risen above the need for such encounters to illuminate his otherwise drudge-filled life, and, alarmingly (3) tooled around in a two-seater sports car in the company of a woman, thus naturally repelling other potential interested parties.

'Are we quite sure this is the premium sales territory boasted by Mr Sp— Beckman?'

The unending vista spread out beyond the windshield. Miss Br— Amaryllis had a point. How had Beckman shifted so many boxes in a nowheresville like this? And hence beat him to the latest—and final—Salesman crown?

No matter; it had worked out for the best—impossibly so, like a blindfolded one-legged cat falling from the Empire State, doing myriad pirouettes and double pikes with a half-twist, and still landing daintily and uninjured on the single paw.

'It has to be, Amaryllis. Beckman is one hell of an honest guy. How far to the turn?'

'No turn. We pull onto the shoulder.'

'Baloney. There has to be a turn. We'll wait for the sign and make the turn. I don't need to be met and escorted like some damn royalty.'

'This is B— Beckman's patch. I'd suggest we follow his instructions.'

He sighed. 'So, how far to the… shoulder?'

She leant over and checked the odo. Of course, he could have kept count, but she'd insisted. It fell under Secretarial Duties, it seemed. 'Three miles.'

Something brushed his nostrils, something he'd not noticed before, even locked in these air-conditioned confines for two hours.

Perfume.

It wasn't odd. Women wear perfume. He'd often noticed it, in the evenings before the mornings wherein he'd wake up with the soft, warm, absent-husbanded.

So, although she wasn't in the same category as those less-than-wholesome conquests, it felt logical that his PA might also choose to scent herself. It wasn't verboten.

It was, well, not very… Miss Broomhead.

Or maybe she'd always done so, and he'd never noticed; they'd hardly spent much time in close proximity under the previous regime. And yet, the sly old fox he was (or used to be) would surely have sensed it. Sensed… an opportunity.

But she had been Malvolio's PA. The office whip-cracker. The untouchable.

No longer.

This wasn't any lingering Old Tyler-ness; this was unarguable. Firstly, Miss Broomhead would have been a frightened mouse to be cocooned inside a sports car with a man she hardly knew. Secondly, she wouldn't have *fitted* in the car—there simply wasn't the headroom, or rather hair-room.

Now, though, the bees had to look elsewhere because their cranially-sited hive had gone. Sure, a lot of hair remained, but it was much less a conversation piece. The hairdresser's floor-sweeper would have earned overtime on the day those towering tresses fell for the last time. Cushions could have been stuffed with the trimmings. Many, many cushions.

When the reality of the new order at Pegasus filtered through, Miss Broomhead disappeared on the first Friday at 5 p.m., and on the second Monday at 8.30 a.m. (sharp, as always), *Amaryllis* arrived.

Tyler could have been knocked down with, if not a feather, certainly a stiff paper napkin.

She looked like a woman. No, that did her injustice. She'd always looked like a woman—except one you might be distantly related to and see on the occasional Thanksgiving, rather than one you might, for instance, be happy to take on a road trip in your new Porsche and not care too much if anyone thought you *weren't* related.

So, was the perfume a new addendum, or merely his perception—his heightened sense she might be more than an efficient colleague?

The jury remained out on this, as on a lot of things.

For example, what kind of twisted person willingly arranges the… untimely dispatching of employees, albeit at the behest of her stone cold-hearted superior? He desperately wanted to ask why she'd served a lowlife shit like Mr Malvolio for so long, without pushing back against—or at least questioning—his methods. He wanted to believe her to be a good person, a likeable person, someone whose once hard edge could be smoothed down until it was at least soft and maybe warm too.

He'd tried to convince himself there must be a logical explanation for what used to go on at Pegasus. She'd have a reason, and that reason would remain, whether or not he asked her about it. He resolved that it was either repugnant, and he'd dislike her (and clearly have to fire her)—and he didn't want to dislike her. Or it was a perfectly reasonable explanation, believable and wholly understandable, which would make asking it a waste of time.

Top of his list was that she'd acted through self-preservation. To go up against a man like Malvolio risked employment termination; to call the cops risked him sanctioning permanent respiratory termination. If she saw it as a life or death decision, he felt glad she'd chosen life. One thing remained immutable; her loyalty, and now he occupied the CEO's chair, he welcomed that loyalty. Not in the face of inglorious misdeeds, merely in support of his infinitely more palatable agenda—to make Pegasus a success for all. Democracy versus dictatorship. Honey, not vinegar.

There would be 100% fewer killings amongst the salesforce.

A penny dropped. No more hitmen to pay. That was a cost saving right there! A hundred grand a year onto the bottom line.

Quickly, any guilt for springing a similar volume of dollars on his current steer was washed away by realising that his new methods had legitimately freed the cash from the business. He'd not even touched the fifty million or so secreted his wall safe—a stash which engendered even more pensive lip-biting than an examination of the moral compass of Miss Br— Amaryllis.

Was it Bad Money? Yes, it was money from the old regime. However, Tyler had no reason to believe it had been obtained by a method any more distasteful than the merciless slave-driving of the salesforce and the subsequent hoarding of the proceeds. Perhaps Mr Malvolio had been a canny investor, pumping those proceeds into stocks. Or was it a legacy of personal inheritance? Had he founded Pegasus on piles of existing cash?

Why had Mr Malvolio kept the liquidity in his office? A show of force? A two-fingered salute to rub the minions' noses in the fruits of their labours while simultaneously keeping it tantalisingly out of reach?

There were a LOT of questions about Malvolio and his relationship with Amaryllis.

Yet the answers would sate curiosity, not make any meaningful difference to the future.

Well, perhaps only his future with Amaryllis. He'd mended his ways and hoped that without the same toxic influence on her life, she might do the same. They would grow together.

Maybe not together like *that*. Although… why not?

He looked across. She dutifully watched the odo, poised to give his next instruction.

She remained Of Indeterminate Age. She managed to appear like she could *be* fifty and *look* thirty, and also *be* thirty and *look* fifty. Simultaneously. It was a hell of a trick. In the last nine weeks, however, the overall estimate skewed younger—less headmistress-y.

Her hair was the most… down he'd seen. A hint of rouge decked her face. Hell, she even had her top shirt button undone, which was unprecedented. She'd been a perennial tight-collar spinster, daily garbed in figure-cloaking attire. Prim, distant.

Malvolio's untimely but very welcome passing had unchained her, as if freed from an invisible shackle, not unlike the visible and iron one with which he'd perpetually restrained Bruno.

Bruno, the killer lizard with only one victim to his name.

One very rich victim.

One very rich victim whose PA was the only other person who knew the combination of that wall safe.

In the immediate aftermath, he couldn't deny this was part of his reason for getting on the right side of Miss Broomhead. Later, his own moral compass told him that filching even ten percent of the safe's fifty million and Brewstering it away with casual abandon would be, at best, a Questionable Plan.

A hitherto unnoticed streak of Real Businessman in him considered the millions were best served as a rainy day plan. He countenanced keeping the money, rather than giving it away to charity, distributing it amongst the employees as a windfall dividend, or, worse, running amok in various high-end malls to furnish a lavish lifestyle which wasn't truly him.

Emptying the safe into a duffel bag and hopping on a flight to Maui never even entered his mind.

Well, it didn't stay there long, even if it had sneaked in.

He'd get too bored laying on a beach for the next forty years and knew he was no natural playboy. Splashing inch-thick wads at a casino might attract the wrong sort of woman for New Tyler, and the fact he was considering, to the tiniest degree, a more-than-merely-businesslike relationship with Amaryllis rang a loud bell.

The enigma, the far from superficial artist formerly known as Miss Broomhead, chimed in. 'We should pull over now.'

He scouted the scene outside. 'I don't get it.'

'Neither do I. But I suggest we follow Beckman's instructions.'

He hoped Beckman had forgiven him for his past indiscretions, insults and temptations. Otherwise, there was a risk his ex-colleague was cunningly stranding them in what appeared to be the middle of nowhere.

He'd keep the engine running after they stopped—as a precautionary measure.

He eased in the beautifully progressive German brake pedal and coaxed the steering to the right.

Then, as fat rubber left the smooth tarmac and spattered through roadside debris, he winced appallingly, flushed with worried guilt about the inevitable impact on pristine coats of paintwork. He shoved harder on the centre pedal, keen to bring the torture to an end.

Stone chips quickly became the least of his concerns as, with a signature pop, something tore into one of the rear Pirellis. He fought the knee-jerk expletive that strained at his throat and risked floating into the ears of someone who he was pretty sure—newly-discovered degree of joie-de-vivre notwithstanding—wasn't keen on such utterances. Instead, he put all effort into steering into the ensuing slither and brought them to rest in a cloud of orange dust.

'Still think it was best to follow to the letter?' he asked with quiet annoyance.

'I'm sure Beckman has his reasons, even if he's not master of every sharp pebble in the county.'

'Get him on the horn, would you?' He tugged open the door and went to inspect the damage.

A minute later, having discovered exactly as many flats as he expected, and a far greater number of square miles of emptiness surround them, he slid back into the leathered bucket.

'I'm sorry, Tyler, there's no signal.' She waved her phone as a gesture of proof.

'Son of a b... gun.'

'Shall I help you with the jack?'

He instantly brightened. Then he pondered the effect on her clothes. Then reflected how his view on a woman and her clothes had markedly changed. Previously his sole concern had been how quickly they could be removed. 'We should wait a spot. In case someone is coming for us.'

'From where?' She scanned the open vista.

'He did say Sunrise is hard to find.'

'There's hard, and there's impossible.'

He sighed. 'You're right.'

They climbed out, and he popped the lid at the front. After busily unpacking a requisite quantity of small brown boxes, they located the jack and tire repair kit beneath.

When they stepped out from behind the open lid, they clocked something beyond both hard *and* impossible.

In front of a tow truck stood a tall, paunched man with a black quiff, snakeskin boots and an eye patch.

Chapter 5

'Sibelius' Finlandia?' Amaryllis asked.

Tyler's eyebrows, already towards the top of their travel, reached the zenith. Then a voice inside his head suggested that her knowledge of classical music (assuming she was correct) was infinitely less of a surprise than anything in the last fifteen minutes.

Their mysterious benefactor—at pains to convince them his name was Saul Paul—glanced across Tyler to where she sat on his other side. (He'd chivalrously volunteered to take the centre seat, unsure whether the tow-truck driver's hands had a mind of their own.)

'Yeah,' Saul replied.

Conversational silence resumed as the new bosom classical buddies enjoyed their fix.

If Tyler considered Amaryllis an enigma, it ranked as nothing compared to a breakdown vehicle arriving without sound, without warning, and at three minutes notice.

And the driver knowing their names.

And liking classical music.

And not smelling like a dumpster.

And did they stock Tyler's required grade of manufacturer-approved tire?

And was there a sone chip repair guy in town?

And had Beckman wanted it all to happen?

What the hell kind of place—and friends—had Beckman wound up with?

Alarmingly quickly, they were not in the middle of nowhere but plainly approaching the outskirts of somewhere. A town sign slid past:

SUNRISE.
Population 4275

Except someone had peeled off the first "P" and stencilled on a "C".

Tyler sniggered. He would have been responsible for such a prank had this been his town at age fourteen.

Saul carefully piloted the big truck and its precious tow through the suburbs and onto the forecourt of his garage premises. As the music's strains died, he killed the V8.

'I'd never have found that turn,' Tyler ventured.

'We knew.'

'How did you *do* that?'

'Experience,' Saul replied, as obliquely as was possible.

Amaryllis heaved open the door and stepped down. Tyler halted the interrogation and joined his PA on the bitumen-jointed concrete apron. Metallic sounds and oily smells tinged the air. He dearly wanted to do a quick walk-round of the car to check for any new scars from the tow ride, but it might come across as dickish, so he held in his concerns.

'I'll check if we have your size,' Saul said. 'Don't get a lot of… machinery like that here.'

'Sure,' Tyler replied noncommittally.

'You want a ride up? It's a few blocks.'

Tyler noticed Saul checking Amaryllis' footwear for heel depth and precariousness, and felt like an ass for considering the guy might have been inappropriate with his passenger. He was now protecting her from an ankle sprain, though it was moot: heels weren't her style. She didn't need to be any taller than 5'8", and certainly hadn't needed to when That Hair had been in place.

She looked at Saul, then Tyler. 'I'm easy if you are.'

'Try "Our Buck's". Tell them I said "Hi".'

By "them", Tyler assumed Saul meant Beckman and Lolita. So long as this "Buck's" place wasn't located off an invisible turn and required him to get a hole in his shoe to find it, he could care less who "they" were. Especially if "they" directed him to an ice-cold soda and a thick steak.

"They" were not Beckman and Lolita. They were solely Beckman because he'd never entertained the thought of the CEO of Milan Enterprises taking time out of her busy schedule to meet a man she didn't care for, to discuss a matter she had no stake in. He wondered how she'd take the news of Tyler's expeditious arrival.

Beckman explained Tyler's situation to Buck, they set up a small wager, then he retreated to Kinda His Table.

During their conversation, he became aware that Buck's attention was repeatedly drawn to a table in the corner. A table for two. Seating one. A tall, female, brunette one.

He'd never seen Buck take an interest in a woman before, yet, the more the man watched the woman, this interest didn't seem to be purely along gender lines—more a kind of curiosity. In a lull between service, as Buck was clearing an empty glass, Beckman subtly nodded in the direction of The Mystery Female. 'What gives?'

'Another customer. We get them, you know?'

'They all get the third-degree surveillance?'

'A man's café is his castle,' Buck declared as a defence.

'Enemy at the gates?'

'Search me.'

'I'd say she doesn't look familiar, except I'm only here ten weeks. And Sunrise is a friendly place, huh?'

'I'm not being unfriendly. I'm… interested.'

'What—five-eleven, brunette in a pantsuit? If I wasn't the happiest gonna-get-married guy in the world, I'd be interested too.'

'It's not like that,' Buck declared.

'Then you're a damn idiot.'

'No. Not like that. I didn't get a "hi" or a "howdy" from Saul. So the "Who the hell?" has a "How the hell?" to go along.'

'Five bucks says in town on business.'

'Hell, even Delmar could spot as much.'

'Smells like big business too. The jacket cut, the hair.'

'The drink order,' Buck added.

'Speak to Kinsey.'

'Figuring she's staying over at the Sunset Hotel? And who was balling me out on third-degree surveillance?'

'Only being practical. Won't want to catch your hand on a hot steam nozzle because your eye gets snoopy for the thousandth time. Just ask. Word gets around— remember? Just, you know… catalyse it.'

'Catalyse, huh?'

Beckman pensively ran his finger around the rim of his soda glass. 'Look at it like this—she can't do half as much damage to this place as I did, and I was the last person in here you probably looked at with your brain turning over. Be nice to her. You might get another regular customer spends a small fortune in here like I did.'

The front door opened and in walked two familiar figures. Except they were not one hundred percent the way he remembered: one had a purposeful stride and sharper slacks; the other had surprising ease to her gait and markedly less hair than previously.

They both bore a familiar expression. One Beckman himself had worn when he first walked up Main Street those weeks ago. He rose, they spied him and walked over, drinking in the decor. Buck backed off but remained in attendance.

'Beckman.'

'Tyler.'

'Mr— Beckman,' she offered.

'Miss Broomhead.'

'Amaryllis.'

'*Amaryllis*?'

'Please.'

Strange things are afoot at The Pegasus Corporation. Which is all your doing, in a roundabout—or actually not that roundabout— way.

There came a pregnant pause, and he remained on tenterhooks, before,

'The lights!' the newcomers chorused in disbelieving wonder.

Beckman caught Buck's eye. The big man gave a gentle shake of the head, surreptitiously slipped a hand into his apron pocket, withdrew it, and casually shook Beckman's hand.

Beckman invisibly pocketed the ten-dollar bill and gestured for his ex-colleagues to sit.

Miss Broomhead has an identical twin with better dress sense, a decent hairdresser, and a zest for life verging on perceptible?

Come on, Tyler, don't tell me you've…? Not already? I thought you'd changed?

Tyler sat. 'This is an… interesting spot.'

'I get by.'

'We got a flat,' Amaryllis said, reminding Beckman that at heart, she dealt in Fact.

'I know.'

'You *know*?' Tyler choked.

'You followed my instructions?'

'Of course,' she said.

'So, I know.'

Buck coughed. All three looked up.

'Sorry,' Beckman continued. 'Tyler, Miss— Amaryllis, this is Buck. This is his spot. Case you didn't make the connection.'

'Great name for the place, very humorous,' she commented.

'Folks. Any word from Saul?' Buck leaned forwards in expectation.

'He says, "Hi",' Tyler replied, confused.

Buck smiled. 'What'll I get you?'

Chapter 6

Lolita arrived home with a sunny disposition, so Beckman made a concerted effort not to put a pin in her balloon.

Walter Whack had signed the Memorandum, meaning; (1) the takeover of EVI Lighting by Milan Enterprises remained on course and (2) a fine wine would be drunk tonight. He might even get lucky later. Hence he didn't mention that Tyler (and Amaryllis) would be in town overnight, owing to Saul not catering for performance rubber.

Overnight. Two rooms—surely? Forget it.

For now, he'd taken possession of the small cadre of Pegasus' product they'd squeezed into the Porsche's 'trunk'. His only task was to deplete the stock as the need arose and claim his kickback from the boss who wasn't his boss, thereby fulfilling his promise to the boss who *was* his boss as well as being his fiancée.

His fiancée uncorked the bottle and served. They toasted.

'We're not counting our chickens, are we?' he suggested.

'Due diligence, another signature, we're done.'

'And… He Whose Name Shall Not Be Spoken…?'

'…Will have to suck it up and see what's coming down the track. I could give a shit what he decides to do.'

'Providing it doesn't involve firearms, obstruction of process, or generally being an asshole.'

'The ship has *so* sailed on the asshole thing,' she observed.

'Tell me again how you're not doing this as petty revenge.'

'*We're* doing this because it's sound business. I can see what's coming down the track, and so can Walter. Cheap imports, industry consolidation. We have to merge to survive. If Carlton stands in the way, he's not the financial whizzkid he reckons.'

'You're telling me he's not twisted enough to bring down both businesses so long as you lose out? He's an FD; he can get a job anywhere. This is your dream. There's a difference.'

'Even Carl— No Name—draws the line at corporate hari kiri. The only people who want both companies ground into dust are the corporate shells at GigantiCorp. Hence the merger for scale.'

'You're the strategic genius, honey.' He offered a gentle toast.

'And you close the sales that make this possible. Without liquidity, we're screwed.'

'Is this a subtle way of piling on the pressure for tomorrow?'

She sidled over on the sofa. 'It's a marriage made in heaven. You, the guy who's probably spent more bucks in Coffee Planet than anyone. An expanding brand with an expiring contract, unhappy with their lighting supplier. You go in, break the ice by mentioning what a huge fan you are, do the trademark Beckman patter of unscrupulous honesty, wield my permission to slash margins, and we're home straight. And I will, unquestionably, put out for you if you seal the deal.'

His face brightened, then fell on the implication that she wouldn't be putting out tonight. Was he that shallow?

'You need all the energy you can for the meeting,' she added.

'Am I that shallow?'

'Don't kid yourself. *All* men are that shallow. The difference is there's only one man I want to be with. And, to be clear, "with" in the general sense, not the bedroom sense. Although the bedroom sense is a factor.'

She leaned in and gave him a quick smooch, wine glass in an outstretched hand whose own gyroscope was a marvel to behold.

You better win that damn contract tomorrow, Spiers.

The perennial pleasure of kissing Lolita Milan was rudely interrupted by a knock at the door. He couldn't ever remember a knock that wasn't the postman, so unless Donnie DiCarlo was running apocalyptically late on today's round, they had Visitors.

He un-puckered and went to the door.

Like you own the place. Free-loading tenant.

Buck wasn't wearing a smile nor a frown. Odd, given Buck never called round—it had to be either Good News or Bad News, rather than merely News.

'You have a phone, I get it,' was Buck's opener.

Beckman waved him in.

Like you own the place. Free-loading tenant.

Lolita appeared. 'This is… a surprise. A nice one, sure. Come in? We have wine.'

Buck shook his head. 'I thought you should know. I spoke to Kinsey. Like you suggested, Beckman. Catalysing. I found out who our mystery visitor is.'

'Come in, Buck,' she repeated.

'Thanks, no. Big day for your man tomorrow.'

'Loss Adjuster, after the warehouse snafu?' Beckman pondered unexpected consequences of the little shoot-'em-up he'd unwittingly precipitated whilst running from certain doom a couple of months previously.

'The roadsweeper guy finally ID'd my guy?' Lolita sighed with a scowl of self-admonishment.

'What?' Buck didn't follow.

'Nothing,' she replied quickly. Beckman looked the other way.

We both had our butterflies that flapped their wings, huh?

'No,' Buck said. 'She's a Dixon… something. Business Development. GigantiCorp.' He gave a half-shrug of resignation. The messenger had done his job.

'How the… ?' Beckman began.

'Sunrise may not be a regular place, buddy, but we do have a thing called the Internet. I took the name from Kinsey's registration book and did something called 'extrapolation'. Good word, huh? So that's your woman. Dixon. I wrote it down.' He tendered a scrap of paper.

'Buck, you are—'

'A legend. I know. And I looked her company up. So, I wish you a lotta luck tomorrow.' He tipped an invisible hat and turned away into the late evening.

Beckman closed the door with pensive solemnity.

'I vote more wine,' she said.

'You want me to fight fire with fire or double vision?'

She sank into the deep cushions, topped her glass and sat back. 'So they have a scout in town.'

'It was only a matter of time.'

'You think this is the first sighting?'

'You make her, them, seem like people from another world.'

'Yeah, a world of venture cap, the corporate helicopter, and swallowing up the little guys.' She took a slug of red.

Corporate helicopter, huh? Could she? Really? Somehow find this place and sneak in under the radar to do her purportedly evil deeds? You're ahead of yourself. She was having coffee and bothering a sum total of zero people. Cut the woman some slack. Innocent until proven guilty.

'Remember how, a few weeks back, you accused me of wild theories?' he said.

'Remember how, pretty quickly, they became real?'

Yeah. There was that.

'You can't—we can't—let it disrupt our stroke. We have deals to close. Anyway, isn't there something about you can't touch a company while it's in process with someone else?'

'Honey, this is GigantiCorp. They'll do anything to anyone, anytime, to get a stranglehold on the lighting market.'

'I was afraid you'd say that.'

You better win that damn contract tomorrow, Spiers.

Chapter 7

'You're gonna want a medal, aren't you?'

'Success is its own reward,' Beckman replied.

'So you'll turn down any additional thanks later tonight?' The patented Eyebrow Raise appeared.

A flash of embarrassment coloured his cheeks, even though there was nobody else in the room.

But being propositioned by the boss is a hell of a thing, huh?

'I'm only trying to repay the boss' trust in hiring me.'

She swivelled absentmindedly on her black leather and steel executive chair, picked up a fat marker pen and nibbled on the end. Then licked it. When she sucked the end suggestively, he turned and went to the full-height window overlooking the drab company parking lot.

He took a couple of calming breaths.

'Some luck though, huh? With the box,' she remarked.

He turned back. The pen was gone. 'At the start. The rest was all me.'

'You expect me to go easy on Tyler now, I guess.'

'Anything short of pushing him under a roadsweeper would feel like a warm hug, coming from you.'

'I'm magnanimous enough to thank the guy. If he hadn't offered you that supply….'

'The Coffee Planet guy would still have his headache, be in a foul mood, not listen to the amazing proposal I'd put together, we wouldn't have a signature, and you wouldn't sit there sucking a pen. *Miss Milan.*'

The Eyebrow.

'That should keep the wolf from the door,' she asserted.

'And show GigantiCorp we're not to be screwed with. They'd have killed for that contract. As would a certain other name in town.'

'Whatever you do, don't antagonise him. Our victory over Carlton Douchebag Cooper will be in our actions, not in our gloating. He'll be out of a job in a week anyway.'

'You go strangely easy on him sometimes.'

She lifted her left hand and flashed the diamond. 'You want to marry a bitch?'

'I want to marry the perfect woman.'

'But she wasn't available, huh?'

'I'm hardly the perfect man.'

'On a day like today, you'll do fine.'

'As a Sales Director, or as a fiancé?'

Before she had a chance to answer, there came a knock at the office door. Her proclaimed policy was "knock and enter", which seldom had drawbacks.

A drawback entered.

'Hi, Jack,' Beckman said.

Lolita didn't disguise her expression of polite tolerance.

Jack offered his hand. 'Congratulations, Beckman.'

'Thanks.'

'Was that all?' Lolita asked brusquely.

Jack raised an eyebrow in response to the implied withering put-down.

Ah! So that's where she gets it from. We can all do The Eyebrow (well, not you, obviously), but he has the Lolita Tone down pat. Or is it her who has the Jack Tone down pat?

Surprised they don't get along better, having so much in common. The Eyebrow. The Company…

That's probably it.

Maybe stubbornness?

Don't say so out loud—you'll get The Eyebrow.

'I do still own a slice of this company,' Jack retorted, in case she hadn't noticed his Eyebrow. 'Just to show I can be civil, and I now recognise you made a good choice.'

'Well, thanks,' she said dismissively.

Beckman had grown used to atmospheres like this.

'So, Walter signed?' Jack asked redundantly—to prolong the conversation, to drag it away from nonverbal mudslinging.

'You got the memo.'

'I'm proud of you.'

'I live for that,' she said flatly.

Jack studied Beckman for some kind of support but received a noncommittal purse of the lips. Beckman didn't want to take sides in this long-standing battle of wills. Poking a tame lioness was one thing; poking a pair of hungry big cats was something else.

With a sigh, Jack turned for the door. 'I guess you have things to do.'

'Always a pleasure,' she deadpanned.

He didn't rise to it, and momentarily the door closed.

Beckman risked a glance equivalent to The Eyebrow. 'You should cut Jack some slack. Remember how I'm not supposed to be marrying a bitch?'

'Forgive and forget?'

'You could at least stop sitting on the fence.'

'About the wedding?' she asked.

'Who else will give you away? Don't tell me—Buck.'

'Says the man whose own father is not on the guest list.'

'I'm not a shining example, I get it. But at least you're on speaking terms with Jack.'

'Don't spoil today,' she warned.

He took stock of the situation and did have a good chance of spoiling the day, and more importantly, the night. 'I need to get the Coffee Planet contract across to Legal.'

'Sure.'

He went for the door. 'Did he mean a good choice as a sales guy or future son-in-law?'

A smile came to her eyes. 'Yeah.'

He didn't get it. Then she eased the end of the pen into her mouth, and he got it.

Quickly, he made himself scarce and returned to his own office, where he sank into the type of leather chair he only dreamed about attaining at Pegasus—though he never stayed in one place long enough to need a chair. The Buick's worn driver's perch had fulfilled most of his ass-resting needs for countless moons.

Being sat down—without simultaneously holding a steering wheel—was only slowly becoming a norm.

He was still thinking about the pen in Lolita's mouth when his cellphone broke the daydream.

The number was familiar, if unexpected.

'Mom.'

'So you haven't vanished off the face of the earth?'

Ah, mom, such loving concern as ever. But then, it's not like you called either, not-so-doting son.

'No, still kicking around on four wheels.' He jiggled the chair left and right on its chromed castors. 'How are you?'

'I met someone.'

Yeah, break it to me gently.

'Really?'

'You sound surprised. Don't you want your old mother to be happy? Or do you not think anyone would be interested?'

Do not pass comment on the attractiveness of a quinquagenarian woman you're proximately related to. Even the thought of her sucking a pen would put you off root beer.

'Er, no, sure. I'm thrilled. Who is it—he?'

Please say it's a "he". Sure, a "she" would be fine, but it would be too left field at the moment.

'We met online. He's a sheep farmer in Australia.'

That left-field enough for you, sunshine?

'Right. Okay. Internet dating, huh?'

'He's *very* handsome, love.'

'Uh-huh.'

'I'm emigrating.'

Okay, mom, congratulations—you just out-Portaled The Portal. Dropped the mic clear through to the other side of the planet.

Is the quirkiness of Sunrise leaking down the phone line to you?

'You're emigrating to Australia to live with a sheep farmer,' he stated.

A silence. 'Can I take that as congratulations, tinged with disappointment that I'll be so far away?'

'Yes. Yes, you can.'

'I sent a picture to your apartment, but it came back undelivered.'

Ah.

'I kinda moved.'

'Moved? You might have told me.'

'Well, it wasn't as far as Australia, so I didn't think it'd mind. Besides, you have my cell number.'

'Why did you move?'

'I… met someone. No sheep, but she's good with pens.'

'Pens?'

'Private joke.'

'Ah.' Silence. 'Is it serious?' Mom asked.

Lame attempt to hide hope and expectation in that voice, old woman.

'We're… getting married.'

Hopefully not too soon.

'That's… amazing, darling. That was quick. As long as you're sure.'

I keep pinching myself.

'Well, not as quick as some, hey mom?'

He heard her studiously ignore the inference. 'So you moved into her place?'

He studiously ignored that inference. 'It all kinda…
happened by accident.'

'Still in Arizona?'

'Still, yeah. The same, but different. Very different.'

*Like a million neon lights, the world's best coffee and root beer.
Oh, and an interdimensional portal. Maybe.*

'Good. Have you seen dad?' she asked.

Does my generally upbeat nature give you a hint?

*Now there's an idea. Maybe dad's emigrated too. That's
Marlon—he loves to move around. Hell, it's the reason for all this—
my life, your apparently soon-to-be-past single-and-US-resident
status.*

*Hang on. It also kinda means he's responsible for meeting
Lolita. So maybe don't be so hard on the old bastard. Unintended
consequences—been a lot of that recently.*

*But he won't have emigrated. Yeah, he'll give up a town at a
moment's notice, but surely not a whole country. Besides, the universe
doesn't have space for any more weird shit right now.*

'Are you having an inner monologue again, Beckman?'

He sighed. 'When do you fly?'

'Next week.'

'I'll text you my new address. Send me a postcard of
sheep, and maybe of Bruce too.'

'He's called Nate.' A breath of motherly despondence
followed the words down the line. 'Send me a picture of
your girl. On the text.'

'So you can give your blessing?'

'Honey, me and blessings quit many years ago. Take a
leaf from my book—if it feels right, do it and be happy.'

'Sure. Oh, by the way, I can see in colour now.'

A small squeak of surprised happiness exited the
speaker. 'Wow. That's wonderful. Since you met your girl,
by any chance?'

'In the neighbourhood of that. All coincidence,
though.'

'Everything happens for a reason.'

'You mean because you're a big fan of lamb steak?'

'Hush your mouth, Beckman Spiers! Nate is a lovely man, and they have a lot fewer twisters than they do here.'

'Watch out for the spiders, mom. I hear they eat old women whole.'

'Less of the "old", sunshine. Now you go help your girl with her pen or whatever. I've a garage sale to fix up.'

'Thanks for calling, mom. Safe flight. Love to Nate and the sheep.'

'Bye, love.'

The line cut.

He pursed his lips and pondered.

Wow. Heck of a lot of happiness going on in the Spiers family right now.

And that's even before we think about pen-sucking.

Mom suddenly an internet bride? Jeez, maybe Sunrise isn't so peculiar after all.

Chapter 8

Lolita tore off the beer bottle's cap and handed him the brew.

Tearing off bottle caps without a wince was one of the many reasons he loved her. She truly was a lioness, and when she roared, he reminded himself that roaring was a facet he had to learn to love too. Nothing is ever plain sailing.

She had purred, reflecting on the day's success, enjoying the process of cooking dinner, when a low growl accompanied the words, 'Did I pass Tyler on the way home?'

He'd had enough dealings with Tyler to appreciate her feelings in this specific case, but he'd learned to recalibrate. Hell, she'd hired a hit-man—not even a "former hit-man", but a live and functioning hit-man—into her Finance team. One who'd tried to kill them both. How could Tyler be worse or less redeemable than that?

'You might want to lighten up on him. Or at least remember the contribution he made today.'

She necked an entire mouthful. 'He got lucky.'

'Without Tyler, argument says I'd never have come to Sunrise. Without his… accident, he wouldn't be who he is. He wouldn't have reached out. I wouldn't have taken the box to the meeting today. How about a little context here?'

'The whole "everything has consequences" is getting pretty lame, honey.'

'I'm only speaking the truth. And it's what you bought into.' He nudged the neck of his bottle against the ring on her left hand.

'I get it, really. Except nobody is that perfect. Don't you ever think lying is a better way out, sometimes?'

'Unless it was to you.'

'Don't think I don't see soft-soaping when it's going on.'

'The only soft-soaping I care about is in the shower later.'

She shook her head in mock disbelief, but with a smile. 'All the quote-unquote water-saving showers in the world doesn't buy you a tidy little housewife. In case you wanted to reconsider this.' She nudged her bottle against the ring.

'Reconsider? Never.'

'So when do the cookery lessons start?'

'I assumed we'd have someone for that.'

'And the cleaning, and the garden? This merger isn't a passport to the kind of desert island mirage you chased at Pegasus. I'm not doing it to get rich. I'm doing it because it's the right thing. It's not so we don't have to work for a living. It's so we get to still be able to. Okay?'

'Okay, boss.' He fired a fake finger-to-temple salute.

'Beckman, it's a good job I love you, because sometimes you're such an idiot.'

'Lolita, it's a good job I love you because sometimes I'm such an idiot.'

'Come on then, idiot, help the little lady at the stove.'

On the "stove" sat a vessel that might have hailed from the set of M*A*S*H. Yes, he liked chilli, but there were only two of them.

Weren't there?

'Eating for two?' he joked.

She spun on the spot with enough assertion to show that his wisecrack hadn't been a laugh riot.

'Number one, if I was pregnant, there would be a lot more redness in these cheeks from the incessant tears of joy. Number two, *Anthony Bourdain*, anyone with half a brain makes extra portions and freezes some. That way, if I get held up at the office someday, running the company which pays your salary, you can whip out something, heat it up, have it on the table when I get home, and feel like the real modern guy, all caring and chivalrous. That okay for you?'

'If I can get my knuckles off the floor long enough, I ought to be able to manage.'

She eased him back against the work surface. Her face came to his, expression set firm.

Gulp.

'You know what you can do with that smart mouth?'

Gulp.

'No,' he peeped.

'Kiss me. And don't feel the need to make it caring and chivalrous.'

So he did. And it wasn't.

Then the doorbell rang. They shot each other a Who Did You Invite? look, and both received a Nobody, You? reply.

'Tenant answer, or owner answer?' he asked.

'I may not have a chef, maid, or gardener, but I do got a doorman.'

The doorman left the kitchen to go to the door and answer it, because that's what doormen need to do, especially when instructed, or even insinuated, by lionesses.

Buck, with more bad tidings?

Carlton, with a scowl, or worse, a gun?

Neither.

In the fading light stood Tyler and Amaryllis. Tyler had something in his hand. Luckily for Beckman and the integrity of his forthright endorsement of former colleague's good nature, it wasn't a gun.

It was a bottle.

Beware Greeks bearing gifts, is what she'd say.

'Tyler,' Beckman said with excess surprise. 'Amaryllis.'

Still feels weird to call her that.

'Nice place you have.' Tyler looked around.

Beckman involuntarily belched out either an embarrassed laugh or a splutter, and wasn't sure any of them knew which. He felt a presence behind him. 'Well, obviously, ah….'

'I told you,' Amaryllis countenanced her colleague.

'Yeah. Shit. Sorry. Should have called. The thing is… Well. You won't believe this, but… Hell, you're a piece of work.'

'That he is,' came a sharp-edged purr.

'We had a call,' Tyler continued. 'From someone at Coffee Planet. They put in an order for a thousand boxes.' He smiled the kind of smile Beckman never recalled seeing; one of contentment unsullied by barb or undercurrent.

Amaryllis eased the bottle from Tyler's grip and offered it across. Beckman took it, then a lioness' paw relieved him of it. The paw's owner peered at the label, probably checking the contents for traces of poisons and formaldehyde and such.

'So that's a little thank you.' Tyler reached inside his jacket and drew out some paper. 'And here's a thousand more.'

Ten Benjamin Franklins glided towards Beckman. He waited for their flight to be interrupted by a dive-bombing paw, but it didn't materialise, so he took the notes and looked Tyler square in the face. He prayed this was a clincher for Lolita's acceptance of the man.

'Tyler. You're… Thanks.'

'Sure.'

Beckman gave Lolita the sweetest smile he could muster, straining every fibre to keep a healthy dollop of I Told You So out of the expression.

She smiled back. They both beamed at their doorsteppers, who returned the compliment. For a good few seconds, they stood there, grinning like simpletons and waiting for someone to figure out what the heck to do or say next.

Beckman stepped into the bear trap. 'Why don't you… come in?'

Are you MAD?

That's a stone-dead mauling right there.

'Oh… no. It smells like you've got dinner on,' Amaryllis replied.

'Well… Ah… '

Social Awkwardness Situation.

Marital Harmony Dry-Run Alarm.

'Yeah. Sure. Why… don't we… you….' He looked around for guidance. From anyone. From the ancient mask hanging on the wall. From Ben Franklin's papery eyes. '…Stay for dinner?'

You what now?

Lolita's expression implied he'd invited a Mr H. Lecter inside for a pot-fresh batch of fava beans and a nice Italian red.

Then, as if a light switch flicked, she gave the Pegasus visitors her best million-dollar smile. 'Absolutely. I always over-cater. Chilli okay for you folks?'

Something is Very Wrong. She's gone all Stepford.

Did you fall through The Portal without knowing?

Is this the parallel universe?

Roll with it. Either you're in an even better place than you were anyway—which is a major stretch—or it's dinner and a fatal mauling.

Hers is a pretty fine chilli, though. Not a bad last meal.

Chapter 9

Ah. This is A Dinner Party.

Except it's customarily planned. And with actual friends. Ideally, ones both of the hosts like.

Ah, well. If we can survive this, maybe we can survive anything. Ideally, by getting appropriately tanked and having no memory of it in the morning.

Which will be a Wednesday, remember.

Or maybe Tuesday Night Drinking is a thing here in The Portal. What if hangovers don't exist here?! Or apocalyptic new-asshole-tearing recriminations?

Perhaps Tyler Being Pleasant and Miss Broomhead Being Feminine was only the start? The beginning of a rip in the fabric of spacetime?

Maybe we aren't actually inside The Portal, but the alternate reality is leaking out into the real world? Soon, everything will be dandy, and we'll be adults who Have Friends Over, and you'll be a salesman who closes big deals as a matter of routine, and have an incredible wife who finds nothing wrong with her husband's appearance, words or deeds. Ever.

No. Way too far fetched.

He seated their guests and went to "help Lolita in the kitchen". Which was code for "try to get a sense of how much trouble I'm in".

'Beckman.' She drew a knife from the block.

'Yes,' he squeaked.

'I want that extra thousand for my wedding dress.'

'I can't possibly imagine a better use for it.'

She nodded at the correctness of his answer. 'So let's have a nice evening.'

'Okay,' he peeped, still massively unsure.

After all, she wouldn't use the knife yet, not while others were in the house. She probably wouldn't even shout. That would be socially unacceptable. Later, though…

'I'll translate for you. Tyler's okay. Amaryllis must be okay too. So we're okay. Okay?'

'Sure?'

'If he doesn't try to look down my blouse or chew with his mouth open, he can stay.'

'Wow. If I'd known those were the criteria, I wouldn't have tried so hard these past weeks.'

'Remember, I'm holding a knife.'

'Oh. Yeah.'

She popped him a kiss, drew over a loaf and began to slice it up.

This working for a living business is challenging. So much easier if you could write a book on how to read women. You'd be a billionaire in a heartbeat.

Yeah, but the fun is in the ride.

Let's see how much of a rollercoaster this soirée is.

He grabbed two glasses from the cupboard and went into the dining room.

The first hour passed without incident. In fact, it passed with civility. Tyler didn't chew like a camel or ogle his hostess.

Lolita didn't serve any remarks with a side order of needling or distaste.

He didn't dredge up old war stories from the Pegasus days.

Miss Broomhead didn't… well, he wasn't sure what she was likely to do, having only seen in her two settings—her office or the parking lot. For sure, she didn't ogle, camel, needle or dredge.

Her eyes did light up when Lolita enquired whether anyone had room for pumpkin pie. That gave him an excuse to engineer another quiet tête-a-tête in the kitchen area.

'Okay,' he said, filling the dishwasher, 'I need your professional opinion. Are they going together?'

She was taken aback. 'I wanted to ask you the same.'

'Because either Yes and they're Oscar-winners of not looking like it, or No, and they're like the school dance wallflowers who you know belong together.'

'Tyler's no wallflower. And he's not totally shed the Venus Fly-Trap persona either.'

'They have this weird… chemistry,' Beckman noted.

'So did Jack and Mary-Ann.'

'Mary-Ann, his PA? The one he was banging on the side? That's the pyromania side of chemistry.'

'I figured Tyler's not making a move because she's too young. Or too old. Which is it?'

Beckman spread his arms wide. 'Search me.'

'Come on. You've known her for ten years.'

'And she looks exactly the same. Some of the guys reckoned she had a painting the attic.'

'But she must have had a birthday party while you were at Pegasus. A milestone. Something?'

'Why—does it matter to you?'

'I'm curious. You were, about the other thing.'

'The Portal? Are you equating Amaryllis' age with an inter-dimensional gateway?'

'If we can't figure either out, then—yeah.' She spooned the ice cream on top of the four servings.

'Why don't you go to the bathroom together? I hear that's what girls do when you want Private Talk.'

'Very funny. You're telling me nobody knows?'

'I swear. If Malvolio had sprung for a water cooler at the office, and if any of us road warriors were ever there—that's the only topic we'd talk about. I mean, purely out of nosiness. Not out of… designs on her… Miss Broomhead. I mean—she wasn't like this person… not that….' He sighed. 'It was like a parlour game.'

'Pin the tail on the donkey?'

'I'd ask for a do-over now. Tyler's taken five years off her. Which I guess makes no difference to any wagers, as we didn't have a clue before anyhow.'

'Then stand aside and let the professional in, honey.'

'You'll never find out how old she is. You wouldn't dare. Not even you. Nobody has dared.'

'Watch me.'

He sniggered. 'You figure out how old she is—to the year—and I'll double that thousand.'

She swept up two plates and pushed her face close to his. 'You watch me, lover boy.'

Dessert devoured, and lips licked, Holmes donned a deerstalker and began to circle her quarry.

'So, Pegasus dates back to the Eighties? Wow. Those were the days, eh Amaryllis?'

…

'Well, Jack remembers exactly where he was when Kennedy got shot. But how many people truly remember?'

…

'I think a person's favourite song of their youth says a lot about their personality, don't you?'

…

'We had a power blackout on the day the Berlin Wall came down.'

…

It was a great spectator sport, and Beckman happily sided with the home team. Even Tyler slipped in his own queries and teasers—signalling loud and clear that, however close he and Amaryllis had become, he hadn't metaphorically penetrated her inner sanctum. The game kept far enough under the radar for her to suspect anything. It ebbed and flowed in the way people who had Dinner Parties might converse.

Yet it came to nought. He could maybe narrow the data range by a few years, but it didn't help discern whether Tyler was the toyboy or the sugar daddy—if indeed anything was happening in that respect.

'Let me help you with those,' Amaryllis said. She and Lolita took the dinner detritus into the kitchen.

'You're a hell of a cook, Lolita. Beckman is a lucky man... if we were being stereotypical about gender roles in the marital household.' She flashed a smile.

Lolita appreciated the compliment but primarily couldn't believe Amaryllis had said 'hell'. What next— swigging wine from the bottle? That could make her a buddy for life.

'I inherited it. Mum was traditional like that.' The smile faded. 'Fat lot of good it did her,' she chided.

'You're smart too. I like you.'

'Why... thanks.' She went crazy and laid a hand on the woman's arm.

'I loved your game too—trying to work out how old I am.'

Lolita's hand slid off into empty air. She swallowed. She tried a facial mix of incomprehension, apology and puppy dog eyes.

Amaryllis gave a very unfamiliar smirk. 'It's fine.'

'You mean you knew?'

'Honey, I may not have the loosest ass in the state, but my mind has the German engineering of Tyler's car. Of course, I knew. I love the dance. I have to—it's been going on for enough years.'

'Miss Broomhead—I think I like you too.'

'And you're not the only one.'

Lolita's gaze flicked to the dining area. 'Hard to get, huh? Not familiar with that approach, I gotta say.'

'I look at it like this. If Tyler is interested in me, he won't care how old I am. If he cares.'

'And you?'

'Tyler? I'm curious. I've always been—maybe I'm actually less curious now. He's a bad boy—I get that, but Mr Malvolio would have shat if we had anything going on.'

Lolita's garden variety eyebrow raise—not the special one she reserved for Beckman—wasn't triggered by the revelation that someone like Amaryllis was attracted to someone like Tyler—not even the legendary Old Time Tyler, but because she'd used the word 'shat'.

Lolita was dangerously close to having a life buddy now.

'We seem to have a thing for bad boys. Previously, in my case, obviously.' Over dinner, they'd touched on the subject of Carlton Scumbag Cooper. She'd been pretty kind, merely running him over without stopping the car and reversing back over the body a few times for good measure.

'I'm hardly the saint myself,' Amaryllis offered.

'That's a whole different conversation.'

'Everybody has reasons for what they do.'

'People like Carlton…'

'…Or Mr Malvolio.'

'…are shot through with venom. Other people make a bad choice, and it runs away with them.'

Amaryllis' gaze darted into remembrance and recognition. 'But they can reform.'

'Apparently so.'

'Tyler? He was always the rough diamond, and it's a trap some people fall into—to believe they want that. All power to them—the risk-takers. But now he's… polished? Maybe I'm interested. So, if he doesn't care how old I am—and he's not asked me, maybe it shows his new shine—all the better.'

'Doesn't the timing worry you?'

'The sudden interest? The soft touch?'

'You can't deny you were the sole barrier to him controlling the company.'

'Us controlling it. I'm not that dumb.'

Lolita conspiratorially lowered her voice. 'So, what's your angle?'

'Angle?' Amaryllis threw her head back and laughed. 'We're not all CEO material. My angle is Tyler is night and day compared to Malvolio. My share is only insurance. In case Malvolio's ghost haunts that big office chair and turns Tyler into a scheming, thieving, self-serving ass.'

'I might be familiar with asses in the boardroom.'

They both laughed.

'So,' Lolita leant in, 'I won't squeal. Cross my heart. Come on, how many candles are on the cake?'

Amaryllis leant in too. Lolita had a giddy surge that felt exactly like a thousand bucks.

'I like you, Lolita.' She winked. 'But not that much.'

Lolita fluffed her pillow with unnecessary exuberance. 'I can't believe she didn't tell me!'

'I think you mistake an icebreaker dinner for true camaraderie.' Beckman clicked off the ensuite light and slid underneath the sheets beside her.

She sighed. 'I get it. Sunrise is a small town with no secrets.'

Except for the Carlton affair. Don't mention Carlton's affair. The one secret everyone kept.

'Yeah,' he agreed noncommittally.

'Apart from the Carlton affair. The one secret everyone kept.'

Their eyes met. Hers were sober. 'Yeah,' he mumbled.

She brightened. 'I thought I'd die when Tyler mentioned the roadsweeper.'

'As opposed to him nearly dying, which is what you intended.'

'But that was for the greater good.' She touched his arm, reminding him who'd been the chief beneficiary of the greater good. 'Plus, look at the guy now.'

'I wonder if a near-death experience would make Carlton a better person?'

'I don't think violence is the answer. If it went wrong, either you'd hate me forever, or I'd hate me forever. And, much as the guy is a cheating, conniving dick, death would be too good for him.'

'Maybe eternal purgatory?'

She lay down, and he spooned her gently. 'I could live with that,' came her mumbled voice.

He flicked off the bedside light.

He, too, had nearly died when the roadsweeper incident came up. A quandary had enveloped him; competing directives. Truth. Loyalty. Friendship. Retaining his Crown Jewels.

It wouldn't help to tell Tyler about the hitman; he'd only end up hating Beckman. Lolita would end up hating him too, and he'd hate her for being the root cause, and she'd argue he was the actual root cause. And things would implode. And he wouldn't be able to do something like spoon her. Which would be a Big Shame.

It was better this way. It wasn't lying. It was… withholding knowledge to protect someone. Well, three people. A man with a penchant for handing out hard currency on your doorstep, a lioness, and a man who clearly wasn't getting any action tonight.

Nonetheless, today had been A Good Day. Tomorrow would be another step on the journey.

Sleep began to welcome him.

The house phone rang.

Really? The phone rings like once a week.

His eyes snapped open.

Five seconds later, it continued ringing, as phones do.

Please get that. I'm only a tenant, remember?

'Who in the hell…?' came a disgruntled murmur.

'Search me,' he replied.

'Humph.'

She wriggled, grumped, threw back the covers and stood. With zombie steps, she reached the hallway, thumbed the Answer button and offered, 'What?'

'It's Buck,' came the voice from the loudspeaker. 'You up?'

'Am now,' she growled.

'Pull on some clothes. Meet me at your offices.'

'At eleven-thirty at night?'

'Trust me. You want to be here.'

'Why?' Her tone was intrigued.

'Because something bad has happened.'

Chapter 10

It was cool out, but warmer where they stood.

A thin sheet of high cloud blurred the half-moon into a glowing canopy. At ground level, an intermittent blue light danced across a few windscreens.

Beckman held Lolita's hand as tightly as he dared, squeezing her fingers yet unable to give a fraction of the support and relief he wanted. Her face was stern, ashen. The gentle quiver in her body betrayed that she was straining at her limits to hold together.

Buck stood a few feet away, giving them time and space.

They all stared wordlessly at the scene of destruction.

Firefighters were still damping down. Only occasional flickers of orange remained.

Milan Enterprises made a very sorry sight. Most of the warehouse stood in charred ruins, and about half of the office space remained intact. The parking lot swam with lakes of water crisscrossed with hoses. Two men reeled up a spent hose into one of the three tenders, its night done.

Near the front of the building, Fire Chief Vern Gallop and Police Captain Oz Bosman were deep in conversation. There would be a lot of conversations over the coming days. Some would involve tears, and Beckman couldn't promise himself to not contribute a few, however strong he tried to be for her.

He sensed someone at his shoulder. They held out an object. It was a flask mug, and wisps of steam rose from its contents.

Buck's hand rested on his shoulder. 'Sometimes, my coffee cures all ills, physical or no. This is not one of those times.'

'Sometimes, friends are all you need,' he replied. 'This is absolutely one of those times.'

'But if you had ten million bucks, or a time machine, or both, that'd be great.' Lolita managed the smallest of smiles.

Buck slipped between them and reached big arms across their shoulders. 'Shy of those, you're welcome to whatever I have that might make a difference.'

'Free root beer for life?' Beckman suggested lightly.

'And there was me thinking my generosity didn't have a limit.'

They fell silent.

After a minute, a new set of headlights played across the lot. They turned as one, like the Three-Headed Knight, to see a silver Mercedes SL slow to a stop.

'And I thought it couldn't get any worse tonight,' she said.

'He's a right to be here.'

'After Oz, that's the second person I didn't want to speak to.'

'Why Oz?' Beckman didn't know the guy, other than that he was PD head honcho.

'Because the cops will blow this thing into a story. And we don't have time for a story.'

Jack slammed the car door and waddled his diminutive frame over.

Can her mood go any lower? If anyone can do it, Jack, you're the guy.

As Jack came in for a paternal hug, Beckman and Buck backed away to allow his daughter room to tolerate a brief embrace.

'I know what you're going to ask,' Jack said, defensive from the off.

'Other than, "Would you mind running out for pizza for everyone?"'

He pulled a smirk, wholly familiar with Lolita's jibes. 'Our fire certificate is up to date. I don't have a lot to do around here anymore—'

'I saw, from the rocketing employee satisfaction rating.'

'—but we're not a sloppy ship on stuff like that.'

'That's a relief. I'd hate for anything bad to happen.' She flung a hand out towards the razed carcass.

'Don't be an ass, Lolita.'

'Why not? It runs in the family.'

'I get it. You're lashing out at anyone. It's the shock.'

'How come you're so damn calm about it?' she demanded.

'Because in business, shit happens, and panicking is no answer.'

'Do you see me panicking?'

'No.' He calmed his tone. 'I see you sad as all hell—and don't think I'm not too.'

'So, nine a.m. tomorrow, I'm straight on the tail of what piece of shit did this.'

Beckman jolted, although she was only vocalising what they both thought.

Jack's brow knitted. 'Who?'

'What? You think this was an *accident*?'

'Ah, that's some accusation,' Buck breathed.

Jack held up a hand. 'I know you're some kind of superwoman, darling, but it's a bit early to leap to conclusions.'

'It's suspicion, okay? Not accusation,' she rapped.

'Well, Oz and I go back a long way.'

'Then you damn well talk to him. We don't need any kind of scandal now. Nothing that might put a spanner in the works.'

'You need to stop being so pig-headed,' Jack suggested.

'I'm only trying to protect the company—or what's left of it. And I'm enough of a *superwoman* to know that wading in with wild theories is not helpful. Especially as the shock is apparently talking here. *You* answer Oz's questions. You might be less partisan.'

'I'll be pretty partisan about things that affect my own—,' he corrected himself, '—our—your company.'

'But without emotional baggage.'

The coffee seeping through Beckman's mind caused a penny to drop. He nodded, catching her drift—the unsaid words.

Sadly, that nod spoke to Jack, who turned his attention across. 'You know something, Beckman?'

Beckman shook his head. He didn't *know* anything, but he might have joined a couple of suspicious dots. Equally, he'd only been in town ten weeks, and there could be a million backstories that left breadcrumbs from way before his time.

Lolita eased across in defence of her beau. 'An accident would be a hell of a lot easier to take.'

'Than what?' Jack asked.

'Things Oz might ask about. Disgruntled ex-employees.' She barely disguised the sneer.

Jack's face swam surprise, then incomprehension. Finally, a dawning, one shot through with, if not guilt, at least reflection.

She saw it. 'What?'

Jack looked away. Not to take in the view, or the rumble of the first fire tender leaving the scene, the hiss of the hoses, the distant barked instructions of the firefighters. He pondered, and his already sloping shoulders dipped. 'Carlton did seem pretty pissed.'

'What?'

Jack sighed. 'You know the way someone's teeth are clenched so tight they're holding something in?'

'Pissed at what?' she demanded.

'Beats me.' But he avoided eye contact, and there was something in his voice—a child crouching in a dark corner.

'What did you say?'

'Nothing.'

She moved closer, a half-head taller than her father. 'What did you say, Jack?' Her tone was cold steel.

'I said... I said it looks like GigantiCorp is in town. You might want to ask if there are any vacancies?' A supplicating smile was received in the same way a fly experiences the outcome of a friendly glass head-butt at freeway speeds.

'You what?!'

Jack attempted comfort with a hand on her arm. 'I was yanking his chain. Come on, he knows what's happening. He's not dumb enough to believe you'd keep him on after the merger.'

She slapped his liver-spotted hand away. 'You prick, Jack! He's a goddamn wasps' nest ready to swarm, and you took a big stick and jammed it right in there.'

'You think Carlton did this?' He jerked his head towards the smouldering carcass.

'Hell, you don't need to be Sherlock Holmes to join the dots. Even Katie Holmes could figure it.'

'I can't believe a simple conversation....'

'Goddamn you to hell! You ruined my company.'

'Our company.'

Beckman took a cautionary step away from the potential blast zone.

Oh, Jack. Now is so not the time for semantics. Stow the table, put the seat upright and brace brace brace.

'Like holy hell it is! You are out of here.'

'Pardon me?'

'You heard.'

'Fine. It's late anyhow.' He turned.

'You're fired, Jack.'

He spun back. 'Pardon me?'

'You heard. You're fired.'

'You can't fire me, I'm—'

She lunged forwards until their faces almost touched. 'You watch me.'

Beckman had seen Lolita break up with Carlton in no uncertain terms, and himself been on the receiving end of being told, in similarly uncertain terms, to leave town. They were angel caresses compared to this mood and tone.

Jack would have been a monumental idiot to offer even a misplaced breath by way of reply. Being a smart guy and an experienced businessman, he eased wordlessly away, turned on his heels, fired up the SL and swung out of the parking lot.

To pass the awkward interlude, Beckman raised the flask to his lips, but they'd all drained it. Out of the corner of his eye, he saw Oz break off his conversation and walk over.

Buck said, 'I'm doing a late-night opening for two customers.'

'I'll start the car,' Beckman offered.

Buck laid a hand on Lolita's shoulder. He pressed a familiar set of door keys into her hand. 'I'll talk to Oz. Just don't burn the café down before I get there.'

Chapter 11

The Usual Table was a loving blanket on a hateful evening.

Not a word had passed their lips since they'd left the scene of devastation (the burned-out version, not the one she'd caused to Jack's manhood).

Soon, the room's silence was broken by machinery; whirring, burbling, hissing. Then by clinking, light footsteps, a rap of china on wood, the scrape of chair leg on the floor.

Buck sat between them. 'The night mom died, you made me come here, about this time.' Lolita looked over, emerging from a dark reverie. He continued, 'I even let you use Bessie.'

It was of exactly zero surprise that Buck had a name for his machine, slightly remarkable it had taken this long for Beckman to hear it, and frankly astonishing he'd ever let anyone near it/her—even near enough his own daughter.

She took a long, reflective draw on her coffee. It seemed to permeate and then melt her, release her from a carbonite prison. 'An honour, never repeated,' she reflected.

'Difference being, mom was gone. Don't mourn; you've not lost anything. Milan Enterprises is still on the operating table, and that machine with the little green wave is still beeping.'

'It doesn't feel like that.'

Beckman reached across and took her hand. 'We'll make it work.'

'There's enough love in the town,' Buck added.

'Love doesn't save businesses or rescue takeovers,' she moped.

'No, but insurance does.'

That lifted her. 'For an executive, Carlton does have his blind spots.'

'Doesn't the guy get a few yards of rope?' Buck asked.

'Absolutely. Even Carlton deserves leeway. I already got the once over from Mister Perfect here for misjudging Tyler.'

She's talking about you.

There are worse terms of endearment. Especially under the circumstances.

'Do you think Carlton would cop to it?' Buck wondered. 'If it was him.'

'I'll take evidence over confession. Oz would, huh?'

'Except he'd follow due process. Slowly, but still.'

'Oh, I'll follow a *process*.'

'Like mentioning it to Randall,' Beckman suggested.

'He's a credit controller.'

'He's a hitman.'

'Outsourcing your revenge is still revenge,' she countered.

'Says the woman who put a hit on Tyler. Even before he'd technically done anything.'

'That wasn't revenge. It was love.'

'Wow. You fell in love quickly.'

With you, dummy. Don't knock it.

'Is that so bad?' she asked.

'Look what happened when you fell in love with Carlton.'

'Trust me, you're not the cheating type.' That came with a version of The Eyebrow, which had a side order of warning thrown in. It was wasted; he'd no inclination to ever cheat on her. Death was preferable to the alternative ramifications.

'Or the twisted firestarter type,' he added.

Buck laid a hand on her shoulder. 'Honey, promise me you won't do anything dumb?'

The only thing worse than going up against Lolita was going up against Buck. What would happen if the two ever came to a significant disagreement? It would make the immovable object vs unstoppable force problem look like a kindergarten playground squabble.

'Yeah,' she breathed.

'Talk to Reba if you don't trust Oz.'

'It's not "don't trust", it's….'

'Start at the end, not at the beginning?'

'We have an advantage over Oz and Sunrise PD—we know some about motivation.'

'You're also civilians,' Buck pointed out.

'What happened to bored small-town cop desperate for action?' Beckman asked.

Lolita turned to him. 'Oh, Oz is desperate all right. For the drug bust of the century.'

'Drugs? In Sunrise?!'

Buck chuckled. 'A few weeks back, he found a gram of weed on a kid who jaywalked. Now he reckons the town's going to hell. He's burning all his time on it. He even picked up this shitty second-hand drug-sniffing dog from upstate. Mutt can't tell weed from a ham on rye, but Oz got an allowance from State to get the thing, plus he always wanted a dog anyhow, but his wife won't allow. So he gets to have one legitimately and come across like this paragon of law-making, but really he's just blowing smoke up his ass on the chance of getting his name in the nationals for breaking a billion-dollar cocaine cartel out here in the middle of nowhere.'

'Sheesh. So I should go easy on a little civilian snooping.'

'You snooped on Carlton once before,' Lolita reminded him.

'I guess. But infidelity is not the same as arson.'

'Being a dick is his M.O.'

'This is big-league now—if it was him.'

'If he's done this to save his job at EVI, and screw the takeover, then if we can prove he did it, that's leverage. Walter would drop the sale price to avoid the scandal. If we're a few million down on account of the fire, that may be our only shot at getting the merger through.'

'He already survived one gross misdemeanour,' Beckman reminded her.

'Because I let him. Because I wanted to be the bigger person. I thought he'd be quiet as a mouse in case I blew the lid on him trying to steal our customers before. Well— the gloves are off now. No more Mrs Nice Gal.'

'And what if it isn't him?' Buck chimed in.

'An accident? Then number one, he'll still be a son of a bitch, and two, I'll feel pretty powerless.'

'I meant… someone else.'

'Like?'

'What time did Tyler leave last night?'

Beckman sat bolt up, shook his head. 'Tyler is a hell of a salesman, but it's an Oscar-winning performance to bring us a bottle, break bread and smile and laugh, then pull off the road on the way home to torch the place.'

'If I could come up with a single legitimate reason, I'd agree with you,' she replied. 'But you might as well say it was Jack—at least he's got reason to hate me.'

'Not even Jack is that big of a dick.'

'Big is the last thing Jack is.'

They all smiled.

'Who else benefits?' Buck downed the last of his own coffee.

'Anyone trying to scupper this deal is living in cloud cuckoo land. It's in all our best interests as a defence against GigantiCorp,' Lolita reiterated.

Buck nodded. 'And GigantiCorp know that. The merger failing would harm both Milan and EVI.'

Lolita sat back, eyes widening. 'I don't like where this is headed, Buck.'

'This woman, Dixon, was just in town.'

'Keeping a low profile,' Beckman said.

'To not be identified. Stay unnoticed. In the shadows. Like the dark ones at the back of the warehouse.'

Lolita swallowed and studied Beckman.

Did she feel the same as him? Would it be easier to take if it turned out not to be Carlton's doing?

Buck stood. 'We should all get some sleep.'

'Go gentle into that good night.' Lolita rose too. 'Because tomorrow is raging time.'

Chapter 12

At breakfast, Beckman suggested they both couldn't tiptoe around Sunrise PD forever and remain silent for fear of saying the wrong thing. Silence might imbue suspicion of insurance fraud, and the last thing they needed was suspicion of anything. They wanted a loose wire, a stray spark, anything to make the root cause an accident. The outcome would be the same, but with minimum ramifications, and their time could be devoted to making good rather than getting even.

But if Carlton's hand held the match, it arguably marked the culmination of a chain of events that Beckman himself had precipitated, and keeping those thoughts from surfacing was an ongoing struggle.

The visit with Oz passed without incident. They answered the requisite questions, didn't give unnecessary information, kept calm, and walked out with one considerable and one small weight off their shoulders. The latter was that, given the time the fire was reckoned to have started, Tyler (and Miss Broomhead) were in the clear, as expected.

When Oz had asked about any potential "disgruntled ex-employees who might bear a grudge", both of them hummed and hawed to disguise the fact that one name raged through their brains. In a town with few secrets, Oz did commendably well not to suggest precisely the same name.

Besides, if Oz mentioned he had an inkling about the culprit, he'd paint himself into the corner of having to actually do something about it rather than pass valuable time walking a dog, drinking coffee, or hunting down non-existent meth dens.

It's a good thing the Coffee Planet supply contract doesn't start until next month. We might have a cat in hell's chance of getting back on our feet by then.

Wouldn't it be ironic if that's what tipped Carlton over the edge? Not Jack's misjudged jibe, but you stealing a big contract from under EVI's nose. That was enough of a statement of intent, a two-fingered salute to the guy who'd tried to bring Milan down.

Ironic?

Make that sickening. Another good deed gone bad. Another ripple.

At 10.30, they were once again standing in the parking lot at Milan Enterprises, staring in wonder. However, this time, smiles were on their faces, not tears.

For one, the damage didn't seem as bad as it had the previous night. Atrocious rather than apocalyptic.

For two, none of the dozen or so Milan employees present stood around wringing their hands. They were all pitching in, ferrying detritus into waiting skips, or rescuing items onto clean pallets.

For three, Jack wasn't there.

For last and not least, an angel had swept down from heaven and deposited a past-its-best Winnebago (later identified as a 2001 Adventurer) near the edge of the lot. An angel with an eyepatch and snakeskin boots who was unhitching his truck from the front of it.

Saul spread his arms wide. 'It don't move, but it does a fine job of not being full of smoke and melted glass. And the seats are real fake leather.'

'It's a mobile office,' Beckman murmured. 'Well, it's an office.'

A brown one. With cobwebs on the windows. And who knows what secrets the pull-out double bed held.

Lolita skipped over and laid a smacker on Saul's cheek.

'Can't stop rescuing people, can you?' Beckman asked.

'Not when they pay in kisses,' Saul replied.

'It may be about all we have left to pay with,' Lolita said sagely.

'Then you may need to demote yourself to Head of Supplier Relations, honey,' Beckman said.

'Meantime,' she plucked a rag from Saul's pocket, 'I confer on you the title of Vice President of Dusting.'

He smiled, but she didn't, so he took the rag and went to see what facilities their new executive suite offered.

At lunchtime, an angel who owned a café arrived with supplies, and they took a break from directing operations and sifting through what was salvageable.

Tobin, Head of IT, went Colonel John "Hannibal" Smith and jerry-rigged a broadband setup using a whole mess of wires and a bigger mess of brain cells. Along with a portable generator, a water bowser and an urn, all seemed pretty rosy.

All the company salesmen fulfilled their scheduled local customer visits.

Randall put calls into all the significant debtors and offered discounted payment terms in the hope of improving cash flow.

Mack, head of Warehousing, busied himself with an inventory list. It didn't appear hopeful. If they couldn't restart supplying customers very quickly, they'd be out of customers, then out of money, then out of business.

Suddenly the late lunch didn't taste so good. And Buck's lunches always tasted good.

'Do you think you maybe went hard on Jack?' he asked.

Lolita set down her pastrami on rye. 'Is that a joke?'

'We already joined dots to put the petrol can in Carlton's hand. It didn't need Jack's jibes.'

'Because he's got this amazing track record when it comes to not making bad judgements?'

'All I'm saying is if you trace the motivation to that one remark, why stop there? It's only fanning the embers that were burning anyway.'

'You mean after I fired Carlton? Or after I shot up his precious car? Or after I dumped him?' She scowled.

'You might as well be mad at me for exposing him in the first place.'

Her jaw set hard. 'You'd like that? Really,? Are you playing the goody goody now, trying to take the blame? Hoping you can wade in again, save another relationship?'

Good job. Fanned your own embers now, didn't you?

'I'm trying to find alternatives. Hell, maybe even it was my winning that contract? It put us in a financially stronger position, them in a weaker one. Carlton would hardly be thrilled about it.'

'Then bravo—well done you. Want I should fire you too?' she snapped.

The air crackled. 'I don't know. Do you want to?'

'I don't know. I want a Rewind button, that's all.'

'To when?'

'Before… all this. When my life was a damn sight simpler.'

'Okay.' He pushed himself up from the rickety table. 'That could work.'

He yanked open the flimsy door and cracked it closed behind him, making the whole vehicle rock on its bald under-inflated tires.

Chapter 13

You wanted that to happen.

He slumped forwards onto the Buick's steering wheel and hunched there. Quickly it became uncomfortable, so he climbed out and walked gingerly to the end of the tarmac.

The quiet stillness pushed in on him.

He parked his backside on the very last foot of blacktop, sneakers planted on the brown-ochre dirt beyond, folded his arms across raised knees and rested his chin onto his wrists.

There had been spots like this, moments like this, in Wyoming too. And Nebraska. And Ohio. And Idaho. And Kentucky...

Some of those times, he'd been in love, or at least thought he was in love. Nobody really knows what love is until they find out what love is when it *really* is.

Some of those times, he'd made a mistake or been an idiot.

Some of those times, dad had been the idiot, or life had been unfair, or at least seemed unfair. Nobody really knows how unfair life can be until they find out it's unfair when it really is.

It's all semantics, though. It's all ripples.

He picked up a pebble. Then, after checking around to make sure he was alone, he took a best guess aim and lobbed the pebble ten yards forward.

It soared twelve feet off the ground and vanished into thin air.

He twitched as if he hadn't expected it to happen, although he had.

Almost like falling through the surface of a vertical lake.

He checked around to be double sure nobody had spotted him. And because they hadn't, he threw another rock.

This is a fun experiment. Even better than throwing rocks into a clear, fast-flowing river when you're nine years old. Except, obviously, without the marvellous sploshing display.

So it was exactly like that, in a cutting-edge scientific discovery kind of way. Unencumbered by any scientific training or qualifications, thesis, method, results, conclusion. Or, indeed, by any motivation besides it being probably the coolest and most dangerous thing a startlingly un-cool and un-dangerous thirty-eight-year-old ex-travelling salesman could do. Especially when he's had a minor hoo-hah with his girlfriend and is hankering for some introspective alone time.

It was a place to go.

A treehouse at the bottom of a scrub garden in Wyoming.

A small graffitied cave in a low range in Nebraska.

Under the eaves in an Ohio barn.

In a clearing beside a river in Idaho.

Up in the loft at the on-base accommodation in Kentucky.

You can't deny all those mused-on problems were solved. Or they went away. Or you got over them. Or they became opportunities or life lessons.

Maybe the life lesson is everything can be figured out, as long as there's a place to do it in.

He threw another rock.

Sunrise is a hell of a place. But this?

It's the polar opposite of all this navel-gazing. Maybe that's its beauty—counteracting dilemmas about consequences by indulging in something with no apparent consequences. Or at least causing a distraction by wondering about the possible consequences of something that was itself unfathomable.

They were right; it draws you in. It reframes you.

What if, on the other side, all these rocks are hitting an innocent baby in the face? What if they are making cataclysmic impacts on microscopic-sized civilisations in alternate realms? What if they are flopping out of an opposite gateway in front of an introspective late-thirties salesman in Uzbekistan or Waikiki or the Orion Nebula?

Probably not.

He threw another rock.

Was there a parallel world where eighteen-year-old Beckman didn't meet Wynona and learn an important lesson about out-of-date milk?

A different reality where you kept quiet about Harlan's cheating on that test and didn't get a black eye?

A place where you didn't call your dad a vindictive asshole and get grounded for a week, missing that three-day outdoor festival?

He threw a pair of rocks at once.

The Portal could handle two rocks; Experiment 2 was complete.

One freeway jam, and here you are.

One freeway jam and one diversion.

One new road. A flat tire. A tow-truck driver appearing from nowhere.

Or through a portal nearby? Saul's own portable Portal? There's a whole new afternoon of wondering there. Or you could ask the guy. Might put his nose out of joint, and you already did that with Carlton—and what happened? You're here...

...Here at the edge of the town. A town not on the map.

Where you saw a girl—a customer.

She could have refused your little brown box. Or taken it and not come back to thank you. Then you wouldn't meet Carlton. Get suspicious of his antics. Hire a P.I. Find out he was cheating on the girl you met and liked but knew wouldn't give you the time of day.

You could have kept your mouth shut. Moved on. Minded your own beeswax.

What if you hadn't got that flat when she threw you out of town? If you'd missed the lobbed beer bottle and sailed on, back to the old life, the life of certainty.

In another world, she didn't kiss you. She didn't accept you back, takes sides in your plight against Tyler Quittle.

A hair's breadth later, and Tyler might have died. That would have been too much.

You still would have left—again, but not returned, even when Randall Ickey and his six-in-the-mag-one-in-the-chamber came hunting.

Any of the bullets flying around the warehouse could have hit you. Or Lolita. Or Carlton.

Wow.

There's a million alternatives even there.

Bruno could have been too slow. Malvolio could have beaten the poor thing to a pulp.

Ickey could have double-crossed you, taken to the hills with the fifty million. Hell, you'd half expected it.

Instead, the money goes into giving Lolita—the woman you now love—her dream.

And she gives you… something. A new start. A… different reality.

Not any of the other million, billion, trillion possible realities— the better ones, the worse ones, wherever and whenever and however they may be.

This reality.

And yet, deep down, a fraction of a slice of a part of you wants to find out what's through that barrier.

Because you're an idiot.

Because this reality is apparently not one hundred percent, Grade A, top of the line perfect.

He sighed, murmuring, 'What an idiot.'

He cast a handful of small stones, in an arc, that popped out of existence (possibly) in the air in front of him.

You have a great job in an amazing, life-affirming, crazy as hell town and an amazing, life-affirming, crazy as hell fiancée.

And in another universe, it was your (her) house that caught alight last night when you were inside it.

So thank your lucky stars in this universe.

He picked up another stone, played with it.

From the quiet stillness came something else. Something that pierced his hitherto lost-in-space. He pivoted at the waist, looking down Latrop Road towards town.

Shit. Miss M is here.

He scrambled to his feet, panicked, glanced at the stone in his hand, pocketed it.

She stood there and put hands to hips, which was one level above The Eyebrow. 'Have you been throwing stones into The Portal, Beckman Spiers?'

For about a picosecond, he considered denying it, then hung his head. 'Yes, ma'am.'

She responded with abject silence, walked closer, The Eyebrow coming into focus. Then she reached into her skirt pocket and dug something out. 'Here's your cell.'

He took it. 'Thanks.'

'I tried to call. It rang on the next desk.'

'Sorry.'

'It's okay.'

Change the topic. Make her laugh. Anything.

'I wish I had a tricorder or something.'

'From Star Trek?' she asked with incredulity.

'I know,' he said, fending off her fiction-isn't-reality disclaimer before it began. 'But, just to figure out—you know?'

She looked at where The Portal wasn't making its presence at all obvious. 'This has really intrigued you.'

'Doesn't it you too?'

'Sure,' she said with the beginnings of a smile.

'Finding Sunrise was great for me. Life-changing. But what if… that… is even better?'

'Honestly? That may be one of the dumbest things you've ever said.' She stepped closer, words echoing a return of concern. 'I mean, anything where you vanish into thin air doesn't reek of being safe.'

'Plus, you'll tell me I'm running from our problems like dad did, and he was a dick. I have you, and that's enough. Or it should be if I can get it into this thick head.'

She took one of his little fingers in her hand. 'I see, and I raise you on the whole dad thing. The difference between you and Jack is you try to do the right thing. He only looks after himself. When he gets round to putting me first, I might forgive him. Until then, please don't interfere. Okay? I know you think you're doing the right thing, but you're too hung up on the whole consequences vibe. Ripples. So be careful of throwing rocks into emotional ponds as well as interdimensional gateways.'

He took her hand in both his. 'Jack hasn't forbidden me from marrying you. So, will you invite him? Knowing he won't come. Or is it not worth the risk in case he does?'

'The way we're going, I've months to decide.'

'Don't you think episodes like this prove that rushing into things after ten weeks together is not a good idea?'

'Why—are you not sure anymore? Looking for a get-out clause?'

'No—absolutely. No. But maybe extra time will help us… flush bugs out of the system.?'

'Look at Jack and mom. It took them twenty years to flush out a pretty major bug. Now, I love the bones of you, but I'm not waiting two decades to get wed on the small chance there's a hairline fracture now which finally blows, and we've waited to live our best lives.' She changed the grip to hold his hand. 'You might have noticed I'm a girl who likes to get things done.'

He nodded but didn't have anything to add.

Silence pushed in again. He wished The Portal did something cool like crackle occasionally to break the silence and help communicate the otherworldly feeling to the place. If, indeed, other worlds were involved, which they'd never find out anyway.

'So, how was the stone-throwing?' she asked casually.

'It was okay.' He gave a gentle shrug. 'Alright, it was *awesome*.'

'You are such a kid.'

'Yes, mama.'

She shook her head and glanced around. 'Can I have a go?'

'Do as I say, not as I do, huh?'

'Because women are fickle. Any other guy will tell you, so you might as well hear it direct.'

'Seems fair.'

She scanned the ground, then spied something closer to hand. 'What about this?' She fingered the bracelet on her wrist.

Beckman was startled. 'Looks expensive.'

'It is. I reckon two hundred bucks.'

'Rocks are free.'

'I know.'

'Okay,' he said, bemused. 'What do you expect to prove?'

'That anything Carlton gave me is about as worthless as a rock.'

'Can't argue. Come over here. This is the best throwing spot.'

Duly positioned, she slipped off the pricey trinket, took aim at an invisible target, and bowled the thing with commendable gusto. Mid-air, it flicked out of existence.

She gave him a wink, and they embraced. It turned into a long soothing hug.

'If Carlton really did start the fire, we can't let him drive us apart,' she murmured into his neck.

'Yeah.' The sun played across the distant mountains. 'Anything else of his you want to jettison into the beyond?

Chapter 14

Ray's was the finest steak restaurant in town, and damn if they didn't deserve it.

The neons in the establishment were predominantly blue, matching the hue they were trying to expunge from their mood.

Ray was also a Milan customer. One whose contract was soon due, although they convinced themselves their patronage that evening was not a factor in greasing the wheels of business.

Beckman and Lolita were there because after the soul-crushing twenty-four hours they'd experienced, damn if they didn't deserve it. Saul was there because he'd ridden to their rescue, so damn if he didn't deserve a 10oz thanking for it.

'Pitcher of margaritas,' Lolita asked their server, milliseconds after her butt kissed the burgundy leather of the booth's ample seat. Kellee, the owner of The Finest Set Of Teeth In Town, flashed the self-same prize-winners and beetled off to fulfil the order.

They'd chosen the booth for privacy, and as there was a likelihood of shop-talking and conspiracy-wrangling, they didn't want anything resembling Jack's faux-pas to transpire.

'You didn't have to do this,' Saul said.

'You didn't have to dredge up The RV from the Black Lagoon,' Beckman replied. 'But we're glad you did.'

Lolita jabbed a thumb at her betrothed. 'Plus, I could use your help dragging Chuckles here out of his own wallow hole.'

'For you, Lolita, I'd walk over hot coals,' Saul replied.

'Imagine what he'd do if you were older and more single,' Beckman suggested.

'She wouldn't need to be older,' he deadpanned. 'But blonder would help.' He winked—or at least Beckman assumed he'd winked, possessing only one good eye.

'It's a good thing you're chain-yanking, buddy. I don't fancy my chances of successfully defending her honour.'

'It's okay,' Lolita laid a hand on his shoulder, 'I'd handle it.' He didn't doubt her for a second.

The pitcher arrived, they ordered, made small talk and learned the RV's colourful back story. Soon, their steaks arrived, served by Ray himself. They were duly honoured. Then he served something they hadn't ordered.

He laid a hand on Lolita's shoulder and lowered his tone. 'I have the contract renewal signed in my office. You folks need all the help you can. Marty from EVI was over this morning, offering me ten percent under your prices. They smell blood. So, I'm only a sticking plaster, but we do what we can, huh?'

'Thanks, Ray. Means a lot.'

'You have a good evening now.' He left.

Lolita sipped. 'What we really need is a power surge, blow all the bulbs in town.'

'Machiavellian, but not the dumbest idea ever,' Saul remarked, chewing.

'If you really were superwoman, with the power over power itself. And if we had the stock to rush-replace everyone anyway,' Beckman pointed out.

'There's always a wrinkle with you, honey.'

'Not that we won't entertain any cockamamie scheme that gets us rolling again.'

'You should give away a pile of those little boxes of yours with every contract,' Saul suggested, juice leaking down his chin.

Beckman and Lolita's cutlery did a synchronised pause in mid-air, and they exchanged a look.

'Sometimes, Saul, you're wasted towing cars,' she sighed.

Saul batted it away with a big paw.

'Head of Business Development?' Beckman ventured.

'If we can pay him in steak, sure,' she added.

'I'll take Head of Bright Ideas, Consulting position,' Saul said, without looking up.

'You have to provide your own decrepit office space.'

'I'll work from home if it's all the same. I do my best thinking in the can.'

Beckman and Lolita sputtered with laughter. Saul (probably) winked again.

Moments into their own meals, the legitimately employed twosome were interrupted by the arrival of a colleague.

Beckman didn't like the expression on Ickey's face. 'What gives, Randall?'

Ickey threw a glance to Saul, and Lolita caught it. 'It's okay. He's almost on the books himself.'

'Contract details pending,' Saul said, not breaking stride on his march through The Best Fries In Town.

Ickey checked around. 'We're not insured,' he said gravely.

Beckman smiled, hoping it would catch, and Ickey's poker-face would be found out. It didn't, and it wasn't.

Lolita shrugged. 'I'll talk to Jack in the morning. Probably misfiled the paperwork, the useless ass.'

Ickey sat beside Saul and shook his head. 'I got the paperwork. Needed it to call the company. They said the policy is voided.'

Lolita set down her cutlery with commendable restraint. 'What?' she asked with a quiet menace directed at the universe rather than the messenger.

'They said our policy was cancelled two days ago.'

'Not possible.'

Ickey nodded sadly. 'The insurance company were told we'd taken our business elsewhere.'

Her face was etched in worry. 'Did we?'

'Not that I can see.'

She shook her head vehemently. 'There must be a mistake.'

'I spoke to the other admins. Nobody has moved us to another supplier.'

'This is not happening.' Colour drained from her face.

'I wish like hell I didn't have to tell you.'

'I wish like hell it wasn't true.'

'Who would do that?' Beckman wondered aloud.

'I asked,' Ickey said solemnly. 'They said the person who called was a Beckman Spiers.'

Chapter 15

Bile rose in Beckman's throat. Lolita's chest rose and fell heavily as she strained to hold herself together. He dearly wanted to hold her—to tell her everything would be okay, even though he could give no such guarantee—but also to keep himself from exploding.

'I've had a margarita or two, Randall, so I want to be absolutely sure,' she said levelly. 'We've lost over half the assets of the business, and we don't have insurance to claim on.'

'Unless I am a Grade-A idiot, or someone at the insurance company is a Grade-A idiot, or worse, a Grade A joker, then, yeah.' His voice trailed off; he barely wanted to breathe the last word.

'Shit. I may have to pay Ray in kisses too.'

'He's worth it.' Saul licked the fine taste from his lips.

Lolita knew he was trying to lift the mood. She cut herself another piece of steak very carefully and would have eaten it with gritted teeth if possible.

'Randall,' she said, 'Tomorrow, I want you to visit the insurance guys in person and discuss this. Check if they have a recording of the call. Because everyone at this table knows a false name was given. And if anyone at this table thinks for a second I doubt that, they should leave now.' Randall nodded dutifully. 'Now, I don't shoot messengers unless they are a male parent of mine, so make yourself comfortable and get a server to take your order. Milan

Enterprises may be staring down the can, but I have a personal checking account too, and anyone showing balls gets the benefit.'

'You're the best, boss.'

'Best, yes. Boss? Enjoy it while you can.'

She tucked back into her meal, and the three guys let the background ambience suffice for a while.

Beckman pondered his personal net worth, if he could liquidate any of it, and whether it would make the slightest difference to their plight.

Probably not.

He considered whether selling an entire semi-trailer of Pegasus boxes within the next day or so to anyone who'd listen was feasible in the slightest.

Unlikely.

He mused the likelihood of Jack lending a hand; remortgaging his palatial abode, calling in favours, selling a Shelby Cobra or two, to help bail out the daughter who despised him so much.

Tricky.

The newly-appointed Head of Bright Ideas wasn't even on probationary yet but was sorely needed.

His own best notion was that The Portal might lead to Aladdin's cave but avoided mentioning it. Besides, the cave's mouth was likely blocked up, thanks to some idiot constantly throwing pebbles at it.

'Now,' Lolita said when the plates were cleared, 'If I was here alone, it would be time for a second pitcher. If Jack was here, he'd be secretly praying I'd burst into tears, proving a woman isn't fit to run this company. As it is, I'm going large on the ice cream order and taking viable suggestions for how we dig ourselves out of this shit.'

'Sounds good,' Randall said.

'And there'll be company bonuses for whoever comes up with the idea that allows us to be able to afford company bonuses ever again.'

'Sounds better,' Beckman agreed, foreseeing the need for the financial wherewithal to keep his future bride in the manner to which she'd become accustomed, assuming they were still able to afford the wedding, or the manner, and she didn't have a nervous breakdown meantime, try to garrotte Carlton with a cheese wire, and end up on Death Row. Worse case, he'd need the money to drive up and visit her once or twice a week and try to slip her a hand-baked Gâteau à la Hacksaw.

When the ice creams arrived, she savoured every mouthful as if she genuinely was on Death Row, although he guessed Ray's recipe knocked the State Penitentiary's into a cocked hat.

Saul hoovered the lot up in about fifteen seconds.

Randall spooned it down with his little pinkie sticking out, which made for the most alarming thing Beckman had discovered about the guy since they'd exchanged gunfire in a now-smouldering warehouse.

'I have some T-bills,' Randall said. He might have revealed a collection of rare Chinese pottery for the three looks he received. 'What? I had some pretty sweet contracts. In my… former life.'

'Which you invested wisely?' Saul said.

'Hiring a credit controller without a decent sense of fiscal responsibility would have been a pretty dumb move, huh, boss?'

'You're nothing if not the most financially astute former hit-man I could find,' Lolita concurred.

'What *is* it with that?' Saul asked. 'I mean, leopards, spots—yeah?'

'I was a repo guy, ten years. It wasn't all muscle; they put me through a numbers thing—for the office stuff. But this,' he gestured to his frame, 'Was a Field Op recipe. So—people pay. It was mostly a softly-softly kinda place. But carrying a Magnum on occasion.' He downed his beer. 'I used to play the shoot-em-ups arcades at the Mall.

Misspent youth and then some. I was pretty good. Turns out they had a scout there, the agency.'

'Hitmen R Us?'

'It's not the dumbest idea—searching for people who can shoot straight. So this guy came over, asked how I could use ten grand. I was already working against schmoes who were crossing boundaries—of a kind. The first guy was about to get acquitted on a stone-cold rape charge. Call me crazy, but I'm not a fan of that. Dot dot dot.'

'I'm in hallowed company,' Beckman said sadly.

'It becomes a job, and numbers on a bankroll. And the devil owns my soul—I get it.'

'Trying to buy it back now?' Saul ventured.

'Straight offer—I'll take a straight answer. Maybe this is me going cap-in-hand for another leg up out of Hell, more than what you folks already gave me. If I can't repay that faith—or try—it's burning pitchforks up the ass forever.'

Everyone exchanged looks.

'How much?' Lolita asked.

'Half a million.'

'It would be a *loan*.'

'Sure,' Randall agreed.

'Okay.' She smiled mildly. 'So we're both one rung out up of Hell.'

'I'll talk to the bank. See if they can extend any more credit.'

'We're already up the wahoo with the finances for the EVI merger.'

'It doesn't hurt to ask.'

'Right now, it feels like the merger *and* staying afloat are two snowballs in that Hell of yours.'

Silence for a moment, broken only by Saul using his spoon to find any atoms of dessert he'd missed the first time. 'On "not hurting", I could speak to Pandora. Her old man is one of those venture capitalists.'

'Venture capital guys,' Beckman said, before remembering that correcting a bear like Saul was about as risk-free as, say, the venture capital business.

'Yeah,' Saul agreed without a blink.

'That sounds like cap-in-hand,' Lolita said. 'Even to your office manager.'

'The way I see it, you have a five percent stake spare if you're closing the door on Jack,' Randall said.

'See.' Lolita tilted her head. 'And they say never hire convicted killers.'

'Not convicted,' Randall pointed out. 'Just Hell-bound.'

Lolita gave Saul a gracious little bow. 'Thanks. I guess… it doesn't hurt to ask.' She flashed Randall a wink.

'I have a signed copy of Born to Run,' Beckman said with zero irony. 'Next to Lolita, it's the most important thing in my life.'

'Saul, I think the shortlist for Head of Bright Ideas just halved.' She shook his hand. 'Welcome on board.' She reached under the table and squeezed Beckman's upper thigh to show he was still very much on the shortlist of her Important Life Things.

'Now,' she continued, 'I guess there are three people in this booth wondering when the boss will step up and lead by example.'

'It crushes my damn soul to touch the money Jack left for me. Because written all across that bank account in invisible, needling, told-you-so ink is that this is for the inevitable day when you realise you can't make a success of yourself in the real world. Well, I have two hundred grand in my checking account, and if I sell off all my business and personal stock of artefacts, there's double. Then I remortgage the house. And, finally, as we're staring at this because *dear* Jack shot his mouth off, I am very much touching that bank account and will proudly tell him it's because of his inability not to be an asshole. So there may be two million, all told.'

'Do you think that's enough?' Randall asked.

'If the wind is at our backs tomorrow, we might have a fighting chance. And if I go see Walter, ask him with my sweetest smile and lowest-cut blouse if he'll overlook this bump in the road, who knows. If he hears this Dixon woman has been in town, and GigantiCorp is sniffing blood, he'll take a merger that safeguards his future over pretty much an asteroid strike.'

'I'll call Tyler first thing,' Beckman said.

'I'll talk to Pandora,' Saul promised.

'I'll get the check,' Randall raised his hand. 'I have a few bucks left from my—what do they call it in commerce—golden hello.'

Oh yeah, the trifling matter of his cut of their cut of Malvolio's stash of loot. A cool million. There must be a chunk leftover after Randall moved his life from whatever anonymous hole he lived in, and relocated to a decent-sized townhouse in Sunrise. After fees, removal costs, price of his first-ever suit.

'Of all the guys who tried to kill me, you're the best, Randall.'

'Well, I didn't officially hang up my gloves, so if you ever… need a guy.'

'If it comes to that, we've all lost,' Lolita said.

'We're not done yet,' Beckman insisted.

Unseen, in the adjacent booth, a recently-arrived wiry man with horn-rim spectacles pursed his lips. His brain began to whirr.

Chapter 16

'You know discretion is my middle name?'

'I thought it was Jennifer.'

'How in hell did you know? Thought I was the P.I. round here?' Reba fixed Beckman with her one real eye.

He tapped the side of his nose. 'I have my methods.'

'Or Randall told you.'

Beckman's shoulders fell. 'Yeah.'

'Good thing I don't tell him any real secrets. He's the yin to my yang.'

'And the two of you are yinning and yanning pretty good, I reckon.'

She smiled. 'He treats me right.'

'And April okay with it all?'

'April has starting fifth grade and obsessing about the new Toy Story movie to worry about. Besides, it's not like he's making to move in with us.'

'I don't envy you that conversation, especially with her Asperger's.'

Reba smiled. 'We all get kicked by change, some more than others. We all deal, some more than others. And her mom has no two days the same in her line of work, so planning can be… a challenge.'

The municipal park was quiet, which is why they were there. No prying ears—not for the pleasantries, but for the business of the day.

He pointed at the swings and, after giving him an intrigued look, she took the hint.

They walked over and took adjacent places on the sun-baked and warped wooden seats. Then, because it was a free country, and the activity was infinitely less inflammatory than lobbing pebbles into a mysterious Zone Of Weirdness, he began to swing.

'Lolita and I do talk,' she said, pushing her petite frame into motion.

'Specifically about… ?' he asked, fishing.

'You and dominoes. It cuts both ways, you realise that?'

'I guess.'

She checked around about them. 'This case—doesn't matter the cause, the motivations—only the perpetrator. I don't tell people how to think, react, self-flagellate, even revenge—if that's how they're built or minded. People want a Yes or No, a name or a photograph. Don't beat yourself up, especially until the jury is in.'

'If you could make me come up smelling of roses, there's a bonus in it for you,' he joked.

'To this girl, you smell pretty fine anyway. The domino you pushed already gave me a case, a payday and someone else to run April around town. The day you walked into Sunrise, the world didn't collapse around you. So lighten up, okay?'

'Yeah,' he sighed. 'So can you keep this on the down-low? Even at home?'

'Jennifer is my middle name, remember?'

He arrived back at their immobile mobile office space as Captain Oz Bosman left, tipping a salute, which Beckman took as A Good Sign. It meant Oz didn't think he'd called the insurance company, set the fire, or done anything else that might involve a round of Searching Questions.

The cop's visit had, however, left the future (aka When I Get Round To It) Mrs Lolita Spiers (assuming she would change her name, which might be a long shot) in not the brightest of moods.

She sat on the real fake leather bench-seat-which-turned-into-a-bed, at the stained dining-table-now-office-table, staring at her laptop. On the other side of the kitchenette, Randall was arranging unidentified paperwork.

Beckman made the international sign for "money". Randall replied with a so-so of the hand.

At least they didn't seem dead in the water yet.

He eased onto the squishy seat opposite Lolita and held up his hands in a heart shape. 'What gives?' he queried.

'We recovered the CCTV tapes.'

'Yeah?' Which was code for "Gotcha, Carlton".

'System was switched off an hour before the fire.'

'Oh, snap,' he breathed. 'By who?'

'Still checking. But an inside job, almost certainly. Not Dixon or any similar sharks.'

'How did it start?'

'Still analysing too. A short could take out the cameras, maybe cause a spark too. It's wide open.'

He nodded, bereft of anything useful to add.

'How was your… errand?' she asked.

'Good,' he replied obliquely.

'Speak to Tyler?'

'Yeah. He liked the idea—Saul's idea. Would treat *us*, this time around.'

'That's lucky, as we may only have two nickels to rub together by the end of the week.'

'Quit on that, okay?'

She managed a half-smile of acquiescence and sat up straighter, emboldened by his gee-up.

He noted her suitable talking-Walter-round blouse. Some guys would be, rightly or wrongly, perturbed by their loved one going out and flaunting, but this was a vital throw of the dice, and he was pragmatic enough to understand that a little cleavage can sometimes go a long way. It was her company, her deal, her body.

'I brought lunch.' He unpacked his careworn shoulder bag.

'And a four-leaf clover?'

'You can do this, and you know it. We have great brains behind this. Plus, I'm sure Walter will see that Milan can still boast some of its better assets.'

He expected The Eyebrow for that remark but instead received a gentle shake of the head.

Behind her, Randall nodded furiously.

It was all Beckman could do not to corpse.

Lolita took the Miata out to the far outskirts of Sunrise, where Walter Whack had set up home some thirty years ago in a house that looked like it hadn't been touched since. Its slightly dishevelled state managed to appear homely and heartwarming rather than uncared for. It certainly didn't want for space, and its aspect below a tree-decked low hill contributed to a sizeable price tag.

Inside, it was outfitted in a manner befitting a longtime CEO, and Walter's mantra was that as long as he was inside it, enjoying the view out, he wasn't looking at the garage doors that needed a new coat of paint, weeds in the long drive, or the few missing roof tiles. It boasted no valet, no prancing stone lions on the gateposts, no ten-car garage. Walter had done okay for himself (and Mrs Whack) but still passed for a pretty regular guy.

Maybe—and apposite on the occasion of such meetings as this—there was an element of disguising the actual state of his financial affairs. He'd be in a better bargaining position if the opposition didn't think he had all the money in the world to play with. "Aw, can't you give me a better price? I'm scratching around here, barely enough money for gas for the ride-on lawnmower."

But Lolita had seen the thickness of the towels in the guest bathroom and wouldn't be duped.

She brushed the brake pedal and rounded the last part of the driveway. The afternoon air eddied, clouds taking the edge off the September sun that bore down on the open cabin.

D-Day.

She came to a halt and killed the engine.

With a deep self-gathering breath, she pulled the portfolio case from the passenger seat and reached for the door handle.

Walter exited the tall, wide front door.

Was this keenness a good sign?

A slight noise cut the air. She glanced around. It wasn't a familiar noise.

Walter stopped.

She sensed it coming from above them and looked up.

It was.

In as much time as it took to absorb what had happened and what would happen, it happened.

A chunk of the brick chimney stack, maybe two feet high, clattered off the edge of the front roof and careered to the ground.

Unfortunately, something blocked its path.

Walter was caught a glancing blow and smacked to the ground, out cold.

Or worse.

Chapter 17

Beckman held her tightly that night.

'Whoever in Sunrise had been under that chimney—even No Name—I'd feel the same. Nobody deserves that.'

'Really? Even… him?' Beckman asked.

She exhaled deeply. 'At the time, yeah, it still would be as shocking. But lying here, now, maybe it would be good riddance. Does that make me a bad person?'

'Let's be bad people together.'

'I'll have Talia send some flowers to the hospital.'

'Throw in some smelling salts.'

'Don't be an ass.'

'Gallows humour,' he said defensively.

'Look on the bright side. It gives Milan more time to get back on its feet.'

'If you're telling *me* to look on the bright side, my work here is done.' He loosened his bear hug.

'Don't let go, Beckman. Mine was gallows humour too.'

He held her tighter again. 'I was afraid of that.'

'So near and yet so far.'

'There's this: nobody can undo anything. They can only *not* sign the merger agreement.'

She wriggled, so he let go. She swivelled round under the bedclothes to face him. A puff of cool air bloomed into the space, so he pulled the sheet up higher and drew her closer, his hand in the soft warmth of the small of her back.

She looked into his eyes. 'Yeah. Carlton and Wanda are the substitute signatories, and if he's dead set against the merger, takeover, whatever—for sure, he's brainwashed her to think the same. The thing is, dear man, if GigantiCorp sees a sliver of opportunity to ride in and gather them up onto their horse, either of them is shallow enough, probably vindictive enough, to take that offer.'

'They would sign away Walter's company while he's in a *coma*?!'

'If they have authority to make decisions, and it'll make them rich—especially if it'll act like a knife in our backs too—they'll do it. Believe me.'

'I'd ask if you were judging them harshly, but....'

'If we get to the bottom of what's happened over the last two days, there's a chance the only person we'll see judging them is a judge. At which point, what I think is beyond redundant.'

'Very magnanimous.'

'Where Carlton is concerned, it's damn easy to be the better person. Hell, there are things living inside the bark of Walter's palm trees that are better people than Carlton Cooper.'

'Less magnanimous,' he smirked.

'Kiss me.'

He did as instructed.

'I don't know how you deal. Are dealing,' he said after an enjoyable interlude.

'I should be an emotional wreck, right?'

'I guess I still don't know you one hundred percent.'

'I'm sure of it.'

'I worry there's a head of water inside you, specifically behind those normally sparkly eyes.'

She gave a sober chuckle. 'I'm not really a crier.'

'Not even when Jack ruled you out from the family business? When you discovered what Carlton had been doing? Even when you thought I'd chosen life on a beach instead of life with you?'

'Sorry.'

'At Bambi? ET? The end of Terminator 2?'

'Uh-huh.'

'Any chance you'd cry at our wedding?' he asked.

'Come on; it won't be *that* bad.'

'I meant tears of joy.'

'Duh.'

'Surely you cried when your mom left?'

'No,' she sighed, introspective. 'Maybe I was born without a heart to break. The only thing at risk of cracking is my soul. My will.'

'And that seems to be holding together pretty well.'

'Maybe because I'm not doing it alone. So, kiss me again.'

They did.

'What are the chances Mrs W — Wilma can sign?' she wondered aloud.

'You said she's never been a part of the business, or not anymore. Both Carlton and Wanda would be apoplectic if they knew Mrs W had a de facto seat at the top table. And Walter wouldn't be a sharp cookie if he allowed a sniff of a chance for a non-business brain to do something to his business.'

'It's hardly his best decision to let the existing pretenders to the throne have a hand on the tiller.'

'We should be praying for Walter, not kicking him while he's down.'

'Whatever I need to work through to get a quiet mind?' she suggested.

'If you want a solid night's sleep, I'd much rather tire you out physically.'

She eased her head away. 'I bet you would, Romeo.'

'I may not be Head of Bright Ideas, but I'm just trying to be practical.'

She narrowed her eyes. 'Hmm.'

'Talk, or sleep?'

'Sleep.'

He smiled and rolled over, clicked off the bedroom light. Silence fell, the glimmer of moon glow through a curtain crack.

'Aren't you going to tire me out then, Romeo?'

Chapter 18

Lolita exited the ensuite, towel-wrapped and towel-turbaned, to find Beckman holding up a hangar.

'I picked this out for you.'

She loosened the headwear and dried her straggly chocolate locks. 'I'm not sure that kinda thing says "kick-ass businesswoman" anymore.'

He laid the navy swing dress on the bed. 'Well, for openers, you don't have any power-dressing meetings today. For second, our office is a vehicle even the Griswolds would shy from. Third, it reminds me of the girl I fell in love with. Besides, I thought it might cheer you up. You used to wear these as two fingers to Jack. How about two fingers to the world today?'

'What did I do to deserve you?'

'You got a headache.'

'Ah yeah.' She stepped closer. 'Want to go back to the scene of the crime for breakfast?'

'Absolutely. There are two things I love about mornings. One is coffee.' He fingered the knot which held the towel in place around her chest.

'Good. Because one is all you're getting.'

They sat at the Usual Table, drowning in Buck's World Leading Coffee.

'She's back,' indicated Lolita. 'Which is interesting as all hell.'

'Only means she has taste in coffee.'

She eyed Buck. 'And maybe baristas too.'

'It looks mutual. The sly dog will scorch his hands unless he watches what he's doing.'

'I've never seen Buck look at anyone. Literally anyone.'

'Well, he's looking at her again.'

'We should tell him she's bound to be bad news.'

'You thought *I* was bad news. Judging a book by its cover. Look what happened there.'

'Exactly. Which is why I need to warn Buck off making the same mistake.'

'You're not funny, *Miss Milan*.'

'I am funny. And it's "Miss Milan *ma'am*". I'm still your boss for a few more days.'

'How does Buck cope with having a Kinda Daughter like you?'

'By the looks of it, he needs a shoulder to cry on.'

Dixon Lewys, in a sharp off-white pantsuit, peered at the menu, oblivious to either Buck's or their repeated glances in her direction. Lolita stood. 'Right. I'm taking a long shot that not all tall, well-dressed, corporate high-fliers are ball-crushing bitches. And I'm going to make nice with her.'

She sashayed diagonally across the floor of the sparsely-populated restaurant. Beckman awaited fireworks.

Instead, something very different happened.

'Hi,' Lolita said.

Dixon glanced up. 'Oh, good. I'll take the Eggs Benedict and a filter coffee.'

'Oh, no… I… '

Dixon sighed theatrically. 'What? Chef not in this morning? Out of eggs?'

'No, it's not that. I… '

'Sorry, is this not your table?'

Lolita forced her raised hackles to calm. 'No. It's…,' she forced a smile, 'I thought I recognised you, is all.'

'Ah. Okay. I never got that before.'

'Never mind. My mistake. Anyway… Eggs Benedict and filter?'

'Please.'

Lolita forced another All-American smile and backed away.

Buck's face was a picture when she reached the counter. 'I don't believe it,' she smarted.

'Me either.'

'Good.'

'With a figure like that, I wouldn't have thought Eggs Benedict was on her diet regime.'

Lolita jammed hands on hips. 'So you *have* noticed her!'

'Who?'

'Dixon.'

'Who's Dixon?'

'That woman. Her!'

'Oh. Yeah. Didn't she come in before?'

'You sly old dog, Buck Travis. You can't take your eyes off her.'

He didn't rise to that; instead set about preparing the drink order. She leaned in, trying to catch his eye.

'What?' he snipped as if trying to swat a fly.

'You should say hello.'

'I already said hello.'

'You're evading.'

'You said she was bad news.'

'Some people think *I'm* bad news,' she asserted.

'No. But sometimes you're a pain in the ass.'

'You're only saying that because I'm right about you and her.'

He set the coffee down and waved away her words. Beckman sauntered over, having surmised what was happening. He flashed a knowing glance at Buck, halving his odds of wriggling out of anything.

'What?' Buck hissed. 'Why would she be interested in an ageing bourbon barrel like me?'

'Because you're the nicest guy in the world,' Lolita replied. Beckman coughed sharply. 'Second nicest,' she sighed.

Buck set both hands on the counter and leant forwards. 'I'll say this.' They both craned in. 'Don't leave your customer hanging, okay? I'm running a café here.'

Lost for words, she looked daggers at him, scooped up the mug and turned on her heels. Beckman's eyes met Buck's, so he snuck out his palm and received an under-the-radar low five. 'How do you get away with that?'

'Because *I'm* not marrying her.'

Beckman almost discerned, through the change in posture, the moment Lolita slipped her pride inside a little box and popped it in her pocket.

The conversation floated across.

'Thanks.'

'Sorry about the wait.'

'That's some machine you have there.' Dixon's gazed at Bessie's six-foot bulk atop the sturdy twenty-foot wooden counter.

'Older than Time itself and more reliable than any man *I* ever met.'

'Oh, they're reliable. To be men about everything.'

Lolita deliberately frowned. 'I can't place your accent. Upper New York State?'

'Lower, actually.'

'I thought I hadn't seen you around.'

'Just in town for a spell.'

Yeah, a black one, like a witch, Beckman mused.

Lolita gestured to the empty chair. 'Not meeting anyone?'

Dixon smiled weakly. 'Not this time.'

'Do we come… recommended?'

'Yes, the hotel desk... Kinsey. And he wasn't wrong. And I like what you've done with the place. Very... ' She looked around, trying to match the decor with its plethora of neons, the wooden tables, the swing dress. She gestured flamboyantly at Lolita's attire. '...Fifties.'

'And I like your pantsuit. Very... out of town.'

They both smiled cordially.

Lolita perched one cheek onto the empty chair. 'So, what line of work are you in, Miss...?'

'Lewys. Electricals.'

'Ah.' Lolita feigned a penny dropping, masking the hour she'd spend researching the woman's company and credentials. 'You've come to the right place.'

'I can see.' Dixon barely concealed the fact that she considered the prevalence and style of lighting in Our Buck's, and indeed in the whole town, to be deeply tasteless.

If Lolita had taken a dislike to her before, it went up a notch. To not love the industry you were in marked you out as a soulless corporate bitch.

This "making nice" business was tricky. Lolita smiled sweetly. 'And we do *excellent* coffee.'

'A+, definitely.'

'Staying long?'

'The person I was here to see is indisposed. Which makes for a long and wasted journey.'

'Well, don't rush away,' Lolita lied. 'This is a very special town.'

Before Dixon had a chance to lie in return, Buck arrived at the table bearing the Eggs Benedict.

Lolita sprang from the chair as if electrocuted.

'Pardon the delay, ma'am.' Buck flicked a stern expression at Lolita. 'She's new here. Sometimes you can't get the staff.' He gave Dixon a longer look than one might expect, but of the exact duration Lolita anticipated, given his appalling denial of any passing interest in this striking—if strikingly dislikeable—personification of what Jack believed his daughter could never hold a candle to.

Lolita, as offhandedly as possible, asked, 'When did you get in?'

Dixon paused her cutlery. 'Yesterday morning.' Then she put on her version of a forced sweet smile that veritably shouted, "Thank you, wench, now leave me to my breakfast."

So the wench did precisely that.

Chapter 19

'She seems perfect for Carlton—utterly dislikeable. Maybe we should hook them up? Because, you know,' Beckman clarified, 'They'd probably kill each other.'

Lolita looked across as he piloted the trusty white Buick. The forecast had given a 40% chance of rain, so they hadn't risked the Miata.

'Or wind up ruling the world, knowing our luck. Either way, we don't burn any bridges meantime. We don't let on—mainly because if we throw mud in the wrong place, we'll be up on slander charges. If I can bite my lip with Miss Almighty Britches back there, we can do it with anything. Besides, if I'd been shaking hands with Walter, things would be very different.'

'Very painfully different.'

'Which reminds me I need to get together a succession plan.'

'Why, planning on going somewhere?' he asked.

'No, but events prove that forces, natural and unnatural, exist. If I'm in bed on a drip, I want someone I can rely on taking the right decisions.'

'It won't be me because I'll be at your beside twenty-four-seven, holding your hand, hoping for the best, whispering sweet nothings in your ear.'

'And trying to fondle various bits of me when the nurses aren't around.'

He focussed very deliberately in the other direction. 'I will take the Fifth on that.'

'I'm not above whispering sweet nothings in old Walter's ear if it means he'll wake up and hold a pen for ten seconds.'

Small though Sunrise was, it did boast a hospital. Legacy of a generous donor some decades ago, although Beckman didn't much care.

They pulled into the parking lot, found a space near the entrance and headed into Reception.

'Here for Walter Whack,' she announced sombrely.

The duty nurse indicated the requisite direction, and they walked down a couple of corridors that looked and smelled like all hospital corridors until they reached Room 122.

Walter Whack—having considerable bucks to his name, primarily on account of having saved many by not repairing faulty chimneys—had a private room. He seemed a lot less sprightly than when they'd met the previous week. Much more... horizontal, significantly bandaged about the head and shoulder, with more wires emanating from him than the back of Lolita's flat-screen TV. Machines and monitors stood guard.

'Are you thinking what I'm thinking?' he asked.

'If it's along the lines of Officer Alex Murphy, then no, and please wait outside.'

Jeez, she's good.

Er...

'I was thinking we should count ourselves lucky. Six inches further left, and we'd be wearing all black.'

She sighed heavily. 'Amen to that.'

'Puts things in perspective.'

'I guess.'

The room's quiet was pierced by three, short, loud hand claps from behind them.

They quickly turned to see Carlton standing there, Wanda a dutiful two feet behind.

A sneer sprang onto Beckman's upper lip, and he looked away to reset its alignment into a less confrontational position. Lolita must have been made of solid brass not to sink a punch clear into the man's midriff.

'Very good. Oscars all round.'

'Excuse me?' Lolita queried.

'If Walter weren't a turnip, he'd see through it as easily as I do. The false sorrow, the introspection, the mock friendly concern.'

'We're here to show we care, that we're shocked by what happened.'

'You're here on a self-serving mission of corporate daylight robbery. "Oh hi Walter, we happened to swing by to see how you were, and you're awake, so sign this paperwork, would you, and we'll leave you to pull your pants on".'

Lolita tensed, eased forwards as if to rush him. Carlton saw it, and a smile tickled his thin lips.

'You weren't even there. You might want to show more respect for my giving your prospective father-in-law CPR immediately afterwards.'

'Because without it, he would have died, and your merger along with it. I'm surprised you're not offering to give blood, whispering sweet nothings into his ear, or playing MTV at full volume to wake him up.'

'It would be a damn sight more than what either of you two are trying,' Beckman interjected.

'You butt out of this, Spiers. You're only a salesman and a lucky one at best.'

'Lucky is right.' He took Lolita's hand.

'Carlton,' Wanda called and reached for his hand to draw him from the fray. He slapped it away.

Wow. A real turnaround in how you treat your lady folk, eh asshole?

The tension cranked up a notch.

After an eternity, Lolita broke eye contact with Carlton. 'Let's go, Beckman.'

The beanpole stood aside just enough for them to pass, and Beckman winced in case Lolita received a deliberately indiscreet brush of Carlton's hand as a last roll of the dice to entice her into detonating like a supernova. Because although he was a shoo-in for Asshole Magazine's Douche of the Year cover shot, Carlton knew she was a pent-up ball of magma. If he triggered an eruption, it would do wonders for his ability to cry foul about pretty much whatever he wanted.

He was an SOB who made Tyler Quittle, even on his worst days, look like Nelson Mandela.

As they walked the short corridors, each in silent reflection, a ghoulish notion popped into Beckman's head, and when they were safely ensconced in the Buick again, he had to let it out. It was one of those disaster movie- I'm The Chief Of The Massive Dam That Overlooks The Town, And I Tell You It's Going To Burst, Why Won't You Listen To Me? See It's Burst, Now Don't You Wish You'd Listened To Me? -type thoughts. It made him sick to his stomach.

'Do you think he'd put a pillow over Walter's face?' he asked gravely.

An expression that mirrored his gut flashed across her face and evaporated. 'It's a step too far. And Wanda's with him. She may be complicit, but she wouldn't stand by everything. You saw how she was.'

'Okay.' But he permitted himself to worry anyway. At least he'd warned the sheriff about the dam.

Warm rain pattered on the windshield as he drove them to Milan Enterprises.

Some day a real rain will come and wash all this scum off the streets.

'Don't you wonder about Dixon?' she asked, above the hiss of radials on the damp asphalt.

'I wonder about a lot of things.'

'She arrived before the fire, left not long after. Arrived before Walter got hurt. Ten bucks says she leaves today.'

'Do we have ten bucks?'

'Humour me.'

'Do I think it's a hell of a coincidence? Yeah. Does she know our warehouse and Walter's house and schedule enough to be responsible? Not convinced, to the tune of ten bucks. Even twenty.'

She nodded. 'Me either. Maybe I'm trying everything to give Carlton the benefit of the doubt. Lord knows why.'

'And to think you were in love with him.'

'Yeah, well, that was before I knew him.'

All of which proved to be a conversation killer.

Soon they rolled to a halt outside the non-longer adventuring Adventurer. She flashed him a weak but well-intentioned smile and skipped up into their centre of operations.

At the table, aged but reliable laptop in front of him, sat Tobin.

When Tobin joined Milan Enterprises some seven years previously, so Beckman had been told, he'd been advised that losing the ponytail was a precondition of his employment. Jack, of course, had standards to maintain, if not his own ones of tolerance.

Yet, even if you never knew as much, you'd see Tobin, a greying forty-something, working in IT, with a predilection for checked shirts and loafers, and think, "I'm sure this guy should come with a ponytail".

When Lolita took the reins, she told Tobin to do what he damn well liked with his locks, because (1) if it made the guy a happier employee, all well and good, and (2) it was unlikely to affect his ability to be a wizard in the Server Room.

Tobin didn't have much of his beloved Server Room left, but he did have nine weeks of hair scraggily gathered in an elastic band, which seemed to have Samson'd his talents.

'I restored the remote system,' he said. 'So if this luxury,' he indicated the vehicle's interior, 'Gets too much for you, you can dial in at home.'

'The captain should stay with the ship at times like these, but thanks,' Lolita replied.

'Don't thank me yet. I managed to retrieve the last online backup. Chief Vern put the fire starting around eleven. There was a complete backup that finished at 22.47.'

'It's a silver-plated lining.'

'Don't thank me yet,' Tobin repeated.

That pulled Lolita's face from sober into apprehensive. 'Okay.'

'Someone logged on and disabled all the site CCTV and fire alarms at 22.30.'

She closed her eyes and put a hand to her forehead. 'Who?'

Tobin bit his lip. 'You.'

Chapter 20

Lolita's apparent login through the remote system marked an investigational dead-end—exactly as if Oz and the boys had done the legwork. The only way they could have gotten lucky was if the perpetrator had accessed the building before the cameras went off to turn off the cameras. As it happened, Tobin had watched the library recordings of the previous minutes to no avail.

This was more than an errant youth with a Zippo; this was carefully planned.

First and foremost, they needed to keep this locked down. Tough, in a town built on openness. Luckily, it was also founded on loyalty, and for Tobin—a guy who dealt in data and security—this was woven into the fabric of his being. He'd never spill a word unless subpoenaed—and they hoped it wouldn't come to that.

Soon enough, Oz would be a-knocking at the door to pursue the same line of enquiry, and he'd doubtless ask for Lolita's whereabouts on the night of the fire. Mercifully, each of them had two independent witnesses to the fact they were at home, making small talk, catalysing relationships, and trying to work out the orbital mileage of a possibly middle-aged woman.

Logically, Oz would want to ascertain the whereabouts of everyone with a connection to Milan Enterprises. The difference was he'd start in alphabetical order or some such procedural baloney.

They, in contrast, would start with the letter C…

…Providing they worked out a method that appeared as natural as, say, a theoretically unsafe chimney falling from a roof at an outstandingly inopportune moment.

Sunrise had a place ideally suited to concocting cunning plans, packed as it was with brain food, brain refreshments and bear-sized baristas who were precisely the right build for bear-hugging Kinda Daughters who were being framed for torching their own premises.

As Beckman chauffeured them through a post-rain townscape festooned with puddle-hosted reflections of a thousand neon lights, a wild thought came to mind.

The kind of thought he wished he hadn't had.

What if Jack did this?

What if his appearance and demeanour that night was a double-bluff ruse to deflect away suspicion?

If he was half as pissed with his daughter as she was with him, then why not?

He had all the necessary physical and digital access, and a motive was easy to contrive. She's wrenched away control of the company, left him with tea-boy duties and a minimal financial stake. Arguably, he'd become a laughing stock at the racket club—or whatever similar clique he frequented. Outmanoeuvred. Emasculated. Beaten.

He could easily pull out a block from the base of the wooden tower as she continued to build it higher. He'd also have the perfect patsy—a man he lost no love for and one who'd already tried to screw his company. A man his daughter hated and who she'd readily believe was responsible.

And Walter? They'd been business enemies for years. Putting him in the hospital or the morgue would be a cherry on the cake of scuppering Lolita's takeover plans. Plus, it wouldn't take Magnum P.I. to put Carlton Cooper top of the suspect pile.

Three poleaxed adversaries for the price of one.

Jack Milan might be an ass at times, honey, but he sure isn't a dumb one.

He hated the notion. Worse, he hated that it had merit. During any spare minute, he resolved to develop viable reasons why it couldn't possibly be so.

Now, though, there was something else to mull. Two familiar figures on the sidewalk ahead, trudging away from Saul's garage towards Main Street.

He slowed. 'Do we want company?'

Lolita peered out the window. 'If he's carrying another thousand bucks, I might flash my suspender tops at the guy.'

Don't think about her suspender tops. The last thing we need is a fender bender.

'Nothing like five seconds with Carlton to make ten years with Tyler feel like a beach vacation in Rio.'

He eased them to a halt a few yards ahead of Tyler and Miss— Amaryllis' position and climbed out.

'I'd know that plate anywhere.' Tyler offered his hand. 'Ride?'

Amaryllis gave a faint nod. 'Sure.'

The passengers climbed in the back. Awkward (logistically, not socially) handshakes were exchanged, then Beckman pulled away. 'Saul have the tire in stock this time?'

'I brought a pickup. Is there a way of getting to this crazy town that *doesn't* involve getting a flat every time?' Tyler asked.

'That's on a need-know basis,' Lolita replied.

'So, how do we get on that Christmas list?'

'Impeccable behaviour and standing us a round of drinks. Actually, that's only the entry criteria to join the waiting list for possible addition to the shortlist of people the town might consider entering the Welcome programme.'

'Was any of that serious?' Amaryllis asked.

'Let's start with the drinks and take it from there. It's been one of those days. Scratch that, weeks.'

Dixon wasn't in the café, which didn't amount to much of a discovery. After all, if wild theories were needed about who had triggered these mysterious 'accidents', Beckman's Horrible Thought About Jack easily outscored Meddling Interloper in terms of probability. Notwithstanding, he wished it could be pinned on Ol' Frosty Pants rather than the person who would, sooner or later, become his father-in-law.

Buck greeted all four and handing Lolita a folded piece of material.

Beckman watched as she unfurled it, curious. Very soon afterwards, the penny dropped. He witnessed, for the first time in his limited sojourn in Sunrise, Lolita ball her fist and, only *fairly* gently, sock Buck in his ample midriff.

Then she backed off, quivering like a dog who doesn't know whether to scrap or play with an unknown mutt twice its size, before throwing her arms about a quarter of the way around the barista's circumference.

'In case you need a few extra bucks on the side. Besides this one,' he said.

'This one is all I ever need.' Lolita disentangled herself, span round and proudly displayed the item, like a spokesmodel. It was a café apron with the word "Lolita" in script on the breast.

'Can you recommend a good table, Miss?' Beckman asked.

'Yeah. One at Jen and Berry's. And don't let the door hit your ass on the way out.'

'Shocking the staff you have here,' Beckman said to Buck.

'Aw, a few whippings and I'll have her straight.'

Without turning, she jammed her elbow into his belly. It didn't even register, apart from the kiss he plonked on the top of her head.

'Alright if I start tomorrow?' she chirped sarcastically.

'Saturday is time and a half. Which I guess you need.'

'For once, mister boss man, sir, the town doesn't know everything.'

'And we know even less,' Tyler said.

'Let's fix that,' Beckman offered, leading them to the Usual Table.

Their hour of beverage consumption was interrupted by Tyler taking two calls. Old Beckman would have considered it asshole behaviour, but the guy had grown into his role as Pegasus' Big Cheese. He remembered Reba's sage words: the consequences of actions cut good as well as bad for anyone in the radius. One upshot of the emergence of New Tyler was that Beckman had lost an enemy and gained a... well, if not friend, at least very tolerable acquaintance. An acquaintance who might facilitate a slight financial upswing in the Milan/Spiers (soon, or relatively soon, to be the Spiers) household.

Must have that maiden-name-change conversation.

So, it could still be the Milan/Spiers household.

But then, a dollar is a dollar.

But then also, a man's dollar is only a man's dollar until he has a wife, at which point it becomes a woman's dollar.

Must have that separate-bank-accounts conversation.

During the hour, the out-of-towners didn't get the whole nine yards about the goings-on at Milan Enterprises.

Was her guarded approach excessive or merely sensible?

Sensible. The more people who knew the intricacies of their current travails, the more likely a word might slip out and enter the wrong ear. He'd learned to his cost that if you are not of Sunrise, you don't know how it works. Just because he'd emerged unscathed (in fact better than that— betrothed) didn't mean Tyler and Amaryllis would be so lucky.

In previously crossing Carlton, Beckman had merely tangled with a viper; now, it was an anaconda.

'Obviously, I don't know this Oz cop guy, but short of a poltergeist, how the hell else does a chimney stack fall off in the exact thirty seconds someone is standing in the way?'

Tyler was only saying what Beckman, Lolita, Buck, Saul, and half the town were thinking.

'Because it never rains,' Lolita replied.

'I didn't move into your apartment yet, Beckman. So, if you want it re-gifting back for some liquidity….'

'You're a pal, Tyler. Hold that thought, okay? Don't want you out on the streets once you leave your mom— leave the place you are now.'

Beckman darted a glance to Amaryllis to see if she'd picked up on his slip but reckoned he'd gotten away with it. If there was the merest chance that *amour* lay in the future for the Pegasus twosome, he didn't want to torpedo Tyler's swagger by broadcasting that he still lived at home. Or maybe Amaryllis already knew and didn't care. Or considered it cute because it meant Tyler couldn't be a bad guy if his mom tolerated him. However, 'living with your mom' and 'sleeping there every night' are not the same, and Tyler's legendaire with the fairer sex was a more significant hurdle for Amaryllis to vault than his specific domestic arrangements.

'You're expecting I emptied Malvolio's safe into my checking account and blew five million on a mansion,' Tyler said.

'The thought crossed my mind.'

'There's something in that office of his—mine. A lingering stench of fiscal responsibility. We have a ship to sail, don't we, Amaryllis?'

'Today's cash cow is tomorrow's steak dinner.'

'That sounds like the old stiff,' Beckman suggested.

'Ignore the methods—in fact, *very* ignore Malvolio's methods: we grew every year. I get the whole "Tyler is an asshat" aroma that wafts through the place but damn if I'm taking the rudder only to steer us onto the rocks.'

'We have a giant octopus grappling with the good ship Milan,' Lolita said. 'Even four hands on the tiller is a hell of an ask.' She grasped Beckman's hand in both hers.

'You have the competition sniffing round—you must be doing something right.'

'Yeah—we stuck our head out of the trench, and now the snipers are having a field day,' Beckman added.

'Well, for what it's worth,' Tyler said, 'We have your back, best we can.'

Beckman and Tyler trailed the ladies up the street; the Pegasus duo were walking back to their hotel.

Separate rooms—has to be.

He's not so reformed that he wouldn't take a sly opportunity—such as now—to boast that he'd enticed Amaryllis into the sack.

And why do you care what happens between them? An idle mind is the Devil's workshop. You've got better things to solve, idiot.

Beckman became aware of Tyler slowing to a halt, distracted by something. He followed the gaze.

Wanda lowered her oversize sunglasses. 'It was a nice thing you did, coming to see Walter.'

'What can we say?' Lolita replied. 'Some fathers are worth the time of day. Even when they're not your own. *Especially* when they're not your own.'

'We hope everything turns out okay,' Beckman said.

Tyler and Amaryllis had backed off to give this discourse some space.

'And we're vested, but all the same….' Lolita tailed off.

'Thanks for what you did,' Wanda said.

'Where were you?' Beckman asked.

Wanda jolted back, more a tic than recoil, and Beckman worried whether he'd let the Devil out of his workshop and into the vocal chord area.

'We… were both at home. Garage door motor was on the fritz. Carlton wanted me to hold a ladder.'

'You don't have a guy for that?' Lolita asked.

'You know Carlton,' she replied, and Beckman saw regret that she'd phrased the comment like that. 'He's stubborn when it comes to fixing things up himself.'

In Lolita's eyes lay a smouldering fire but also steely self-control. 'Yeah,' she replied noncommittally.

'Anyways.' Wanda dug out a small smile, nodded to everyone, replaced her glasses and set off across the street.

Tyler watched her go. Amaryllis watched him watch her go. Beckman watched her watch him watch her go, then watched her go. Except Tyler wasn't watching her go *like that*. He was watching her go *to that*.

A red '65 Mustang parked two cars down.

'Never figured you for a pony guy.' Beckman hoped he'd correctly interpreted the item that had piqued Tyler's interest.

But if he's looking at Wanda, so what? It's a free country.

The Mustang is a safer bet, though. Better lines.

If it was blue? Don't get me started. I'd hate Carlton even more—if that were possible.

'No, not really,' Tyler responded distantly.

Wanda slid into the seat, and the car burbled away.

Tyler span back to face them, his mind clearly working. He looked at Amaryllis, then back at Beckman. 'Any more in town?'

'You're kidding? Museum piece like that?'

'Only… I saw one. That night, after we left your place.'

'Everyone has to go to the late-night liquor store.'

Tyler shook his head. 'Coming out of the Milan factory. I reckoned maybe your overnight security guard—if you paid them really well and they had great taste in Detroit metal.'

Lolita stepped into the fray. 'Darren Deeks drives a Civic and finishes at midnight.'

'After we left your place was about, what, Amaryllis? Ten thirty?'

'About that.'

Lolita's eyes widened. She and Beckman had both done the sums.

'Holy crap,' they chorused.

Chapter 21

Lolita's perennially excellent cooking tasted like so much ash in their mouths that evening.

Unspent ire crackled in the air.

The angels and demons on both their shoulders were at it, hammer and tongs, ninety-three rounds into a twelve-round bout, with neither showing signs of flagging.

'I need a walk.' She slapped the dishwasher door closed.

'With or without company?'

'Totally with.'

He pulled two beers from the fridge. 'Packed and ready.'

They dropped the hood on the Miata, and she tossed him the keys. 'I trust you more than I do myself.'

'Not to ram-raid the Cooper residence.'

'This is why marriage, Beckman. This is why. Buck is the only person who gets me like you do, and he'd fairly squash me in bed at night.'

He fired the ignition and decided the whole Lolita-might-be-sweet-on-Buck thing was (1) beyond crazy and (2) shouldn't be touched with a ten-foot pole either way.

The air hung still, and the heavens were painted above, all the way out of town until they reached a favourite spot.

One day, or maybe one evening, we'll happen upon someone else out here, in the middle of nowhere, behind the crumbling shell of a roadside gas station. Whoever it is will discover the silence, the slight eeriness, the whiff of illegality in being here.

Crazy to think that, in such a wilderness, anyone should hide behind a building in pursuit of whatever they were there to pursue.

For Beckman and Lolita, the first time had been a romantic liaison. The second time was a business proposition from Tyler. The third, a picnic.

This time it was… what? One rung below sitting at The Portal, throwing rocks and trying to solve all life's ills. Yet it didn't matter—it was what she wanted and needed, and it would do him no harm either.

The car ticked as it cooled. The Apache cicadas peeped. The stars winked.

'Cover your ears, honey.' Her expression told him this was no joke. So he complied.

She eased out of the car, stood, threw back her head and screamed loud enough to trip out the decibel meter in Sunrise's theatre, many miles away.

She's human, after all. And what she lacks in willingness to cry, she more than makes up for in the ability to bellow raw anguish.

There was enough in that outburst to cover his despondency too. It was a good thing to do. Certainly preferable to going postal on someone.

As the noise rippled across the innocent landscape, she gazed around the low lux vista and meandered, lost in thought.

He felt awkward, so he hopped out and caught up with her.

She slipped a hand into his. 'Sorry if I gave the impression I'm a strong person.'

'Even iron stretches if you apply enough force.'

'Damn it, Beckman, sometimes you're a poet.'

'Maybe. But not even Shakespeare could find the words to extract us from this.'

'You're looking for words, and I'm looking for actions. All the while, I'm only discovering actions that make things worse.'

'Don't think I'm not looking either,' he insisted.

'You know what this is? It's a temper tantrum. And what do you do when a kid throws a temper tantrum? Ignore it.'

'If you can ignore this, then whatever is stronger than iron, that's what you are.'

She squeezed his hand. 'But I'm not. I'm a pan of popping corn. I'm a charged-up thunder cloud. So I need a lightning rod.'

'Those kinda things have to be perfect, I'm guessing. To avoid scorching everything they touch.' He brought their walk to a halt and faced her. 'Jeez, you don't ask much.'

'What we have—us—is a ten-week-old baby. It shouldn't be dunked in scalding water. We should test it with our elbow first.'

'Pretty good, Keats.'

'Problem is, Carlton ran the bath.' She gave a gentle shrug.

'Okay, now you might lose me. Metaphorically.'

'With one proviso, he's doing a fine job of trying to break us up.'

'Proviso?'

'Circumstantial evidence. Take away all the baggage, all the reasons it should be him; we have no proof. Neither does Oz. How about that? I'm being objective.' She gave a sad chuckle. 'Never thought I'd see the day.'

Is this the time to mention the Jack thing?

No. Close call, but no.

It's only more theorising.

'Do we need to come out here every night for a good scream, save you from exploding?' he suggested.

'What we need is a smoking gun.'

'Providing it wasn't pointed in our face a few seconds beforehand.'

Her face fell even more serious, which he scarcely believed possible. 'There's something you need to know.'

In that split-second, myriad horrible thoughts coursed through his brain. The kind he didn't like having and needed to jam deep down inside—assuming they weren't crushingly on the money. Things like the Jack Did It theory.

A new one crossed his mind: the She Did Log In That Night gut-punch.

Then he comforted himself that anything as unpalatable and downright ridiculous as most of the things he invented would undoubtedly be much worse than the actual reality of what was about to pass her lips.

For instance, "I'm Pregnant" would be a hell of a sideswipe but redolent with infinitely more joy than disappointment.

'Yeah?' he asked apprehensively.

'We may not get a fair crack from Oz. His son is married to Carlton's sister. And believe me, she's not the kind of person to cross. And Oz is not renowned for making waves, and these would be in his harbour.'

'I don't like where this is headed.' He squeezed her hand.

'We may have to make our luck.'

'Sounds dangerously like vigilantism. Which I won't be a part of. I screwed up already by taking matters into my own hands.'

She sighed. 'Let's hope it doesn't come to that.'

A heavy silence fell.

The stark beauty of the ill-lit place was in tune with their hearts. He scanned overhead, and the faint stripe of the Milky Way lifted him. He felt wonder.

Wonder that he existed at all. Awe at Nature. Fortune at having this lioness beside him.

Amazement that of all the six billion people on the planet, they should be saddled with the presence of Carlton Cooper and all he bore and wrought. Or appeared to have wrought.

Which, he reminded himself, was unproven. And there was the rub.

'How did the scream thing work for you?' he asked.

'I looked at it like this—it couldn't hurt.'

So he took her hands and laid them over her ears.

Then he let rip a scream that would impress Munch and a volley of words that would heartily displease mom.

Chapter 22

The morning after the night before; the night before being devoid of restful sleep and blissful dreams. Breakfast tasted like breakfast. Coffee tasted like coffee.

The unspoken between them was: today is another day on the road to recovery. Eat the elephant a bite at a time. Hope for a swathe of good luck to balance out the week of bad.

Don't get mad, or even. Get finding solutions.

The first order of business was to get down to Saul's and relieve Tyler of his stock of Pegasus boxes.

They took 12 BECK, his trusty white Buick, to the rendezvous.

Saul had agreed to store it at five percent commission and hawk out the product to any customers as he saw fit. He'd seen over the past weeks how easy it was for Beckman to sell the brown boxes, and it only became easier as word got around.

Amaryllis was getting to know Pandora, Saul's office manager, and Beckman made a note to interrogate the girl later vis à vis her views on Amaryllis possible age.

He popped the trunk on the Buick and discharged Tyler's pickup's load bay into it. Then he filled the back seats.

'You know the irony?' Tyler asked when they were done. 'Keep this up and, by numbers, you'll be Salesman of the Year this year.'

Beckman snorted an ironic laugh. 'Two years in a row, huh? Never would have happened under Malvolio.'

'Why, because you should be six feet under, or the fact you're not even legitimately an employee?'

'What would a smart boss do, Tyler? He'd list himself on the sales payroll and put me down as a distributor. That way, he'd get the figures, and he could bonus himself.'

'Why?'

'In case you get a schmoe on the team who comes to you at the end of the year and says, "Hey boss, and what the hell did you do all year except sit behind a fancy desk and take a million in salary?".'

'They'd never say that to Malvolio.'

'Not if they wanted to live,' Beckman agreed. 'But you're the caring, sharing, taking feedback kinda boss now, huh? It's Saturday morning, and unless you're paying your PA overtime, let her have a weekend, okay? Ironic as hell if you treated her worse than the last guy did.'

'It's fine, honestly,' Amaryllis insisted.

'Still, take him for overtime anyway.' Beckman winked.

Tyler was about to offer judgement when a car lolled onto the forecourt.

A familiar car.

Lolita eased her body close to Beckman. 'High Noon,' she breathed.

Yet Carlton merely noticed the foursome, then, with an air of disdain, went into Saul's office like the most natural thing in the world. Which it probably was.

Stupidly, the foursome stood and watched him like a sideshow freak, inwardly tense at the expectation of a contretemps which was in no way inevitable, yet equally fearful of firing the first shot.

Carlton's gaze was sucked towards the gallery of spectators. Then he exited the door and came to see what all the fuss was about.

'Feeding time is one o'clock,' he sniped.

Beckman took a deep breath and turned away. The opening bars of the Jaws theme played in his head.

'We saw your car.'

Tyler, you ASSHAT!

'Pardon me?' Carlton asked.

'We saw your car, the night of the fire,' Tyler reiterated.

'Do I know you?' he said with quiet menace.

Tyler shot out his hand. 'Tyler Quittle, CEO, Pegasus Corporation. Great vehicle you have there.'

'Pardon me?'

Lolita shouldered into the fray. 'Your car was seen leaving our property on the night of the fire.'

A look of distaste washed across Carlton's face. 'What proof do you have?'

'I saw you,' Tyler said for the third time.

'This,' Carlton thumbed towards the New Guy In Town. 'This your alibi?'

'Absolutely,' Lolita confirmed.

'Very convenient. A little soirée with friends, which you expect Captain Bosman to swallow as proof you weren't at the factory.'

'Hey, Carlton,' Beckman interjected, unexpectedly growing a pair of balls. 'Number one, why in hell would we be there anyway? Number two, you know nothing about this guy.' He jerked his head towards Tyler.

'I know enough. Pegasus. Loyalties run pretty deep, huh?'

'Loyalty? This piece of shit?'

Tyler's eyebrows arched way into the stratosphere at Beckman's words. Even Lolita was taken aback.

'If there's one person at Pegasus I wouldn't want on my side, it's Tyler Quittle,' Beckman continued, desperate to catch the man's attention. 'He's lower than the Mariana Trench. He owes me nothing. Jeez, it's all I can do to stand next to the guy without punching him.'

Tyler became the first human to officially send his eyebrows into orbit. Whilst still wearing them.

'He'd never stand up for me because I *asked* him to! He'd sell his own grandmother's body parts to pay for a custom paint job on his look-at-me German sports car in order to bed an even longer succession of vacuous blonde housewives. You think we had dinner with him and his... colleague because we *like* him? Polite society in Sunrise means you invite anybody in, even unfailingly godawful human beings like Tyler, and sit and smile and drink their frankly shoddy highway liquor store crud, all for not burning bridges and trying to prove we're a damn sight better than people like him.'

Lolita was holding in the ruse with every fibre of her being. 'He barely knows me—and it's my business at stake. Why would he say he was at our place if he wasn't? Come on, Carlton—if he pissed all over Beckman for twelve years, why lie to protect the woman his nemesis is dating? Conclusion—he was there.'

'Although we wish like hell he hadn't been,' Beckman added. 'We could stand the suspicion, but having to break bread with the guy? That's a whole level worse.'

'The fire was almost a mercy. Made us forget what went on before.'

Carlton stood dumbstruck, but nothing compared to poor Tyler, who looked exactly like a man does when his beautiful blonde Texan wife of ten years tells him she used to be a Bavarian male wrestler called Ernest.

'Come on, Tyler,' Amaryllis urged, taking his upper arm and leading him towards their pickup.

As they left, Beckman's stomach tossed on a hurricane gale. 'And good riddance,' he called.

Amaryllis turned her head, saw Carlton studiously looking the other way, and risked a quick wink at Beckman.

His stomach settled to a storm.

'Should we agree we all have alibis?' Lolita asked with a level tone that belied her raised hackles.

'Absolutely,' Carlton replied. 'After all, I'm not the one who has to prove they didn't switch off the CCTV.'

'How in hell do you know that?'

'Come on, Lolita, this in Sunrise. But I have to admit; it's pretty ballsy. I know you hate Jack, but torching the business when it's not his anymore? Feels pretty dumb.'

Her hands flexed, balled into fists, then relaxed.

Beckman prayed she'd hold it together; the last thing they needed was to be slapped with a charge of common assault.

'And I cancelled the insurance for an extra kick in the balls?' he said.

'Why the hell not? You've done enough around here already. You play the nice guy, Beckman, but do any of us truly know you? Ride in on your white charger, save the princess from an apparent ogre, bribe everyone with a mystery box that probably causes brain cancer, run amok in her warehouse like goddamn Jesse James, and force a longstanding businessman out of work. And you've got the gall to accuse *me* of being underhanded?'

Suddenly, Tyler's ten years of jibes felt like an angel's caress.

'You can't be serious,' was all he could muster.

'I can't be sure what the hell happened here, but sure as eggs is eggs, it's all down to you. You lit the match, or her, or Jack. Even that objectionable shit Tyler. Maybe this Dixon person who's snooping around. I may be an accountant, but you don't need a college degree to do the math. Everything was fine until you walked into town.'

There it was; the gut punch. And Beckman had to lie there and take it because it was true.

It was even in Lolita's face, the ring of truth. Yes, some of the specifics were arguable, and though he'd lit no match, nor made that insurance phone call, the line of dots could still be joined.

'And the crowning turd on the woodpile?' Carlton asked. 'You got a taste for pinning the blame on somebody else once already when you hired that P.I. to snoop on me. And now you're trying to frame me again. I know you've had someone following me. Taking pictures. Trying to construct a nice little frame-up. Once, I could forgive as an innocent misstep—the actions of an outsider who doesn't play nicely in Sunrise. But twice?' He shook his head. 'Somebody has to stand up against that kind of bullshit. So I am. You don't belong here, Beckman.'

'Carlton,' Lolita began.

He swatted a hand in her direction, then stepped in towards Beckman, good and close. 'I'll be the bigger man and play nicely. Just once. Sunrise doesn't want you. You've done enough damage. You should leave.'

'Are you going to make me?'

Where the hell did that come from?

'Do you want me to?' Carlton asked.

That might involve a trip to the hospital. Better to stall for time.

'No.' He looked away. 'I'll make the arrangements.'

'Good.' Carlton flashed them both a sneer, walked to the Mustang, slid in and fired the V8. The signature move would be to light up the tires and snake down the road. Instead, he tickled the car off the forecourt, giving Beckman and Lolita a long hard stare as he went.

When he was long gone, they drew together.

'It's true, isn't it?' he asked.

'Beckman,' she began.

'Isn't it?'

'Listen, you're the man I fell in love with.'

'Yeah, well, some things can be undone. This can't.'

'Now you're being an ass.'

He tilted his head towards the now-departed Mustang. 'You have a thing for those, it seems. And *that's* what started this.'

Her face lit with hurt. A palm stung his face. He stood there, cheeks tingling, waiting and hoping for a retraction of her knee-jerk response.

None came.

So he turned away and climbed into the Buick. As he fired the ignition, she spun on her heels and marched away towards town.

The stars weren't out, and the place was too built-up, so a scream was out of the question.

Instead, he laid his forehead on the worn-down plastic of the steering wheel and waited for his heart to implode.

Chapter 23

There was a knock at the window.

He peered up. Saul extended his open palm towards the door.

Beckman sighed, killed the engine, removed the keys and cracked open the door. Saul stood back to allow him egress.

Beckman deposited the keys. It was the first time he'd been prevented from not-drink driving.

Saul laid the free hand on his shoulder. 'The coffee's not Buck's, but come have some.'

As had happened before, with Buck as well as Saul, these were not requests. It would be no more fruitful than a monorail driver having a steering wheel.

They paused in the garage's atypically clean and orderly kitchenette, collected a mug each of steaming filter from the jug, then walked out back to Saul's dirty secret: a yard filled with all the junk that didn't belong in the main premises.

There were odd fenders, unpainted wings, a stack of assorted tires, the obligatory teetering tower of pallets, old drums, something uncannily like the shell of a Ford F100, and the maroon bench seat from maybe an Oldsmobile Cutlass.

Saul lobbed away an errant track rod end, and they eased onto the mottled leather.

'You're being an ass.'

'Wow—Breaking News,' Beckman replied sarcastically.

'You going to be an ass to Uncle Saul as well?'

He sighed. 'No.'

The whole "Uncle" thing was a curio in itself: (1) it was self-proclaimed, (2) guys don't tend to pick up new uncles when they are thirty-eight, and (3) especially when these uncles are not old enough to be real uncles.

Plus the smothering irony that he'd had more words with this fake uncle in the last ten weeks than any of his real uncles in his entire lifetime, and more than with his real father in the previous ten years.

'I may not have the best eyesight in town,' Saul circled his one pupil, 'And I don't lip-read. But I have a few years on picking up people who are broken down.'

'What did I ever do to deserve you?'

'As I recall, made a turn off the freeway—if we're using Beckman logic. Which is kinda wearing thin, so let's drop it. Anyway.' He sipped pensively. 'Back awhile I had a guy working for me by name of Burton Browning. Because I'm this approachable boss, this is a team game, all that baloney, sometimes I run out for lunch—subs for the guys.'

'Okay,' Beckman said, not being able to relate at all. The only "sub" Malvolio ever treated his salesmen to was a sub-machine gun. The business end.

'So one day I walked into the motor shop. Burton was in the inspection pit, taking a break grinding rust off an underbody. Chevy Impala, maybe. I toss him the bag. I'm no Dan Marino on the best day. It landed about a yard short.' He waved a hand like skimming stone. 'Didn't bounce—sandwiches don't do that. Only kicked up a mess of rust spots. Burton caught one clean in the eye. He knew right away. I knew. Number one is I don't toss subs—or much else—anymore.' He slurped.

'Number two?'

'We go to the hospital. It's right in there, this thing. He could lose a lot of vision. I'm crazy as all hell. You think I call you an ass? It's nothing to what a dumb move tossing that sub was.'

'I know where this is headed.'

'No, you don't. So they're examining him to see how to go, and something turns up on the scan. Turns out a symptom of a heart problem. Don't ask me; I'm a mechanic. Never would have spotted it otherwise.' He drained the mug. 'They fixed the eye, gave him medication for the heart thing—good as new. In fact, better than new.' He stared at his back seat companion. 'You follow, or you need the CliffsNotes version?'

'I get it. Except nothing here is better than new. I'm King Midas ass-backwards. I roll into town, yada yada, Lolita, Delmar. Carlton goes from Jekyll to Hyde. None of this is Breaking News. But every time I try to fix things, it gets worse. Even hiring Reba to get the drop on Carlton this week—and he finds out. All I do is poke the wasp nest some more. I can't let my actions harm the business and the pretty fine girl who runs it. Day One here, and I'm suddenly an Okay Guy? Is that what an Okay Guy does? Catalyses a girl's dream and then lets it die? Helps it die? Carlton may be an ass in a league I'll never graduate to— but he has the benefit of logic.'

'He's an accountant. They make the numbers fit where they want. He does it with words too.'

'Why do I get the feeling all this is special treatment for the New Guy? When do I stop feeling like I'm on the outside looking in?

'When you marry her.'

Jeez, not you too. How much is she paying you?

'How does that make a difference?'

'It means you're serious, and you know the stakes of doing wrong by her. Figure what the town will think if you do wrong by her.'

'Carlton did wrong by her.'

'Exactly. Sunrise is Okay Guys and Okay Gals. Which is why he's the one who should leave, not you.'

'Life doesn't work out like that.'

'Clearly.'

'You can't hold my keys forever. Besides, I have two good feet.'

'You remember what I said on day one? This is not Hotel California. I can't make someone do the right thing or the wrong thing. Not even Carlton. Remember Burton? I was getting a lunch order for Chrissakes. You were trying to stop a woman from doing the wrong thing. You were coming from the right place. That's not a crime. All bar one person in town will tell you so.' He reached across, took Beckman's hand and pressed the Buick's keys into them. 'Maybe tell yourself?'

Beckman took a good long look at the keys. 'What would you do?'

Saul rose. 'Same thing I always do. Whatever fixes things.'

Chapter 24

The walk up Main Street helped Lolita drop from DefCon 5 to a solid 3.

Still, it was her choice to storm off. The slap was another matter; she didn't appreciate people opening old wounds, even people she thought she was in love with.

Was in love with.

Thought?

Was?

She shook her head to cast out that demon.

Mercifully, nobody she knew besides Buck was in Our Buck's. She couldn't face polite conversation. She'd struggled to face polite conversation for most of the week. Beckman had been lucky to get away with a slap. She'd bubbled over rather than going the full Old Faithful.

Buck approached.

'I hit him,' she announced without context.

'Finally,' Buck breathed.

'No, Beckman.'

'Ah.' His face fell. 'Apple pie?'

'And Jack Daniels. Yes, at eleven-thirty in the A.M.'

'Well, our new waitress hasn't shown up, so I'll get onto that.'

She wanted to hug him for the second time in two days, except with a side order of pouring a gallon of tears into his apron front. Instead, she held it in, as always, and squeezed his Yule log upper arm as best as her small hand could.

The Usual Table felt odd. Lacking something.

Someone.

Buck set himself, a plate, a fork, and a tumbler down.

The tumbler barely grazed the tabletop before she upended it into a grateful throat. 'Don't bring me any more of that.'

'Yes, ma'am.'

She dug fiercely into the pie, and it lasted two minutes. Two minutes in which each mentally circled the other, mulling the best opening gambit.

'Couples fight,' he ventured. 'I bet even the Obamas.'

She attempted to extract the one last drop from the bottom of the tumbler, and when it didn't coalesce at her whim, she ran her index finger around inside and licked it. 'Absolutely don't bring me any more of that.'

He pursed his lips. 'The customer is always right.'

'What about when they're not a customer? When they're going about their lives?'

'Nobody is always right,' he stated.

She cocked her head. 'You know the "It's not you, it's me" thing? Do you think it's me?'

'I don't have the specifics.'

She gave him the specifics. 'Now you have the specifics.'

'I'll say again. Couples fight.'

'*We* never fight.'

'We're not a couple,' he stated.

'Not like that, no. But we're closer than a lot of couples we know. Hell, fathers and daughters fight. I wrote the book.'

He absentmindedly scraped away at the last remnants of the apple pie, assembled enough to cover a dime, and ingested it through lips pressed together like a mangle. 'I'm not your father.'

'Yeah. I was aware. Which is why I'm here.'

'Honestly, Lol, I think it's you.'

She exhaled heavily. 'Because why?'

'You're using the past to analyse the present and predict the future. You were screwed over by a travelling salesman, what, five years ago, and by a fiancé this year. Now your new boyfriend is a travelling salesman. You're walking into that with so much baggage they'll have to switch for a bigger plane.'

'I went and put a bomb on the flight too, huh?'

'Snakes, at very worst,' he snarked.

'And if Carlton has a point?'

'There's a butterfly who flaps his wings. Then there's a coyote who lights a trail of gunpowder leading to a big rock beside the highway. Which one of those put a ring on your finger before, and which one has it there now?'

'The question is whether I want a butterfly. Or if I'll squash it without meaning.'

'You mean if *you* took some actions which happened to screw things up? Like a butterfly.'

She caught the inference. 'Or a black widow.'

'A bee, at worst.'

'I already stung once. That means I'm done for. And the guy I stung is pretty damn unhappy about it.'

'He shouldn't have tried to swat you. It was self-defence. Besides, only honey bees die after stinging. Most don't.'

'Great,' she grumped, 'Leaving me plenty of punishment left to hand out, huh?'

'Bees are pretty amazing things. They ought to remember that sometimes.'

She half-smiled, rose and went to the counter, leaving Buck somewhat dumbstruck. She returned with two small glasses containing a yellowish liquid. 'Look, I made honey.'

'You said no more of that.'

'I told you not to bring me any more. *You* didn't. I did.'

He shook his head in disbelief. 'Bees are a piece of work sometimes.'

She raised her glass, and he followed suit. 'To the oddest conversation we had in twenty years.'

'It was a buzz, huh?'

'If you think I'm laughing at that, you're very wrong.'

She necked the shot, then he, and they set down their glasses. With a slight smile, he caught the glint in her eye, and she sputtered into giggles.

'So,' he said, 'You want the waitress job?'

Chapter 25

Beckman took the Buick up Main Street and went to an ATM.

With his back turned, he didn't spot a guy looking out of the grocery store opposite. Nor did he notice the triangular-framed, buzz-cutted individual raise a pocket camera to his eyes, run the zoom out long, and commit two images to the SD card.

Beckman returned to the car, dug into his shoulder bag, pushed aside the one brown Pegasus box he always carried, and fished out an envelope.

A wad of bills went into the envelope.

He pulled his cell from a pocket, scrolled and dialled.

He tutted as it went to voicemail. 'Hi, Reba. Stand down 'til further notice. I'm leaving the fees at the office. Thanks for what you did.'

He hopped out, climbed the street and slid the envelope into the mailbox outside the premises of "Taylor's."

Zoom. Click-click.

Back in the car, he sat for a few minutes, had a notion and set off.

Zoom. Click-click.

As the Buick slid past Our Buck's, a woman in the window watched and wondered and cogitated.

Buzz Cut pulled out his cellphone.

Beckman eased in the brake and stopped twenty yards short of the end of the road.

No point in parking too close.

He got out, closed the door and let the surroundings take him in.

The distant murmur of town. A fly buzzing past.

As he paced around, hands in pockets, bathed in the early afternoon sunshine, the odd ray winked from slivers of glass scattered on the ground.

For sure, bottles have been thrown in there.

His shoe tapped a stone that rattled away a few feet. He followed it, kicked it deliberately. As it skittered again, he got his bearings and, with the following two nudges, lined it up for launch.

Of course, he checked around, because he was an idiot.

Then he kicked it, relatively deftly if he did say so himself, into The Portal.

Poof!

He was disappointed it didn't make a noise.

He scoured around and found another loose brown pebble on the road margin, encouraged it towards a similar launch site, and toe-stubbed it into Wherever.

Another one felt the outside of his shoe as, audience-free, he showboated it into the invisible doorway.

He'd found the next innocent rock to launch to its doom when the silence was broken by a familiar noise: the buzz of a two-litre in-line four.

He abandoned the penalty-taking and waited for Lolita.

Will the lioness purr, or roar, or maul?

She closed the small, curvaceous driver's door (rather than slamming it), so he was confident that a mauling was unlikely.

He didn't attempt to look Not Guilty, Your Honour.

'Hey.'

'I'm sorry I hit you.'

'I'm sorry I bad-mouthed your dating history.'

'You're not an ass.'

'Sometimes I'm an idiot, though.'

She looked into his eyes to assess his mood. 'Yeah. Sometimes.'

'And you?'

'Sometimes. Maybe less sometimes than your sometimes. But sometimes.'

He pulled out his cell, swiped and held it up. 'You want to say that to camera?' He knew it was a risk, but some playfulness danced on her face.

'You filming?' He nodded. She put her shoulders back, addressed the tiny camera like a reporter. 'I, Lolita Milan, on this seventh day of September, do hereby declare for the record that… Beckman Spiers is an idiot. Sometimes.'

He looked past the phone, eyebrows raised, awaiting the second part. Or, technically, the first part—the admission he'd expected, the ammunition to use against her in future (probably in jest) if she ever insinuated she was without flaw.

She drew a finger across her throat. 'And that's a cut. Great scene, well done, everybody.'

Beckman thumbed the red circle on the screen. 'Either I'm never speaking to you again, or….'

'Or… ?'

He stepped in closer, ready to kiss and make up.

The squeal of rubber meeting tarmac, and eight cylinders worth of air-petrol mix being exploded thousands of times a second, washed in on them.

He watched the approaching Mustang. 'How did you know I was here?'

'Because sometimes I'm not an idiot.'

'How did *he* know you were here?'

'Because we underestimated him? Again.'

In the distance, another vehicle did a U-turn and retraced its steps. Beckman filed that image, aiming to revisit it when this latest confrontation finished.

The V8 fell silent. Carlton emerged and walked to their position, leaving Wanda in the passenger seat. 'Still here?'

'You're sharp. I can see why Walter hired you,' Beckman replied. Lolita flashed him a Don't Mess expression.

'Maybe I didn't make myself clear.' Carlton reached into the small of his back.

Beckman and Lolita had a simultaneous moment of not being idiots and knew what was coming. They both involuntarily took a step backwards.

Carlton let the gun fall loose at his side. 'I clocked the P.I. still following me. I get the insinuation. I see the cause of all this ruin and heartbreak is still inside the town boundary.'

'He certainly is.' Half of Beckman was cleverly oblique, nicely snide and taunting, whilst staying the right side of Don't Mess. The other half recognised, as had been true all along, that Carlton's logic was sound. It didn't justify the guy's actions, but Beckman wasn't in control of those.

'Time to leave town, Beckman.'

His shoulders fell. 'Okay.' He moved towards his car.

Do you know what you're doing?

No, but if it gets me further away from that gun, I'll take that as Step One.

But Carlton raised the gun. 'Not that way.'

Beckman stopped as if he'd stepped in a bear trap.

Then, which way?

Oh, snap.

Carlton waggled the gun like a finger, pointing over Beckman's shoulder.

'Okay, Carlton,' Lolita snapped, trying to take control. Yet, there was a tremble in her voice. 'Time out. Enough with the Dirty Harry.'

In response, he swung the gun over in her direction. She yelped, did a little hop and snapped her palms upwards in surrender.

The gun, having gained the desired response, returned to Beckman. 'Nobody needs you around, chasing scapegoats for what you caused.'

'You know that's not true.'

'I'm only cutting out the cancer in Sunrise. Turn around and walk.'

'You are kidding.'

'You should have left before.' Carlton cocked his head for a second, caught a notion. 'Actually, no. This way is better. There's no way back.'

'How do you know? How does any of us know?'

'Because *nobody* has come back.'

'Only because nobody has been dumb enough to go in.'

'Then congratulations, asshole—you can make history.' He waggled the gun in a manner with only one interpretation.

Beckman eased backwards, heart hammering and legs jellying with every second. He fought for the headspace to find a way out.

'All I am is *your* scapegoat, Carlton. I'm not the only one who knows—yeah, knows—what you did.'

'Not that I did anything, but I'm pretty sure anyone else who thinks the same will have a change of heart when they hear, or especially see,' he glowered at Lolita, 'What happens to assholes who screw with me.'

Beckman very gradually slowed his pace, hoping Carlton wouldn't catch on. Hoping for some words to hit him. Hoping for a diversion. An intervention. An earthquake. An eclipse. An alien invasion.

Carlton caught on. He jabbed the gun encouragingly, stepping forwards to hammer home the point.

Beckman cursed, sick to his stomach, and picked up the pace as little as he dared.

'Everyone else will stay quiet,' Carlton continued. 'Or end up here, or worse. But look on the bright side—at least if that happens, you'll have company in Hell, or the wilderness, or an alternative dimension—wherever that thing leads.'

Beckman risked a glance over his shoulder. Ten yards to go. Ten yards of his life. It was funny; he'd never imagined measuring his lifespan in yards. He'd been hoping for decades.

Decades in the company of a lioness who stood, toothless and clawless, watching the king of the pride take out his rival.

He dug deep for the last vestiges of his invention and courage. 'Such a poor loser—is that why you started the fire?'

Carlton smiled. 'Oh no, you don't get me like that.'

'Come on, at least give me the satisfaction. Something to take to the grave.'

'You've been watching too much James Bond. Besides—I don't like an audience.' He glanced at Lolita, whose fists clenched and unclenched in vain.

'Does that make you the villain of the piece? The Blofeld?'

Carlton shook his head slowly. 'No dice. Accidents happen.'

'This here is no accident.'

'Unless my gun accidentally goes off while you're refusing to step back there.'

'There are witnesses.'

'Maybe there will be a second accident.'

'How can I be sure there won't be one anyway after I've… gone through.' And when those words passed his lips, it became Very Real. He wondered how his heart hadn't detonated, bowels hadn't let go.

'You have to trust me.'

Somehow, Beckman formed a grunting scoff. 'Because you don't shoot ladies. You only lie to them and cheat on them.' He looked at a helpless Lolita, then at an impassive Wanda.

And I thought so much better of you. Can't you be Vader to his Emperor right now? Cast him into the void as he electrocutes me?

Yet, she sat there. Maybe stunned, maybe complicit, perhaps powerless.

Maybe listening to an MP3 player.

'No,' Carlton replied. 'Because a line exists between people this town would miss like crazy and people who don't belong here.'

That means you, sonny, in case you weren't keeping up.

The firing squad are taking guard, Beckman.

One last request for the condemned man?

'One last request for the condemned man?' he asked, in vain hope.

'Hey, I'm not a monster,' Carlton lied with world-class panache.

Beckman was about to request a farewell kiss (from Lolita), but they already had memories of many. Better to stall for time, hope she'd understand, and take a practical step.

'My shoulder bag,' he said, knowing there was probably nothing on this incredible Earth that he could take into the Great Unknown which would deliver him from asphyxiation, annihilation, transmogrification, inside-outification, or even plain eternal boredom.

He might as well have asked for a hubcap from a red '65 Mustang, a tall root beer, or a spare pen.

'Okay,' Carlton said with a shrug.

So he stepped forwards. But Carlton had a limit to his graciousness, and that step had... overstepped it.

The gun waved. 'You get it,' the accountant instructed Lolita.

Beckman froze. On the plus side, he was one step further away from the invisible probable-nemesis.

Wow, a whole extra few seconds on the planet.

Par-tay.

Lolita gathered herself and, as slowly as she could get away with, walked to the Buick.

Stalling. Good girl. Who's to say the cavalry aren't on the way?

It was still fruitless, but zero was precisely the amount of harm it did.

A half-minute later, she approached, shoulder bag in hand. Her face was rent in agony, body fizzing with nerves, hatred and anguish.

She proffered the bag, shaking. 'Don't go,' she said through gritted teeth.

He cast the bag over his shoulder. 'Maybe if there are aliens, they'll have headaches.' He shrugged as nonchalantly as possible, which wasn't much. 'It worked at Coffee Planet.'

She tried and failed to smile. 'Don't go.'

'I'm a travelling salesman. This is travelling. Maybe a whole new territory. Imagine if they need neons as well as brown boxes. We'll be rich!'

'Don't go, Beckman.' Her voice cracked.

'I'm out of ideas.'

'He'll never shoot.'

'Sure?'

She took a step away. 'You'll never shoot, Carlton,' she yelled as bravely as possible. Which wasn't that bravely.

A bullet zinged off the ground a foot away from her. She shrieked.

'Time to move on,' Beckman said, scooping the last ounce of bravery from deep, deepest inside.

'Not any more.' She shook her head, and tears welled. 'You are here. You belong here. Go through there, to… wherever, whatever—how will you get back? Ever?'

'I'll find a way. I found Sunrise. I found you. Maybe my luck will hold. Maybe there's something even more amazing on the other side.'

He doubted it, ninety-nine point nine percent. Recurring.

'Now!' Carlton yelled, holding the gun ramrod straight.

Beckman swallowed some bile, drew himself up as best as he could, and stepped to where he reckoned The Portal lay.

'Any last words?' Carlton sneered.

Wow. You're spoiling me now. Next, it'll be a last meal, a last phone call. Maybe even a night in solitary to consider again what a Bad Boy I've allegedly been.

Unlikely.

'So… Goodbye? No, those can't be my last words. What if people ask what they were? Give me a second. How about, "This is one small step for a salesman"? No. Corny. "Beam me up, Scotty"? Hmm. Hold on; I've got it. "None of your business, asshole".'

He took one more tiny step.

This was indeed the end of the road, the buffers on the Rocky Mountain Railroad ride.

A freeway jam. A flat tire. A girl. A headache. A private detective. A breakup. A hookup. Number One. Bruno. Randall. Diamonds. A takeover. A fire. A falling chimney. A dream.

A dream that died.

He gazed at Lolita. There were no tears in her eyes, not any more.

They cascaded down her cheeks like Niagara Falls.

He gave her the best smile he could. Which wasn't that smiley.

He turned to face the invisible door to whatever the future held for him, however long—or more likely very, very short—the future lasted.

He reached his right leg out and, at the last second, because neither his tormentor nor his love could see, he closed his eyes. Not that it would have helped in any way. But because he was an idiot.

He stepped through.

Chapter 26

Neurons sped through his cortex.

Oxygen diffused into his blood through myriad alveoli.

Electrical impulses danced around limbs.

Photons pelted eyeballs and transmuted into information.

For one second, Beckman Spiers continued to be.

Then two seconds.

Five seconds.

Ten seconds.

Instinctively, he'd ceased forward motion.

Now he was Hillary planting the flag. Franklin flying the kite. Aldrin opening Eagle's hatch.

Stiff as a board, yet fizzing with nerves, his mind an impossible maelstrom of senses and emotions—many he was experiencing for the first time—he dared himself to breathe.

A sniff or a lungful—the result will be the same.

So his next breath was a deep one. Literally do or die. Or possibly do *and* die.

It felt exactly like… breathing.

His eyeballs swivelled in their sockets.

It looked exactly like… Arizona. With an annoying difference. A familiar one. He parked it.

He peered down.

He seemed exactly like… Beckman Spiers.

Gingerly, he spun on the spot. His shoulder bag swung and tapped into him.

Behind, now in front of him, lay more Arizona. Or what looked like Arizona. If this was a simulation or a parallel world, the creator/builder/architect/programmer had done a fine job. You could barely see the join.

Without will, he'd taken more breaths, and they hadn't flooded him with poisonous air. At least, not yet.

His life would at least be measured in minutes and not seconds.

Next, he wished he'd been a Boy Scout, equipped with at least rudimentary survival skills for situations like these. Or, on second thoughts, situations very unlike these.

Robert Baden-Powell's missing chapter: Alternative Realities And What To Do When Forced Into One By A Jealous Rival.

Yet, with a stroke of genius, he slipped off his belt and laid it in a line at his feet, like the starting mark for a hundred-metre sprint.

Thanks to Lolita's cooking, and the loving contentment she'd engendered, he'd put on a couple of pounds in the past ten weeks, so his pants didn't summarily fall down.

Not that there was anyone around to see.

Lolita.

He examined the space in front of him. It appeared the same as on the Sunrise 'side,' i.e. there was nothing there. He gingerly reached out a hand.

It kept going. And going.

His arm hit full stretch. He reached more, praying for it to disappear into an invisible curtain and signal that a swift return to civilisation was available.

He toppled forwards, hand very much intact, caught his fall and regained his two feet.

The door had closed. Or vanished.

He willed himself to believe the former. He stepped back, checked the belt line remained intact, and heaved a monumental sigh.

Lolita.

Well, it was good while it lasted.

I hope she'll be okay now.

She most certainly was because at that instant she appeared out of thin air and clattered into him.

He yelped in shock and surprise.

Which made her yelp.

Which made him yelp.

Which, luckily, didn't make her yelp, or things would have got ridiculous.

Strike that, *more* ridiculous.

Her face was a Picasso of every emotion in the dictionary from Addled to Yearning—he couldn't think of a Z.

They fumbled each other upright.

Every other letter in her face vanished, leaving only Joy. She embraced him hard enough he'd turn to spaghetti. So he kissed her hard enough that they'd probably both need dentistry, assuming there were dentists here.

Her cheeks were red from crying. He stroked them with his thumb, felt soft skin and knew the remainder of his life was much less likely to be spent alone. Which made him feel very selfish.

'You didn't get the memo.'

Her eyebrows creased. 'Memo?'

'The idea that I get out of your life, you stay in Sunrise and work things out. Maybe find another mug, too. Obviously not as good as me, but you could try.'

'I see going through The Portal hasn't made you any funnier.'

'Seriously, baby. I thought we were on the same wavelength. It doesn't bode well for our future.'

'At least we have one now.'

'For a few minutes, anyway.'

'Why did you do it?' she asked, a plea in her eyes.

'Because you said he's a pretty good shot, so it was either certain death or marginally less certain death. Besides, like I said, I like to see the country.'

'It was very… Captain Oates.'

'I thought so.'

'It was… weird.' She glanced back over her shoulder, shuddered.

'I didn't expect a magic carpet ride.'

'You know—and this sounds crazy—it felt like….'

'…going through a potato ricer and being reconstituted on the other side.'

Her face lit surprise. 'Exactly!'

'Maybe *this* is the real Twilight Zone.'

'Maybe.'

'Poor potatoes,' he said, mind drifting.

'The jury is still out on Brave versus Dumb, you should know.'

'I'm a curious person. Comes with the territory. I see a girl in a swing dress on a café stool holding her brow, and I think, "I wonder if she has a headache". And I also wonder, "Why is she wearing a swing dress?". And pretty soon after, I wonder what she's like without a swing dress on.'

'Yes?' she replied with both inflexion and The Eyebrow.

Ah, The Eyebrow works here too. Good thing, or bad thing?

Let's park that.

Bigger fish to fry, in case you hadn't noticed.

'Answers being Yes, Because, and a solid nine out of ten.'

She shook her head gently. 'How can you joke at a time like this?'

'Well, the alternative is crying, except you're here, so why would I cry? Maybe if you'd done what you were supposed to and stayed the other side, I might cry. Not right away. I'd wait at least until I missed you. Say, a couple of minutes.'

She pressed her lips to his. 'Really, why did you come through?'

'To try and make your life better. Why did *you* come through?'

'Because like you said, what if there's a tiny chance it's okay here? My life in Sunrise is for shit without you, and I have a lot of what I have *because* of you. As Carlton said, it is absolutely all your fault. Without Pegasus, we wouldn't have had Malvolio's money, even a chance to be part of dad's business.'

'Without Sunrise and you, I'd have no sales. Without you putting the brakes on Tyler, I'd have lost the Salesman race.'

'Sounds a lot like teamwork.'

'One hundred percent,' he agreed.

'Which is why I came through. We're a team. For better or worse. Without the business I dreamed of and the man I love, why bother staying?' Her face hardened. 'Plus, I didn't want to give Carlton the satisfaction of gloating twenty-four seven, three hundred and sixty-five because he got his own back.'

'And guess what? I was right—there is something amazing on this side. You.'

'Back at you, partner.'

He held her tight. 'Thank you for coming. I didn't want you to, but I'm glad you did.'

'Thank you for going. I didn't want you to, and I'll never be glad you did.'

They loosed. She gazed around. 'So, any ideas what this place is?'

'No. I skipped Portals 101. But I'll take a wild guess it's not black and white.'

Her shoulders sagged. 'Oh, baby, no.'

'Yeah, the old Beckman is back.'

'That sucks.'

'Of all the possible outcomes here, monochromacy feels like first world problems.'

'I guess.'

'Kinda forgotten what it was like. But then, that was before I had you, so I've had better things to be doing.'

Her brow creased. She eased her tinted glasses down. 'I'd swear my eyes weren't so sensitive out here.' She looked around, blinked a few times.

'So it heals you, un-heals me.'

'As I said—it sucks.'

'Even more than the irony of a light-sensitive woman running a neon lighting company?'

'Yeah, it's damn hilarious.'

He puffed out a heavy breath. 'Sorry. Hardly the time or place, baby.'

She nodded, subdued, and glanced down because her foot had snagged his belt. She shot him a query. 'Why did you…? Oh no. You weren't…?'

'No!' That kind of thing hadn't even crossed his mind. Although, now she was here… 'But, you know, now you're here….' He moved in to give her a sly embrace.

She backed off. 'You *have* to be kidding.'

'Why? What else is there to do?'

'Any normal man lost in a wilderness would be focussed on food, water and shelter.'

'Any normal man doesn't have you,' he asserted, knowing it was futile.

She put her hands on her hips. 'Well, Mister Not Normal, unless you want a dried-out husk of a fiancée, you'd better get a plan together.'

'I guess.' He stroked his chin theatrically, then pulled out his cell.

No signal.

He swiped and tapped.

'What are you doing?' she asked.

'No signal. Putting it on Airplane Mode, save the battery.'

'Why not turn it off?'

'In case… we need to use it quickly?'

'To phone who? You said there was no signal.'

'In case we…,' he fumbled for a response, 'Need to use the torch.'

'It's daytime.'

'For now. Who knows when night comes? Or how quickly?'

'Or if ever?'

'Exactly.'

'You just shot down your argument.'

'So, the phone is a non-starter,' he said. 'Now, let's hear one of yours.'

'How do you even know there's a way out?'

'Know? I don't. But you have to believe. Don't you?'

She turned and waved her arms, at first carefully, then with more thrust, in the direction of where they'd come. Or at least what they perceived as that direction, supposing such things as directions existed here, wherever here was.

But there was no door. She looked like, well, like an idiot.

She gave up. 'You could believe. Or you could face facts.'

'This.' He tapped his left lower eyelid. 'This. I always believed there was a chance this could change. I did face facts—black and white facts—for years. But deep down, there was always a spark, a burning ember, that there might be deliverance. And I'm looking at her. Who knows how or why. But it happened. Don't tell me you never had your own ember that Milan Enterprises would work out for you?'

She pulled a sheepish face, which told him everything. 'Okay.'

'The belt, Miss Mind-In-The-Gutter, is a marker. Only a crazy idea that we don't want to lose our spot. Assuming, of course, The Portal is two-way, it doesn't move and is still there.'

She grimaced. 'Problem is, we know what's waiting on the other side.'

'You're crazy! You want to *stay*?!'

'I'm only saying, this world feels a hundred percent less full of bullshit already.'

'But we could starve looking for a better life. And wouldn't that mean he'd still win?'

'You're saying the way to win is to get back through?'

'Love, I'm not thinking about winning right now—only surviving. Kissing is a pretty fine pastime, but I'm pretty sure it's not that nutritious.'

'On that—did you get lunch already? she asked.

'No. You?'

'Does JD and apple pie count?'

Beckman did a ready-reckon of the day's timeline. 'So I've already turned you into a morning drinker. Wow. I dated Mercia Jackson for three months. She's lucky she didn't wind up in the Betty Ford Clinic.'

'So the headline is that food is a priority. Anything in that bag of yours, Ford Prefect?' She'd tried to be snide, but it had a strange irony.

'When you're touring the Galaxy.' He gestured grandly around.

'Can I take that as a "No"?'

He dug into the bag, desperate to prove her wrong. 'I got some Trident.' He offered up a squashed half-packet.

'At least our last breath kisses will be minty-fresh.'

'There's worse ways to go.'

'I don't want to go. I want to *go*.'

'So let's try, huh?'

He manoeuvred her closer to where he reckoned The Portal should be, just beyond where his belt lay in the probably ochre, seemingly Arizona, allegedly dirt.

'Ready?'

'No way it's this easy?' she wondered aloud, worry and disbelief on her face.

She had a point. A very significant one. After all, to the naked eye—even his compromised ones, the vista spread out in front as it did to left, right, and behind. A desert landscape without so much as a house visible, let alone a whole town.

'Maybe there's a way into Sunrise that even Saul doesn't know?' he suggested.

'I'll buy that.'

'Believe, okay?'

Because why not? It might not make a difference, but it couldn't hurt.

The actual Going Back Through could hurt, of course. Maybe worse than being riced. Maybe this direction is like driving over Wrong Way tire spikes.

At least they have medical care in Sunrise, which is a heap better than the facilities here, which frankly suck. You probably can't get a takeout, much less an Uber.

They have inexplicably loyal and caring lionesses, though, so it's not all bad.

'Okay,' she agreed.

He moved forwards, but she tugged his hand and held him back. 'What?' he asked, concerned and perturbed by her intervention.

'Love you,' she chirped.

'Love you too,' he beamed.

Then he took them a giant stride forwards.

Chapter 27

Randall Grover Ickey (his parents were strangely fixated on the 22nd and 24th presidents) shifted his grip on the picnic hamper strap and reached his other hand out towards Reba Frances Garrity.

Randall had never considered himself the marrying kind. After all, who'd sink so low as to hitch up with a hitman? Probably someone with designs on his savings, especially as his lifespan was likely to be shorter than the average Joe. Best case, he'd wind up in prison for a long stretch, and Mrs Bide-My-Time Ickey would abscond with the contents of his bank account, knowing Mr Frustratingly-Still-Alive wouldn't be able to hunt her down because, well, prison bars.

When he pocketed a cool million for not killing a certain Beckman Spiers, he sensed potential suitors might appear from thin air. These would be a different strain—aware of his U-turn into a humdrum trade and hence more likely to be in it for the long term.

He didn't expect it to be a private investigator eleven years his junior. A single mom eight inches shorter than he, with a glass eye, the word "April" tattooed on her right shoulder, and cropped straw-coloured hair.

But technically, he'd been *her* suitor, and, in his defence, he didn't have a *type*. Except perhaps those who didn't mind if it was an hour, a day, a week, or a month of togetherness. Women in his life came and went, like the heartbeats of the people beyond the end of his gun barrel.

Reba Frances Garrity was unquestionably not that type. He didn't know her type, unless there was a type shot through with determination, balls, curiosity, tenacity, kindness and surprising maternal grace.

A Grover and a Frances had been together once before, and it fostered encouragement of possible mileage a second time.

She took his hand in hers, a small but strong right hand with the short fingernails and slightly weathered feel of a person whose stock-in-trade is a camera, a keyboard and a Sig Sauer P938.

They trudged up the hill, sun at their backs, thin grass under their feet.

'You're quiet,' he observed.

'Trying to figure why Beckman pulled the case. Something in his voice. Not disappointment... Deflation. Resignation maybe.'

'That you wouldn't find anything?'

'You don't bail that early on a case. There's no proving a negative.'

'Is that disappointment I hear?'

She looked across. 'I guess it is. I'm sure there was dirt on Carlton.'

'You're supposed to be impartial.'

'Honey, this is Carlton Cooper we're talking about.'

'A new case? A fresh start? Ignoring priors.'

She pointed them in a different direction and tugged his hand. 'You're serious? Hell, why do I ask? You're from out of town. Cooper has form. He's a leopard.'

'I have form,' Randall noted. 'I used to kill people. I stopped. You may have noticed.'

'Yeah, but that was a job. Cooper is doing what he's doing because he's a piece of shit.'

'As opposed to me being this great saint.'

'I don't date pieces of shit,' she said.

'I still pinch myself, you might know.'

She drew him to a halt. 'You're still the new kid on the block with this Miss, remember.'

He studied her up and down. 'Every day. That's why the pinching.' He embraced her. 'But I'd much rather it wasn't me I was pinching. He gave her a quick nip on the backside.

Her eyebrows shot up, and she looked around nervously. 'You're about thirty years too old for that, Mister.'

'At my age, you take what you can get.'

She rolled her eye, one thing which slightly disarmed him about her charmingly individual monocularity. 'The only thing getting laid on this rug today is our lunch. Capisce?'

'Yes, ma'am.' He checked the environs. 'How's this spot?'

'Fine, Jeeves,' she commanded in an appalling British accent.

He gave her a playful whack to follow the pinch, then set about unpacking the picnic basket.

She meandered around, breathing deeply, gaze cast first to the cloud-bedecked sky, then went to look over the town spread out a hundred feet below. Sunrise's topography didn't win any National Geographic awards for beauty, but the relative lushness of the low hills counterpointed the brownish scrubland stretching beyond the town boundaries.

'I never realised how close Walter's house was,' she remarked.

'I guess all the best spots are away from what passes for hustle or bustle around here.'

She plonked herself down beside him. 'Spoken like a pure-bred city boy.'

'If I'd wanted to put my very questionable past behind me and move to a little out-of-the-way place, I should have done it somewhere where I hadn't announced my trade in ten-foot capitals.'

'Ten-foot *neon* capitals.'

'I have a hard time believing *you're* a straight-A student at Sunrise Finishing School.' He raised an eyebrow.

'Well, I can't hold a candle to you when it comes to tearing up the landscape; that's for true.'

'You never had a halo to slip. Right?' He quaffed from a bottle of soda and risked a belch, which passed without comment, reinforcing a growing feeling that this girl might be a keeper. If she'd let him.

'I picked a lock or two, even before my time on The Beacon.'

'Why, they teach that in journalism school?'

'What I'd wish they'd taught is how to look busy at a local paper when there's damn all to do. Luckily Elmer gave me something to do.'

'Yeah, kick the shit out of him.'

'I had to prove he'd earned the right to be an ex-husband first. That's not really what investigative journalism is supposed to be about. Especially when you don't want there to be a story to find.' She looked down, reflective.

He gave her a supportive rub on the upper arm. 'He's lucky you didn't put a bullet in him.'

'Maybe he judged me well enough to believe he could have an affair and live to fight another day.'

'Better if he hadn't, though, huh?'

'Why? A Saturday picnic with me not doing it for you?'

'Every second with you does it for me, Reba. And almost every other second, I wonder when the veil will fall.'

'When I'll wise up? When someone in Sunrise will point out the blinding obvious?' She chomped into a hardboiled egg.

'You think anyone can be redeemed?'

She nodded. 'Even Carlton. But he has to want to.'

'I wanted to.'

'Not the same. There's a difference between revenge, anger, hatred and doing a job of work. Look at what I do—it creates divorces, lawsuits, jail time—but it's just a job. One of justice.' She licked her finger and thumb. 'I'm sure you never killed any saints.'

'Beckman was the most saintly job I ever had.'

'And you didn't even kill *him*. Nobody's perfect. Even April is as sweet as, but I'll wager she stomped on a bug for fun. She can lash out when she's provoked. It's the Asperger's.'

'Best I don't teach her to shoot.'

'I've seen you shoot, Randall. If anyone will do it properly, it's me.' Her brow creased. 'Besides, you think you'll still be around for when she's old enough?'

He paused, mid-sandwich bite. 'I guess this is the first "What are we doing?" conversation of my life.'

Her face softened. 'Sorry. I wasn't fishing. Hell, you think I want to rush into marriage again? I knew him since we were fifteen, and he still let me down.'

'The fact you used the M-word is enough to make most men run for the hills.'

'We're on a hill already, so I guess I did your work for you,' she said with a smile.

'You're just too smart and irresistible—that's the problem.'

She saw what was in his face and braced for the advance. There was something of the stuntman about the way he piled carefully on top of her, scooped her up and rolled them both sideways, ending up on the grass astride her and pressing his lips to hers.

She acceded for a second, wriggled, and he gave ground.

'Ow,' she snipped.

'What d'I do?' he asked, worried.

She shook her head. 'Nothing.' Her brow furrowed, and she wriggled again as if she'd found a sharp rock. He moved away to let her sit up. She shifted sideways and checked where her backside had been.

Two pieces of brass glinting in the green.

Knowing what they were, he reached out a hand.

She slapped it in admonishment. 'Hey, matador, leave this to the gumshoe.'

She crabbed over to the picnic rug, snatched up a light blue paper napkin, and, channelling CSI, used it to pick up one of the objects.

'They cover this in Journalism 101?' he asked.

'No, but I bet they had it in day one of Sniper School?'

'May I?' He gingerly took the flimsy paper from her and peered at the contents. Meanwhile, Reba went onto all fours and scoured the nearby ground.

'.220 Swift,' he called.

'I defer.'

'Yeah. Don't see a lot of these.'

She crawled back, having found no further perfectly formed metal deposits, then surveyed the area again.

'Walter shoot?' he asked.

'No,' she replied pensively.

'I'm guessing not Wanda.' He watched her. 'What's the deal?'

'I shoot at the rifle range. A few folks have spaces out back of their property. Ones who run into open country.'

'You have access to the gun register?'

'No.' She sat cross-legged on the rug and cracked open a soda. 'But I know stuff.'

'Like who shoots a sniper's rifle.'

'I have some ideas.' She scanned around again. 'But it's not the who. It's the what.'

'Don't follow.'

'Somebody dropped bullets. While out for a walk on the hill? Unlikely.'

'So?' He shrugged. 'Sniping at game.'

'Look around.' She spread her arms wide. 'Why here? To piss off the community? You've got a million miles in any direction. Walter spies you; he's not the kind of guy to roll out the welcome mat.'

'I'm only a humble credit controller.' He tucked into a chicken wing.

She ignored that, stood and walked a few feet away, hands on hips. After a good minute of surveying the townscape below them, she rejoined him on their lunch table. 'I never shot rifles. You?'

He nodded. 'Some.'

'Could you hit Walter's chimney from here?'

Chapter 28

Both their feet landed on solid ground.

Then, the momentum took them forwards another step. They stopped.

Beckman couldn't help feel crushingly disappointed. She was too.

'It was a long shot,' he said, trying to brighten.

'I know.'

The belt still lay on the grey scrub ground four feet behind them. 'At least there's this,' he began.

'What?'

'I still love you.'

'Yeah. That would suck—if The Portal erased our memories.'

He led them back to where they'd failed the exit manoeuvre. 'Maybe. Or you might fall in love with me again, except without knowing all the crap I'd caused.'

She sighed heavily. 'Why do you blame yourself for everything?'

'You mean, besides the obvious?' He unslung the bag, dropped it on the rough ground and parked himself down, like a hitcher waiting kerbside.

She joined him. 'Cause is not the same as blame.'

'Semantics.'

'No.' Her tone was firm. 'It isn't.' She tapped his forehead. 'What have you got in there?'

'Is this the time?'

She made a pantomime of looking around. 'I have a window in my schedule. Besides, if we're doing this—at some point,' she fingered her engagement ring, 'I have a pretty low tolerance on secrets and asshole behaviour. You may have noticed.'

He picked up a jagged pebble of grey, possibly Arizona rock and tossed it pensively in his hand.

'I was fourteen, which makes it... Nebraska. I came back from tooling around on my pushbike, and I heard my parents arguing. So, like a little shit, I found a space to sit and listen.'

'We all did that.'

'Mom said she didn't want to move again. She wanted me to have stability at school. Dad said it's your fault anyway for having him.'

'Because, of course, virgin births were all the rage back then. What an ass.' Lolita was well-placed to pass judgement on the asshole-ness of fathers and shook her head—a mild rebuke.

'Thing is, it was her fault. Well, maybe not *fault*. She'd lied and stopped the birth control without telling him. He wasn't ready. Not that he didn't want a kid, it just had to be on his terms.'

Her mouth fell open. 'Even though it's not his body.'

'He wanted something on his terms. His career was always out of his control—or that's how he saw it.'

'Except it wasn't.'

'No. He quit every time he didn't get the promotions he thought he deserved. He didn't stay the course. Anywhere. Blamed others for unfair rolls of the dice. And now another thing happened he didn't want or expect.'

'So he always resented you.' She tried to find his face, but he remained too introspective, absentmindedly pursuing a game of Five Stones with the collection of pebbles.

'Yeah. I was to blame for everything. He always wanted to get on, to get a promotion, but now he *needed* to. To feed me, clothe me, keep me out of mischief. And not getting those breaks made it worse. My appearance on Earth created our lifestyle.'

'When actually, your mom is to blame.' She clasped his hand. 'Or thank.'

He gave a small smile. 'Aren't all mothers?'

'She had reasons for what she did. So did you, the day you walked in and hired Reba to watch Carlton. Good reasons.'

'But still... ' he protested.

'But nothing. I didn't walk through only because I love you. Although, before you say, that's a big enough reason.'

'I have the house keys in my bag?'

She gave him a friendly shove. 'Carlton was pissed on account of being followed.'

'I got that. The straw that broke the camel's back. I already called off Reba. Maybe she didn't get my message. Anyway,' he shook his head, 'I was past fighting him.'

'Reba's not who he spotted. It was Delmar.'

'What the hell was Delmar doing? Wanda hire him?! Jeez, does nobody trust the guy?'

'No, honey. I hired Delmar.'

'Why?'

'Same reason you hired Reba. To find out whether it was him who set the fire.'

'You could have told me.'

'You could have told *me*. It's my business that went up in flames, don't forget.'

He was about to point out they were in this together when it became shatteringly clear there was no better demonstration of their togetherness than the fact they'd both tried the same method to extricate themselves from the situation.

'So,' she continued, 'Say after me. "Lolita is to blame for what happened".'

He nodded.

She gently pinched his chin between thumb and forefinger and waggled it up and down, so his mouth opened and closed. He tumbled out a staccato, 'Lolita is to blame for what happened,' as if he had a mouth full of novocaine.

That tickled her, which raised a smile, which raised his smile, and they both corpsed. It was much needed.

He inspected the pebble in his hand, turned and lobbed it over the belt-line into the beyond. It kept going, as he'd expected.

'You think it's gone? she asked. 'The Portal?'

He shook his head. 'We need the key.'

'Or there's one entrance and one separate exit.' She contemplated the landscape. 'Somewhere.'

'If you're suggesting we walk around like idiots, looking for another invisible something, when there's one right here, I'm calling that out as a dumb move, survival-wise.'

'Okay. Agreed. You're the one who's travelled all his life. If there's anyone with a nose for the best spots, a cheap room, the right direction, I'm talking to him. Hell, you can probably sniff a Coffee Planet at fifty miles.'

He pretended to doff a cap. 'All the same, it's warm, it's light, and there are no inter-dimensional monsters in the neighbourhood, ready to chomp on stranded foxy executives, so I vote we try and pick this lock, okay?'

'So get us through that door, Kerouac. Or Gateway. Membrane. Whatever you want to call it.'

He took her hand. 'Come on, Alice. Let's get you back to Wonderland.'

'*To*?'

'Which of these is the amazing place, filled with colour and quirky characters, and which is the lifeless nowheresville?'

She smiled. 'You have a point. What does that make you—the rabbit?'

'Happy to be a turtle or a caterpillar—any form of life that's not as low as Carlton Cooper.'

'Amen to that.'

They stepped up to his makeshift borderline. 'On three, a good, strong, two-footed jump forward,' he instructed.

'You think?'

'It's all spitballing. Ready?' She nodded. 'One, two, three!'

Well, thought Beckman, as they fairly sailed through the air, *Mr Oswin, my sixth-grade gym teacher, will be proud of me. Actual leaping. No "Try harder, Spiers!" now. I'm a veritable Bob Beamon.*

And dad will be proud too. I'm holding hands with an Actual Girl.

A relationship who you won't be able to break up by being a peripatetic underachieving asshole.

Though, being honest, the relationship might not have long to it anyway. We'll be dead of hunger and sunstroke inside a week.

Unless this works…

They landed with a thud. On earth, not tarmac.

Oh, snap.

They exchanged a disappointed, sober look and walked back to the start line.

To regain their breath, he tried something a bit more cerebral.

'Open Sesame,' he proclaimed grandly, casting his arms wide, before taking her hand and, with startling predictability, failing to step back into Sunrise.

Back to the belt.

At the risk of getting The Eyebrow, or more likely a blank expression of total loss, his next gambit was, 'Swordfish.'

Defeated, they returned to the launch position.

He pondered for a minute.

They failed to conga back to Sunrise.

She had an idea.

They failed to limbo back.

And reverse back.

And run back.

And crawl back.

And get back one at a time (which required her belief and trust to be turned up a notch).

And walk back diagonally.

And walk back while enunciating, 'esirnuS.'

Then he suggested they try it naked, to which she reminded him there might still be people on the other side. He responded that a flash of God's exquisite handiwork was a small price to pay for avoiding certain death.

'Besides,' he added. 'Carlton has seen it all before.'

'Well, that remark guaranteed I'm not doing it.'

'I *would* do it, but I wouldn't want to leave you here—if it worked—so I guess no point.'

'Whatever you need to tell yourself, Adonis.'

'I guess it was a long shot.'

'We're eleven for eleven on long shots.'

He sank to the dirt. 'So let's take a break.'

'I need to make it a comfort break,' she announced as if it was the most natural thing in the world. Which, technically, it was. Whatever world you're in.

They scanned around. There were no bushes.

This is another relationship landmark.

'You think the aliens will mind us whizzing on their land?' he asked.

'I could care less.' She found a spot about ten yards away and began the necessary process.

'I'm turning my back,' he called.

'Whatever!'

He walked ten yards in the opposite direction, so they were both clear of the standing/sitting/thinking/jumping/conga-ing zone. Oddly nervous, for a million reasons he couldn't put his finger on, it took a few seconds, then nature took its course.

The ground didn't disappear, turn to acid, or act as a miniature trampoline, so he duly zipped his fly and went back to Base Camp.

'Okay?' he asked unfathomably.

'Aside from the oddest and most definitely out-of-town place I've crouched, yeah, I had a good whizz, thanks for asking.'

A pregnant pause fell.

'Is it sinking in yet?' he asked sombrely. She frowned as if weirded out. 'No, not the… ' He loosely gestured around. 'The *situation*.'

Realisation dawned, then sobriety. 'It's down to the marrow, Beckman.'

He took her hand. 'If things were different, and I hadn't already, I'd propose to you right now.'

'All it took was a mutual whizz in the desert to cement the bond, huh?'

'No, I mean—'

She smiled. 'I'm kidding.' Her face neutralised. 'Anyway, it *is* different.'

'Couldn't be more.'

'No. I mean, you didn't already propose.'

'Yes, I did. At the… I mean, when I….'

A metaphorical lighting bolt, not unlike (although much less real than) the one that had crisped poor Esmond Belcher and precipitated all the events of the last ten weeks, shot through his brain.

Oh, snap.

He froze. Non-existent birds took simultaneous flight from non-existent treetops. Non-existent dark clouds rolled in. Non-existent chattering crowds fell silent.

She had him on a technicality.

Quite a significant one.

A planet-sized one.

But he *had* proposed. Hadn't he? Surely.
That time…?
Or was it…?
Maybe?
Please?
Oh, snap.
If you weren't already, you're dead for sure now.

Chapter 29

She laid a hand on his arm. 'Relax. It's not like I can make your life any more unbearable than it is.'

He saw the truth of it in her face and exhaled with overt drama.

Maybe I should do it now? It would be a pretty memorable place.

You can keep your Mount Rushmore proposals, your Washington Memorial surprises, a Statue of Liberty bended-knee.

This is how to do it. In a parallel dimension… probably.

That'll be something to tell the kids. Popping The Question while Not Actually On Earth.

What better time could there be?

Yeah. Let's do it now.

'And please don't ask me now,' she continued. 'That would just feel desperate.'

Sure. Wasn't going to anyway.

'Okay.'

'Ask me when I won't expect it. Make it fabulous. Make it quirky. Make it "Beckman".'

'That sounds a lot like it'll put the date back even further. And I'm already not doing too good on that score.'

'Don't remind me,' she grumped.

He sighed. 'Is this really what you want to talk about? Right here? Right now?'

'Of course not. I wish it was already a done deal. And, being honest, every day makes me the smallest bit more nervous that there's a second thought washing around in that idiot brain of yours.'

'Well, for one, there's not a second that I have a second thought.'

'That's very sweet, but I'm not sure there's a guy in the world who doesn't have a second thought at some point.'

'Want me to mention that, right now, I'm not necessarily a guy who is actually *in* the world?'

'Are you relying on semantics to get you out of this?'

'No, I'm relying on honesty. It's one reason we're in this hoo-hah in the first place.'

'Maybe you want to try *not* being honest sometimes.'

'I'm not about to start now. Not where this is concerned.'

'So—honest away, husband-to-be,' she instructed.

Come on, Beckman. No regrets, especially if this is the beginning of the end.

'I know you want my dad there. I know you want me to call him. But I've got to say, that's a hell of a double standard, given you and Jack. Dad will never be happy for me. He'll always find the downside in any situation I'm in. Hell, he'd say, "Why didn't you pick a blonde?". I don't want a scene. I don't want to spoil your day. So I won't invite him.'

He stood and took a couple of steps away, jammed hands in his pockets and waited for the bomb to explode. When it didn't, he continued, 'Besides, I don't have his number. He moves around—I may have said.'

She processed for a while, then reached a conclusion. 'Okay. I understand. You're right.'

That could have gone worse.

But the other thing?

Good luck with that.

'Thanks,' he said.

She embraced him. 'Thanks for saying so. Besides, it's one small part. As long as I have the church, the white dress, the flowers—you know, the dream—why jeopardise all that spectacular wonderfulness with family squabbles?'

His stomach turned—butterflies on top of the growing hunger. He forced a smile. 'Let's hope it goes ahead at all.'

She touched his cheek. 'What did you tell me? Believe. We'll fix this. We'll get back through, and we'll have our wedding. And it'll be amazing.'

He took her hand down, held it in both his and dared himself to look her in the eyes. 'No, it won't. I'll hate it.'

She pulled her hand away, more in shock than anger. 'What?' she whispered.

'I'm only being honest. It's what you asked.'

She backed away, face swirling with emotions.

You've done it now.

Two minutes ago, you were going to die young and in love.

Now you'll be alone.

And understand this; whatever else went before, this one thing is undeniably your fault.

He crumpled to the floor as if weakened by the loss of a demon that had both possessed and strengthened him.

A tortuous two minutes silence passed.

He knew it was two minutes because he surreptitiously slipped his cellphone out of his pocket, checked it still had some battery and mentally noted the time, which triggered his brain to remind his stomach it was way past lunchtime (at least in Sunrise), so his stomach reminded his brain that it was much too empty.

He flicked off Airplane mode. Still no signal.

You can't even text anyone when she dumps you.

Well, that'll be something to tell the not-kids. Losing the perfect woman while Not Actually On Earth.

She sat beside him.

'Sorry,' he murmured because it couldn't do any more harm than had already been done. You can't burn ashes.

She held out her left hand and raised the fourth finger. 'Why did you buy me such a small ring?'

He expected humour in her face. There was none.

Ah, payback time.

Better be honest, sonny. After all, look what a roaring success that's been over the last four minutes.

Think of it like this—kill or cure.

Kill?

Hmm.

Would she really kill you and eat you to survive?

Wow. Things took a significant emotional nosedive there, didn't they?

Let's aim for single and alive, huh? Let's call that a heck of a result at this point.

He took a deep breath, corralling ideas and strength.

'What we have—or at least thought we had—is about here,' he touched his chest. 'Not trinkets. Sorry if that's corny, but I'm a simple guy. I know we have money... well, did have.' He paused, reflecting. 'I reckoned it was better to invest in our future. No ring in the world costs enough to represent what you mean to me, what you've done for me, how much... idiot you put up with from me. I just... I just thought you weren't that shallow. That's all.'

He hadn't looked up at her the whole time. He still didn't. He felt too guilty.

She gave a quiet snort. 'And I thought Carlton was the penny pincher.'

'Wow. I have to love being compared to him, huh?'

'Sorry.'

The post-apocalyptic silence of Wherever It Was pushed in on them briefly. The total absence of the sounds of civilisation, nature. It almost triggered goosebumps, the most embarrassing, visceral, pregnant pause imaginable.

Think, idiot.

He took her left hand. 'You want me to get you a bigger one? Or...' He forced himself to voice the hateful alternative, 'You want me to take it back?'

'Why do you do it, Beckman? Risk everything to be a good guy?'

He shrugged. 'I guess if I'm going down in flames, I'd rather do it by being honest and doing the right thing.'

A smile crept across her lips. She pressed them to his. 'Then that's the kind of man I want to marry. However. Whenever.'

'Once we get out of here.'

'Kind of a prerequisite. Pretty light on pastors round about.'

'But the first licensed person we see on the other side, I'm marrying you.'

'I didn't mean you had to jump into it that fast. I only wanted a ballpark.'

'Life is short enough anyway. Right now, more so.'

'What are you doing next Saturday?'

'Let me check my schedule,' he joked, pulling out his cellphone and scrolling to the Calendar.

Before he could announce what they already knew—that his schedule was wide open and ripe for a Social Engagement Of Huge Significance—they both jumped out of their skin.

Because the ringtone chimed.

Chapter 30

'You ever hear of a little thing called trespassing?'

'You're kidding me, darling?' Reba came to a halt, which triggered Randall to do the same.

He shrugged. 'What?'

'Number one, I'm a PI, so hell yeah. Number two, you're a paid killer, so—'

'Was,' he corrected.

She let it pass. '—so I'd think you're not averse to some trespassing yourself. Number three, we're doing these folks a favour trying to pin the case on someone. For four, nobody is home—Wilma is on visiting hours at the hospital—I saw her car leave earlier.'

He let her words hang there for a second. 'There a five?'

'Yeah. Grow a pair of balls, you big lug. I haven't even crossed the Police tape yet, and I damn well will be.'

She resumed her purposeful stride, taking them on an arcing path down the scrub hillside and towards Walter Whack's impressive property. Sunlight glinted off the outdoor pool.

'That's not a job for Oz?' Randall hefted the strap of the picnic hamper up his shoulder, caught up to her and slid his spare hand into hers, in the way a man does when he wants to soften the words of an assertive query which might otherwise be met with a steely glare.

'Honey, in nine weeks here, did you ever hear a siren?' She didn't wait for an answer. 'There's an actual dimple in Sergeant Oz Bosman's desk, inside the near edge, where his heels have worn down the wood.' She gave him a matter-of-fact glance. 'The fire is the most exciting thing to happen in Sunrise since Kelvin Hammer decorated the front of Palmer Garret's clothing store with his Plymouth Neon on account of his dyscalculia. And that was six years ago.'

'His dyscal—'

'He forgot how many bourbon's he'd had.'

'Textbook open-and-shut case.'

'Exactly how Oz likes it,' Reba confirmed. 'Those potato chips and Twinkies don't eat themselves, you know.'

'I guess I'm not built for judging people.'

'Hell no. That'd be a liability in your line of work.' She caught herself and voiced the rejoinder before he did. 'Would have *been*.'

He flashed a wink. 'Yeah, can't be seeing the good in the people I'm supposed to be putting a bullet through.'

'Like me,' she recalled. 'Shooting at you in the warehouse.'

'You probably get into a lot more unsavoury shenanigans than I ever did. Personal lives. Character destructions of people you thought you knew. Pretty brave in a small town, putting yourself up to make enemies, then pass them on the street every day.'

'I said to Beckman one time; you can't turn off curiosity. And if anyone's going to wade into this or go off on wild theories, I'd rather me than him or Lolita. At least I have the slightest clue what I'm doing. Plus, Carlton would think twice about picking a fight with me over it.'

'Hell, *I'd* think twice about picking a fight with you.'

'Elmer John James Garrity didn't even try.'

'But he was a cheating asshole.'

'We do seem to have a thing on those round here, huh?' She flashed an eyebrow.

'If it keeps you in ballet classes and picnics, let it roll.'

'Not that I'm averse to becoming a kept woman instead.'

He helped her over a patch of jagged rocks. 'Ah, the M conversation again.'

'Honey, you don't have to marry me if you don't want to. So long as you stay, do right, and let me spend your money while I watch April grow into a tough little lady who won't fall foul of people like Elmer Garrity.'

'Or I watch over April and bring her to the penitentiary once a week for visiting after you get put away for tampering with evidence.'

She stopped dead. 'Randall Ickey, if you don't want this to be your fight, speak on up. I get that it would be a hell of an irony, if after all you've done, being an accomplice to interfering with police business finally gets you jail time. But maybe if a guy like Beckman had forgiven me for trying to rub him out by handing over a million bucks, I'd be nervous about not being able to walk the streets and spend all those dollars instead of taking a chance to repay that gratitude.' Her expression put an inked-in period to that soapbox proclamation.

He pointed at his head. 'This is me thinking twice about picking a fight with you.'

'If you want to pick a fight, do it with whoever is playing Joker here in little Gotham. Because the Bat-team is assembling, and I'd sooner have you on it than not.'

'Well, if you love me for my special skills *as well as* my bank balance, I can't recall a better offer.'

She tugged his hand, and they paced the last hundred yards to the side of the property. After a careful scan of the area, she led him to the front drive, where an area about six yards square was marked off by police tape lazily held in place on the ground by a few chunky rocks.

She checked around a final time before crossing the Do Not Cross into the centre of the makeshift quadrilateral, where the remains of a century-old chimney had splatted onto the shingle.

Randall couldn't believe there wasn't more blood.

'Lucky does not even cover it,' Reba offered, mirroring his take on the situation.

'The luck, and the accident versus design, are two different things. What gets me is I don't like either accident *or* design. They both feel off.'

'Like how?' He took up an inspection position diametrically opposite his infinitely more qualified girlfriend. He peered at the bricks, without a clue what he was looking for, other than presuming it would be obvious when he found it, if he found it, and if it was even there to be found.

'If this is an accident, Walter should play the state lottery because these are killer odds.'

'It's more unlucky than a lightning strike.'

'And on the flip side,' she pulled a pen from her tunic pocket, 'You'd have to be a physics major or a construction expert to predict exactly how this stack would fall.'

'So that makes you have to rethink our list of potential perps.'

'The thing about my job, it's a lot about the Who and not the Why. I mean, the Why is usually because people are greedy, or liars, or idiots. The Who is what makes the conclusion, and when you have the Who, you ask them the Why. Either they give you the bird and tell you to take a hike, or they come over all repentant. The motive here is, in some way, to get Walter. But it doesn't change what we're looking for.'

'Which is?'

'Evidence that it's possible to hit that rooftop from the hill with a .220 Swift.'

He scanned the debris. 'Good luck with that.'

'I don't need luck.' She indicated a spot on one of the broken bricks. 'I've got half as many good eyes as most people, but that's all I need.'

He crabbed over to see. He half-expected to find a shell, although even the lackadaisical Oz would spot a spent bullet nestling in plain sight.

What Oz hadn't noticed, amongst the fracture lines, sharp edges of brick, shards and powdered mortar, was what appeared very much like an impact site. Possibly, if they were even half as lucky as Walter Whack, from a long-range bullet strike designed to take out a corner wedge of chimney stack and send it careering to earth.

Chapter 31

No number showed on the phone, but Beckman jabbed the green circle without hesitation. Whoever was calling, and whatever they said, could hardly make their predicament any testier.

'Beckman?' came the voice.

Okay, now this HAS to be a parallel universe because this sounds suspiciously like Sergeant Marlon Spiers. Well, Sergeant last time we spoke, so allowing for career progression in the intervening years, based on past trajectory… Sergeant.

'Dad?'

Lolita's mouth fell open. He'd seen that kind of thing in Tom and Jerry cartoons but never believed it happened for real.

That's parents for you.

'How are you?' came the stupendously original follow up question.

Sadly, Beckman's mind wasn't cut out for answering questions. It was too busy fizzing like a firecracker, leaping like eleven Lords, a needle in the red segment of the dial while klaxons blared.

'Yeah, I'm… good,' his vocal cords offered by way of a stalling mechanism.

'Where are you, son?'

'Oh,' he looked around. 'Out of town.'

'Which town?'

'Oh, you wouldn't know. It's hard to find. Even when you're nearby. Where are you?'

I guess we're doing the superficial pleasantries thing, avoiding the elephant in the alternative dimension, until he gets round to asking me for money, or telling me he's getting remarried, or whatever other reason there is for this asteroid strike of a phone call.

'Duluth,' Marlon replied.

'Uh-huh. Why the call?'

'I saw your mother.'

Ah. Now the penny drops. She showed him the diamonds I sent. It's a money call, sure as God made little green apples and unfathomable portals and astounding women who are staring at me, having shuttered those wondrous lips.

'Why? What did she do to deserve that?'

'Still the wiseass, Beckman.'

'At least one of us is wise.'

'Mom showed me the diamonds. You come into money?'

'Why, are you asking? If so, you picked a hell of a time.'

'You come into money?' Marlon repeated.

'Is that why you called?'

'I don't appreciate the insinuation.'

'Wow, big word. Why'd you see mom? Really?'

'I was passing.'

'And she opened the door. I thought better of her.'

Beckman's noticed Lolita pointing towards where the portal was (or at least should be) and planning to walk to it. He covered the mouthpiece. 'Don't go without me,' he called. Mercifully, she stopped. Being on the phone with dad was bad enough, but if she left him behind, he'd have nobody to bitch about it with afterwards.

'Who was that?' asked the tiny speaker pressed to his right ear.

'Just a friend.'

'A lady friend?'

'Yes,' he said with a reluctant sigh.

'Finally.'

'Finally? You're the one who always stopped me from making my way with anyone.'

'Remember it whichever way you want.'

'You're serious?' Beckman replied in disbelief. 'We moved. That could be Janelle now.'

The person who wasn't Janelle, but in counterpoint to his argument was very much worth the intervening twenty-year wait, had stopped trying to escape back into Sunrise and now took hold of his free hand.

'My son dating a girl with a name like that?'

'Because, of course, you despise odd names,' he sniped.

'Always me at fault, huh?'

'You call me up to tell me what name girls I can hang out with? "Lolita" okay for you?'

She smiled. He replied with an Emmy-worthy eye roll.

'I guess,' Marlon said.

'How very magnanimous of you.'

Beckman heard a heavy sigh. 'I guess I was an asshole to think you'd be over all this.'

'Or maybe you're just an asshole.'

'This may be news to you, but I did what I did for good reasons. I'm not dumb. I know you didn't enjoy it. But I was never being pushed out. Never running away. Not away. I was running *towards* something. Towards opportunity. Opportunity for better things. Everybody wants that.'

Beckman had no smart Alec rejoinder: his recent upswing proved that a sensible guy always chooses the gold at the end of the rainbow, whether or not it wears swing dresses, cooks a demon pot roast and puts up with the sensible guy's idiotic foibles. 'I guess,' he admitted.

'I always moved to get a promotion, to earn more, do the best for you. You could have embraced it, taken it as a life adventure, but you chose to be the ass.'

'I guess,' he admitted, again.

'I was at Duluth when you were about two centimetres across. My CO, Val Biagi, was a dick. We didn't see eye to eye. He'd never promote me in a million years. So that was the first move out. Anyway, seems Val's boat sank last month, and luckily he was on it. So they have a new CO. And I have a shot.'

'Well... I guess that's good.'

'Hence moving back. Word to the wise, son: Don't pick a fight you can't win.'

'I'll remember that,' he said because he felt he should.

'So maybe I'll call you with news of promotion.' There was a calm, almost apologetic tone to his father's words. 'That be okay?'

'Sure,' he replied, being the magnanimous person he'd sought before.

'Look after yourself.'

'Yeah.'

And before he had the chance to find anything better, more upbeat, more searching or less confrontational to say, the line cut. He slowly lowered the phone and stared at it.

No signal. Only the time, 13:44, overlaying his wallpaper image of Lolita, lips puckered, looking over the rim of her glasses.

Wherever They Were returned to its natural silence.

'I'll be a son of a—'

'Asshole?'

'I might need to downgrade him to idiot after that. Or at least call the jury back on asshole.'

'Is that how I am with Jack?'

He snapped out of his reverie. 'What do you want me to say?'

'The truth. Always.'

'Then, yeah, you are. But without my biting wit.'

She laughed. 'The second part I know is a lie. See, honey, you can do it—lie.'

'Only in jest.'

She kissed him on the cheek. 'Let's call that a start.'

'If it's all the same, I'll cling desperately onto the notion of being as honest as the day is long. Though, out here, who knows how long the days are? Maybe it's perpetual sunlight.' He gazed skywards, searching for the sun, and couldn't find it.

Weird. I'm sure I left it around here someplace.

Surely enough, if he'd believed the place wasn't unfathomable enough already, this took the biscuit. A whole bumper family pack of them. The sky was a cloudless blue (grey), the hills brown and green (dark grey) and the ground a brown-ochre (a different dark grey). Yet no sun shone—no apparent source of illumination. It was merely light as if by—and he'd keenly avoided even thinking the word before—magic.

Luckily, there was no such thing as magic, so he ascribed it to physics or chemistry or Stuff Really Clever Guys Write Equations About On Blackboards.

It made no difference. They were where they were, and wherever they were was terminally short on root beer and coffee, and staying in places like that seemed Not Much Fun, notwithstanding the company.

Company which had, for reasons he still hadn't understood, followed him into potential oblivion.

He took Company's hand.

'Do you think he called to ask for money?' she asked.

'He could have called to say he was emigrating to Tuvalu to live as a rainbow fish, and it wouldn't feel weird. Calling is crazy enough anyhow.'

'Enough emigrations going on anyway, you said.'

He nodded, remembering mom. 'Yeah, but mine wins right now. Just so long as it's temporary.'

'How did he get your number?'

'He's always had it. I never switched. But ability and motivation are not the same thing.'

'Like you always had the ability to tell me you didn't want a big wedding,' she suggested.

'Just not the balls.'

'So why now?'

'Nothing to lose. And because I don't think you'd really try and walk back through without me.'

'I wasn't. I was hoping for… inspiration.'

'I can't even lose you, which right now is pretty important because that's all I have. Plus, my shoulder bag. Which I do like, but not quite as much as I like you.'

She pressed into an embrace. 'And I quite like you too. You're thoughtful, you do the right thing, and you're not the worst looking guy in the world.'

He kissed her. 'Darling, stood here, I'm absolutely the best looking guy available.'

They held each other close.

'Why are we so calm about all this?' she asked finally.

'Maybe we've achieved some kind of peace, and that's enough. Or it's all we have.'

'It's a hell of a good place to start.'

'I thought if I was honest about this one thing, it would hurt you. That's why I avoided the topic.'

'And I thought being honest about this one thing would hurt you.' She raised her ring hand.

'Better to be honest with each other all the time.'

She waggled her head. 'Maybe not *all* the time.'

'Really? Any other secrets you want to take to the grave? Which, I'll remind you, could be any time now unless we figure this return trip.'

'That shirt does nothing for you.'

'Ah, holding back the big stuff, I see.'

She shrugged. 'You asked for honesty.'

'You look better with bangs.'

'You have a wonky tooth.'

'I don't like that picture on the dining room wall.'

'You're not as funny as you think.'

Cut. To. The. Quick.

'Okay, that's enough honesty for now.' He smiled to show he was deadly serious—in a friendly way.

'One more thing.'

'What?' He braced for impact.

'I love you, like crazy much.'

'I could take or leave you.'

Her eyes lit, her lips cracked into faux shock, then she whacked him on the ass. 'Any last words from the condemned man?'

'You say the nicest things. Well, some. Well, a couple.'

'Just so we're clear where we stand. In case that Saturday idea was to pour water on things.'

He shook his head. 'Not a bit of it.'

'Do you want to move, or stay in the house?'

'Here, a house of any kind would be a blessing. But yeah, your place is good.'

'Invite your dad to the wedding?' she said.

'Rain check on that, okay? One phone call is only a sticking plaster over the Grand Canyon.'

She nodded. 'Okay.'

'I ask one?'

'Sure.'

'Can we get a parrot?' he asked.

She frowned. 'Can we get a parrot?'

'Seriously.'

'Seriously?'

'One who repeats everything I say.'

'One who repeats everything I say?'

'You know, to double the number of annoying personalities in the house.'

'Double the number of annoying personalities in the house?'

Beckman had a soft spot for parrots and passed endless fun teaching Cousin Ichabod's sidekick plenty of hilarious phrases, chiefly designed to get the guy in trouble with as many people as possible. The problem was shutting the damn creature up.

The creature in front of him, however, was easier to summarily silence. So he mashed his lips to hers with an uncompromising undercurrent of "Shut Up Darling".

When they came up for breath, the resonance of gallows humour hanging in the air, he made a pronouncement. 'You've just made the whole parrot idea seem very unappealing.'

'Then my work is done.'

'So turn your mind to something more important, Einstein.' He pointed at where his belt lay. 'If you want marriage so much, marriage is teamwork, and we need to teamwork the hell out of here.'

'I'll pass on the part where we compare GPA and find out you're the nerd.' She took his hand and led him back to where The Portal, they hoped, awaited them.

'Maybe it's luck that gets us out of here and not bright ideas,' he said hopefully.

'How long do we keep trying? Sooner or later, we have to work on survival. And I'll remind you that kissing burns calories—calories we need to save.'

'Not that I needed any more incentive to get back home, but that went to the top of the list.'

She put a hand to his cheek. 'Ah, my dear, sweet, honest, and deeply shallow man.'

'Hungry. You left out "hungry".'

'Damn. I wish you hadn't said that out loud. My stomach heard you, and now it's pissed as well.'

'So let's walk. Huh? I'm fresh out of ideas, and I'm fed up with standing here and pretending everything will work out in the end if we simply hope it will. I have no more clue than you about how this… thing…,' he flung his arm in the direction of the invisible gateway, 'Work—'

She yelped as if in pain. Her eyes were saucers, aghast at something. He followed her line of sight.

The end of his left arm was missing.

He didn't yelp. He didn't leap back. He didn't curse, although it was a gloriously perfect moment for doing so.

Instead, his conditioned brain took observation, instinct, a good dose of circumstantial evidence, and threw in a whole barrel of hope and desperation.

He grabbed the nearest part of her arm and hauled them violently into The Portal.

Chapter 32

As Reba gazed up at the roof of Walter's property, Randall had a good idea what her next good idea would be. He didn't like the idea, but liked that he had an idea of what the idea might be. It meant he was getting to know her, to get fully on her wavelength.

'If you're figuring to find a ladder and go hunting for where that .220 lodged, you're SOL, baby.'

'How's that?'

'I just think it's a bad idea.'

'Why, scared of heights?' she joked.

'No. It's pushing our luck.' But his face left a small clue, like a bullet scrape on a shattered brick.

'You're scared of heights!'

'I'm not keen on either of us getting caught on that roof if she comes back.'

'Randall Ickey, you're a scaredy-cat!'

'Okay.' He put his hands up defensively. 'You have me bang to rights. Rib me all you like. Only not when we're on someone else's property without even the most half-assed of excuses, which we haven't even invented yet.'

'Find the bullet—that's the smoking gun—to use an ass-backwards analogy.'

'Then up you go, Sherpa Tensing.' He waved towards the roof. 'You explain all to Wilma if she arrives. You explain to the doctors if she doesn't come, but you fall off the roof and bust your pretty keister open. Or you explain to Oz, when you find the smoking gun, bullet, whatever, how you didn't trust the guy's grasp of crime scene technique and went rogue.'

'I'm so tactless, huh?' She pushed towards him in gentle confrontation.

He hugged her, taking the heat out of the situation and minimising the opportunity for her to throw a right hook.

'All I'm saying is, it's been a good day's work. For a Saturday, which is supposed to be "us time". Let's roll with what we got. And, hand to God, if you still want to button it up good and tight, let's do it properly. We'll figure a way to keep Wilma off the property long enough for you to do what you need, and get an open comm channel setup or something so I can warn you off, like all that movie heist shit.'

She stroked his stubbled chin. 'You're not so bad for a sidekick.'

' "Sidekick" is it now?'

' "Boyfriend" makes me sound eighteen. Got a better idea?'

'Probably. Let's get back to "us time", and we can agree some mutually acceptable terms of endearment—for when I'm announcing who I am to the guards at visiting hour.'

She gave him a little sock in the ribs. 'Deal. Sidekick.'

So he hefted up the picnic basket, and they took a direct line towards where their car sat parked on the far side of the hill.

As they burbled back to Reba's place on the west side of town, Randall allowed himself a smug smile of satisfaction when, a couple of minutes into the journey, they passed Wilma Whack's pricey German saloon heading in the opposite direction.

'Get over yourself,' Reba said, without giving him the gratification of meeting his eye.

He could only wonder, for the millionth time, why Elmer JJ Garrity cheated on this rare find of a woman, but Elmer's loss became his gain, so he wasn't going to lose any sleep over the guy's blind spot.

At her request, they detoured via Zander's Homewares on Diode Street. It was a ramshackle place with a parking lot at the rear that was being reclaimed, weed by weed, by the open country beyond.

They had skirted the side of the store when Reba barked, 'Stop!'

He jammed on the brake. The Corvette stopped on a dime, thanks to his foresight in fitting aftermarket pads as part of the fifty grand makeover to his ten grand machine.

'What?' he rapped, perturbed.

'Back up.'

Assuming her command was driven by some P.I. Stuff, rather than because he'd run over Zander's prized pet Shih Tzu, he slotted R and gassed them back twenty feet.

Instantly they came to rest, she opened the door and hopped out.

Reba pressed herself to the building's wall and crept forward to peer around the corner and into the parking lot where they'd erroneously strayed for about five seconds. Perhaps she was curious to observe some ancient Rite of Freemasonry which was trying to remain secret by being undertaken in broad daylight in a public place… admittedly in a town nobody knew about or could ever find.

Whatever she saw, it took about thirty seconds, after which she climbed back in and announced that the shopping errand could wait and he should take them home.

'Why the cloak and dagger?' he asked.

'Aside from it's my job?'

'What happened to "us time"?'

'Subversion is no respecter of schedules, honey.'

'So what gives?' He jerked his head in the vague direction of where they'd come.

'Carlton Cooper and Pollard up to something.'

There was only one Pollard in town. Like there was only one Carlton. One Randall. He'd not met Pollard McGary, one of Reba's colleagues at Taylor's. 'Any chance they were shooting the breeze?'

'A lot of privacy for a breeze-shooting happenstance and more passing of brown envelopes than I'd expect.'

Was she kidding? She was not.

'Pollard an off-book kinda guy?'

'If it had to be one of us to stoop so low, it's him. Delmar doesn't have the brains or balls, Zeb is too straight and honourable, and I need the wage packet too much to get fired for going freelance on the side. Pollard is ex-military. He's never said *which* military, which makes us think it's the under-the-radar kind. Not that he lasted long, based on calculation. All piss and vinegar. The crew-cut is for show. Twenty years older, and he's the kind of guy who'd say, "You don't know about 'Nam, you weren't even there, man", despite only doing a week in a supply depot thirty miles behind the lines.'

'Strikes me not a good idea to ask either of them what went down. Beyond the obvious fact, Pollard just did Carlton some favour.'

'Question is—what, why now, and why under the radar? Cooper was large as life when he hired Delmar to tail Beckman a few weeks back. It doesn't do Pollard's CV any good to be seen taking counsel like that, not if we figure him for the chimney and the fire. If we can find a .220 Swift-bearing rifle in the vicinity of Carlton Cooper, and his prints on those two shells in your pocket, the walls are closing in fast on the guy.'

'So who is Pollard following?'

'Ten bucks says it's related to Milan.' She bit her lip. 'Cooper was laughing. I don't recall ever seeing that.'

'So?'

'I don't like it.'

'Because normally he's Time Man Of The Year?' he scoffed.

'Because I get a nasty feeling that if there's a case hiding here, we've already lost.'

Chapter 33

The hard glare of the mid-afternoon sun hit them square in the face.

He stumbled, feet slapping the tarmac, and clutched onto her to steady himself, which unbalanced her, so she clutched him, and they danced like drunken windmills until her backwards topple met his forwards totter, their arms yanked tight, and the two-body gravitational system found equilibrium.

His heart hammered in his chest.

Yes, it *was* tarmac beneath his feet. Rich, deep grey tarmac, but not a greyscale grey—a grey flecked with ochre dust and glinting with the tinge of a truly yellow sun that really existed in an actual sky above a familiar town.

The space next to him erupted in a howl of unbridled joy, as if Lolita had won the state lottery on the same day she'd read in the newspaper that she'd been voted Sexiest Woman Alive, while in a limousine on the way to collect her Nobel Prize for securing world peace.

He crushed her in his arms and terminated her yelping noise using the method he'd successfully employed to halt her earlier parroting.

She felt and tasted like ambrosia.

He would have continued frolicking in the glow of their deliverance—and her utter magnificence—if it wasn't for a nagging feeling in the back of his skull that they were being watched.

So he let go of his purring lioness and turned to look.

They *were* being watched.

None of the people was pointing a gun at them.

But one had an eye-patch, one sported a bar apron, another rose from a nonchalant pose on the prow of a new sports car, and the last was of indeterminate age.

He wanted to jog across, arms wide, in glorious slo-mo, and startle more than one of them with a highly unexpected fat wet kiss. Hell, if dad had been there, he'd even stretch to a handshake with the objectionable SOB.

Norman Rockwell's G.I. never had this level of relief.

'You two done?' Buck called.

In response, Lolita dropped Beckman like a dog bored of a chew toy and pelted over to her Kinda Father, clattering into him and squeezing so tight he could almost feel it. She'd have got more joy trying to shrink the circumference of a sequoia pine.

Beckman took a more casual stroll to the foursome, exchanging handshakes with Tyler and Amaryllis, and half-hugs with Saul and Buck.

'There goes the quarantine we had lined up,' Saul said.

'Quarantine?' Beckman queried, before seeing the glint in the tow-trucker's solitary pupil and knew his leg was being pulled. Buck, now freed from the constriction of a swing-dress-wearing traveller from (possibly) another dimension, pulled two takeaway cups from the cab of his Chevy Silverado.

Beckman tipped the brown nectar into a grateful throat. It was still nicely warm.

Were we only gone ten minutes? Felt like a couple of hours.

The Twin Paradox made real?

'How long were we gone?'

'Best guess, couple of hours,' Saul replied.

'How did you know we were... in... there?' Lolita asked Buck.

'Thank Tyler.'

'Why, he develop your sixth sense?' Beckman asked Saul. 'On which, are you slacking? Two people, very much in need, stranded?' He was only half-kidding.

'You think I'm taking a truck in there after anyone, you're about as dumb as I would be crazy.'

'Give the guy a break,' Lolita supplicated.

Saul waved away Beckman's query, dismissing it as the universe-hopping after-effect equivalent of "It's the beer talking".

'Well, don't keep us in suspense,' Lolita said. 'Days go by, nobody with any brain comes out here. Aside from idiot man-boys wanting to hock stones. So why the four of you, all of a sudden, and bang on time?'

"Man-boy"?

Fair call.

Tyler stepped in. 'Amaryllis and I were getting a soda in Jen and Berry's, in walks Carlton and Wanda, so we keep our heads down. She was kinda spiky, asking whether straight-out murder was the type of thing she should have to put up with.'

'She could have stopped him,' Beckman interrupted, remembering how passively she'd sat in the car while her beau forced them through The Portal at gunpoint.

Tyler continued. 'Cooper said he couldn't prove you weren't right as rain on the other side. He told you to leave town, and that's what you did. Bonus being you were a hell of a lot less likely to come crawling back.'

Beckman saw Lolita: her jaw set hard, eyes fierce, fists balling. She possessed anger enough for them both. The challenge now would be how to keep her out of Very Serious Trouble for a precipitous double homicide. If Oz was running scared from the small matters of arson and property destruction, a couple of bodies found crushed by an especially heavy Egyptian artefact would make the guy's desk pen explode.

'So we did the best thing we could think; we told Saul,' Amaryllis said.

'Things like that are in danger of getting you the first hug in twelve years,' Beckman smirked.

'Or twice in a week here.' Lolita stepped in for the embrace. 'Thank you.'

Beckman's brow furrowed in remembrance. 'Anyway, I thought you were leaving town yourself?' he asked Tyler.

'My greatest performance since Third Sheep in the Grade Five nativity.'

'He knows you love him really,' Amaryllis added.

'Love?' Beckman asked. 'I'm already taken, thanks all the same.'

'After that, because Jack's daughter was in danger, I did the only sensible thing,' Saul said.

'You didn't call him,' Lolita guessed. 'And for that, I'm grateful.'

'She called someone better,' Buck said.

Beckman emptied his cup. 'Absolutely. I hear Jack makes the worst coffee.'

'How come it's so fresh?' Lolita asked, drinking. 'If you charged out like the cavalry, it'd be cold by now? What kind of witchcraft is this?!'

'Oh, we brought the whole damn store.' Saul gestured to the two pickups.

Beckman went to investigate. Between the two cabs and two load bays sat a generator, folding chairs, a giant flashlight, a crate of water, towels, a first aid kit, a host of edible provisions, tow rope, an oxygen bottle, a defibrillator, and a small coffee machine and a fridge, both of which had been rewired to work from either a car battery or a generator.

Beckman felt guilty that they hadn't come back more in dire need of assistance. 'Were you going to *sleep* here?' he asked, dumbfounded.

'Well, not all of us,' Buck replied. 'We had a rota. Clint, Reba, maybe Randall.'

'Wow,' Lolita said, the extent of their warmth sinking in. 'Looks like all you were shy on is actually going in after us. Kidding, by the way.'

'I said we could back the Silverado in there, so you could grab hold of the rear fender,' Saul said. 'Buck not too keen on that.'

'In case The Portal sucked both me and it inside,' Buck explained. 'I suggested the Ranger instead, but….'

'Neither of you dumb enough to suggest the 911,' Beckman ventured.

There was a chorus of laughter, capped by Tyler's, 'Love only goes so far, fella.'

'So, want to enlighten us about your adventure?' Buck glanced towards the invisible barrier at the end of the road twenty yards away.

'Absolutely,' Beckman replied. 'But somewhere with comfortable seats, fresh food and decent root beer, okay?'

Chapter 34

After the nirvana of Deliverance From Certain Doom, Beckman and Lolita were brought crashing down to earth by Buck's sage summary of the situation: Carlton wants you gone, thinks you're gone, and won't exactly be skipping gaily down Main Street, tossing rose petals asunder when he finds out you're both very much alive and kicking.

Discretion, of a wholly understandable and not Falstaffian nature, was the better part of valour on that particular Saturday afternoon. As such, the CEO and her Sales Director were hidden under a jumble of blankets arranged across the rear seats until they arrived at the rear of Our Buck's.

In fifteen years, Lolita had never entered the café through the back entrance, let alone been smuggled in like a reluctant celebrity. Beckman didn't even know the place had a back entrance, sensed the way his betrothed felt about the whole affair and tried to convince her it was done for the right reasons.

'Revenge is a dish best served cold,' he said, because (1) it felt apposite and (2) it sounded cool. Even under the obscuring gloom of their makeshift tarpaulin, he heard The Eyebrow leap into action, thereby confirming it was neither (1) nor (2), but (3) incredibly lame.

Neither denied the wisdom of circumspection, yet he knew she simmered with ire: Carlton had them creeping around like frightened mice. Jerry was stranded in the kitchen with Tom on the loose, and seeking refuge behind table legs and stacks of plates was a precondition of survival. Thankfully they had Spike the dog to look after them.

Spike the dog parked his Silverado tight up to the back door, pulled the key from his pocket and created an entrance for his friends to bolt into, which they duly did. He locked the door behind them and went to the main entrance to reopen his premises.

The makeshift sign on the front door read, "Back when I'm back". He tugged it from its sticky tape mooring, flipped the switch on the door jamb, so the neons in the window read OPEN instead of CLOSED, and went inside to fire up Bessie.

Buck's backroom was, as all such backrooms are, a bomb site. Its disorder made Beckman feel uneasy, thriving as he did on order and predictability. Still, it was infinitely better than being inside The Portal.

He was taking an inventory of the surprisingly capacious pigsty when Buck opened the inner door, thereby reminding him he wasn't Hannibal Smith and therefore not expected to summarily escape from the room using only an oxyacetylene torch and the Aladdin's cave of useful parts.

'Bessie is putting her face on,' Buck said, flicking on the light switch and handing over a tall root beer. Beckman passed the glass to Lolita, who drank deeply and handed it back for him to drain.

'You've done a lot for me, Buck, but this is right up there,' she said.

'Counts double here,' Beckman added. 'What can we do?'

'Lay low and don't get your asses whipped again.' Buck hauled a couple of boxes away from two dusty bar stools, tugged a rag from his apron pocket and roughly wiped them down.

'I meant by payback.'

'Don't kill the guy and wind up in Perryville for fifteen to twenty.' Buck's glare underscored his deadly seriousness.

Lolita raised her hand in testimony. 'Swear to God.'

'Or hire anyone to do similar.'

Her hand went up again, silently.

Hence Beckman got the undertakings he secretly hoped for, because whilst he could never be an accomplice to murder, he couldn't be confident he had the fortitude to stop her from doing what she arguably had every right to. He might beg her with every last breath, but the only sure way to restrain her was actual preventative incarceration, which would make for a pretty sucky marriage. That was, assuming they made it to next Saturday's planned nuptials without further crime, conflagration, injury, destruction, conspiracy, revenge or impromptu trans-dimensional awaydays.

He scouted around their holding pen, put two and two together, and asked, 'Lay low?'

Look on the bright side; at least there's coffee and root beer on tap 24/7.

Without a shower here, though, keeping the flies off after a few days could be a challenge.

'Surely we can go home?' Lolita suggested.

'Somehow, Carlton knew you were at The Portal. You want to take a chance that he's nervous enough to keep the spies roaming?'

She let out a sigh and pinched her forehead. 'I guess.'

'Look, I don't have all the answers. But playing dead is the smart move until we get a better idea.'

'Playing dead feels like he keeps on winning.'

'Tortoise and the hare. What happened out at the gateway is "he said, she said". No independent witnesses. And Oz has come up empty so far on the fire and the

Walter thing. So I may not be Atticus Finch or Columbo, but Carlton is sitting pretty, and we all need to suck it up until the cracks appear.'

'Don't pick a fight you can't win,' Beckman mumbled pensively.

'What?' she asked.

'Nothing. That is, something.' He gestured around. 'We can make this work, honey.'

Buck stared. 'If you want to sleep here, be my guest. But I figured you'd come over to the house.'

'What?' Lolita asked.

'Unless you reckon different. The only rules are No to your own cars and your own house. Your rides stay out at The Portal, so if Carlton swings by, he still thinks you're in there. Find a place you can hunker down, guest of someone who's got your back. My hat is in the ring, is all I'm saying.'

Beckman stepped over to Buck, rapping his knee on the edge of an arcade machine that he couldn't believe ever looked at home in the café proper. 'We'd be honoured to stay over.' He shot Lolita a glance.

She pecked Buck on the cheek and offered thanks.

'Right answer,' Buck said. 'Now, sit there, wait while I get your coffee and such, call Esme to come take over until closing, then we'll all go to the house, pull down the drapes and lie on the floor for the rest of the day.' He winked to show the last part was hyperbole.

But before he reached the door, the handle turned.

Beckman and Lolita, Red Alert klaxons blaring through their skulls, hit the floor and scrabbled for a place to hide within the two seconds warning they'd received.

It was no use.

Chapter 35

In his defensive desire to block the view, Buck rapped into the opening door, causing the inbound interloper to yelp in some alarm.

A female yelp. Wanda?

Frozen in fear, Beckman angled his eyeballs up from his prone position, seeking a few seconds pointless warning of any approaching nemesis. Or nemesises. Nemeses?

Now there's a word I never thought would cross my life's path.

Malvolio and Tyler were very separate nemeses. Meaning each one was a nemesis on his own. They didn't work together. Very separate agendas.

But now? Carlton and Wanda were joined at the hip, and as she'd shown no signs of reigning in her beau's antics, she had to stand shoulder to shoulder with him when it came to being viewed as a nemesis.

So they were nemeses.

Or merely one gestalt nemesis?

Well, this is a fun game. Lying on the floor of a junk room, fiancée spreadeagled by my side, something sticky under my right hand, something else painful digging into my ribs, waiting for the axe to fall on us both for the second time today, and I'm damned if I knew whether a pair of adversaries are 1 × nemesis, 2 × nemesises, 1 × nemeses or 2 × nemeses.

If there's a last request granted again this time, I'm asking for a dictionary. Never too late to keep learning. Even if it is the final

moments before succumbing to whatever our... nem... nemis...
nemes... opponents have planned for us.

Buck backed away, allowing the singular or plural nemesis or nemeses into the room.

Beckman wanted to call out a warning, tell the big bear not to be such a sucker, except: (1) calling out a warning when you are trying to remain silently hidden is Peak Idiot, and (2) it wasn't Wanda after all. Or Carlton.

The person in front was a woman, but not of Wanda's frame. There was only one person with such... diminished stature. Behind her stood a less diminished shape, and two such outlines which, often seen together, were easy to identify, and hence classify as the opposite of nemeses, whatever *that* word was.

Should he ever get that dictionary—very preferably long, loooong before he shuffled (or was pushed) off this mortal coil—he'd make a point to get clued up on "nemesis" and related synonyms and antonyms. Then, armed with that knowledge, he'd hope only to have cause to use such words in nostalgic remembrance of these less than delightful but undoubtedly *interesting* times. For instance, when recounting tales of Portal crossings, backroom cowerings and a deplorable lack of English language skills, ideally for the amusement of two children he hoped to bounce on his knee one day.

'God, Reba, sorry,' came Buck's voice.

While Beckman took precious seconds to satisfy himself that Reba would have the good sense never to touch Carlton Cooper with anything less than a handful of bargepoles duct-taped together (lengthwise), Lolita liberated herself from horizontal discomfort. 'You might have knocked,' she sniped.

Beckman scrambled up, dusted down, and beheld the glorious sight of their visitors.

Reba held up her hand in apology. 'Okay.'

Randall smiled. 'Future reference, the "laying" in "laying low" is not literal.'

'One day, Randall Ickey, I will swing for you.' Lolita slapped dust from her red and blue skirt.

'Maybe after we've finished doing favours for you.'

'How so?' Buck asked.

'Come on in.' Beckman waved. 'Plenty of room for a pow-wow, now there's not two idiots trying to swim the length of the place.'

'I'll fix those drinks,' Buck said, passing into the doorway. 'Move what you need.'

So, five minutes of hasty rearrangement and dusting down later, with beverages in hand, Lolita recounted the events of the day for the benefit of the sleuthing twosome. Outside in the café, Tyler and Amaryllis were charged with being an early warning system.

Throughout it all, Beckman mused on the lack of interrogation about what had happened *inside* The Portal. He considered inventing stories of a wild world, replete with luminous blue dragons, lava pools and endless wide-grinned realtors in check shirts. Perhaps a place where everything was a different shade of yellow, everyone walked upside-down and lived on blueberry tacos. He might even try talking about snow, fauns, a wicked witch and a mysterious lion, and see how long the audience took to realise their chains were being yanked.

'So what's it like in there?' Randall chirped.

Caught in the headlights, Beckman was about to give the unsullied truth, chiefly because he didn't have the energy or chops to try and drag out a lie.

Lolita waved it away. 'It wasn't hell. We survived. Eyes on priorities, okay?'

'So, these favours?' Lolita continued.

Reba apprised the audience of their discovery at Walter's house and, being the dutiful P.I. charged with finding evidence rather than making accusations, kept everything fact-related. Then she chugged on her diet soda and awaited questions from the audience.

'Is Carlton a good enough shot?' Beckman asked.

'If he owns the rifle, has prints on those bullets, and can't hold onto an alibi for the time of the quote-unquote accident, then yeah, he's a good enough shot,' Buck said.

Lolita shook her head gently. 'I knew right off the bat that Carlton had done it, but… actual murder?'

'Attempted murder,' Reba corrected.

'For now,' Buck corrected her correction. 'Unless coma leads to worse.'

'If it was him,' Beckman said.

'You're trying to give the guy the benefit of the doubt? After what he did to us?' The Eyebrow hovered in readiness.

'Not 'cos I want to, but yeah. Give the guy enough rope to hang himself.'

'On which,' Randall piped up, 'We saw him paying off Pollard. We reckon off-book surveillance.'

Lolita clicked her fingers in realisation. 'His was the car out near The Portal. He turned tail when he'd led Carlton to the scene of the imminent crime. He's how the shitbag knew Beckman hadn't left town like he was supposed to.'

'You're sure about this?' Buck asked.

'No smoke without fire,' Randall said.

Buck laid a big hand on Randall's similarly broad shoulder. 'Bad analogy, fella.'

Lolita waved it away. 'But wanting to kill Walter? Like you said, a hell of a lucky shot to get everything to fall right. Carlton's an accountant, not Stephen Hawking.'

'It's a hell of a stack of bricks,' Reba suggested. 'Probability was on his side. Either way, it was meant to look like an accident, like the fire. Sure it's an odd scheme, but if Oz found no evidence at the warehouse, why would Carlton break cover and shoot the guy directly? It makes all the stealth earlier for nothing.'

Beckman shrugged. 'Unless he didn't set the fire. Unless it was an accident—a really happy one if you're Carlton Cooper.'

Lolita put both hands up to call a halt to things. 'Carlton is up to no good—we just don't know exactly what. Big problem is we have to rely on you folks to help us out.'

Buck nodded. 'Because you are in the inner circle now. Six people know these two are back in town, and it needs to stay that way. Any of those six let slip, I will personally break something fragile. We have to keep a lid on this for two reasons. One, if Carlton finds out you escaped, he won't carry on doing whatever the hell he is doing to screw your merger—if that's his game. He has to carry on, so he can leave breadcrumbs, letting Reba and Randall sniff him out. Two, if he finds out, he'll plan a better way to make your departure a lot more permanent, and I'd be dumb to bet against a .220 Swift being involved.'

'Which makes it even more important you don't get spotted,' Lolita said to Reba. 'You were called off the case. If we're over the hills and far away, you have no client, you have no job.'

'How do we know you're over the hills and far away? Carlton is hardly likely to be running around the streets, bragging on how he ran you out of town the hard way. Are you Missing Persons suddenly?'

'Our cars are abandoned on the road. No sight nor sound in four hours. Footprints in the dust leading into oblivion. Fall or push, maybe the two of us went in there?' Lolita gave a sad shrug as if writing her own epitaph.

Buck stood. 'Carlton will get suspicious if the whole town acts like nothing's happened. Like our friends haven't vanished. Like they're not missing, presumed dead.'

'So we have to act like you are?' Reba asked.

'No tears,' Lolita said. 'That's too much, too soon. There are no bodies, no proof. But two frankly wonderful people are missing, and that needs to seep through town, so Carlton sees he's won.'

'I'll do my best,' Buck said. 'But compared to genuinely losing you, my act of being utterly crushed will be pretty lame.'

Chapter 36

The ignominy of a second back-seat ride like a couple of stowaways was worth it for the relief of collapsing into armchairs in Buck's lounge and having cold beers pressed into their hands.

Buck ordered in pizza—a service that Beckman hadn't experienced in Sunrise.

'So, really,' Buck said, tearing off another piece of pepperoni-topped scrumptiousness, 'What's it like in there?'

Lolita wiped stray tomato sauce from the corner of her mouth, 'If you took Sunrise off the face of the Earth but left us where we were, that would be pretty close.'

'Except no creatures of any kind. Oh, and no sun. Only light. Like… the whole place was lit by a giant softbox,' Beckman added.

Buck eyed them both and shrugged nonchalantly. 'Okay.'

'That it?' Lolita asked.

'I figured it wasn't total heaven or godawful hell. I mean, you were happy to get back, hardly shellshocked.'

'You make it sound like a cakewalk. You want to have a try?'

'I dunno. How'd you get back? You didn't rush. Guessing you weren't sightseeing. So—you stay away to make sure Carlton was gone? Fool him into thinking it was a forever thing?'

Beckman looked at Lolita.

Lolita looked at Beckman.

They both looked at Buck.

Beckman drained his beer.

They looked at each other again.

What had happened, exactly?

'I… we….' he began

'We tried a few times. It just… didn't work.' Lolita screwed her face up, trying to fathom an answer to such a simple question—one they'd not challenged themselves with before. Chiefly because they'd been too busy with relief, gratitude, subversion, drinking coffee and rattling themselves around a broom cupboard.

Buck waved a big paw. 'No matter.'

Lolita shook her head. 'No. It does matter. Now you've got me thinking.'

'We're out, baby, who cares how?' Beckman consoled.

'What happened to Beckman—student of the human condition, enquiring mind, the man who figured Malvolio's scheme and found a way to beat it?'

'Call me dumb, but since I've no desire to go back, I'll not need the exit code a second time around.'

'I guess because you've not lived with the thing for three decades, you've not got attached to it like I have,' she said.

'Says the girl who was telling me to keep clear of it.'

'No, I was telling you not to spend your days like a skater boy, hocking half the landscape into it.'

'It was a… scientific experiment,' Beckman pleaded weakly, pushing his luck.

'My ass,' she scoffed.

'Don't get me started on your ass, honey. That's a whole other amazing feat of nature.'

Lolita rolled her eyes theatrically. 'Why do I get the feeling there'll be a lot of days I wish I'd left you in there?' she asked Beckman.

'Children, children.' Buck shook his head, took empty bottles from them both and went to the kitchen for replacements.

Lolita blew out a heavy breath, containing fifty percent CO_2, thirty percent frustration and twenty percent melancholy.

Beckman slid an arm round her shoulder. 'Life isn't perfect right now, but we have what we need to make it that way. Trust me—I've had the hot breath of extinction on my neck not so long ago. Randall was a professional; Carlton is an obnoxious teenager throwing a hissy fit because you confiscated his dirt bike.'

Buck stood at the partition door. 'Difference being a hitman is predictable. A teenager is a rollercoaster.' He handed over their beers and sat. 'A year ago, I'd never have predicted he'd cheat on you, let alone anything he's maybe guilty of. Either we have him wrong, and these are accidents, or the Dixon woman, or another agent, or—more likely—he's gone off the deep end. Either way, cool heads is the winning strategy here.'

'Winning?' Lolita drank. 'Winning what?'

'Winning back your lives, and maybe a few other lives too.'

'Is that code for you want us out of your house in double-quick time?' Beckman inferred.

'Beckman, I don't do 'code'. I speak as I find. You have my two cents; take it or don't. But I hope you do. We'd still be out at The Portal, eight hours later, if you hadn't come back. You leant on us already. Don't stop leaning because you feel bad for it. Someone once told me to accept help gracefully.'

Lolita smiled. 'Yeah, I remember.'

'So rest up, and tomorrow we'll convene the brains trust.'

'For a way out,' Beckman surmised.

'Ways, plural,' Buck replied. 'The way I see it, you want to get that merger through, with or without Carlton blocking the road. We have to pray Walter wakes up. We have to prove two accidents or not, without help from Oz. You have to do it all while laying low or find a way not to lay low. And we have to figure what to do about Carlton in the long term.'

Lolita raised her bottle in a mock toast. 'Way to make a girl feel motivated.'

'You missed the important one,' Beckman said. 'We're getting married a week today, and fixing that up is not the work of a minute.'

Buck sat upright and checked Lolita for confirmation.

She gave a nonchalant shrug. 'I knew he'd come around eventually.'

A smile spread across Buck's face. He raised his bottle to meet her distant toast. 'So, to back up aways, what you've got is this: there's only one thing up at the bat— happy ever after.'

Chapter 37

At 08.15, Randall had a brainwave.

By 08.30, he'd made enough of a nuisance of himself, beaming with self-congratulation, mimicking the roar of applause, and even holding his breakfast bagel up like a medal to his chest, that Reba capitulated.

'Okay, what do you want to shut up?'

'Help me wash my back?'

She scanned his face to make sure he was deadly serious (beneath the playfulness turning up the corners of his mouth), then, in search of an easier morning, conceded. 'Okay.'

'I hope you know it's still only an idea,' she said, raising her voice against the hiss of the spray.

He raised his arms, luxuriating in the wash-down like an ape enjoying having his ticks methodically picked off. Besides, brainwaves that landed deep in Reba's area of operation—and hit home as having merit—were few and far between.

'It beats crawling to Oz for help or trying something more underhanded,' he replied.

'I'm not crazy about what happens if we have to present this as part of an actual case.'

'Let's hope it doesn't come to that.'

She sidled around and sponged down his chest, the edges of the faucet's canopy of warm rain tickling her cheek. 'How else do we hold the guy to task? Assuming the prints match. Assuming we can get a pair. And assuming my forensics 101 is up to the task.'

'I have nothing but confidence in you, my love.'

She smiled. 'You're only saying that because you've got me naked and treating you like a Lord.'

'I can't deny I've had worse Sunday mornings. But you're a pretty fine gumshoe all the same.'

They dropped April off at her doting maternal grandmother's place an hour later and went to Our Buck's.

Seeing Carlton and Wanda on stools at the bar, Randall resisted the urge to punch the guy's lights out. Instead, he put on his best polite face, noted Reba do the same, and they wandered over to assess the lie of the land.

'Morning, Buck.'

'Morning, folks.'

'Carlton, Wanda,' Randall said with a courteous nod.

'Oh, hey Randall. Hey Reba.'

Reba mustered the best smile she could, but her eyes were busier, noting the backpack at Carlton's feet.. 'You folks look all packed up.'

'Day out at the Petrified Forest,' Buck told them. 'And a good one for it.'

Randall did a quick double-take that this apparent scourge of the town was taking his dame out on a date exploring the tracks of dinosaurs. But then, nobody ever considered him capable of (possibly) burning down a warehouse, (probably) shooting out a chimney stack and (definitely) cheating on Lolita Milan.

'Yeah,' Carlton said, draining his coffee mug with an air of dismissiveness. 'Been a busy week. Need some air.'

Randall felt damn sure the guy had had a busy week, much of it of a deeply unsavoury nature. 'Bring me back a six-foot femur,' he offered, a tone slightly less offish than the one he'd been thrown.

Carlton dropped a couple of notes on the bar, scooped up his bag and belle, gave Buck a nod and walked away.

Buck's hand reached out for the dirty mug.

'Good to see you this morning, Buck, you old son of a gun!' Randall's hand shot in, cutting off Buck's reach and clenching the guy in a good firm handshake. Buck was taken aback by this sudden over-friendliness. Nonetheless, Randall kept on shaking, like he hadn't seen the guy in twenty years, until Reba touched him on the shoulder.

'They gone?' he asked.

'All clear.'

Buck withdrew his hand. Before he resumed his clear-and-clean duties, Reba was a step ahead, yanking a napkin from the holder nearby and deftly using it to pluck Carlton's mug up by the rim.

Buck backed away half a step. 'Okay. You got me.'

Reba checked quickly around. 'Ten bucks for the cup. Put it on the bill,' she whispered.

Buck scrutinised them both, and his posture softened. 'Either April broke your last crockery, or you're shooting for Carlton's prints.'

Randall eyed Reba. 'I told you he'd be cool about it. Didn't I tell you?'

'Doc Watson here thinks the ol' Garrity magic extends to building a case based on some hokey forensics and a ton of circumstantial.'

'Does the ol' Garrity magic include missing a golden opportunity?' Randall jerked his head towards the door.

Randall lowered his voice. 'Mister Congeniality and his silent partner are heading out for the day, so...?'

She got the message and patted him on the shoulder. 'Excellent, Watson. You may stay.'

Buck didn't wade into the banter. 'Bring the cup back tomorrow, and I'll waive the ten bucks. I got customers. Have a good... whatever you do this fine day.' He moved off to attend to the table of Sandy Vale and her octogenarian mother.

Reba and Randall took a seat—Beckman's Usual Table—knowing Beckman nor Lolita wouldn't attend the café that day. Or possibly any day until this whole mess got sorted out.

'Throwing yourself into the part, huh?' Reba asked.

'Like you said before, Beckman gave me a lifeline, Lolita gave me a job, and Carlton is a total douche, so it's about as hard of a choice as asking you out that first time.'

'Aw, that's sweet. Not so much comparing Carlton and me, though.'

He slurped his coffee. 'So it's not the dumbest plan you ever heard?'

'Even if it is, you keep coming up with enough dumb ones, we're bound to get lucky on one eventually. Simple statistics.'

'Thanks for the vote of confidence, Sherlock.'

She winked her good eye. 'Let's see how good of a guard dog you are.'

They left her tired 2005 Jeep Wrangler down the street from Carlton's place and walked up. The house looked impressive if functional, with a double garage and plenty of land backing onto open country, like the owner's prospective father-in-law enjoyed.

Randall found a spot beside a roadside tree and hunkered down for a long wait, his body shielded from clear view but with a clear sightline towards town.

Reba went to the front door, bold as brass, and rang the bell. Act One: pretend to be a regular visitor.

After receiving the lack of response she'd expected and desired, she skirted the house curiously—as if checking whether the owner was in the rear garden: Act Two.

Then she disappeared from view for Act Three: seeking evidence.

Randall set his cell to vibrate and began scanning the area whilst behaving as nonchalant as possible. The house opposite was owned by an old couple who took long summer vacations to New England. The next closest properties had minimal chance of spotting either of them, so Reba hadn't regarded the enterprise as particularly fraught with risk.

Problem was, the two mugs of fine coffee had gone right through him, and taking a piss would soon be a necessity. He marked himself down on his Stakeout Scorecard for a schoolboy error.

Reba's return made him jump. That took his tally down further.

She'd been away barely five minutes.

'I need a whizz,' he said as soon as the Jeep's doors slammed closed behind them.

'You want to talk about your bladder or my brilliance?'

'The bladder thing wasn't going to be a TED talk.'

'You want to hear what I found?' She spun the car around and headed towards town.

'I want to hear what you found.'

She pulled her phone out and handed it across. He thumbed through to the photos while she narrated. 'He shoots targets; I knew that. Reason he wasn't a crack shot in the warehouse debacle; it's all about statics. He mostly shoots fifty-metre pistol, but there are a two hundred, maybe five hundred and eight hundred rifle bosses out there. There are also a whole heap of brick stacks.'

He'd found the image on her device and met her gaze. 'Brilliance is spotting things in plain sight now, huh?' he joked.

In response, she freed a hand from the wheel, dug into a pocket, and reached over.

Two shells tipped into his palm.

He took a closer look.

.220 Swift.

'Okay, I'll give you the benefit,' he admitted.

'Thought so.'

'Whizz?'

'I'm going to swing by the hospital. Clench 'til then.'

'Reba Garrity for Walter Whack.'

The receptionist checked her computer. 'I didn't know you and Walter were tight.'

'He hired me once. Few years back. Don't tend to broadcast my clients.'

The receptionist smiled. 'Sure. 118, down the hall.'

'Thanks.'

Randall joined her as she moved away from the desk, a much less pained expression on his face.

'You shake properly?' she jibed.

'Yes, ma'am. You get us in?'

She lowered her tone. 'Why'd you make it sound so covert? It's visiting time. We're visiting.'

'A guy in a coma? I'd like to see you work the 'ol Garrity magic on that.'

'Give me a break, honey. I figured we're on a roll here; what can it hurt? Carlton is out of town—it would be a hell of a coup if Walter woke up this afternoon and gave us something. Not even Oz had a word out of the guy.'

'Can't fault the logic.'

'It's only: Select Target, Locate Target, Engage With Target. Even if you're not putting a bullet in someone, it's a pretty solid way to go.'

As they approached 118, he heard a noise, and Reba put her arm out protectively, slowing their pace. The door stood ajar. She walked quickly across, peeked through the gap, and crossed the corridor to a water cooler.

'Orderly?' he asked.

'No. Woman. Tall. Suit.' She pulled a tiny cup of water and drained it.

He racked his brains but came up empty. An EVI employee? Not Wilma—she didn't wear a suit. Not Wanda—she was away ogling dino footprints. Secretary? Mistress?

Reba shook her head like flicking away a fly. 'Why are we standing out here? What are we afraid of?'

Apparently, nothing, as she went to the room, knocked gently, pushed open the door and entered.

The woman inside was slightly startled and moved back from the foot of the bed—but Randall caught a whiff of guilt. She hadn't been trying a pillow over the guy's face, for instance. Yet that thought lodged itself in Randall's cranium, and he resolved to dig it up later for cross-examination.

'Oh, I'm sorry.' The woman flashed an awkward smile.

'No problem,' Reba replied, damping down any conflict.

'I was leaving anyway.'

'Sure.'

With an awkward mental and physical dance of hello-goodbye, don't-know-you-so-don't-know-whether-to-greet-or-just-bail-out, the woman nodded a courteous farewell and left.

'What was she afraid of?' Randall suggested.

Reba scanned the room for signs of disturbance or questionable practices and came up empty. 'Feeling guilty about standing watching a guy sleep?'

'Know her?'

'Know? No. Have an idea? Maybe.'

'Okay.'

'Beckman told me there's a stranger in town, snooping around the merger. Name of Dixon.'

Chapter 38

'I hereby convene the War Room,' Buck said, setting the homemade chilli down at his surprisingly accommodating dinner table.

Randall was first to spoon into the vast rice bowl. 'Not much of a war if I can't shoot the guy,' he muttered.

'We already did this,' Lolita said.

'Come on. I never killed anyone for free. It'll be a new experience for me.'

'You're better than that, Randall,' Reba insisted. 'Don't sink to Carlton's level.'

'Okay,' he conceded. He served her some rice. 'What if I shoot him in the knee or something?'

'No!' they all chorused.

'He have a dog?' Randall tried.

Reba rapped the back of his hand with her fork (splines upwards).

'Randall,' Lolita said, 'The depth of your support is noted.'

'It's not like I don't have a stake, working for you and all. Hell, it's only another two weeks 'til my probation is up and I get a raise.'

'The shallowness of your support is also noted,' Reba chuckled.

Lolita dolloped out some chilli. 'But, given it's my business at the root of all this, and, yeah, I was dumb enough to date the guy and smart enough to can him, it's my call that there's no violence. It would be exactly like the SOB to press charges, even with his last breath.' She looked around the table. 'This may be the Magnificent Seven, but the parallel stops there.'

Buck held up a paternal hand. 'Brain food first, brainstorm after.'

So that was that.

Fifteen minutes later, the plates were clear. Seventeen minutes later, the table was clear, except for another round of bottles.

They all looked at Lolita.

Behind Beckman's gaze lay an all-encompassing, primal desire to pull a wand from his pocket and magic this all away. To produce a panning dish and shake it vigorously until the detritus of their lives vanished, leaving only the gold that illuminated her inner and outer beauty. To click his fingers and have a perfect idea, without compromise or side-effect.

Lolita took a breath. 'Whether or not Carlton is behind the fire or the chimney, he has a beef. Either he or the beef needs to go away. He's hurting me, and Beckman, and the business. We have to fix this. He's like a wounded lion, and what's to say it won't be Jack or Beckman or me under the next chimney.'

There were nods; everyone wanted the same thing.

'The way I see it is this. You've got five options.' Buck counted them on chunky fingers. 'Kill him. Scare him so bad. Get him in a cell. Just get him out of Sunrise for good. Make a truce, whatever compromise that means.'

'Well, two of those are not happening,' she replied.

'We're trying to get him in a cell,' Reba offered. Earlier, she'd recounted their finds at Carlton's house.

'I already offered scares, up to whatever maximum value you want,' Randall said.

'It's not only him; it's the juggernaut he's driving.' Tyler toyed with his bottle. 'Like you said, the grudge may be personal, but the game is business, and he's got Wanda's ears in whatever he does.'

Lolita nodded. 'Problem is, it's a sure bet that in Walter's absence, Carlton is a signatory on our merger, and he'll rip it up in a second. If Wanda's a co-signatory, she'll follow his lead, like she did at The Portal.'

'If only we could communicate on his level,' Tyler said.

'Sadly, I don't speak dickhead,' Lolita confirmed.

'I feel like a lynch mob, trying to run him out of town,' Reba admitted.

Lolita fingered the label on her bottle. 'He's already like an angry wasp or the Terminator. He'll come back.'

A solemn silence fell.

'Is a truce so bad?' Amaryllis asked quietly.

Lolita looked over. 'It would be all take and no give. Right now, he has no legal black marks. He has a financial upper hand. His opening bid will be whatever he wants us to give up to get him off our back, personally and professionally. Or it should be—it's what I'd do.'

'Harness that fighting spirit, Lol, that's all we need,' Buck said.

'Or take the easy path,' she mused. 'Beckman can find another great sales position—hell, even with you, Tyler, if you still want a local guy on the team.'

Tyler shrugged. 'Offer's there.'

'And the Egyptian artefacts game is a pretty safe bet. I've done okay. Plus, I hear they have a position open at that café in town.' She flashed Buck a weak smile.

'Sorry, Lol. Can't give you the job. You're over-qualified. You're the damn CEO of a corporation. You have a responsibility to your employees. Reason one being, if they're out of a job, where do they get the money to come into my café and buy my coffee?'

That made her laugh, which was precisely the idea.

Amaryllis cracked up too. Beckman didn't ever recall seeing her so loose, not even on the night they'd stopped by unannounced. Tyler's eyes watched her, and Beckman got lost in a tangential train of thought. Back to the innocence of under a week ago, where the only needling issues were how he'd ever tell Lolita, he couldn't face a full-on white wedding, how in hell he'd pull off the Coffee Planet contract, and how come nobody this side of The Portal knew how old Amaryllis was.

Good times.

Conversations broke down after that, meaning no further forward momentum.

At around eleven, Buck pretty much threw everyone except Beckman and Lolita out: 'Much as I love you all, a man's gotta sleep, and this is no slumber party.'

Beckman found Buck's spare bed smaller and harder than he would have liked and immediately felt an idiot about it.

Twelve hours ago, you were being forced out of town—hell, probably out of this reality—at gunpoint. A night on the hard desert ground would have been a heck of a result.

This is the next best thing to an angel's caress.

Then an angel caressed his head. 'How are you doing?' he asked.

'Squirming on the horns of a dilemma.'

'How so?'

Lolita sighed. 'I can't see beyond sinking to his level. And that sticks in my craw.'

'Well, someone has to sink. Unless we get a better idea.'

'Not you. You're not a bully; I get it. You want to make this right. But don't trash yourself on account of it.'

'Exceptional circumstances.'

She shifted around to face him. 'That's when Mr Hyde comes out? I can't believe you ever so much as hit anyone.'

His face creased in memory. 'Violet Sunnerson. Her ears stuck out. Bullies always find something—only sometimes they don't have to dig too hard. She was sweet.

God, she made me laugh. I could never concentrate in Math; she was always passing notes. And I mean *good* notes. Like SNL good. A wonder we both didn't flunk out or get thrown out. We never... I don't know. I don't think she was into guys. No matter. She was more like a sister I never had. Franklin Dymes got pretty jealous, even though nothing was going on. She'd turned him down flat. So he was always on her case. Mostly about the ears. One time he said how nobody would take her to the prom on account of her ears, but he'd be this great *friend* and take her. But she wouldn't. So he gave her both barrels on how nobody would ever date her.' He shook his head. 'So I socked him.'

Her eyes widened with surprise, then creased with affection. 'You took her?'

'No. We were shipping out the next week. Didn't want to get her hopes up. Why d'you think I hit the guy? He couldn't make my life hell as I wasn't going to be there.'

'He socked you, though.'

'Oh, real good.'

'What did Marlon say?'

'He said about time I showed some balls.' He sighed. 'So that's my Ali moment. Something tells me you had a few.'

She reflected for a second. 'I hit Jack pretty good one time. Cruel, huh? You shouldn't hit anyone shorter than you.'

He smiled. 'Good thing Carlton is taller. Although hitting him won't solve anything.

'No, but it makes you feel a whole heap better, believe me.'

'Even you didn't hit him that day—the break-up.'

'I wasn't prepared to find out whether he'd hit back,' she asserted.

'Not if he knew what was good for him. If life were a movie, you'd be at the punchbag, working out for the day the mouse roared.'

She stroked his cheek. 'Somehow, these mice have to roar.'

'We'll figure it out,' he promised. 'We've already been to hell and back today. And that was a breeze.'

Chapter 39

Randall reached the sorry-looking Milan Enterprises premises in good time that Monday morning. He'd dropped April at school and headed over.

As he took a passing interest in how the gutted building was being cleaned up, he casually asked whether anyone had heard from Lolita or Beckman in the last 48 hours. Nobody had. Then again, nobody was unduly alarmed. He was probably projecting his knowledge of the truth onto their unsuspecting minds. He wanted people to be worried about the CEO's absence, to give a sense the pretence was working.

In the makeshift Winnebago office block, he reviewed the last week's figures, caught up with suppliers, and found out some of the requests for additional funding had been denied. He even tried to persuade the insurance company that they'd been the victim of a hoax, and the policy cancellation was false, but it fell on deaf ears. News of the fire must have reached them via other means, and understandably they wouldn't reinstate a policy if five seconds later they'd be slapped with a huge claim.

Business is business.

Which was what had gotten them all into this catastrophe in the first place.

At 11.04, Reba called, and 'suggested' they meet for coffee at Jen & Berry's.

He found her at a table in the corner, half a coffee ahead of him, and he surmised that the choice of table was driven by privacy. Of course, privacy could equally well be achieved at home, out on the hills, or in the car, but none boasted the second best coffee in town.

'What gives?' he asked Reba after Berry had taken his order.

'I passed on a case today. I gave it to Pollard.'

'Why does this sound a long way from generosity?'

'I considered giving the guy the third degree, or trying to catch him off guard, so we can get a hundred per cent on the fact Carlton hired him.'

'And?'

'There's nothing on file about it, which makes it off-book. I could tell Zeb and see what happened, but Pollard's mostly a good guy. I don't want to screw him over—we might be wrong, and wrong or not, he could be another enemy we don't need. Another complication.'

She fell silent as Berry returned with Randall's coffee and donut.

When she left, Randall asked, 'So what am I missing?'

'Pollard bought me a milkshake to say thanks.'

'I don't believe I've forbidden you to have milkshakes from other men.'

She laid a hand on his. 'First, you couldn't anyhow. Second, he left his cell behind for three minutes.'

'You didn't...?'

'I'm a P.I. Damn straight I did. There are texts from Carlton about the whole thing. He wanted the word when Beckman left town—any noise to indicate he wasn't playing ball. Pollard tailed Lolita to the Portal. Just like she reckoned.'

'Why does this feel like an over-zealous spite of jealousy?'

'Because it's a tug of war.'

Across the room, the diner door opened smartly, and the man of the moment barged in. But Carlton hadn't seen them, and his evident beef was not with them.

'Son of a bitch!' floated across the room, causing other customers to look round.

Wanda attempted to tug her fiancé's hand in restraint but received short shrift. Carlton led her to a nearby table and thunked down into a seat, growling. Then he snapped an order at Jen, who summarily left, and began bitching to Wanda.

'Take a leak, honey?' Reba suggested.

'Huh?' Randall grunted.

She peered towards the bathrooms, which lay close to Carlton's position, and slid her cell across to him.

'I'd go, but I'm a P.I. He'll get antsy. I'd be ambling, on a "phone call", on the way to the john. And on the way back. There's a breaking story, mister sidekick. And there's a special dessert in it for you, catch my drift?' She flashed a conspiratorial smile.

He scooped up the phone, held it to his ear, and paced languidly across the room, slowed as much as he dared, and disappeared through the swing door. When he emerged, he paused, feigned incomprehension of the non-existent caller, looped around and rejoined Reba.

'What's next after "Sidekick"? "Assistant"?' he asked, a knowing look in his eye.

'All promotions have to be approved by the management. Now spill, or I'll choke it out of you. Honey.'

'Best I can gather, Carlton is off the board of signatories. He doesn't have control over the merger.'

Reba sat back, exhaled softly. Randall drained his coffee while she processed the news.

'Doesn't make sense,' she said eventually.

'How so?'

'Obviously, add a "hypothetically" to all this because, you know, innocent until proven guilty beyond all reasonable doubt, yadda yadda. But why try to kill Walter if he couldn't take control of the company and the merger in his absence? If the magic falling masonry trick isn't for screwing the merger or inheriting the business, or both, well,' she threw up her hands, 'I'm out of ideas.'

'And if you are, a sidekick or assistant sure is.'

'This would be a damn sight easier if Oz gave any of this more than a passing interest. Problem is, he'd never implicate Carlton in anything. He's as scared of Carlton's sister as anyone. Woman's a fruit loop.'

'That's still a hell of a breakthrough I just made,' he suggested.

'One fly-by doesn't make you Philip Marlowe.'

'Does it get me that dessert?'

'Honey, if you put as much effort into detecting as you do trying to get me in the sack, we might have to tell Delmar he has competition on his hands.'

Chapter 40

Mondays.

Not most people's favourite day of the seven.

Habitually, Beckman witnessed Lolita almost spring from the bed, her desire to drive Milan Enterprises forward always undimmed by the all-consuming Mondayness of the day.

Today, she had moped around Buck's house.

He couldn't recall ever seeing her mope.

Maybe she moped when she thought she'd lost you that one time? Or when she discovered Carlton had been very much less than committed with his fidelity.

Today, the lioness was dozing when she wanted to be stalking.

For the first couple of hours of the morning, he kept his head down, not wanting to antagonise her. It fell in the category of "If you can't say something smart, don't say anything", and as he didn't have anything to help their plight, he focussed on trawling the circumstances in search of a breakthrough.

Mid-morning, she called Randall and asked a favour.

Half an hour later, Tobin turned up. This increased the size of the cognoscenti to nine. It wasn't done lightly, but she needed to have at least a finger or two on the rudder of the business, so Tobin brought their laptops and set up the secure connection.

'Did Oz ask about the CCTV yet?' she queried.

Tobin tightened his ponytail. 'I said it was down for maintenance.'

'You lied?' Beckman asked.

Lolita waved a hand for him to calm. 'Perspective, honey.'

'Lying to the police is perspective?'

'The system was down. We have no record of who did it. We have no CCTV footage. Therefore we have nothing to help or hinder anything Oz does.'

'I don't like it,' Beckman reiterated.

'Well, it's done. It's a dead end. Oz should be working on other things. Following up alibis, finding an empty gas can, a loose wire, canvassing for witnesses.'

Is it technically a lie if you give someone what they want, even if what they want is of no use?

'So my logon is only known in this room?' she continued.

'Hand to God,' Tobin replied.

Beckman felt relieved the secret was safe. Yet something didn't sit easy, and he couldn't put his finger on it. Like a disconnect somewhere.

Soon, Tobin left, and Lolita hunkered down, seeking solace in things she understood—running a lighting supplies corporation—rather than pondering things she didn't—like how to deal with an ex- who wants to crush you, your business and your man.

For lunch, they raided Buck's fridge and mostly ate in silence.

He'd never seen her so introspective yet understood why. Hell, even when he was being chased by a hitman, his Pegasus dreams in tatters, his heart torn out by a girl who'd said she never wanted to see him again, he'd still had an option. A clear, large as life, safe as houses option.

It was logical those weeks ago: to run to a safe place. Maybe that was the unspoken option. The path of least resistance. It had worked out before—why not again?

He took a deep breath. 'Did it ever cross your mind the universe is telling us this is not meant to be? That we're pursuing a dead-end?'

'No,' she replied flatly.

'It's not healthy. Don't give yourself a coronary out of revenge. Out of trying to prove Jack wrong.'

Her eyes flared, but there was restraint, a bell that chimed in to say that squabbling is what Carlton wants. 'I thought I knew you better. I thought we had something worth fighting for.'

'Only if it's a fight we can win.'

'Don't you believe it is?'

'The jury is out. I wanted to say what was knocking around in my head. You know, for honesty.'

She nodded slowly. 'Yeah. Well, don't be afraid of it. We've done pretty well on that score lately.'

'Except Carlton's lies are winning.'

'And the easy way out is to sink to his level. Lies and violence.'

'The easy way, sure. When it's the only way, we—you—have to decide whether it's the path to take. If you'd feel better, or worse, as a result.'

'Honey, I don't have the ammo for a decision. I'm too pissed off at being cooped up here. Powerless. Like a captain who's taken his ship back to port, afraid of the storm.'

He took her hand. 'No. You're more like the master of a submarine. Cruising with the periscope up. Radar out. Ready to torpedo the skulking SOB in your waters.'

A faint smile appeared. 'Sometimes, Beckman, you're a poet. A pretty lousy one, but a poet.'

'I'll take that. Try this one. A CEO doesn't do the work themselves. They have a corps of people to help, to use their special talents to keep the wheels turning. We have a great Board on our side. We have our spies out. Run silent, run deep, baby.'

'Better. Still no Wordsworth, but you'll do.' She lifted his hand and kissed it.

'I'm trying to convince myself that High Noon outside The Portal is the end of Carlton's story. That the guy has redeeming features. Because we're all boxed into this one cause, and if we're all sucked in by what we *want* the answer to be, we might be missing the real answer.'

'Which I'm guessing you don't know,' she said.

'No. You'd be the first to know. We have two facts. Someone cancelled the insurance, and it has to be a guy because a female caller isn't a Beckman. So a guy is involved. Fact. But maybe he has a partner. Or two. Maybe a woman.'

'Like Dixon?'

'Paid by GigantiCorp to put us on the ropes. We'd beg for a takeover then, huh?'

She shook her head vehemently. 'Not if they've done the research. They can beg on all fours. I'd sooner go under than sell to them.'

'Maybe it's a gamble. What have they got to lose? Worse case, they pick up expiring contracts because we can't service them? Death by a thousand cuts.'

'So this insider is also the one who cut the CCTV?'

'Anyone with access to your credentials.'

'Why do I get the sense you're pointing at Tobin here?'

'Because he lied. Maybe to cover his ass because he doesn't want Oz to dig into the records and find out the truth.'

She let go of his hand and sat back. 'I preferred it when we had no answers.'

'You mean you prefer it when I provide answers implicating people you hate rather than those you trust?'

'Well, people I hate are more likely to hate me and more likely to want to screw me.'

'It's still an insider. No way Dixon, or Walter, or Wanda has your ID password in their Rolodex. You ever piss anyone off?'

She disliked that remark—heard an inference that wasn't there: she was hard to work for, work with, be with. She riled people. Her tone was stern. 'I've been there ten weeks. I'm sure as hell not the master of human study you are, honey, but if I pissed anyone off in that time, it's a hell of a trick. Jack and I are old news, and Carlton was out on day one.'

'No way he sneaked back in?'

She shook her head. 'I always had him escorted. Plus, his ID was suspended anyway. He couldn't login and check the database for my ID.'

'Or anyone else's?'

'It would never be anyone else. He'd want to twist the knife. Give Oz a dead end or, worse, make it look like I torched my own company. If he could, he'd find a way.'

Beckman waved it away. 'Water under the bridge.'

'Yeah,' she said sadly.

He rose and went to the kitchen for coffee.

'Oh God,' came her voice.

He thunked the coffee pot down and darted back into the living room. 'What?'

Her face was etched with anguish.

'What?' he repeated, looking around for the source of her distress.

She swallowed. 'He knows my password.'

'How?'

'Because I hate passwords. I suck at them. It's my Kryptonite. So I always have the same one. Bank, online shops, whatever. He said it was dumb.' There was a catch in her throat. 'He joked. In a… being endeared by it. The irony. The little woman on a hundred grand. The self-made businesswoman. Can't juggle a dozen passwords.' She blinked, her eyes glistening. 'Safe, predictable, Lolita.

It's all fine when you're in love. When it's hate, it's a noose around your neck.'

A million bucks in single pennies simultaneously dropped through Beckman's skull. 'I knew something bothered me. Outside Saul's, Carlton knew you switched off the CCTV. I figured Oz told him, or word got around like word always gets around. But the only people who *know* it was your ID are you, me, and Tobin. Because, like a goddamn genius, your trusty IT man lied. He kept the faith. So the only way Carlton knows about the ID....'

'...is if he was the one who used it.'

Chapter 41

Tyler became aware of being watched.

Luckily it was from across the table. He raised his eyebrows towards Amaryllis in query.

She withdrew her hands from the tap-tapping on the laptop. 'Something tells me you miss the old life.'

On reflection, he was surprised how it had been such a clean break. How he'd so quickly and smoothly cast away the peripatetic drudgery (and its soft, warm, absent-husbanded perks) in favour of being arguably just another guy in another office in another town.

She had it wrong. Or did she? What was he doing now if not scouting for business, ever the insatiable salesman, always poised for an easy buck?

'Not miss, Amaryllis. More like… get sucked back into.'

'Pegasus is down a fine salesman without you.'

'That's very kind.'

'We all want success, Tyler.'

'Only some people have a funny way of going about it, huh?'

'Malvolio, or Cooper?' she asked.

'Two sides of the same coin.'

'Is this why we're here? Helping?'

He hadn't considered that. 'Because Malvolio screwed over a lot of people—me and Beckman included—and now we have a shot at intervention this time around?'

'Or to repay the favour because Beckman got you out from under the gallows.'

'From a hitman I'm guessing you hired.' Then as she jerked her head away, he regretted the words.

He waited for a comeback, a detonation, a storming out. None came. Tentatively he touched the edge of her hand, where it lay on the table. 'Sorry.'

'I'm trying to make it ancient history. I'd hope you are too.'

She hadn't withdrawn her hand, but he removed his, not wanting things to get too weird. 'Out of curiosity, how many people were at his wake?' He tried to move the subject away without it appearing like a guilty U-turn.

She looked back. 'Seven.'

'Maybe I'll aim for eight,' he said dejectedly.

Her eyes widened with surprise. 'There's probably eight in Sunrise alone.'

'Let's not get ahead of ourselves. And thanks.'

'All we can do is the right thing, whatever went before. We all have skeletons. Some scarier than others.'

He smirked. 'I'm not sure Beckman has a single bone. Well, apart from the time he stole my car. That's the summit of his cruelty. Though I kinda provoked him.'

'Because you're a salesman, Tyler. You want to succeed. And if I'm any judge, you still do. Which is why you're people-watching, waiting for a chance to hawk a box.'

She wasn't wrong. It was in his DNA.

It didn't hurt that Pegasus' box was a miracle cure, a product that almost sold itself. The only challenge he'd encountered was potential customers who thought it too good to be true; snake oil, a magic bullet, Professor Clarence Arbuthnot's Old Timey Cure-All. When it happened, he relied on inbuilt charm and honed patter (although good looks were no hindrance).

It was never a hollow pitch, a con, a triumph of technique over outcome because he was genuinely selling something people needed, something that worked. That's what he held onto in the few dark hours when it felt like a never-ending treadmill. That, plus the fringe benefits in suspenders and negligees.

He'd spent many hours, probably weeks in total, people-watching.

A girl approached the counter across the room. Twenty, he reckoned. Petite, brown flared pants, denim shirt. Yellow macaw on her shoulder.

Yellow macaw on her shoulder. Bold as day.

She ordered at the register. Waited. Plucked something from her shirt pocket, held it up to a grateful beak. Took her takeout milkshake. Bold as day.

'Email from Portman,' Amaryllis announced.

He looked up. 'Yeah?'

'They found another snafu in the wiring. Going to be an extra day.'

Tyler closed his eyes briefly in annoyance. There were worse problems to have. Like the whole business going up in flames. He chuckled. 'Do it. Make the place A1.'

'Book an extra couple of nights at the Sunset?'

'I don't have a better idea. Working out of places like this,' he gestured to the room, replete with neons, delicious smells and the background chatter of a happy community, 'Versus in an office crawling with nail guns and exposed ass cracks.'

'Plus, we might make a sale or six.'

'If you might allow the boss to indulge, what with our man on the ground having bigger problems.'

'The boss can indulge what the boss wants to indulge,' Amaryllis said with a smile. 'Because he's the boss.'

'Creating an extension of fifteen years of a downtrodden woman.'

She shook her head. 'Not a bit of it. Malvolio wouldn't spring for so much as a new desk jotter. Three months in, and you've already signed away on a new office.'

'The world keeps turning, Amaryllis. Happy workforce is a productive workforce. Complacency is death. I wonder how long Malvolio would have left the status quo before he realised there were warning bells in the air he couldn't hear.'

She gave him a puzzled look. 'Something I should know?'

'No. But look at Milan Enterprises. Fending off suitors on two sides. One day you're grazing in your safe meadow, next day, there's a wolf inside the gate. Nothing says what we have can't be imitated.'

'How do you defend against that?'

'I don't have an idea. Yet. But recognising inertia is a start.'

'Malvolio would simply work everyone harder, building up a bigger war chest.'

He waved it away as unthinkable. 'Innovation, not exploitation. Diversification. Expansion.' His gaze drifted across the room, past the litany of neon tubes, to the counter.

More customers, he mused. 'Is it a US or World patent?'

'World, I think. But we only serve the US.'

'Why?'

'Because expanding requires risk and effort. I'm not sure Marion had those in his lexicon.'

'Marion?' Then he got it. 'Malvolio? His name was Marion?!'

'I was sworn to secrecy.'

'Marion?' he repeated. 'Jeez. A hundred bucks says he got bullied at school. Two hundred says that's why he was a twisted SOB, revenging on the whole damn world.'

'We all have our crosses, I suppose. Some more than others.'

He nodded in agreement, then wondered what her cross might be. Not the time or place to broach.

The diner door opened with a thud. It was sticking; they needed to have a guy come and shave an eighth off the lower edge.

In walked a girl of about nine. No, not walked, roller-skated. Bright red and blue, Stars and Stripes roller-skates.

On her head balanced a foot-high teddy bear.

Tyler and Amaryllis exchanged a look of mutual curiosity. His gaze flicked up to where her beehive wasn't.

The girl didn't stand still for a moment; she jiggled and swirled around, conversing with the server at the register.

Tyler and Amaryllis were both so transfixed that they didn't hear the waitress come to their table.

'Cara Hickock. Eight hours off the world record.'

Tyler looked round. 'Pardon me?'

The waitress nodded towards the girl.

'For roller-skating with a bear on your head?' Amaryllis asked.

'It was either that or hula-ing on the roof of a moving car, but mom wasn't keen. So keep a watch on the sidewalk, today folks.' The waitress winked, scooped up their empties, and left them to their stupefaction.

As Cara presently glided out of the door and hopefully into the history books, Amaryllis chimed in, 'I could never live here. I'm not nearly interesting enough.'

'Amaryllis, fear not. You're an enigma wrapped in mystery as you are. Only with fewer wheels than some.'

That made her chuckle.

He liked that. He liked it when she was three-dimensional.

Another thud announced the arrival of the next customer. Would they have wheels? Or wings? Or be astride two proud Bengal tigers?

They were neither, but they were plural.

He immediately snapped his gaze away and hunched over. Amaryllis flapped the laptop screen up vertically and buried her attention in it.

'Do you think he'll run us out of town as well?' she whispered.

'I didn't leave before, and I'm not doing now. He's nobody. He's an ass. A bully. I know. I was one.'

'Who's that with him?' she murmured.

'Not sure. Not Wanda.' He couldn't see now; his back was turned to the couple, and he wanted it kept that way. Not because he was a coward, but so they could linger as long as possible and gather whatever evidence might be available, ready to report back to Beckman. 'What are they doing?'

'Finding a seat.' Her eyes scribed a line of sight, following their path, until they came into his field of vision, still across the room, maybe forty feet away.

They sat, Carlton's back to them and his female companion facing vaguely in their direction but engrossed in whatever conversation they were having.

'Can you get them on your webcam?' Tyler asked

Amaryllis fiddled around on the keyboard, then rotated the laptop on the table, so it pointed over her shoulder. 'Is this technically legal?'

'Because you accidentally knocked your computer during a conference call and filmed the background?'

'I can see why you made CEO,' she joked. 'Recording.'

'It's nice only to have to do something *marginally* questionable for the boss, huh?'

She frowned. 'Are we going back over that again?'

He briefly closed his eyes, cursing his insensitivity. 'No. And if I bring up the subject again, please make a note of it. Every time, I'll give you a thousand dollar bonus. Deal?'

'Generous. In spirit and reward.'

He shrugged. 'I don't think there's a price for this—you and me. I mean, us. Working together, that is. Working well together. Trust. Understanding.' He waved away his fumbling sentiment.

She smiled. 'Sure.'

Across the room, Carlton Cooper rolled in his seat.

Tyler pushed the laptop's lid quickly down. 'Shall we people-watch somewhere that does Mexican food?'

'Maybe with a margarita on the side?'

Well, Amaryllis Broomhead, he thought, we pretty much have that rod all the way out of your ass now, don't we?

Chapter 42

The doorbell rang.

Beckman and Lolita exchanged a nervous look.

'Got it,' Buck called.

Redundant, as neither of us is likely to rush to see who your visitor is. Sure, it's probably one of The Inner Circle, but there's plenty of other people in town. Beggars—or stowaways—can't be choosers.

Beckman grabbed Lolita's hand, led her off the sofa, and flattened them against the dividing wall.

It's come to this: high-stakes hide-and-seek against four thousand people.

Or rather, one particular individual.

An individual whose voice regrettably drifted in from the front of the house.

'Buck.'

'Cooper.'

Beckman's now-saucer sized eyes met Lolita's similarly distended baby blues. He wanted to curse, but even a tiny misstep could blow their free-bed-and-board cover.

'Do for you?' Buck continued curtly.

'Have you seen Lolita?' Carlton asked, with quite staggering nerve.

'Like I said this morning, no,' Buck replied with gravity. "Getting kinda worried, being honest.'

'They had a deal lined up with Walter.'

'I'm aware.'

'We can't have the Pause button on that forever. It damages the company, the uncertainty.'

Well, boo-hoo. Excuse me, Buck, while my heart bleeds on your carpet.

'What do you want me to do about it?' Buck asked.

'Maybe you'd want to file a Missing Persons?'

'On account of it works for you like that?'

'On account of you two are close.'

I underestimated you, Carlton. Your balls are galactic in size. But I'd much rather have small balls and a clean heart.

Lolita shook her head in disbelief, shifted her position. Her wrist grazed the wall, and her watch thwacked. Beckman held his breath. Her face creased in anguish.

Carlton's words came through the house like bullets. .220 Swifts. 'Sorry—you got company?'

Beckman swallowed. Lolita mouthed something unladylike.

'Ah, no?' Buck replied, holding in a hint of fluster. 'Ah,' he tutted, 'Damn cat.'

'Cat?'

'Shoot, yeah.'

'You don't have a cat,' Carlton reminded Buck. And Beckman. And Lolita.

Say you bought it today. As an impulse. To get over the anguish of Lolita—and me, why the hell not—being missing. A comfort in tough times. Middle age crisis. Call it what you damn will, man!

'Nah, she's a stray. Comes in sometimes if I don't close the back door.'

'Really. I always wanted a cat.'

'Uh-huh.'

'Can I stroke it?'

Beckman made a throat-throttle with his hands. Lolita cocked her finger to the side of her head.

'What?'

'Can I stroke it?' Carlton repeated.

'No. I… it's quite aggressive to strangers.'

'But aren't you a stranger?'

'Well, we've become quite close.'

'Have you given it a name?'

Buck coughed. 'Samson.'

'It's a guy cat then?'

'I guess. I mean, yes. Well, it looks like a guy. Cooper, it's not a good time, okay?'

'The cat ill?'

'No, I mean the Lolita situation. Missing and all.'

'Sure. You want me to come in, talk about it?'

Lolita threw back her head and bellowed the most silent, most screamy, silent scream the world had ever seen but not heard.

'That would be the last thing I would want.'

'Okay. Like that is it?' Carlton asked, recognising what was blindingly obvious to anyone, specifically two people, within earshot.

'Yeah. Because if I let you in, you take a shine to the cat, the cat thinks it can stay as long as it wants, come in whenever it wants, maybe eat what the heck it wants out of my kitchen, and pretty soon I have a cat, and I work long hours, and I can't give it the love it needs, and I have to buy one of them special dustbusters with the pet hair attachment, and pay for its shots, and keep the cat in on Fourth of July in case it gets scared, and miss out on a great party, and frankly, I'll need a damn good party more than once a year if my Lolita has skipped town without rhyme or reason. So, on balance, you go home to Wanda, and I'll call you up the second I hear anything. Okay?'

Beckman and Lolita, wall-mounted statues already, held their breaths.

'Sure,' Carlton replied after about a billion years.

Buck must have given the outstandingly unwanted visitor one of his trademark hard stares because a few seconds later, the door banged closed.

The motionless twosome permitted their eyeballs to swivel left and right, chests still full, not wanting to believe the overweight opera star had hit her final note. Then Buck appeared and was hit by two Force 10 gales as lungs were summarily dumped of their stale contents.

'I'd like to thank my manager, my producer, the director, in fact, the whole team who made this moment possible.'

Lolita pushed up on tiptoe, grabbed Buck's head, drew it downwards and plonked a smacker on the guy's cheek. So did Beckman.

'Frankly, Beckman, that was horrible. I hope Lolita gets better.'

She shrugged. 'Meh.'

'If it's any consolation, that's the last time,' Beckman said (to Buck—he was nowhere near tired of kissing Lolita. Maybe in fifty years.)

'Especially as we're not waiting around for it to happen agai—' The words were strangled in her throat by…

…the doorbell. Again.

'Coming,' Buck yelled, deafening them whilst covering up the noise of him unceremoniously but protectively, shoving them back against the wall.

'Meow?' Lolita murmured.

Buck flashed up a stern admonishing finger and went to the door.

They held their breath.

At this rate, we'll be world experts at breath-holding. Maybe I should try out for some underwater free-diving records?

Sound of the door opening.

'Hey Tyler,' came Buck's voice.

They exhaled loudly and crumpled, limp, against the wall.

'I'll break his neck,' Lolita said through gritted teeth.

'He's a friend. Save the neck-breaking for people who deserve it. Person. Person who deserves it.'

Buck led Tyler and Amaryllis into the room. The visitors halted abruptly; Beckman and Lolita were hardly giving off welcoming vibes.

So he shook Tyler's hand to break the spell but still countenanced, 'Next time, call ahead, okay?'

Lolita brushed past and flopped onto the sofa. 'Except there won't be a next time.'

Beckman sank onto the sofa beside his beloved. 'So? Bring takeout? Crate of root beer? Chest of pirate gold?'

'Evidence.'

Lolita perked up at Tyler's words (word). 'Spill.'

'Cooper is talking to someone. Maybe more than talking.'

'It's not a crime,' Buck countered.

'Who?' Lolita asked brusquely.

'Don't know. But tall, long hair, pantsuit.'

'Dixon', Buck and Lolita said in unison.

'More than talking?' Buck queried. Was there jealousy there?

Irrelevant. More important things to do. Buck may be sweet on Dixon—he's entitled.

That's not the news here.

'We didn't wait to find out.' Amaryllis perched on the edge of the sofa, dumped down her bag and withdrew the laptop. She flipped it open to show the stowaways the mooted evidence. 'But we recorded this.'

Buck nodded. 'Dixon.'

After a few seconds, they all looked at Lolita for a reaction.

'This could be anything,' she said, which was infinitely less reactionary or inflammatory than Beckman had expected.

'Or it could be vultures circling,' Tyler suggested.

'Or the monkey meeting the organ grinder,' Beckman added.

'Or the SOB getting back on the two-timing horse,' Lolita said. 'Point is, with respect, Tyler, Amaryllis, unless you had a directional mic on him, we have a shot of two people having coffee.'

Tyler's shoulders fell. 'Yeah.'

Amaryllis closed the laptop.

'Not that we're not grateful,' Lolita added.

'Devil's advocate here,' Buck said. 'If it's business, why is Wanda not there? And why have we not seen this before? This is Dixon's third time here.'

'Maybe we've been unlucky.'

'Or he's deliberately trying to stay under the radar.' Buck perched on the arm of his sofa, the guests having occupied all the soft places. 'Look at it like this. If this could be anything, we can *make* it anything. Show Wanda that image, and it'll go one of two ways. Either she'll be part of it, or it'll be news. If it's news, we can make it bad news. We can stretch the truth. It's a crack we can jam a jemmy in and push them apart. We do that; there's a chance she'll let something slip.'

'Convince her he's having an affair?' Lolita suggested.

'Whatever will crack those alibis wide open. Cooper has a weak link in his chain of destruction. Break the spell on Wanda, and the whole tower of cards might come down.'

'No counting chickens, okay?' Lolita warned.

Somewhere, on a cloud, on a throne, in a lair, an Omnipresent Being, a Fate, or a Gamesmaster Trickster cackled inanely. Nobody had even begun working on their fowl abacus.

The doorbell rang.

Beckman and Lolita exchanged a look. Again.

This time her eyes burned. She rose from the sofa. Buck rose too and held up a warning hand.

She shook her head vehemently. 'Not again.'

'Don't be an ass, honey,' Beckman said.

She swivelled on the spot. 'I've had enough. I'm not cowering any longer.'

'What if it's Carlton come back?'

She strode for the door, fists balling. 'Then I hope he's got a good dental plan.'

Chapter 43

Randall and Reba, teeth intact, took seats where they could find them.

'Next time, I'll have to sell tickets,' Buck said, scanning the whole room.

'I don't see any takeout bags,' Beckman said to the new arrivals. 'So is this a welfare check-in, or did you find Carlton's footprint out back of the warehouse?'

'No, and no. What I did do is bump into Oz and buy him coffee and pancakes,' Reba replied.

'I'm guessing not on account of charity,' Tyler ventured.

'For idle curiosity. One detective to another. Well, one detective to one test pilot for BarcaLounger.'

'And?' Lolita queried.

'You know "No News is Good News"? This is more "No News is No News",' Randall said with a sigh.

'Oz is never likely to upset any apple carts, mostly because he's never seen an apple cart and has a crippling allergy to apples.' Lolita patted Buck's nearby thigh. 'Times like this, I wish you'd gotten into law enforcement twenty years ago instead of making lattes. We could use someone who gives a shit.'

Buck laid a hand softly on the top of her head. 'There are five people here who give a whole manure truck.'

'Well, thanks for trying,' she said to Reba.

'We didn't get to the Good News part.'

'You said there wasn't.'

'Not there. But later on, new Kojak on the block here,' Reba nodded at Randall, 'Pulled a scoop.'

'I'd call it a sting,' Randall said.

'Call it a ham on rye or the Rosetta Stone. I could care. Just talk.' Lolita leant forward encouragingly.

'Walter wrote Carlton out of the succession plan. He has no control over the merger.' Randall beamed unapologetically, either due to his detective skills or the news itself.

Lolita's mouth fell open.

'A break, finally,' Beckman breathed.

'Yeah, but who does have control?' Lolita asked.

'Whoever,' Randall said, 'I'd bet a fat steak they're a damn sight easier to lock horns with.'

'If it's Wanda, it's even more important we split them up before he has the chance to exert pressure. Because sure as God made little green apples, Carlton will find an angle to get her to do what he wants.'

'So she's in danger,' Reba remarked.

'Then let's hope for her sakes there's another co-signatory required.'

'Who?'

Beckman was staring out of the window, watching a pair of squabbling birds, when Lolita jabbed him in the ribs to bring him back to the matter at hand. 'Unless Walter has managed to transcend the material plane, his U-turn happened before the accident. Why?'

She shrugged. 'He saw sense. Realised he didn't want to leave his company in the hands of a manipulative ass like Carlton Cooper.'

'But why would Carlton try to kill Walter when he was already out of the game? I mean, killing for an inheritance, it's prime-time TV 101. But if you're not part of the estate? Carlton has an evil streak as wide as monster truck tires, but dropping a ton of brickwork for fun is a hell of a stretch.'

'You didn't see him this morning,' Randall said. 'He was mad as a wasp. This was out of left field. Walter screwed his plan—pretty impressive for a guy flat on his back.'

'That's a sixth sense even Saul would be proud of,' Buck suggested. 'We got in a pre-emptive strike.'

'Or he got a tip-off,' Reba said.

'When I find that tipster, he just might get a flash of my suspender tops.'

All eyes turned to Lolita. Beckman waited for her to call "Psych!". And waited.

Hmm, a glimpse of rather attractive upper thigh in exchange for the rescuing of our collective livelihoods?

I could live with that.

Either way, you'll have to live with it, sunshine, whether it happens before or after Saturday. Whether or not she's technically single. Regardless of a ring on her finger. Some things aren't worth a push back.

Still, I'd rather she'd offered to buy the mystery benefactor a pizza or a lifetime of free neons.

If someone, somewhere, has genuinely made Walter Whack wake up (not physically, or at least not right now) and smell the coffee, perhaps, just perhaps, we had a shot at pushing this merger through. If it gives Carlton the teensiest aneurism, well, that's a bonus.

'One thing is for certain,' Buck said, breaking the silence. 'Let's hope whoever is controlling the merger now is blessed with some foresight. One more gust of wind in our direction, something that puts a smoking gun in Cooper's hand, and EVI will be tarred with that brush. Any customer with a conscience won't deal with them after that. I wouldn't, and neither would half the town. If that happens, whoever has Walter's pen now, they'd sign that merger if they had any sense.'

'There's no smoke without fire,' Reba said. 'Even if it's only theories that Carlton is playing fast and loose, wagging tongues is enough. He's a liability. He's the first domino. An honourable man would jump before he was pushed. He'd fall on his sword to save the company.'

'Problem is, Carlton is not an honourable man. He won't leave on his own accord. Not until he gets what he wants.'

'Which we won't give him,' Beckman said.

'Then he needs to be out-thought. He needs to think he's getting what he wants.'

'Which is?' Randall asked.

'The moral victory. And money.'

Beckman looked at Lolita. 'That sounds a lot like handing him the business and leaving town.'

'What it sounds like, and what it is, are different things.'

'And what is it?'

'Not a clue. Not yet. But smoke and mirrors. Somehow. A big empty box, tied up with a golden bow. The promise of a happy ever after.'

Randall shifted in his seat. 'Say that Carlton believes you tipped off Walter to change his Will? You ready for that backdraft?'

'He'll be pissed off enough that you escaped the Portal,' Tyler said.

'Hopefully, it'll make him so determined to win, so blinded by reason, he'll make a mistake, take a gamble.' Steely determination returned to her eyes. 'He's not untouchable. He's a damn accountant for Chrissakes. If this room can't figure a way to beat him, then handing him the business and leaving town is all I'll have left.' She scanned the group. 'After sacking the whole damn lot of you as friends and colleagues.'

Buck laid a hand on Lolita's shoulder. 'Which I find a damn sight scarier than anything Cooper might do.'

Chapter 44

At 02:36, Lolita had the idea.

Technically, she'd had the idea a few minutes earlier, but 02:36 was showing on the circa-1995 bedside LCD in Buck's spare room when Beckman's eyelids were rudely unshuttered by her egregious shaking of his lately-slumbering body.

'This better be good,' he mumbled, Grinch-like.

It was good.

And when she'd finished explaining her idea, she made amends for waking him with a kiss that would work as a penance for starting WW3.

'Now get some sleep, beautiful man, and in the morning, tell me why it won't work.'

'That would be puncturing the world's biggest party balloon.'

'I'd rather you did the bursting than some other prick.' He sensed her smile, even in the near-darkness.

'I hope to hell your plan is better than your jokes.'

She gave him a soft poke in the midriff and turned over. As his mind whirred, her breathing descended into sleep, which warmed his heart, and soon he too was adrift on the nightly ocean of unconsciousness.

In the morning, over an early breakfast before Buck went to open the café, they unveiled the plan.

'So it gets your seal of approval?' she asked.

'If it means I get my house back, you bet your ass.'

'I love it when you come over all mock righteous and snarky.'

'Only promise you won't rattle his cage too hard,' Buck countenanced.

'It's not about bearing teeth,' she replied. 'It's about rolling over and playing dead.'

'You want a hand making calls?'

'Let Saul know. Beckman and I will do the rest. Then we've got an alibi to crack.'

As a longtime student of behaviour, Beckman saw Lolita's bravado and confidence were tinged with an undercurrent of nerves—and he felt the same. Neither had the racing driver balls or the pugilistic puffed-up air of invincibility to swan around Sunrise, casually inviting all-comers to see and hear and do as they wished.

Their movements were calculated and circumspect, even though the first job of the day involved walking right up to the dragon's lair. They'd reasoned that if a confrontation was coming, there was no point in delaying the inevitable: Carlton would be a million shades of surprised and confused and mad fit to burst. If it happened outside his front door, so be it. You don't make an omelette without breaking eggs.

As Beckman casually rolled the Buick up the street to the appointed address, his fingers tensed on the wheel. He craned his neck in the direction of the driveway.

It was empty of red Mustangs.

The white spots on the back of his hands drained flesh-coloured again.

'If he's bribed them, there's no competing with that.'

'Glass half-full, okay Beckman? Power of positive thinking.' She swung open the door; he climbed out and followed.

They went up to the front porch of Carlton's left-side neighbour, and Lolita rapped on the screen door. Beckman scanned around for approaching nemeses.

The door was answered by a kid of about fourteen, faded Wildcats tee, jeans with myriad holes. Beckman expected a grunt, but the youth pulled himself up straighter and gave what passed for a welcoming smile.

Beckman understood at the very basic level: meeting Lolita Milan made anyone want to be the best version of themselves. Hell, he'd dedicated his life to being the kind of person she deserved, or at least less of an idiot.

'Miss Lolita.'

'Hi Robbie.'

He eyed them both curiously. 'I heard…'

'The reports of my death are greatly exaggerated,' she replied.

'That's good to know.' He cocked his head. 'Mark Twain?'

'You're a good study, Robbie.'

'If it's about not being in school today—'

'Honestly, we could care less. I'm not your mom. Hell, I'm not even your neighbour.'

'Dodged a bullet there,' Beckman murmured.

'I heard about the fire. I was real sorry about that.'

'Thanks. Listen, last Thursday, were you at home?'

Robbie thought for a second, then nodded sharply. 'Had my cousin over from out of town. Last visit before the new semester.'

'Video games, that kind of thing?'

'Messing about. Hoops. Football.'

'Robbie is holding out for quarterback,' Lolita added, giving Beckman a sideways glance.

'Got an arm on you, Robbie?'

'I don't know about that,' the kid replied sheepishly.

'We had to toss your ball back enough times,' she recalled.

'Sometimes, my aim is not so good. Plus, Jonas sucks as a wide receiver. Mr Cooper is pretty piss—' Robbie checked his language in front of a lady, 'Hacked off with throwing it back over the fence.'

'On Thursday?' Beckman said, fishing.

'Twice. Except not Mr Cooper; he were out.'

'Afternoon, this was?' Lolita's brow furrowed.

'Yeah.'

'They were mending the garage, though?'

Robbie looked like someone had skipped a page. 'No. Well, not I saw. Car was gone. Miss Wanda was on the back porch. She fetched the ball.'

'Sure?'

Robbie shot them a look like this was a trap. 'I do something wrong?'

'If we ask Jonas, he'll say as much?'

'I think the second time he did it on purpose, just so's he could see Miss Wanda again.' Robbie's face coloured red. 'I shouldn't a said that. Don't tell Jonas. Don't tell Miss Wanda.' He inspected his feet.

'Jonas took a shine, did he?' Beckman asked, an echo from his own misplaced crush on a rather svelte English teacher some twenty years earlier.

Lolita touched the boy's shoulder. 'It'll be our secret.' She pulled a ten-dollar bill from her skirt pocket and proffered it. 'Buy some phone credit or whatever you kids do.'

Robbie looked up. 'I couldn't.'

She tucked it into his shirt pocket. 'Just until pro ball starts paying real money, okay?'

He nodded. 'Yes, Miss Lolita.'

Beckman tapped the side of his nose. 'We were never here.'

Robbie glanced around furtively. 'How was The Portal?' he hissed.

'A lot less safe than your back lawn,' she replied. 'And I don't want to have to report your death, exaggerated or not, to your mom. Dan Marino did fine enough without playing chicken with physics.'

'Yes, ma'am.'

Robbie was sensible enough to recognise the end of the conversation, so Lolita and Beckman gave him a nod and headed back to the car.

Beckman turned the key, and the V8 coughed into life. 'Well, she lied for him. Next up on Ripley's Believe It Or Not, a bear takes a steaming dump in the woods.'

Chapter 45

The trip to Our Buck's passed uneventfully, although it was good to resume some normality, or what passed for it in the rollercoaster circumstance.

Buck intercepted them as they got through the door.

'What?' Lolita asked, worried.

'Jack was in.'

'It's a free country. I mean, you serve assholes the same coffee we drink, but you're entitled to a wage.'

Buck pointed surreptitiously. 'Over there. With Dixon.'

Lolita's shoulders slumped. 'Oh, shit.'

'Did he ask where we were?' Beckman said. 'Were his eyes red from the loss of his beautiful daughter? And maybe from the disappearance of his gallant and wholly innocent future son-in-law?'

Buck shook his head. 'They sat there, they talked low, and didn't shake hands.'

'Because watching Dixon is your new favourite pastime.'

'You'd rather I *wasn't* your spy?' Buck asked.

Lolita touched his upper arm. 'Sorry. Maybe it's the pain of another knife in my back.'

'Maybe a man is innocent until proven guilty?'

'I can't remember Jack ever being innocent of anything.'

'She came to sit at his table, not the other way around.'

'All the same, it takes two to tango.' She set her face hard.

Buck held out a mollifying hand. 'Remember, she's not Sunrise. It isn't personal. It's business.'

'Good. We agree on something.'

She strode towards the edge of the room, and Beckman followed dutifully. When Lolita stood over Dixon—Death without the cape and scythe—he sank quietly to the adjoining table.

He wondered if Dixon worked out. Then, whether Lolita could floor her with a single punch. A small part of him wanted her to. The small, thrill-seeking, idiotic part.

Yet violence wouldn't bring answers, merely consequences. Besides, she needed to save her knuckle strength in case a more deserving cause came along. A tall, bespectacled, CPA-qualified cause.

The women eyed each other for an eternity. Then Lolita did something he didn't expect. 'What can I get you?' she trilled.

'It's okay, Lolita. I had my fun. We're grown-ups.'

'So you did know?'

'I'm sorry.'

Beckman, if nobody else, was taken aback by this revelation.

It Apologises.

Perhaps it hadn't been sent by a machine race from the future.

'Wow,' Lolita said. 'Mind if I take that at face value?'

'Be my guest.'

'You knew who I was.'

'I'd be a pretty lousy M&A exec if I didn't.'

'I'm curious why the misdirect. Either talk to me straight, or play a game. Don't give up halfway and apologise. Or is that to show your human side?'

'You have me wrong, Lolita.'

'I hope so.'

'Sit?' Dixon gestured at the chair opposite.

'Why, making you uncomfortable?'

'You have no idea.'

Would Lolita concede and step inside the dohyo or retain her position of authority by standing?

She sat. 'So, Round One was the belittling. Round Two is you go behind my back?'

Dixon tucked a lock of stray chestnut hair behind her ear. 'Honestly? Round One was fear.'

Lolita laughed. 'Surprised you can spell it.'

'You want to give yourself more credit. You have a pretty fierce reputation. I heard you were a tough cookie, and maybe I wasn't ready to lock horns.'

'You? Afraid of me? Big, corporate ball-crusher like you?'

'Like I said, you have me wrong.'

'I'll take that under advisement.'

'It's a man's world.'

'You don't need to tell me.'

'So, needs must when it comes to walking the walk.' Dixon set her elbows on the table and entwined her fingers.

Lolita eased back in her chair to maintain a safe distance. 'This is all an act? Underneath you're sweetness and light, Miss Suzy Homemaker?'

'Hard shell, gooey interior—that kind of thing?'

'I guess. You tell me.'

Dixon shrugged, took a sip of her latte. 'Work is work; love is love.'

'And how is "work"?' Beckman heard the air quotes.

'Right now, interesting.'

'And love?'

'Not as interesting as it is for you.' Dixon spied Lolita's engagement ring.

'Like I said—hard shell, gooey interior.'

'We're not so different. A hard shell pursuing the dream of a corporate hotshot. A gooey interior dreaming of a good man to take out the spiders and reach the high shelves.'

'I think you have a shelf or two head start on me,' Lolita regarded Dixon's slim frame.

'Just not a good man.' Dixon glanced across to where Beckman sat.

His cheeks tinged with warmth.

Just don't ask me to take out the spiders. Being shoved into an inter-dimensional gateway is one thing, but spiders? No thanks.

'One who'll throw himself under a bus for you?' Lolita sniped.

'That's not a prerequisite.'

'I thought that was your line of work. M&A throws a lot of good employees under buses.'

'Is that what you're afraid of, Lolita? Your people? Or losing your company to a vacuous corporate shell?'

Lolita gave her a strychnine-laced smile. 'Oh, I wouldn't call you vacuous, Dixon.'

Dixon opened her mouth to correct Lolita's misunderstanding, then sensed she'd received the gentlest mauling from the lioness' partly-exposed claws. Instead, the interloper mentally circled her opponent for a few seconds. 'I know you're not on best terms with Jack.'

'And meeting you won't do that any favours.'

'But see it from my view—or his. The world keeps turning, in your absence—permanent or temporary. Money talks. Money saves companies.'

Lolita rose, brusquely. 'We don't want your money, your fake concern.'

'I gathered as much.'

'Then we're done here. You're done here—in Sunrise.'

'Are you trying to throw me out of town?' There was a steely edge to her tone. The icebreaker was over—it was back to pistols at dawn.

'I tried it once.' Lolita looked at Beckman, who was transported ten weeks into the past. 'It worked. For a time.'

'I wasn't aware you carried a tin star.'

'There's a lot of things you're not aware of.'

Dixon rose. 'I'm finding that out.'

'Blood might be thicker than water, but the water runs pretty thick anyway round here.'

Dixon looked towards the long bar. Buck was watching the three of them. 'Yeah. You're spoiled like that, Lolita.'

'Tell me about it.'

'I wish things were different. There's a lot of... opportunities in town.'

'You want to buy out the café too? You'll have to go through me.'

Dixon chuckled—the first glimpse of humanity. 'I wouldn't do that to either you or Buck. He seems... too good for that.'

'There goes that gooey heart of yours again, getting in the way of screwing over the little guy.'

'Or the not-so-little guy.' Dixon smiled.

Wow, two for two on human gestures inside ten seconds.

'Buck's heart is by far the biggest thing about him.'

'I've no doubt. Certainly makes up for my tiny, old, dead one.'

Self-deprecation too. Getting dangerously close to the outside edge of likability, Ms Lewys.

'Nah,' Lolita replied. 'I'm sure it's not that old.'

Dixon pulled out her purse and dropped some bills onto the table to pay for her check. 'Before I go, for my curiosity, is Buck single, or always that friendly?'

Lolita weighed up the correct response. 'Maybe. But probably not to you.'

'Ah.' Dixon nodded. 'Do you always judge people so harshly based on reputation?'

'Normally. It's a great defence mechanism.'

Lolita gave a smile of remembrance. But it faded. Beckman had been a no-good salesman. The enemy. An unwelcome interloper. A vacuous shell. A corporate peddler of false promises, cons and schemes.

And in five days, she was marrying him.

'Listen, Jack wanted you to have a company to come back to. I wanted my time here not to be wasted,' Dixon said.

'So you went to Plan B.'

'Actually, Walter was Plan B. But he's not really up for negotiating.'

'Hence you spoke to Carlton.'

'Just trying to do my job.'

'We all are. At the moment, mine is keeping my people and securing their future.'

'I get that.'

'So why try to do the opposite? I know GigantiCorp—it's a slash and burn operation.'

'You ought to read beyond the headlines.'

'Educate me.'

Dixon pointed at the door. 'What happened to throwing me out of town?'

The sparring jabs were coming thick and fast now. But Dixon had thrown Lolita off-balance. To stall, Lolita turned to Beckman and said, 'Be a doll, would you?'

His caffeine-starved bloodstream interpreted that one way, and he gladly went to the counter to slake their thirst and take a breather from the tension of the gladiatorial arena.

'Lolita ahead on points?' Buck said, packing coffee grounds into the portafilter.

'I feel like I've gone six rounds myself.' He pointed to where Lolita and Dixon retook their seats. 'Frost/Nixon gets a reboot.'

'She's bad news; I get it.'

Beckman held up his hands defensively. 'No way in a million years I'd tell you who to date.'

'All the same, no need to encourage her to stick around, huh? Poking her nose, screwing your plans.'

'Unless there's a chance she's *not* the Devil incarnate. As we already have one of those in town.'

'For now,' Buck said with a wink.

Bessie did her age-old thing, and Beckman carried three mugs over to where the tête-à-tête was unfolding. There was no blood spatter on the floor nearby, so he surmised all was well and pulled up a chair.

'All I'm saying is—dominoes,' Lolita was explaining. 'You can deny that manpower cuts are your stock-in-trade, but I'm a businesswoman too. Probably more than you. To you, they're numbers in a town you'll never see again after the signatures are done. You can ride off into the sunset with your bonus. To me, they're real people. She pointed across the room. 'Norris there services our forklifts. Velma works in purchasing.' She indicated another woman who sported an Alice band, had a cellphone glued to her ear, and drank from a takeaway cup. 'Mabel The Bagel delivers to the warehouses.'

'GigantiCorp have people too; you might know,' Dixon insisted.

'In anonymous offices in big cities spending dollars with big brands. Throw those three people there on the trash heap, and fewer dollars go in Buck's pocket. The domino train snakes around every street in town.'

'Is this supposed to tug on my heartstrings?'

'Only if you have a heart.' Beckman slid the coffee across in front of Dixon. 'You keep coming back in here—is it honestly just for the coffee?'

She shrugged. 'I like the place.'

'Then don't mess with the status quo,' Lolita said.

'Is that code for "Leave my man alone"? or "Let my business fail by itself"?'

'Number one, Buck is big and ugly enough to take care of himself. He'll smell a bad rat if that's what you are. Number two, Milan is not done yet. Carlton Cooper doesn't hold the strings he thought he did.'

'I gathered. Which is why I'm looking for alternatives. To save someone's bacon.'

Lolita sipped. 'Ah, the white knight, riding in to save us all from ourselves.'

'I'm sure we can find agreeable terms.'

Lolita's eyes flared. 'Are you making a direct approach, Ms Lewys?'

'Whatever you think about your father, Lolita, he wasn't about to go behind your back to sell the company out from under you. So, in your terms, I'm going to the organ grinder and not the monkey.'

Lolita was disbelieving of the woman's audacity. The cloak-and-dagger was over; the direct approach had arrived.

A small part of him knew it made perfect sense: save the company, end the nail-shredding financial heartbreak, and put the kibosh on Carlton's scheme. The ass would be smiling on the other side of his face when it became clear that EVI couldn't compete against an emboldened Milan Enterprises. Sure, they'd have faceless corporate overlords. Still, if GigantiCorp sprung for a shiny new warehouse, negotiated Milan some volume discounts from suppliers and opened up more nationwide contracts, EVI would soon be the minnow in town, and Lolita would love the chance to grind Carlton's dreams into the dust.

All we have to do is sell our souls, and then we'll be happy.

Chapter 46

The look from Lolita was enough to dispel that idea, like a campfire in a forest clearing being bombed by the entire load from a C-130 firefighter.

She took a calming breath. 'It's all just black and white? All just numbers?'

'Once an accountant, always an accountant,' Dixon replied.

She softly closed her eyes. 'Jeez, not you too.'

'Numbers make the world go round.'

The eyes snapped open. 'So do humanity, humility and love.'

'I get it, Lolita. Honestly, I do. I've heard enough whispers about you and Carlton Cooper. Accountants are not your favourite.'

'It used to be salesmen,' Beckman interjected.

Lolita ignored that. 'But you transcended that career, huh? Moved on to bigger and better? Extra zeros in the plus column, a few individual minuses but only human ones, so no harm, no foul?'

Dixon's voice was commendably level. 'You can't fight economics—you're smart like that. Your merger with EVI is borne out of financial security, and you can't tell me there won't be job losses.'

Lolita sighed. 'I'm beyond bored of this. No dice. No sale. Think of it as corporate suicide if you want. Ride off into the sunset with a knowing grin on your face. Purse your lips for an "I told you so" a few weeks down the line. Your bonus will have to wait.' She looked Dixon up and down. 'The new tailored pantsuit. The new convertible.'

'You could just call me a soulless self-serving bitch to my face. I wish you would.'

'Because you'd have an excuse to throw a fist?'

'Wrong, yet again. Because it would prove how fallible you are. It would show the chinks in your armour. It might even educate you, rub away the harsh judgemental edge. You're not like that inside; you talked about how saving Milan Enterprises is for the people and not your own pocket. Your pantsuit. Your convertible. Is that what scares you about me? I'm the person you think you want to be but can never be because you're too human? Isn't it *you* who's putting up the facade of the strong businesswoman? Trying to fake it until you make it?'

Lolita's jawline hardened as she clenched her teeth, restraining herself, not wanting to be taunted into a mistake, a cheap bar-room brawl that would do nothing to extricate themselves from the bigger problem at hand. They couldn't let Dixon be Al Capone's tax evasion charge.

Beckman laid a comforting—maybe restraining—hand on her arm.

'You're wrong. But what if I was?' Lolita said through thin lips.

'It'd be a mistake. Judging your insides by someone else's outsides is a path to disappointment. We all only show what we want to be seen.'

'So this is all an act?'

Beckman's gaze flicked between the two women, who were now bent forwards over the table like Kasparov and Karpov.

No way in a million years, Dixon will crack, open up, show her softer side. Pluck out her wallet and flash pictures of the endangered primates she's sponsoring in

Borneo. Roll up her sleeve and reveal a delicate tattoo of two cute cats paws.

A nascent smile flickered over Lolita's lips. A smile of victory.

Dixon sat back. 'Do you like me?'

'I'll take the fifth.'

Dixon nodded gently. 'Buy me pie.'

Lolita shot Beckman a query, which he returned. She shrugged. 'Okay.'

Beckman did his duty and went to fix the order. When he returned, it was clear that not a single word had been exchanged in his absence. Pie seemed to be the key to the door, Dixon-wise. He'd brought them all another coffee, for good measure, which was welcomed with a nod verging on genuine gratitude.

He sincerely wanted to like Dixon. After all, it was unarguable that she and Lolita shared something in their character—was it the hard shell / gooey inside they'd joked about?

Dixon picked up the fork and clipped off the nose of the pie slice. 'Some people are born strong, some people become strong, and some people have strength thrust upon them.'

'My mistake,' Beckman said. 'I must have asked for philosophy pie instead of pumpkin.'

'My sister was the strong one.' She clipped off another piece but held both of their gazes. 'It didn't save her.'

Then she wordlessly devoured the rest of the pie, downed a slug of refill coffee, and wiped her mouth with the blue paper napkin. 'She died six years ago from a rare condition. She was stronger than I'll ever be. Real strength, not show. Fortitude, bravery, not puffing out a chest. I will never love anyone so much.'

Then, as if to prove Beckman wrong, or at least tease it, she slid a thin purse from her jacket, plucked something out and laid it on the table.

The business card listed Dixon as Chair & Patron of The Adelaide Foundation.

'It's a charity set up in her honour to find a cure. Fifty percent of my salary goes into it. I don't do what I do for me; I do it for her.'

Lolita puffed out a small breath. They had passed with unerring speed into the eye of the storm, and all the wind had vanished from their sails.

Dixon sipped her coffee, looking alarmingly unlike the cat who had got the cream, which was a feat in itself. Perhaps she was used to pulling the rug from under naysayers. 'I haven't found her level of strength, only enough to make headway in an old boys' network. To play the bitch to climb the ladder to get the promotion to get the money to run the Foundation to pay the scientists. You might call it the dictionary definition of a means to an end.'

'People still lose their jobs.' A plaintive tone entered Lolita's words—her argument was flagging.

Dixon shrugged. 'If not me, someone else would be sitting here. This way, maybe some lives get saved.'

Lolita sat back, taking it all in. 'We're still not for sale.'

'Sure.'

'But you have my permission to date Buck.'

'Who says I'll stick around?'

'Because you don't seem like a woman who gives up easily. Maybe you go down fighting.' Lolita's face fell reflective. 'Like Adelaide.'

'Then maybe you and I do have something in common.'

'I have no desire to go down at all. Which is why I'm fighting.'

At the other side of the room, the café door opened. Out of interest, Beckman flashed a look. He froze.

It was Carlton.

Seconds Out. Round Two.

Chapter 47

'I knew it.'

Carlton's words carried from all those yards away.

Beckman lowered his voice. 'By which he means he didn't know it at all, not in the slightest, but the Ol' Superiority Complex is hard to shift when you are technically the most superior asswipe known to humanity.' He glanced at Dixon. 'Pardon my language.'

'Not at all. I only met him to find out if he's *my* kind of asswipe.' She winked.

Ms Dixon Lewys was growing on Beckman with every minute. But compared to the lanky, bespectacled nemesis striding towards them, she was Mother Teresa in what were, on reflection, probably mid-range pinstripe pants.

Lolita sprang from her seat. There was no point in ducking a confrontation, and seeing as they'd come out of the face-off with Dixon on at least equal terms, she looked fit and ready for another battle of wills. Plus, as it was a public place, the chances of Carlton hitting her (or him) were minimal. In fact, he didn't recall Carlton ever hitting anyone. Perhaps because it was too easy.

'You knew it?' Lolita ventured sarcastically.

Great opener, honey. Pure balls.

'Yeah, I knew it.'

Credit to the guy—he can lie at the State level, maybe even have a shot at the Nationals.

'Then why send us in there? You don't throw a boomerang and walk away with a smug-ass grin. Or did you get appointed Professor of Quantum Physics at MIT?'

Carlton's hand clenched and unclenched: she was getting to him already. He didn't verbally rise to the taunt. He looked square at Beckman. 'What part of "Leave town" didn't you get?'

'I left the oven on.'

Carlton sneered. 'How d'you do it?'

Beckman shrugged. 'One foot in front of the other.'

'Wiseass.'

'It's a hundred percent the truth.'

Lolita nodded to confirm his words.

'You think that makes you a hero? Walking into The Portal and coming out alive?' Carlton locked his killer stare.

'Well, you were there. Going in wasn't exactly my choice, and coming back out was self-preservation. Anyone would do the same. It's not quantum physics.' He turned to Lolita. 'Or is it?'

'At some level, it's all math anyway.' She glowered at Carlton. 'So maybe it *is* your kinda thing.'

Carlton shook his head as if casting away demons. 'Who gives a shit. You're back. That was against orders.'

She stepped into his personal space. 'Orders, is it?' she whispered.

'He will leave.' Carlton lowered his voice too; they were ten feet from Dixon, the nearest customer. 'And I guess you—if you love him. Make no mistake—I'm only getting started.'

'You mean the fire, Walter's accident, the gunpoint threats?'

He gave a thin-lipped smirk, not about to be caught off-guard. 'Like I said before, the root of all recent misery in this town is the arrival of… him. Your employees are facing the unemployment office. It's not only me who wants to see the back of him. So, because I'm a nice guy,' (Beckman nearly snorted out half a mug of finest Java), 'I'll ask nicely. You should both leave.'

She examined his face, then half-turned to see how Dixon was taking this encounter: with apparent disinterest, although the angle of her head and the flick of an eye betrayed her.

'Saturday,' Lolita said. 'We have some things to put in order this week, and a... personal engagement, then after that, I promise you won't have to share Sunrise with us.'

Carlton leant back; he hadn't expected a capitulation. 'You're conceding?'

'Someone has to be the bigger man. Show some balls. What an irony that it's a woman.' She gave him the most challenging stare in her armoury and reached out a hand. Beckman took it and the cue and escorted her towards the door. The slow swivel of Buck's head tracked their path.

Nobody heard Beckman's heart thumping.

Behind them, as the door closed, Buck walked over, curious to see whether the expression on Carlton's face was hitherto uncatalogued by mankind or merely unusual for its owner.

Before he got there, Carlton had engaged Dixon, and Buck caught the words, 'Did I imagine that?'

'You mean that they were here or that they conceded?'

'You heard?'

Dixon smirked. 'There's a reason I don't wear earbuds when I'm sitting in a succession of coffee shops. Amazing what gems you pick up. Gems can be leverage.'

'I guess that makes you the Queen of leverage round here,' Buck interjected.

Carlton turned. 'I want your opinion, Travis; I'll ask for it.'

'You forget; I'm the barista. Listening to my opinion is Café 101. Especially where Lolita is concerned.'

A slight sneer creased Carlton's lips. 'You knew all along.'

'Well, that makes one of us.'

'Ass,' Carlton breathed ever-so-lightly. 'So, did they tell you how they did it?'

'They told you—one foot in front of the other.'

'I don't buy it.'

'That makes about as little sense as anything I've heard. What—they flapped their arms and flew back out of The Portal? Found an abandoned DeLorean with the engine running?'

'I'm saying that all being right as rain is fishy as hell. They not tell you what was in there? No need for counselling? No PTSD? No medical once-over to check The Portal doesn't give you cancer, or whoever is on the other side hasn't been sticking probes where the sun don't shine?'

Buck shrugged. 'I tend to live and let live. You may want to try it sometime.'

Carlton opened his mouth for a louder rejoinder this time, then reflected. 'Maybe I should be grateful it didn't scar them so much they'd be prepared to take issue with me.'

'You mean, more issue than before?'

'Yeah, well, we all know about that.'

'Yeah, I guess we do.' A pregnant pause, then, 'You gonna leave? My café, I mean.'

'The pleasure will be all mine.' Carlton turned on his heels and left. The clang of the door evaporated into the silent atmosphere.

'I think the pleasure was probably all yours,' Dixon piped up.

Buck contemplated her, mulling. 'I'd bet a free lunch that you have about as little time for Carlton Cooper as most people around here.'

Dixon licked her lips pensively. 'Why, is that a prerequisite for being a *persona grata* for you and your friends?'

'Lunch I can do in about five minutes. Being accepted into polite society might take a stretch longer.' He smiled, and she caught it and threw it back.

'I don't have to like people I do business with, but it helps. Seeing as I can't do business with Carlton because Walter made him *persona non grata*, I can judge him independently. So, yes, lunch would be fine. Thank you. Buck.'

'Your judge of character is nearly as on-point as your Latin. Lunch it is.' He nodded courteously and turned to go.

'Join me?' she asked.

Chapter 48

'Your ability to not lie—technically—may be my new favourite thing about you.' Beckman selected an apple from Lolita's fruit bowl and took a bite.

'Don't start counting chickens, honey. In fact, don't even count eggs. You can lead a horse to water....'

'Swear to God; I'll not take any farmyard inventories until this is done.'

Lolita collapsed gratefully onto her sofa. 'It's good to be home.'

'I ask you a serious question?'

'Always.'

He sat beside her. 'Worse case, would you leave on Sunday?'

'That sounds a lot like planning to fail. I'd rather take the time to work on Plan B than go straight to all-out defeat.'

'With planning a wedding too, we'll be living on caffeine and adrenaline for four days.'

She popped him a kiss. 'Yeah, but I'm worth it.'

He returned the kiss, which became an embrace, which became more intense. Soon they weren't sitting on the sofa but lying on it. After a few minutes of intense activity, followed by two hours of indolence, the doorbell of 1002 Edison Avenue rang.

Lolita made herself presentable and, without it even crossing her mind that the visitor might be a tall gun-toting accountant, went to answer. Her gait told Beckman as much; it was neither dukes-up nor timid mouse. Almost like everyday life had resumed, although he had scant experience of what everyday life for her, or both of them together, looked like. It had been an... atypical twelve weeks.

'Reba?' floated her voice down the hall.

Probably Reba.

The door closed.

Definitely-Reba took an empty chair and laid a small salt cellar on the antique wood coffee table between them.

'Genie took your voice and went back inside?' he said.

'Your Groom's speech is going to be a real riot,' Reba replied, deadpan.

'Think you're invited?' he replied in kind.

She picked up the salt cellar and unscrewed the lid. 'Definitely.' She tipped something into her palm.

Beckman and Lolita craned forwards.

It was, to all intents, a microchip.

He put two and two together with remarkable alacrity, given he wasn't the detective in the room. 'A bug.'

She sat back and beamed. 'If matron of honour isn't taken, I might be your gal.'

'Depends what and who you recorded,' Lolita said.

'Our friend Dixon.'

Lolita waved it away. 'Boat has sailed. We had a lovely eye-to-eye. She's not on my Christmas list yet, but she's not our problem anymore.'

'Three hours is a long time in Sunrise right now.' Reba pulled out her phone, swiped through and set it on the table.

A recording played.

Ten minutes later, Lolita was pacing the room.

Beckman and Reba watched her for a while.

Lolita swivelled on the spot. 'That answers the question of who Walter left in charge. Why the hell didn't we interrogate her when we had the chance.' Lolita pointed at the salt cellar. 'That proves she's easily led. We could have turned her.'

'From the Dark Side?' Beckman quipped, then wished he hadn't.

She flashed him a disapproving look that was one rung below poking her tongue out and half a ladder below The Eyebrow.

'You don't reckon Carlton would do the same in her position?' Reba asked.

'I absolutely do. I just thought she was better than that.'

Lolita jammed hands onto hips. 'You forget, she's had him browbeating her for weeks to try and spoil our merger, to put the squeeze on daddio. Now she's gone one better than bypassing us—she's cosied up to the big blue whale so they can treat us like plankton whenever they want.'

Beckman sighed. 'It was inevitable. Dixon found a way to walk away as the heroine.'

'I can't believe Carlton sanctioned it.'

'I'm not sure he did.' Reba plucked a stray feather from the seat cushion. 'He's probably finding out about the same time you are.'

'You heard Dixon,' Beckman added. 'What she offered them was a hell of a deal—at a personal level—which is what's important to Carlton.'

'And it still screws us, leaves us bottom of the pile.'

'Plus, she's bound to have overheard what we said to Carlton. If she thinks we're out of town by the weekend and knows Jack won't sell, Milan is a dead-end. She has to put all her effort into closing a deal with EVI.' He sighed. 'I only wish there wasn't an upside—which there is. Dixon will get a fat bonus, and maybe the cure is a step closer.'

Lolita threw her arms up. 'Well, thanks for the moral downer, honey.'

'Yeah, the silver lining nobody wanted.'

A silence descended.

'Do you want a beer, Reba?' Lolita asked. 'Least we can do.'

She nodded. 'I should bring bad news more often.'

'Don't you dare.'

Beckman purloined three bottles from the fridge, and they began to drown their sorrows.

'You have to admit, she's a smart cookie, that Dixon,' Reba ventured. 'Going where Wanda hangs out for her regular PM smoothie. Finding a way to win.'

Beckman put an arm around Lolita's shoulder. 'If I were a glass-half-full kinda guy, I'd say we have a better shot convincing Wanda to retract her offer than we would if Carlton was holding the ace cards. At least she has a good side to appeal to.'

'And don't forget we have the incriminating evidence of Carlton and Dixon's liaison,' Reba added.

'That was wholly innocent.'

'Probably,' Lolita said. 'But if it's the sharp end of a wedge we can use, the magic tool that picks locks, we'd be dumb not to try.'

'That sounds a lot like lying,' he warned.

'It's... insinuation. Like the insinuation you're responsible for everything that's happened. The insinuation I disabled the CCTV. The insinuation Sunrise would be better off with you long gone. So, what's wrong about fighting insinuation with insinuation?'

He bit his lip.

They weren't married yet, but she'd started Being Right About Everything five days early.

Chapter 49

'Are you sure about this?'

'I know enough about Wanda. EVI would have to be on its knees for her to be at the office past 5.01.'

Beckman checked the Buick's rear-view mirror: the suburban street stretched out empty. 'Yeah, but are you sure about *this*?'

'Baby, I'm not sure about anything anymore. But look at it like this—we went into The Portal, we got out. Safe to say that stranger things have happened. Maybe our luck is turning.'

'Predicting the workings of an interdimensional gateway is tough, but have you ever tried reading a woman's mind?'

She gave him a solid thump on the thigh.

Something caught his eye, and he checked the mirror to see a Merc SL cruising up to their position.

'Showtime,' he said.

They hopped out and watched as a curious Wanda Whack emerged onto her driveway, then they went to sate her curiosity.

'Afternoon Wanda,' Lolita sung.

'Lolita,' came the guarded reply.

'Drinks on the rear porch?'

'I don't follow.'

'Invite us for drinks on the rear porch,' Lolita repeated. 'We have some news.'

'Good news?'

'Invite us for drinks and find out.'

Wanda eyed them both, still unconvinced, but waved towards the door, which they took as the aforesaid invitation.

The rear porch was expansive, as Beckman imagined from the size of the property. Carlton Cooper seemed to have as much of a task keeping track of his bank balance as he did counting the beans at EVI Lighting. The porch overlooked the land that stretched away for hundreds of yards, peppered by a few trees and some makeshift shooting targets.

They sank into three of the six chairs.

'Soda, or something stronger?' Wanda asked.

'Soda, for now,' Lolita replied. Wanda duly disappeared into the house. 'But you may want something stronger later, honey,' Lolita added.

Beckman shifted uneasily in his seat. The late summer sun continued its inexorable, imperceptible warping of the boards, and the gentle chirrup of insects echoed in his mind like the quietest opening chords of John Williams' famous marine theme.

Wanda set the drinks down and sat.

Lolita sipped. 'First off, we're doing this because, and I can't explain this, we think you're a decent person.'

'I'd hope so.'

'And Beckman and I both had a crossroads this year. You have yours.'

Wanda's brow wrinkled. 'If this is about marrying Carlton….'

Lolita held up her hand. 'Absolutely not. I'm the last person to give relationship advice, especially with him.'

'Yeah,' Wanda said, discomfort on her face.

Beckman wasn't revelling in the social awkwardness of sitting with his fiancée, in her ex-fiancé's house, talking to her ex-fiancé's current fiancée about their past and present relationships.

'I'll get to the point.' Lolita set her soda down firmly. 'We know you gave a false alibi for the afternoon when Walter was hurt. You and Carlton weren't working on the garage door. We know he wasn't here. We know he shoots rifle bullets like the one lodged in Walter's chimney. He's been practising.' She jabbed a finger towards the far garden. 'And his car was spotted on the night of the fire.'

The colour drained from Wanda's face. She wriggled uncomfortably in her seat. 'I can explain,' she began, but Lolita held up her hand.

'Let's put that all on one side of the teeter-totter, okay?' Lolita didn't wait for acquiescence. 'Word is you've agreed on terms with Dixon?' When Wanda nodded curtly, she went on, 'You're selling your soul to the devil, you get that?'

'I'm doing what's right for us,' she protested.

'You're doing what Dixon's convinced you is right. What Carlton's brainwashed you into thinking is best. He wants it for spite, not practicality. It's long past being about EVI—it's all spite and revenge against the company and me. He never wanted our merger because it would strengthen me and my business. It might even wind up with him being a casualty of streamlining. His defence was to kill the merger and hope we lost ground. He'd even have engineered a reverse buyout so he held all the cards— or at least convinced Walter to hold all the cards—so he could enjoy getting me pushed out, just as I pushed him out.'

'You can't deny you did push him out.'

'Absolutely. Because he's a liar and a cheat. I don't have people like that in my company. I'm not a blind ass like Jack. So, because he can't kill our takeover or mount a counter-bid, he's rubber-stamped Plan B—you let GigantiCorp take a stake. Milan can't compete with that market presence, certainly not now, with half our inventory up in flames. So, Wanda, honey, what you agreed with Dixon today just signed our death warrant. He's got you wrapped around his finger tighter than the ring you're wearing. The one he put on my finger not six months ago. Which is a whole other story—one you've got co-author credit on.'

'Is that what this is about? Trying to screw my engagement because I screwed yours?'

Lolita shook her head firmly. 'You didn't screw my engagement. He did, by sleeping with you for, what, nine months? I'm being kind, of course—you knew exactly what you were doing. Unless you're dumb as chalk?'

Wanda sprang from her seat. 'Get out of this house.'

'No.'

'Pardon me?'

'I said no.'

'Do I have to call Oz?' Wanda warned, narrowing her eyes.

'Go ahead. We'd still have six weeks or so before he did anything about anything. Or maybe you'd get special treatment, being inside the inner circle.'

Wanda's gaze—a blend of indignation, bravado and fear—roved over her guests. She sank into the chair.

'So,' Lolita continued, 'On one side, we have you being an accomplice to a whole bunch of unsavoury stuff, and I'd be the one making the call to Oz about that. On the flip side, you have an opportunity to reconsider your agreement with Dixon. They'll asset-strip EVI within weeks, probably relocate the factory out of state, and most of your friends who enjoy little soirées on this palatial deck will give very polite refusals of your invitations because you screwed over a ton of your employees for a pay-check and the offer of management positions which I'll bet Dixon has no intent on honouring.'

'I can't go back against Carlton.'

Lolita looked at Beckman, which was his cue to present evidence for the prosecution. He pulled out three glossies, screengrabs of Randall and Reba's snoop, and passed them across.

Lolita narrated as Wanda pored over them. 'A year ago, I'd never have thought that Carlton—my Carlton as was—meeting a woman in a coffee shop was anything but business.' She met Wanda's gaze. 'And look how wrong I was about that.'

Wanda shook her head. 'This was about the merger.'

'Possibly. Possibly not.'

'He wouldn't.'

'Like he wouldn't give a false alibi about being at home when the fire started. Like he'd force you to lie about him being at home when he was out shooting the chimney—which, you don't need reminding, came about an inch away from killing your father. All to try and grind me into dust because I caught him cheating.'

Beckman wanted to point out it was *he* who had caught Carlton cheating but avoided being an idiot.

'The thing is,' Lolita continued, 'I know you. We go back aways. You're not dumb as chalk. Go ahead—love the guy—see if I care. The heart can be a strange organ. But selling out to GigantiCorp is not in anyone's best interest. And I don't mean because I want our merger to go through. We don't want Big Lighting in town. We're better than that. EVI and Milan can survive, separate or together. Carlton is an accountant. He does what he does—makes the suggestions and chess moves he does—because it's good business sense. Hell, he was trying to steal our customers to give EVI the edge. Remember that? The way he was cheating my whole company as well as me? On some level, he was doing it to make EVI stronger. Not now. He doesn't care about you any more than anyone with an EVI pay-check. If he'd crush his prospective father-in-law with a hundredweight of rubble, it's no leap to say he'd sell your firstborn into white slavery if it meant I ended up penniless and howling in a padded cell.'

Lolita drained her soda and stood, triggering Beckman to do the same. 'You could both be in a cell—not the padded type—by the weekend. Or you can call time on being his patsy. Someone wise once said they would do anything for love, but they wouldn't do that. Sleep on it, wake up and smell the coffee, dammit, Wanda. You're at your own Portal. On this side is Sunrise. On the other side might be perpetual night.' She gave a hopeful look. 'Thanks for the soda. We'll see ourselves out.'

So they did.

Beckman started the car.

'How did I do?' she asked.

'Ask me tomorrow, I guess.'

'You think she's a good person underneath?'

'Why are you asking me? And what's all this about you two going back aways? Something I missed?'

'We went to school together.'

'Late-breaking story!' Beckman scoffed. 'So, what, was her affair some deep-seated revenge? A best friend, seventh grade spat she never forgot?'

Eye Roll. 'No. We just went to school together. Not even the same year.'

'So, she didn't pull your pigtails, steal your boy, or get you detention? Or vice versa?'

'No, she was that awkward middle ground between the nerds and the cool, edgy kids.'

'Which were you?'

'Can you guess?'

Damn. Now you've started it.

Check the look in her eyes. Hmm. Not quite testy, not quite playful.

An awkward middle ground.

'What did you score on your SATs?' he probed, wincing.

She shook her head. 'No clues.'

He paused for a moment, pondering, feeling the aircon wash the interior of the car that had simmered, unoccupied, in the warm late afternoon Arizona sun. The Buick's V8 burbled away, his hand still on the shift.

'Is this a litmus test for our marriage?'

'I think that boat has sailed,' she replied noncommittally.

He took that as a good sign because there was enough anguish anyway, without rocking that specific boat by wondering whether he was cut out to be Mr Lolita Milan.

Think, dummy.

'Even before Milan, you didn't exactly suck at the artefacts business. Doing the whole job is arguably even harder than being a CEO. Which means you must have book smarts. Which makes you the nerd. The whole rebel, swing dress, taking no prisoners thing—that happened after Jack walked out. A reaction, your balls dropping. The cool kid you wished you'd been at school.'

She took an age to answer, drawing him good and long across the tenterhooks. 'Looks like I'll still see you front and centre on Saturday.'

'If we survive that long.'

Chapter 50

Amaryllis had chosen the wrong outfit that Tuesday morning, and now, nine hours later, it resulted in a mental tussle between the Anakin and Darth in Tyler's skull.

She'd bargained on a cooler-than-usual day, based on the early signs, and chosen a heavy blouse. Now, as the heat of the day peaked, her cooling move was to loosen a button.

Billions of women wore bras. Tyler had seen hundreds; in shops, in the drawers of sundry bedrooms, on the floors of disparate bedrooms, and uncovered or partially covered on the torsos of various owners. It was of absolute, sun-coming-up-next-day certainty that Amaryllis wore them. Not only today but for countless days and years past.

Yet when a half-centimetre of black strap peeked out from behind the blouse that early Tuesday evening, as they both loitered outside the gates of EVI Lighting, Tyler thought he'd found a lost Da Vinci or discovered Martha Stewart used to drop acid.

Darth, aka Old Tyler, dragged his eyeballs across for another glimpse, all the while Anakin, rent with confusion, slashed his lightsaber through New Tyler's conscience, willing him to understand what a sexist, opportunistic ass he was being.

The puerility of it hit home, although too late to stop a second look, and he resolved to give himself a good stern talking to in the hotel mirror that evening.

Damn you, weather—it's all your fault.

It brought to a head another conundrum that had raged within him for a few days. He was interested—no denying it. Yet, there were two hurdles to clear.

Point One: He was deeply, overwhelmingly—and also unnecessarily—preoccupied with Amaryllis' age. Annoyingly, here was another conundrum within a conundrum: should he care? New Tyler—no—not if he was the reformed man he professed (or self-professed) to be. Old Tyler—definitely yes. Perhaps, on a tail-of-the-bell-curve occasion when a particular bored housewife looked especially appealing for her years. But to date? A possible fifty-something? It would turn Old Tyler's stomach to stoop so low, to look outside the perfect age range, especially when there were so many eligible thirty-something specimens who would make better alternatives, be easier on the eye and humour of his friends.

To New Tyler, it simply shouldn't matter. So what if she was 43, 48, 51? Age was merely a number. It was the person, not the skin, and Amaryllis was good company, friendly, reliable. Easy on the eye.

The mirror in his mind reflected his unspoken—possibly un-confronted—notion that Amaryllis represented a line in the sand. Like the boy's First Time that makes him a man, she was his rite of passage from shameless, sexist, playboy to caring, upright, one-woman (at least concurrently) man. If he could get over his misplaced age-related angst and successfully date her, he'd prove to himself he'd become the kind of guy who could date a person like Amaryllis Broomhead.

Which messed with his mind a little.

The sure-fire outcome was he'd have to set aside any cares or concern about her age, chiefly because the alternative was to come right out and ask her. This plan failed in two key respects; a gentleman never asks a lady how old she is, and if Tyler considered himself a contender to the category of gentleman, he could never take this shameless route.

Secondly, it would reveal to Amaryllis that he considered it a necessary line of pre-qualification in the dating stakes, thereby showing he was an identically-spotted leopard and not worth her time. She might even take such offence as to leave Pegasus—an undesirable baby-out-with-the-bathwater outcome.

The sensible decision was to actively not care.

New Tyler was nice, or at least in line for graduation into Nice.

And Nice Guys asked women out on dates. They didn't hijack friendships, have wandering hands or make lewd suggestions. They did it properly.

He caught himself. Looking down a woman's blouse was not Nice. It was opportunistic and arguably woven into the fabric of manhood but not ideal. Or rather, being caught wasn't ideal—it would give Amaryllis enough ammunition to suppose that New Tyler was Old Tyler with a Velcro-fastened mask.

He took small comfort in being interested enough, even at a primal level, to seek a glimpse of underwear. It implied she was a regular woman with a figure he wanted to see more of. If he was unsure before, a happenstance slip in the afternoon sunshine outside a lighting supplies building in a mysterious town somewhere (he still didn't know where) in Arizona had shown he was undeniably interested in dating Amaryllis. However old she was.

'How long do you want me to keep taking pictures?' she asked, lowering the point-and-shoot.

He checked his watch, did a ready reckon. 'I think we're out of the woods now.'

They were about to walk back to his Porsche, which he'd left a hundred yards away (pointlessly, in retrospect) when a familiar figure caught his eye. He halted as Carlton strode across the parking lot towards the gates, wearing the demeanour of a man on a mission.

'This is private property,' Carlton barked from ten yards away.

Tyler checked down at his feet. He and Amaryllis were standing on the road side of the boundary. He hoped Carlton wouldn't duel in semantics.

'Hey, we're outside. Just passing by. You know, tourist snaps.'

The slack tie and creased shirt betrayed a long day at the coal face, but Carlton's height advantage and his look of thunder indicated he wasn't shy of rounding off the shift with some trademark haranguing. 'Since when are you still in town? That always the case with supposedly travelling salesmen at Pegasus? Forgotten the travelling part?'

'It's a free country.'

'And I was free to ask you to leave, which I did. Remember?'

Tyler nodded. 'Absolutely. And we took that request under advisement.'

'Like your pal Beckman? He doesn't listen either.'

'So I hear. Well, I would if I could hear. Which apparently I don't.'

'Wiseass.'

'Well, journeyman salesman—the travelling kind—to CEO overnight? Yeah, there's got to be some wisdom behind that.'

Carlton stepped into Tyler's personal space. 'Do I have to put you in The Portal too? Huh?'

'Should I have my PA note that as a polite query, or a threat?'

'Do I?' Carlton repeated, unamused.

'I can think of worse things.'

That confused the beanpole bean counter. 'What?'

'There are worse places to go. So I hear. You know, if I—'

'How d'you figure?'

'I think my colleague—my friend, Beckman—you remember the guy?—found the whole episode quite... enlightening.'

Carlton scoffed. 'Enlightening?'

'He certainly appeared buoyed by it. I mean, yeah, I'd be scared shitless going in, but actually, he came out a better person. He said he felt richer for the experience. So, if you're querying, or even threatening, then being honest, I could do with being a richer person. What about you, Amaryllis? Would you risk The Portal to come back a calmer, happier person? A woman richer than before?'

She nodded gently, not over-egging the pudding, but still a mite unnerved by the ongoing encounter.

Carlton eased back, perplexed.

Tyler swore he heard the faint ting! of a lightbulb popping into existence above the six-foot frame opposite. 'Anyway,' he continued, a theatre-goer scooping up their coat as the final applause dies, 'I promised to call my distributor back by end of day. He works longer than either of us, Carlton, but no point in taking liberties, that right?'

Carlton's gaze alternated between mid-air and the faces of his two technically-not-trespassers. 'Yeah. Sure. Just don't... hang around the gates. Lot of lorries come through here. If you're gonna leave town, no point in it being in an ambulance. Don't need the litigation, being honest. Now get lost.'

Tyler willingly took Amaryllis upper arm and guided her away. He held on all the way to the car, and she didn't ask him not to.

Chapter 51

Randall Ickey wasn't a religious man, but he'd spent the last couple of days praying things worked out for Beckman and Lolita, and thereby for a lot of other people, including him.

It wasn't purely out of job-salvaging personal interest, but to quieten the demons in his head, which insisted the surest way to get Carlton out of town was to shoot the guy. After all, he'd shot plenty of people in the past, and those hits had only happened on the say-so of someone else: he'd no proof that he was erasing unworthy assholes—festering boils on the backside of humanity. Here, though, he had first- and second-hand evidence that Carlton Cooper was easily worth a bullet or six. It would make a lot of things easier and happier.

Yet Lolita said no, and as she and Beckman had catalysed his new life in Sunrise, to go against her wouldn't be biting the hand that fed him but unceremoniously removing it with a chainsaw.

The leaf he'd turned over needed to remain face down.

He and Reba sat at the long coffee bar, sipping their brews and nonchalantly watching Beckman and Lolita at their customary table, or returning their attention to Buck's zigzags around the room. They were also keeping a watch on the door.

All of them occasionally looked up and inwardly cursed one of the ceiling-mounted aircon units which, that

September day, had developed a rattle. Buck's customary technical cure-all, turning the thing off and on again, had failed. A call to Sunrise's odd-job engineer of choice, Evan Freely, was needed. But there were more important matters to attend to.

Carlton entered the cafe.

It said a lot about the quality of Buck's wares that, despite the man's contretemps, and the habitual presence of the even more despised Beckman, Carlton couldn't stay away. Either that or Winston's Coffee, three blocks down, had suffered a power cut or similar. Winston's was fine, and Carlton got on infinitely better with the guy, but there were no grounds on which to compare the grounds.

Or, Randall thought, perhaps Carlton is hiking the staircase to Cloud Nine, knowing Beckman will be gone in four days, and trying to rebuild bridges with Buck in anticipation of a return to the pre-Beckman normality of life in Sunrise.

Carlton and Buck's exchange was cursory, but of more interest was Beckman and Lolita's swift adjournment of their morning interlude. They kept a respectful distance from their nemesis and intercepted Buck further down the bar.

'Got the keys?' Beckman asked.

Buck fished into his pants pocket, produced the requested item, and laid a hand on Beckman's shoulder. 'You sure about this?'

'Safe as houses.'

'I'm talking about the Silverado, not you.'

Beckman smiled. 'You're talking about Lolita. Maybe the Silverado. Possibly me, on a good day.'

'Is it worth it?'

'It's no risk, all reward.'

Buck paused, then set the keys in Beckman's palm.

Randall felt a nudge. Reba jerked her head imperceptibly towards Carlton, who was doing a fine job of pretending not to hear.

Lolita hugged Buck, Beckman shook his hand, then they passed Carlton in a wide loop, blanking him with laudable skill, and left.

Randall watched Buck watch them go, watched Carlton watch them go, then watched Buck belatedly serve Carlton his coffee. Then Buck came over.

'I never saw you loan your pickup out to anyone,' Reba said to Buck.

'Lolita's not just anyone.'

'Are they after hauling a load?'

'I don't get the lowdown—even me. They said it would solve all their problems.' Buck wiped the counter.

'Well, we all want that,' Randall replied.

'Amen,' Buck said, nodding. 'Rather them than me. They know what they're doing out there.'

'You mean—?'

'When you've sunk this low, it's not even a gamble. Lolita—she's no dummy.'

'She may be the smartest person I know,' Reba agreed.

Whether it was that remark, the fact Carlton had received the takeaway he came in for, or that he'd heard enough, the outcome was that the door soon closed behind him.

Buck, Reba and Randall exchanged the same worried expression.

'What'll be, will be,' Buck proclaimed.

'We can only do what we can do,' Reba replied.

'On which,' Buck beckoned her with a finger and walked down the bar a couple of paces.

Randall strained to hear, as Buck pulled a piece of paper from his apron pocket.

'I need you to find this guy and give him this message.'

Reba scanned the paper, gave Buck a querying look, and nodded.

Randall was intrigued but didn't pry; enough was going on in Sunrise without having something else on his mind. Anyone in town was allowed secrets.

So long as nobody, least of all the woman he loved, got hurt.

An hour later, Beckman was getting used to the vagaries of the Chevy Silverado's sloppy steering as he guided it towards the outskirts of town. Beside him, Lolita's hands nervously tapped her leg.

Conversation had been minimal.

'I love you,' he said for something to say, not that it was a throwaway comment.

Love may not be blind, but it sure as hell can get you into some tight spots. But, like you said—no risk, all rewards. Or, at worst, no risk, no reward.

Whatever comes, just marry her Saturday. That day is always some kind of watershed, however much a person may dismiss the fact.

How much of a watershed, though?

He checked the rear-view mirror.

'I love you too, Beckman.'

Something in the aircon unit, deep within the dash, rattled. Maybe the café caught it from the Chevy. It didn't matter: the vehicle was a means of transport. It wasn't the glorious Mustang; it wasn't the breezy, carefree aura of the Miata. Just a set of wheels with a load bay, and that's all they wanted.

He checked the mirror.

'Take a left here,' she said. So he did.

The V8 gurgled along. The town thinned.

'Do you think someday we'll laugh about all this?'

'I'd settle for not having an ulcer. Besides, you make me laugh enough anyway.'

'Sometimes deliberately.'

'Aw, don't do yourself down. When you're not an idiot, you're quite sweet.'

'Whoah, let's not get carried away here.'

'I didn't think this was the time for shallow flattery,' she said by way of defence.

'Baby, I'm always in the mood for shallow flattery.'

She gazed with curiosity, as if taking in the view for the first time. 'Anyone ever say you had a Tintin vibe about you?'

'Whatnow?'

'The kind of abrupt hair, the boyish good looks. The jamming your nose into everything and getting into a whole mess of trouble.'

He gave her a fake snarl. 'You dare buy me a white puppy for Christmas; I'll swap you for two guys with moustaches.'

'Christmas? Hell, let's get to tomorrow first.'

'Yeah,' he said quietly.

The Chevy swung onto the penultimate street. He checked the mirror. A red Mustang was gaining on them.

He put his right hand beside his left on the wheel and gripped it tighter. 'Showtime.'

Lolita swivelled in her seat and watched through the letterbox rear screen.

Calmly, Beckman indicated and took the turn onto Latrop Road. Inside, his heart thumped.

The Mustang followed.

As the road straightened, an aggressive rumble came from behind, and the Mustang gassed past in full cry.

Seconds later, a hundred yards ahead, Carlton showed his fifty-year-old steed precisely zero mechanical sympathy as he tugged on the handbrake and slewed the car perpendicularly across the road in a cloud of spent radials.

Beckman jammed on the old drum brakes, snapping seatbelts into both their chests and brought the pickup to a halt with ten yards to spare. Had they been doing anything more than thirty, Carlton would have been the next person to utter the word 'insurance' shortly before washing some crumpled pony car with his tears.

'You okay?' Beckman asked.

'Yeah.'

Carlton sprang from the car, familiar steel in his eyes and an equally recognisable piece of steel in his hand. He walked towards the pickup, gesturing, with arrogance rather than menace, for the two of them to get out.

Not being an idiot at that moment, Beckman complied. Lolita, never having been an idiot—

—*except for all that time she dated Carlton, thinking he was a decent guy*—

—did likewise.

'Going somewhere?' Carlton shepherded them away from the Chevy.

Well, duh!

'What's it your business?'

Carlton ignored the question. 'You going in there?'

'What's it your business?'

'I don't like it.'

Beckman shrugged. 'It's a free country.'

'Look, Carlton,' Lolita began.

He raised the pistol to her. 'Be quiet.' She did. He gestured to the Silverado. 'Why the pickup?'

'Change of scene?' Beckman tried.

'Need to collect something in there? Is that it?'

'What's it your business?'

Now the eye of the pistol came to glare at Beckman. 'Keys.'

'I'm not sure Buck—'

'Keys,' Carlton repeated.

Beckman backed up slowly, removed the key from the ignition, and retook his position much closer to the barrel of a gun than he'd rather be.

Wanda had opened the Mustang's passenger door but sat there, spectating.

He looked at Lolita, ostensibly a rabbit in the headlights, and tried to draw her attention to the fourth person at the scene.

His mind raced. 'We thought it was a gamble taking one vehicle in. Worth it, yeah. But two? Especially your *beautiful* Mustang? What if something went wrong?'

'Like how?' Carlton asked, aim wavering.

'Time is a funny thing. Certainly in there. Go in convoy—you might end up in a fender bender. Then where would you be? A busted engine. Hell, even a flat. A hundred bucks says Saul doesn't make house calls through there.'

Carlton straightened his aim. 'Honey!' he rapped.

Like a dutiful puppy, as she had proven to be, Wanda hopped out and walked over. Carlton didn't take his eye off them for a second.

Give the guy credit; when it comes to thuggery, he's well drilled.

'Run the car onto the shoulder, then come back with the keys.'

Obediently again—although with nerves—she did, then dropped the keys into his outstretched hand. Carlton offered a satisfied smile.

'Would this be a bad time to tell you I can hot-wire?' Beckman asked.

'Guy like you? Right?' Carlton scoffed.

Beckman shrugged. 'Sure. Whatever.' That messed with Carlton's mind deliciously.

Pride comes before a fall, idiot. Don't shoot for any Tony Awards.

Beckman and Lolita exchanged an expectant glance.

Come on, Carlton. The sensible thing is to shoot out the Mustang's tires. Except it's your beloved pet, and that would hurt it. Besides, it would cost precious money to get new ones.

Carlton turned to Wanda. 'You okay if I do this by myself?'

Lolita, unseen by Carlton, nodded vehemently.

It caught Wanda's eye. She thought for a second. In her defence, there was a lot to consider. 'You... you want me to stay here and watch them?'

'That's my little Annie Oakley.' He handed across the gun and pecked her on the temple. She shifted her grip and retook the uncompromising arm-outstretched warning stance. 'Now get away from the pickup,' Carlton instructed them.

They scooched over to the far side of the road, watched by a muzzle.

He climbed into the cab and slammed the door. 'Kneecaps first, then shoulders, okay honey?'

'Uh... sure,' Wanda replied.

'Back before you know it.' He started the engine and looked at Beckman. 'One foot in front of the other to get back out—that's what you said?'

Beckman nodded. 'Or one wheel in front of the other.'

Carlton slotted Drive and burbled away down the short remaining stretch of tarmac.

Beckman swore there was some reticence to the pickup's speed; even Carlton couldn't be one hundred percent sure of his ground. Then, just when it seemed the douche might be human after all, the engine went up a notch, and the rear fender receded faster.

He held his breath. Beside him, Lolita did too.

Even Wanda wore a mix of curiosity and dread.

The pickup disappeared into The Portal and snapped out of existence, rather like a stone being lobbed by, on reflection, not such an idiot after all.

Chapter 52

For a full minute, nobody spoke.

Then, catching Lolita's eye, Beckman winked. Wanda wouldn't notice—she was fixated on The Portal (despite there being nothing to see).

Lolita's response was a "maybe, maybe not" grimace-slash-smile.

Credit to Wanda; whilst her attention wasn't entirely on her hostages, her gun arm was pretty solid. She'd probably crack off a shot if she'd sensed any movement. Even if she didn't hit either of them, it would serve as a mighty warning to Stand The Heck Still.

'Would you shoot?' he asked.

Wanda looked round. 'Try something, and we'll see,' she replied noncommittally.

'I know you're a good shot, but I'll bet the value of that car we can stand here, dead still, longer than you can hold your arm out.'

'He'll be back soon enough.'

Lolita sighed with deliberate intensity, her sonic puff crossing the five yards to Wanda, and held out a gentle hand. 'Wanda. Here's the thing: he's not coming back.'

'You won't get me like that.'

'There's no getting to be done. The getting is over. You stayed this side of The Portal. Why? Because it was the right thing to do.'

Wanda shook her head. 'No. I stayed to watch you. To help him. He doesn't need me in there, doing what he's doing.'

'And what is he doing?'

Wanda regarded them like they were mad, or at least strangely unaware of the knowledge they'd ventured. 'Collecting the treasure.'

Beckman indulged in a mental lap of honour.

Nearby, Lolita's mouth creased into a semblance of satisfaction. She fixed Wanda in a serious look, a teacher not exactly telling off a pupil but explaining, without the possibility of misinterpretation, how life worked. 'You need to know two things. There is no treasure. And Carlton is not coming back. Certainly not in the next ten minutes; probably ever.'

Wanda chuckled, a lamentable impression of an evil villain that was cracked apart by a thick vein of nervousness and incomprehension. 'No.'

'Yes. By encouraging you to get out of that car, to stay here, we saved your life. And by taking that advice, listening to what we said yesterday, by leaving Carlton to do his own dirty work, you've shown you're a reasonable person. You've seen which way the wind is blowing. So put the gun down.'

'But there has to be treasure! He said you said there was!'

They both shook their heads. 'Ask anyone in town—that word never passed our lips. All Carlton is chasing is a dream—a dream of rubbing our noses in the mess of his making. And guess what? The irony is the root cause of everything that's happened isn't Beckman; it's not his wandering into town. It's Carlton's lying and cheating—which was going on before! Long before. And who was his chief accomplice? You. And how have Beckman and I repaid you? By not spilling everything to Oz and stopping you from making a one-way trip into The Portal. He had to go. You didn't.'

Wanda was fixated on Lolita's words, not her actions, which had been to ease closer.

Lolita reached out. 'So you won't shoot Beckman or me, and I'm going to take the gun now.'

Wanda recoiled slightly, steadied her aim. Lolita was three yards away.

Beckman held his breath. Wanda wouldn't need to be any kind of Annie Oakley to hit Lolita square in the chest at this distance; she could be Annie Lennox.

I hope like hell she doesn't hold a schoolyard grudge. Irony being, we'd all be better off in The Portal because that's not a fatal encounter, or at least not as damaging as a .38 slug at two yards distance.

Which is where Lolita had reached.

Before he asphyxiated himself, he released the breath and held another.

Because everyone knows that holding your breath stops your fiancée from getting shot.

He had half a mind to rush Wanda and create a distraction, but it was one hundred percent likely to startle her and inflame the situation, possibly resulting in injury, probably resulting in death, and certainly resulting in a pre-marital dressing-down of biblical proportions.

So he stood his ground as, at the one-yard mark, Wanda's hand drooped, then her shoulders, and the gun arm fell limp.

He blew a pent-up hurricane from his lungs.

Lolita calmly and deliberately prised the gun from Wanda's grasp and lobbed it over to Beckman, who impressed his former sixth grade gym teacher Mr Oswin, for the second time in about a week, by actually catching the thing.

'I… I don't get it,' Wanda said. 'He said if we went through there, we'd get rich.'

'Richer for the experience. It... I guess... banged our heads together. Made us admit some home truths. Brought us closer. Emotionally richer. Stronger.' She gave a gentle shrug. 'Don't even ask. I'm no rocket scientist.'

'The point is,' Beckman took Lolita's hand, 'We got lucky. You might not have. In fact, we're banking on it. Look at it like this: in Sunrise, you have an easy way out. Inside The Portal? Who knows.'

Wanda's looked back and forth between them.

The cicadas chirruped.

No pickup trucks came thundering back from the edge of nowhere.

'What easy way out?' she asked.

'You go back to Dixon and say you were mistaken—a rush of blood to the head. You retract the deal and reconsider ours. The one that's best for real people who believe in real community, not corporate shanking, vendettas, or hijacking a car at gunpoint because you think it's heading to the end of the rainbow.'

'But Carlton would—,' she began to protest and realised circumstance was one step ahead. She bit her lip. 'Couldn't I just walk through there, find him, and explain things?'

'Absolutely. If being with him is the most important thing. We were only there a few hours. I'm sure you could manage longer. Maybe years. But you couldn't come back to Sunrise. We've played real nice up 'til now—someone had to—but if you did get back, make no mistake, we would crush you.' Lolita's expression matched her words.

'Honestly, Wanda, and I know I'm the new kid around here, but there's plenty of wronged women in this country who, a few weeks ago, would have visited you and Carlton with one of these in her purse.' He waggled the gun. 'You're getting off easy.'

Her eyes met his, then Lolita's, and the last bricks of resistance flopped out of her wall. 'He's okay, though?'

'Almost certainly. Unless he's been even more of a damn fool than the last year or so.'

'He's probably already found someone to cheat on you with,' Lolita added gleefully before backtracking with a mumbled, 'Sorry.'

'Is there food?' Wanda said.

'A million questions—we had them all. Think of him as a new… Livingstone. Cousteau. Columbus.'

'Carlton is an accountant, not an explorer. Hell, he wasn't even a Boy Scout.'

Beckman and Lolita exchanged a shrug.

'Okay, you win. I'll throw him a bone.' He set off at a loose jog, covered the couple of hundred yards at about the same slack pace as Mr Oswin had witnessed, and paused in front of the invisible barrier. Then, partly against his better judgment but not against his broad streak of humanity, he lobbed the gun casually out of Sunrise's universe.

'Man's gotta hunt,' he mumbled to nobody.

He tried and failed to avoid reaching the Mustang in a sad, perspiring, breathless bag of uselessness. But, on the brighter side, he stood a good chance of living with himself, a better chance of living with the love of his life, and a high chance of both of them living without the scourge of Carlton Cooper.

Despite not being one hundred percent sure on that last one—which irked—he mentally set it aside as there were still bigger fish to fry. He perched on the toasty red hood of the quinquagenarian automobile. 'So, are we calling Saul, or do you want me to hot-wire it?'

Lolita looked at him like he'd danced a perfect Dying Swan. 'Not in a million years can you hot-wire a car, Beckman Spiers.'

In response, he swung open the driver's door, slid into the seat—commendably setting aside the boyish rush he got from meeting one of his automotive heroes—and fiddled around the steering column.

Very soon, he had an audience. Wanda was curious, casting glances towards The Portal as if seeking approval from the departed owner. Lolita had hands on her hips, and lips parted like a blow-up doll.

After a minute, he sat back in the soft, mottled leather seat. 'Okay, confession. I haven't the vaguest clue.'

'I knew it.'

He pulled a sheepish grin. 'Had you for a while, though, huh?'

Lolita was about to lean in, and he prepared to be literally hauled out of the car by his ear, schoolmarm-style, when Wanda elbowed past and dropped into the seat.

'Scooch over,' she instructed wearily. 'I'll do it.' Then she bobbed her head down, tore off a piece of trim, and began searching for wires.

Beckman and Lolita shared the same expression and the same two words. The kind that mom and Amaryllis didn't like to hear.

Chapter 53

Beckman spent the rest of the ride back to Buck's—him in the passenger seat, Lolita squeezed in the back— wondering how attached Wanda was to the Mustang and whether to make an offer she couldn't refuse.

Then he remembered (1) there were more important matters at hand, (2) they'd pushed her good nature far enough for one day, and (3) they were flat stony broke. Saving Milan Enterprises made Saving Private Ryan seem a cakewalk, so it wasn't the best time to spring for a new set of wheels, especially as they still had a wedding to fund. Besides, Lolita wouldn't consider the Mustang to be the ideal wedding gift to themselves anyway.

Women: no appreciation of priorities.

After they parted company with Wanda and took a long celebratory root beer (on the house) with Buck, Randall and Reba, it was back to the dour everyman-ness of 12 BECK for the ride home.

They should have been on Cloud Nine Million, but the atmosphere was oddly restrained.

He tried not to think about the moral angle, and when he failed to not think about it, he consoled himself with the fact the guy had it coming. When the victim's fiancée is pretty meh about the loss of her lover, it's a decent barometer of whether, on balance, it's the right outcome.

'Can we go see Walter?' Lolita asked out of the blue.

'What, you mean to break the good news?' he replied with deliberate irony.

'Strange things bring people out of comas. A touch. Favourite music.'

'Hearing your daughter's wedding is indefinitely postponed, and you need to hire a new FD?'

'Alright, Mister Goody Two Shoes—maybe I want to do something kind to wash the taste out of my mouth, okay? It won't hurt to leave the guy new flowers or something. We need every bit of ammunition on this charm offensive. Hell, Wanda might sign our papers, but the rate we're going, Walter's bound to be awake by the time we raise the money to get the deal through. I'm damned if I'm not buying a shitload of flowers every week if it'll keep him onside. Okay?'

That was an I Have Spoken-type "Okay".

So he figured where they were relative to the hospital and made the next left turn.

They approached Walter's private room with unnecessary reverence—like he was a departed leader lying in state, rather than merely a longtime enemy whose business they wanted to buy out.

If she wants to whisper sweet nothings in his ear, it can't do any harm. If I was him, and the first face I saw after marathon zeds was Lolita Milan's, it would be a tough call whether I'd woken up on earth or gone to heaven.

Except Walter's taste is almost certainly his own wife, rather than yours. Well, yours soon enough.

You lucky son of a gun.

The door was slightly ajar, so they entered gingerly, but the room was empty, bar its sole slumbering guest. They watched him for a minute, exchanged an eye-shrug.

'Hi Walter,' Lolita said redundantly. Walter, being in a coma, didn't have much by way of response. She turned to Beckman. 'He's so peaceful, like a deep sleep.'

'He's certainly slept through plenty. He won't have to touch the news channels for days—there are a lifetime's headlines just in town.'

'I hope they make sure he's good and stable before the nurse takes him through Page One. "Oh, hi Walter, nice to have you back. Apropos of nothing, your future son-in-law has vanished into thin air, so you may want to get Human Resources on the horn pretty quick before the EVI abacus rusts up".'

At which, Walter Whack sat bolt upright.

Lolita screamed.

Beckman, recognising a split second too late that he'd never live it down, also screamed.

Walter screamed.

Something clutched Beckman's arm. So he screamed.

It was Lolita's hand, so he had another thing never to live down because why stop at one episode of making an ass of yourself?

Then, because further screaming would have gotten silly and caused an orderly to call the cops, they all fell silent, as if guillotined. Walter didn't have a coronary. Neither did Lolita. Neither did Beckman, which was great news because he'd certainly never live it down if he went and died too. A couple of screams were plenty.

What goes on in the hospital, stays in the hospital—isn't that the expression?

So long as I don't appoint Walter my Best Man so he can bring up the matter on Saturday, my reputation is fine.

Probably.

'Walter?' Lolita queried shakily, which was by a sizeable margin the dumbest thing Beckman had ever heard her say.

No, honey. It's just a really good Frankenstein's monster.

'You're… ' She trailed off before saying "awake", which was a shame because he was desperate to not be the biggest idiot in the room.

'You were faking this whole time?' Beckman asked, weighing up the probability of being a brilliant detective versus coming across as very insensitive and also leapfrogging Lolita into the top spot on the Idiot rankings.

Walter tried to chuckle, but it came out as a splutter, a cough, then a sneeze, which fortunately took the wind out of his attempted scoff at Beckman's prize-winning idiocy. 'No,' he croaked. 'Only the last few minutes.'

'Why?' she asked, nonplussed at both the sudden awakening and the ruse behind it.

'I heard someone coming, then I got that it was you two, so I played dead in case you said something juicy.'

Beckman's mouth opened and closed, fish-like.

'So when did you wake up?' she asked.

'Couple of hours ago? The nurse called in; I guess they do all the time. But she was a different one. Anyway, she had this perfume… like Wilma used to wear, back when we were dating. I guess that tickled more than my nostrils. She was bending over me, but I shut my eyes pretty quick. I didn't want her to know what I'd seen when she leant over, so I kept quiet. Then I was working out what the hell happened to me when I heard your voices.' He coughed again, took a shaky sip of water from beside the bed. 'I thought about shouting Boo! and scaring the living shit out of you, but you're good people. So, what happened to Carlton?'

'It's a long story,' Lolita replied.

Walter nodded at the small corner wardrobe. 'There's money in my wallet—go and get a beer and explain it to me.' He held up a finger. 'But don't tell anyone I'm awake. Maybe that nurse will come back while you're gone, and hopefully, that button is still missing.'

With that, he shuffled back into a horizontal position and shuttered his eyes.

Beckman and Lolita exchanged a stupefied look—one which was worryingly familiar of late—and headed to the door.

'I'm not sure beer is on the permitted list here,' she said.

'Well, you wanted to woo him with flowers. Looks like the way to a man's signature is through his liver, not his nostrils.'

'Unless I put on some of that perfume.'

'You're sure as hell not flashing Walter, the work of the divine potter,' Beckman cautioned.

'Come on.' She tugged his hand. 'Let's find a liquor store. You may not be James Dean enough for a car thief, but you could rescue your manhood by smuggling some contraband back in here.'

'And for gratitude, get to admire God's handiwork later?' he suggested with a wink.

She shook her head in amusement. 'Go for your life, young buck. In three days, we're married, so it's separate beds from then on.' Her look was deadpan, but the sparkle in her eye gave her away.

He still gave her a playful whack on the ass for good measure.

They pulled the blinds down and locked the door.

Walter tore the cap off the bottle and drank gratefully. Captain Blackbeard and his scurviest wench drew seats up to the side of the bed.

'So, did he clean me out before he left? Do I still have a company, or are you here for last rites?'

Lolita précised the events since the night of the fire, calmly outlining the evidence against Carlton. Walter took it all in, accompanied by a range of facial cues and the odd whistle of surprise, then took a few moments to post-process, sipping his beer.

'Truth is, I was never very keen on the guy. Not as an employee, just the other stuff. But would I tell Wanda? No. Hell, remember what happened when Jack told you what you could and couldn't do.' Lolita nodded sagely. 'Who to marry is her choice. Her lookout. But if half the shit you've told me is true, I'm grateful to you. It only takes one man to sink a battleship. So good riddance to him. EVI can hire another beanie, easy as anything.'

'How grateful?'

He raised an eyebrow at Lolita. 'So I'm awake an hour, and it's back to business, is that it?'

She shrugged. 'I'm thinking of what's best for everyone. Why not go ahead with the merger? We had the prelim signed.'

'So while I was asleep, you got a ton of VC funding, won the lottery or robbed a bank?'

Lolita's shoulders fell. 'No.'

'So I don't see how it's full steam ahead.'

'But it's not off the table?'

'I have to do what's right for the company at the end of the day. Problem is, I also have to do right by Jack, after the heads-up he gave me.'

'What heads-up?'

'About a week back, Jack found out there was this woman in town, on the prowl to snap someone up. Jack had heard bad things. He also knew what a... driven person Carlton is. Was. Is? Never mind. The point is, he suggested, I might want to rethink my list of signatories. So I pulled Carlton—all on the QT. The thing is, Jack was right. Not a day later, Carlton comes to me with a business plan, showing how tying up with GigantiCorp was a damn sight better for us than your merger.'

'But it isn't,' Beckman interjected.

'Spiers, I may not be the king of ones and zeroes, but I'm aware Carlton fiddled those figures.'

'Because all he wanted was Milan out of business,' Lolita said.

'There's something you should know,' Beckman began. The look of apocalyptic daggers he received from Lolita strangled the rest of his planned sentence. In a fraction of a second, he realised what an idiot he'd almost been. So he dug like hell to get out of the hole. 'That is, I, er, bought you a bag of chips too.' He rifled round in his trusty shoulder bag, found the foodstuff and tossed it loosely across to Walter, who tore it open, looking slightly perplexed.

For good measure, Beckman scooped up Walter's empty beer bottle and replaced it with a second full one, casting a concerned glance at the door. It was like the three of them were ten years old and indulging in a secret midnight feast.

Lolita had been taking it all in. 'Why would Jack help you?'

'Help *you*,' Walter corrected. 'He doesn't want your business to fail. So he protected me from the enemy within. It's not like he didn't have experience of Carlton trying to bring down Milan Enterprises from within. Honestly, you need to give the guy more credit.'

'Spotting that Carlton Cooper was a self-serving ass is not exactly rocket science.'

Walter nodded, and started on the second bottle. 'I still wouldn't have him down for trying to kill me.'

'We don't think he was,' Beckman said. 'He was trying to scare you into realising life is short, accidents can happen, and maybe you want to sign the company across to him and Wanda, then take a back seat in the boardroom.'

Walter pulled a face. 'Maybe. I hope the irony's not lost on him that he'd gotten less power, not more.'

'Nothing like a pre-emptive strike,' Lolita agreed.

'Maybe if we'd all come up with your Portal ruse a week ago, we could be toasting a combined future.'

'Champagne on ice, Walter, okay? Now there's no rabid dog on our tail, Beckman and I can concentrate on finding you the money to keep you in beer and potato chips.'

'Not to forget a new chimney,' Beckman added.

'Well, make it quick. I may have been flat on my back for a week, but I'm tired, and you know what? Carlton was right—it's dangerous out there, and retirement is looking pretty sweet. I like you, Lolita, but business is business.'

Chapter 54

Lolita finished her bagel. 'You don't have to come along. If ever there was a time I didn't need you to hold me back, it's today.'

'AKA the day you thought would never come.'

'Don't jinx it, baby. Jack is a past master in being an ass in the least expected situations.'

'I'm not too shabby on being an ass myself when the mood takes me,' Beckman joked, downing his OJ.

'Just don't make a career of it. You're about to marry the most eligible woman in town—'

'Says you.'

'—and she'd like to think it's third time lucky when it comes to finding a non-ass to share a house with.'

'Then, this morning at least, I'll leave the court clear unless Jack wants first call on asshole-ness.'

'You deserve a day off. I can't believe you nearly told Walter that Wanda had cosied up to GigantiCorp.'

'My bad. Anyway, what he doesn't know won't hurt him. She's scratched the deal, and Dixon's checking out today. Empty-handed.'

'You think maybe our luck's changing?'

He smiled cheesily. 'I'm not one to talk about luck. I used all mine up on the day I met you.'

'Please don't make me bring my breakfast back up. This is a new dress.'

As they approached Jack Milan's palatial suburban abode, Beckman instinctively checked out the chimney.

It seemed in excellent condition, metaphorically shutting the stable door after the horse had bolted into a mysterious interdimensional portal in search of non-existent treasure.

Less of a horse, more of an ass.

He makes Jack look like a reasonable guy.

The reasonable guy met them at the porch. He wore an expression of a man who has been told by the daughter he loves (but has his horns permanently interlocked with) that she's coming over, with no reason given.

When Lolita got within six feet and opened her arms wide for a hug, poor Jack Milan must have thought Stepford were making Daughters now as well.

'Nixon comes to China,' she announced.

Jack cocked his head, unsure. He didn't take up the hug offer.

Beckman held his breath. At this rate, he'd be getting enough regular practice to become a pearl diver.

'Stick to Egyptology, honey. I think I'd be Nixon, and you'd be China,' Jack said.

Lolita's arms flapped down. 'There's always something I do wrong, isn't there?'

'What's this about?'

She shook her head. 'Never mind.' She turned back to Beckman and took the first pace away from the house.

'Would China like to come in for pancakes? I just made a batch.'

Come on, honey. (1) I can't hold my breath much longer, and (2) you do love pancakes.

Beckman had never seen the inside of Jack's place, and if that wasn't a cutting edge, supercomputer-powered barometer of Lolita's relationship with her father, nothing was.

It had an understated luxury, the kind of place where nothing looks over-the-top fancy, but you don't recognise any of the brands because they're not in your price range. Nevertheless, Beckman didn't begrudge Jack his lifestyle, as the guy had worked for decades building Milan Enterprises into the kind of business which stood a chance of surviving an impromptu gutting and filleting by his once future son-in-law.

They stood at the kitchen island.

Jack drank his coffee. It was in a mug bearing the faded legend "WORLD'S BEST FATHER".

Alanis Morissette missed a real trick by not including that little gem in her song.

Has Jack done it deliberately—today, or does he daily cling onto such a heinously wide-of-the-mark belief?

'Is this kiss-and-make-up on account of your near-death experience?' Jack asked.

Why did some people make reconciliations so damn hard?

Like you ever tried.

Lolita chewed the pancakes and gave Jack the evil eye. 'You told Walter to put Carlton in the dog house.'

Jack shrugged. 'It took a lot for Walter to agree to your merger. I had a vision of a saboteur in the machine, a puppet-master in waiting. Hell, look what Carlton tried before. I didn't want Walter making the same mistake I did.'

'Or I did.'

'I can't promise it'll keep the vultures from circling, but I didn't need to give him an easy win. I wanted you to succeed or fail on your own merits—because that's what *you* wanted.'

'Oh, the vulture has flown now,' she said nonchalantly, scraping up the last of her impromptu second breakfast.

'Flown?'

'He's gone into The Portal. Long story. Maybe another time.'

Jack's eyes were saucers. 'How the——? Why the——?'

'Because your daughter and future son-in-law won't give in to a bully.'

'Somebody wise told me only to pick a fight you can win. So we changed the rules of the fight,' Beckman added. 'And unless I missed something, we won.'

Quoting one asshole father in front of another one has a weird kind of circularity, doesn't it?

'With your help, Ja— dad.' Lolita face creased affectionately—a look Beckman hadn't seen in the presence of Jack.

Jack's face did likewise. 'I know I'm an ass sometimes, but I don't stretch to schadenfreude. I'm glad as hell you won. And not because it's—was—my company. Because you're my daughter.'

She searched his face. 'Do I get that hug now?'

'How do you know I won't screw it up?' Jack asked with a smirk.

'I'll risk it.'

They embraced Lolita's two-inch height advantage, augmented by the swing dress, seeming to make it more of a mother-son clasp. Beckman listened for any muttered apology on either side, but none came. Maybe this was a sufficient easing of tensions for now.

'Do I get away with saying that if you'd gone ahead and married Carlton, none of this would have happened?'

Lolita stepped back and stuck her hands on her hips. 'If I'd married Carlton, I might have debated longer about sending him into the beyond, but I'd be able to plead mental cruelty. Plus, I'd be able to asset-strip the asshole or at worst take half his everything.'

'The paintings would be a start.'

Her eyes lit up. 'Jack, I could kiss you.'

'I think it's allowed.'

So she pecked him on the cheek. As she stood there, her lips pursed. 'Something is happening on Saturday you need to know about.'

Chapter 55

'Welcome to the Cooper residence. Everyone pick a painting you like.' Lolita gestured theatrically.

They peered around the spacious hallway; Randall, Reba, Tyler, Amaryllis and Beckman.

'Oh, come on, Amaryllis,' Lolita continued, seeing the woman's doubt. 'Want me to leave an IOU?'

'It's just that....'

'There are three people here who are out of a job if we can't raise funds in the next few days. Or maybe you don't know Carlton like we do.'

'I'll also remind you whose legacy pays your bills,' Tyler added, easing one frame away from the wall.

'Gentle as mice, okay,' Lolita said. 'I don't want you wannabe Hudson Hawks scratching thousands of bucks worth off these frames.'

This time around, they legitimately borrowed one of Saul's ageing P150s with explicit intent to use it rather than deploy it as a sacrificial lamb.

Lolita cut to the chase. 'If you're agonising, I will write that IOU.'

'Just tell me to stop feeling like a heel,' Beckman replied.

'Here's the deal—when we get home, we'll compare what Carlton did to us with what we did to him. If you still feel bad, I'll write a blank check. Not that he'll ever cash it, but I know you want the principle.'

'Can I help it if you're dating a schlub?'

'Just yin to my yang.'

He switched the steering wheel to his left hand, making sure to avoid potholes that would jolt their seven-figure cargo, and laid his hand on Lolita's skirt. 'I'd assume you have a potential dealer in mind?'

'No reason not to go back to the guy who Carlton bought through previously. But there's someone else too; we've crossed paths at auctions.'

'Want me to point out Carlton is still the rightful owner? How will you work magic with the paperwork?'

'Remember how he used my password against us? I've had his signature down pat for a while. Benefits of being engaged to the guy and practising for a life together.'

Beckman took his hand off her knee. 'That means you have mine forged already too?'

She met his eyes. 'Only way to find out is to break up with me.'

'I'd get rid of you straight away anyhow. Probably push you in The Portal. Or create some fiction to make you so curious you'd go through.'

'Believe me, honey, there's nothing you could put on the other side of that door which would make me willingly go through. Remember who else is there. A whole universe of separation distance is my minimum restraining order for Carlton Cooper now.'

After offloading the paintings at Lolita's place and sending photos to both potential dealers, they dropped the pickup back to Saul's. Two crisp hundreds were pushed into the tow-trucker's hand—money they could ill-afford, but necessary investment to facilitate the sale of the paintings they hoped would repay their faith many times over.

Our Buck's was busy—the hands of the big iron wall clock read twelve-fifteen—but one customer stood out.

'Kinsey said she checked out of the hotel,' Beckman murmured.

'If her head's telling her to leave, it's fair to say her heart is having a harder time.'

Buck was standing at Dixon's table, and the two were all smiles.

'In other circumstances, she'd be a hell of an asset.'

'Hire Dixon?' Lolita's brow furrowed.

'She might be a ball-crusher, but she's good. And she's not the worst person in the world. Buck's a pretty good judge of character.'

'Yeah,' she said dismissively, 'Like little old Milan could ever afford to poach her—on a good day.'

'So let's be civil people. You rebuilt a burned bridge already today. No point in setting another one on fire. You never know when you might need a favour.'

At that point, Buck noticed them, so they walked over to exchange final pleasantries.

'Ms Lewys is leaving us,' Buck said.

(1) That's not news, and (2) Is that disappointment in your voice?

'I'm sorry your time here was wasted,' Lolita offered.

'It's certainly… an unusual set of circumstances and an unforgettable place.' Dixon's gaze briefly wandered to the proprietor.

'I suggested she shouldn't be a stranger,' Buck said.

'Pleasure, not business, would be fine,' Lolita suggested.

'Well, you won't sell, and Wanda had a backtrack, so I guess that's it. Carlton is… out of town… apparently, and if I wait for Walter to wake up, I could miss some other opportunities elsewhere. You know the type, Lolita—nasty, corporate ball-crushing, hard shell activities.' Dixon gave a knowing smile.

'It's the gooey interior I'll remember you for most,' was Lolita's rejoinder.

Dixon's smile screamed, *Touché!*

Lolita offered her hand. 'Safe trip.'

Dixon stood and took the olive branch. 'Good luck. You'll need it.'

'We're due some.'

'It could be a phone call away,' Beckman added.

If Carlton's art collection scrapes eight figures, then even you, Dixon—in your fancy triple-glazed, concrete and steel, fingerprint-security, allocated parking space, high rise office—will hear the cheers all the way across the State line.

The café door clicked open.

Wanda entered, gave Lolita and Beckman a wave, and returned her attention to her cellphone call. 'Of course I'm not reporting it. I'm drawing a line under the whole thing.' The hard wooden floor and furniture bounced her voice across the room like a thistles-deprived Tigger. 'Nobody needs to do anything. I don't want to talk about it.' She listened for a moment. 'Yes, okay, fine. Bye, dad.'

Beckman wanted the floor to open up and swallow him. Plus, Lolita for good measure. Certainly, Wanda, who must have seen something in Beckman's face—probably the fact he was white as a sheet—as she pulled the expression of a person who has just committed a major faux pas.

'Anyway,' Dixon said, 'It was good to meet you all.'

Then she left.

Chapter 56

Buck slotted the last of Bessie's cleaned nozzles back in place and gave her a pat for good measure.

He heard a tapping, checked nearby, scanned the empty room, and ended his survey at the door.

'Well, there's a thing.'

The iron wall clock stood at 5:40. The yellow neon "OPEN" in the window was off. The brown coffee cup neon wasn't dancing in the window. The interior walls were home to dull tubes of glass.

Yet, someone wanted to come in.

Buck Travis opened the door to most people, at most hours—seldom to serve them, often to simply be there for them.

This time was no different, although he had mixed feelings about doing so. He unlatched and swung open the full-height glass door, upon which a fingernail had been pecking.

'It's okay; anyone can forget to leave a tip.'

'I may be here a couple more days,' Dixon announced. 'I thought it was… polite to tell you.'

'Gooey interior?'

'Something like that.'

'Will you come in?'

'You're closed.'

'True enough. Not available for business transactions. Not true everywhere in town, I'm guessing.'

Her eyes roved his face. 'How did a smart guy like you get to be doing a job like this?'

'Gooey interior,' he said.

Silence fell, pockmarked by a passing car and the hum of the under-counter refrigerators.

'I'm not going to be popular, am I?' she asked rhetorically.

'Do you do it to be popular?'

'I do it to please the suits.'

He looked her up and down—which wasn't a chore. Five-eleven, low heels so as not to be *too* overbearing, faintest of pin-stripes in her navy pantsuit. Long brown hair, brown eyes, diamond ear studs. High cheekbones.

The suit was all he was looking at, but the rest framed it nicely enough.

'I get the irony,' she replied.

'Well,' he said with a smile, 'Can't say Sunrise won't welcome a few more tourist dollars.'

'Sunrise?'

'Yeah.'

Another awkward silence.

She thumbed over her shoulder. 'I should go tell… Kinsey?… my checkout was premature.'

'Okay.'

She flashed him a smile, moved away, and had a grip on the door handle when he said, 'Need a good place in town for dinner?'

She paused, let loose her grip, and turned back. 'Is that a line?'

'Yeah.'

She ran the numbers on that. 'Can you walk me up there?'

In Ray's, he pulled the seat out for her and took a pew opposite.

'No man ever pulled a chair out for me,' she said.

'If someone's welcome in Sunrise, they're welcome.'

'Nobody else in Sunrise pulled a chair out for me.'

'Maybe they don't know you like I do.'

'Know me?'

He shifted in his seat, masking emotional disquiet by feigning physical discomfort. 'I'm not used to this, okay?'

'You think I am?'

'I know you so well, huh?'

Her hand laid on his. 'Shall we go out and come in again?'

'That means I'd have to re-seat you, and I'm not sure you could handle the chivalry overdose—twice in two minutes.'

She laughed. 'The problem with chivalry is it's too easily faked by people with other agendas.'

'Sounds like you speak from experience.'

Dixon was about to respond when a server arrived and presented the menu, so they diverted off the main conversational road, made food-related small talk, ordered, then doubled back onto the highway.

'What convinces you I'm different?' Buck asked.

'Not sure. A feeling. Besides, we're only getting dinner. It's not verboten.'

'What other chairs were people pulling out for you? Office chairs? Bar stools?'

'Maybe for "chivalry", read "flattery".'

'When does truth slip into flattery? Or does it depend on how you view yourself? Someone with low self-esteem considers anything is flattery, regardless of how they look.'

'I'm not the worse looking woman in the world.'

'That kinda saves me a compliment,' he said with a chuckle.

'I'm okay on a date—dinner engagement—but it's after that things get tough. I guess you could say I'm difficult to handle.'

'I'll have to take your word.'

'And the four guys who've divorced me.'

Buck let out a low whistle and subconsciously sat back. While he was lost for a response, the drinks arrived, which offered valuable thinking time.

Dixon bypassed the glass and drank from the bottle. He'd imagined she'd have a cocktail, possibly drink it with a straw, or at worse, slowly sip a glass of wine. Proof positive he didn't know her at all—though the drink order was nothing compared to the discarded men who she churned in her wake.

Had he picked the wrong woman to have a soft spot for?

'Is this a warning that you're damaged goods?' he asked.

'If it is, you're the first person I'd have warned. Read into that what you will.'

'Maybe you're older and wiser now? Written the pages of history, read them back, and didn't like the stories.'

'That's poetic, Buck. But if either of us is the older and wiser, I think it's you.'

'I know so.'

'So, do you want to get the check?'

'I thought you'd be the one paying, on account of I bet you wear the pants in any relationship. Plus the corporate expense account.' He made a decent attempt at a deadpan face, but she saw through it.

'I guess we find where chivalry ends, huh?'

He lifted his bottle, and she chinked it. 'Touché.'

'So—never any Mrs Travis to be part-way chivalrous for?'

'Is this, "I show you mine, you show me yours"?'

She shrugged. 'We could talk about the weather or where you source your coffee.'

He tapped the base of the bottle on the table, ran its moist lower rim round the dark circle it had made on the napkin beer mat.

'I was engaged,' he admitted, not meeting her eye. 'Long time ago.'

'Why did she get away? Or why did she let you go?'

'Dena was… a strong person.'

'Hard shell, gooey interior?' Dixon smirked.

'And tall, brunette.'

'Maybe you need to be reading a history book too.'

'Once is a… blip. Four times is….'

'A reputation?'

He sighed. 'Not so chivalrous anymore, am I?'

'You're fine, Buck. Just fine.'

He drank some more; Dutch courage. 'Dena worked insurance here in town. We dated two years. Then she got a job offer in Phoenix. Money, car, apartment. The logical thing was for us to go there. There isn't the money in coffee and root beers, which won't be any kind of surprise to you. I was dumb enough to think that town, and me, were enough for her to stay.'

She stroked his hand again. 'I'm sorry.'

'So it was the girl or Sunrise.'

'She had to do what she thought was right.'

'We both did.'

'I hope she's as happy as you.'

He shook his head. 'No.'

'Wow—schadenfreude much?' She slugged from her bottle.

'We write,' he stated. 'We didn't fall out.'

'Write? Real pen?'

'Yeah. It comes from taking notepad orders. So, we stay in touch.'

'I guess that makes you one of a kind.'

'Everybody is one of a kind. Only some are more so.'

'Poetic. Again.'

'Dena's got the dream—the man, the two kids, the commute and the forty-hour week. Is she happy? Yeah, but maybe a little dead inside. And no, not from missing me—my head is not that big.'

'So, what's "happy" for you? Sunrise, the café, friends?'

'If you mean "do I have regrets"? No. She did what she had to; I respect that. Doesn't mean she didn't have a heart of gold. Maybe it's why I have such a spot for Lolita. Strong but not too strong. Stubborn.'

'People only do what they believe is right, best.'

Buck stroked his chin. 'Is that why you did what you did today?'

She sat back, met his eyes with some steel in hers. 'Business is business. I like Lolita too, but I have a boss to please. A quota to make.'

'You like your colleagues, your boss?'

'Not especially.'

'What would you do for people you did like?'

'It's also for Adelaide,' she stated.

'I get that, really I do. Do you think she'd want you to help the charity at all costs?'

'Do I tell you how to make the best coffee in the state?'

He sighed. 'Is this how it started with the four? Talking business politics—the beginning of the end?'

'But you and I are not even at the end of the beginning yet. Besides, I don't make my charity work public. Certainly not at work. It's hard enough being part of the white-men-in-suits brigade anyway, without them knowing I have a business on the side, and one so polar opposite to the corporate ladder-climbing bullcrap.'

'Never let them see the gooey interior, huh?'

'Only special people get to see that.'

Chapter 57

Everybody wanted alcohol. Even Amaryllis.

It was Friday. 10 a.m.

Usually, they'd at least wait until 6 p.m. Especially Amaryllis.

Maybe 5 p.m. on a Friday.

Instead, Buck served them all their various choice of coffees: Beckman black, no sugar. Lolita white. Tyler black with sugar. Amaryllis a latte. Randall black with sweetener (habitually, it had been two sugars, but meeting Reba made him want to be a better man—a better man with an inch less on the belly).

'Okay, I'll say it,' Beckman calculated he'd said plenty more idiotic or inflammatory things in the past thirteen weeks, and Lolita still wore the ring on her finger. 'Who'd have thought Carlton was a big phoney?'

Lolita looked deflated: events of the last twelve hours had sapped her energy for being snippy.

'Two million is two million,' Buck said, ever one to err on the bright side.

'Kind of academic now,' Randall suggested.

Lolita nodded. 'Honestly, even after everything, I thought better of Dixon.'

'That makes one of you.'

'I'd expect you, more than anyone, to appreciate that people can change.' Lolita offered the ex-hitman a hint of The Eyebrow.

'Amen to that,' Tyler said, casting a glance to Amaryllis, who responded with a smile.

'I think you still judge her harshly,' Buck said.

'Ah, but you're biased,' Lolita pointed out.

'Says the woman who took an immediate dislike to the man she's about to get hitched to. Knee-jerk judgement is not always the best. I mean, people like Tyler and Amaryllis, who've only known me a couple of weeks, assume I'm a good-natured guy with a fatherly love for Egyptian artefact dealers and a soft spot for tall, slim, kick-ass brunettes.'

Lolita looked at him askance. 'But you are.'

'Yeah, but I also like to pull the legs off spiders.'

'You do not.'

'Okay, I don't. But you get my point.'

She was perplexed. 'What point?'

'Pardon me?'

'What point?'

'What were we talking about again?'

Tyler interjected. 'We were trying to figure out whether you took Dixon home last night.'

Buck was taken aback. 'That was absolutely not the point. Even if it was, I resent the implication.'

'Because she'd spent the afternoon screwing someone else over?' Lolita asked. 'Like your favourite Kinda Daughter.'

'I'm sure it wasn't designed like that.'

'Now she's called in the cavalry, and because Carlton was a *big* fan of forged artwork to impress gullible people—yes, me included—we have no chance of matching GigantiCorp's offer. Definitely not by the end of today. You have to say this about her—she's a pretty patient fisherman, but she reels in the line like a Bulgarian weightlifter. And I do mean a female one.'

'GigantiCorp's raiding party is not in town yet,' Beckman noted.

'Baby, I love you, but we need to take a hint. We leant on this town already. I'm not duct-taping Saul in his bathroom so he can't pick them up. I'm not taking our line of dumpsters out and scattering glass shards over every road into town. We're not giving up on Milan, only on the merger. Maybe this buys time to bootstrap ourselves for when Dixon rides into town again, and we can kick her ass for a second time. Because she sure as hell deserves it.'

Buck held up a defensive hand. 'You're still being harsh. She's not that one-dimensional.'

Lolita set her coffee down hard. 'Problem is, you're not looking at the same dimension we are. I thought you were on our side.' She rose from the table and left.

Everyone exchanged glances.

Buck scooped up the empty vessels. 'It doesn't mean anything unless she's tried to throw you out of town—that right, Beckman?'

He nodded. This was a mere scratch in relationship terms. For Milan Enterprises, though? A deeper cut. More than ever, Beckman wanted to drown his sorrows. It was over.

Buck went back to his bar.

'We should be leaving too.' Tyler rose. Amaryllis followed suit.

'How come?' Beckman asked.

'Something to take care of.'

'Weekend away?'

Jeez, insinuate much?

'Something to take care of back at the office. Maybe see you later if we get it fixed up.'

'Thanks for everything, Tyler, Amaryllis.'

'We only scratched the surface. You pretty much took a bullet for us, remember?'

Randall coughed nervously.

'Yeah, well, a lot of water under the bridge since then,' Beckman suggested.

'And more to come.' Tyler nodded, touched a hand in the small of Amaryllis back, and guided her towards the door.

The ripples of circumstance died away. Just the low hubbub of the morning coffee crowd, the clink of mugs and glasses, the hisses and thunks of Bessie at work. And the spectre of doom fairly blotting out the skyline.

'Are they going together?' Randall asked.

'Tyler and Miss B?'

'Yeah.'

'Search me. Where's a good detective when you need one?'

Randall nodded his head towards the door. 'Reba is out of town, an errand for Buck.'

'What kind of errand?'

'What do I look like—a detective? She's out of town, an errand for Buck.'

'What kind of errand?'

'I've got it—if Milan doesn't work out, maybe you try stand-up?' Randall smirked over the rim of his coffee cup.

'Sure. As soon as there's something in life to laugh about,' he replied dejectedly.

'We figured it out before—we can do it again.'

'Are you Chief Motivator now Buck has the hump with us because we cast aspersions on his girlfriend?'

'Girlfriend? Are they going together? He was pretty clear about that. I'm not sure even I'd argue with him.'

'Guess we'd need a detective to be sure if they were or not.'

'Reba is out of town, an errand for Buck.'

'What kind of errand?' Beckman asked with a smile.

'What do I look like—a detective? She's out of town, an errand for Buck.'

'What kind of errand?'

'She's on a year-long road trip to find someone who'll laugh at your act.'

'We could do with the brains back here,' Beckman said.

'Why—you and I not good enough to come up with a way out on our own?'

'Is that a poorly camouflaged way of saying we shoot Dixon and her guys before they get to Walter to sign the papers? By which I mean, *you* shoot them. By which I'm not suggesting we do shoot them because it would be putting the gun to my own head, marriage-wise, or possibly even more terminally.'

'You could deny all knowledge. Say I went rogue; you tried to stop me.'

'Sometimes, Randall, I wonder if you're cured of your old habits.'

Randall downed the rest of his coffee. 'It's like riding a bike. You never really forget.'

'Then I'll make sure never to cross you.'

'Good plan, buddy.' Randall tapped a heavy hand on Beckman's shoulder. 'Good plan.'

Chapter 58

Sunrise had once had a blacksmith. Not back in old times, but up until Buck was a young man. When he casually told people about Sam White, there was enough romance and potential embellishment that not everyone believed Sam ever existed.

The five-foot diameter, finely-wrought timepiece in Our Buck's was a testament to the facts. It hung on the wall opposite the long wooden bar, so Buck could see it easily and be reminded it had been an engagement present from Sam. The poor guy had had a hard time covering his excitement that his daughter had escaped the low-rent small-town life for a career in the big city, even if it meant he wouldn't be spending long hours hammering out a subsequent wedding present.

The hour hand nudged 2.

The café door opened to two guys in suits.

'Back home, the garage would have the courtesy to run me up the street,' one sniped.

'Not sure I want ol' Dr Hook there driving me anywhere more than I need,' replied the other.

Oh joy, Buck thought, GigantiCorp do most of their hiring directly at the swamp's edge.

'Two coffees, buddy,' called the first, heading to a table.

Each unbuttoned their jackets, loosened their ties a notch and pulled out their cellphones. Both then found, to their surprise, they had no signal, and had to put up with something as old fashioned as talking. Plus, admiring the array of neons which decorated the place, much to their amusement.

Buck took his own sweet time making their coffees, wondering whether to call up Saul and tell him to add twenty percent to their tire bill for good measure.

Dixon walked in. She saw her colleagues, saw Buck, and debated which to choose. Gingerly she approached the barista.

'I was never here for a popularity contest,' she said.

'You still have one fan.'

'You're very sweet, Buck.'

'You are too. Somewhere.'

She leant on the bar. 'None of this hurts Lolita—you get that?'

'Not exactly. But you could have given her another week. Would that be so hard—staying in town a mite longer?'

'You know it wouldn't.'

'So why call in,' Buck nodded towards the newcomers, 'Curly and Moe?'

'Actually, it's Brandon and Corey. The one on the left, trying hard not to look at me, is Brandon.'

'Because he's a sexist pig running the errands of a mere woman?'

'Because he's one of the four.' She gave Buck a "They're the breaks" shrug.

'That's a nice reward for your efforts from on high—sending him on the raiding party.'

'Compared to Cooper, the guy's a pussycat. Asshole, but still a pussycat.'

'Business is business, though, huh?' he said pointedly.

Her forehead wrinkled in sadness. 'Maybe I can dream that one day you'll forgive me.'

'Maybe one day I'll be the kind of guy you want forgiveness from. Either you're a magician with blusher, or you slept fine last night.'

'What do you want me to say, Buck? I lay awake rubbing my hands together with glee because I rode roughshod over hopes and dreams? I'm that cold? Or dinner with you made me regret seeing Walter because it torpedoed any hope of us being friends?'

'What I think is maybe in your head the Venn diagram—you business folk like that kind of thing—has no overlap between business and friends. They are parallel worlds.' He shook his head. 'Not in Sunrise.'

'You know why I do it? For the greater good.'

'Absolutely. For Adelaide. For love, in a roundabout way. Because, deep down, you're a good person.'

She looked at her two colleagues. 'Well, I score better than some, I reckon.'

He slid her coffee over. 'Into the lions' den, go on— you have a five o'clock deadline.'

He watched her go—partly to see how she carried herself emotionally, partly to watch her physically—and sensed a struggle.

He busied himself at the counter, making more beverages and snacks, keeping the place clean, waiting on the ten or so occupied tables. Still, his attention was never far from the trio, trying to interpret, perhaps catch the odd word, find a chink in their collective amour.

Could he save Lolita's business?

Fifteen minutes later, they rose, the one who wasn't an ex-Mr D Lewys tossed a few notes on the table, and they headed for the exit. She managed to flick Buck a sheepish smile.

The door banged open.

'Phew, we caught you,' Lolita puffed.

The two suits eyed her and Beckman with curiosity.

'Caught us?' Dixon asked warily.

'Yeah. You're seeing Walter, right?'

'You know we are. What's it to you? Is this an intervention? Going with strong-arm now, Lolita? Last throw of the dice? Ask daddio over there to roll his sleeves up for you?'

'Violence is never the answer,' Beckman reassured her.

Lolita nodded. 'You won't have got the message. Walter's doc said he should get plenty of air, so he went for a spot of fishing.'

'Fishing?' one of the two nondescript jocks said. 'We've got a damn meeting!'

'You think a businessman like Walter Whack hasn't got a fishing lodge on the lake for times like this?'

'The lake?' Dixon queried.

'What, a week in town, and you expect to know every inch, Ms Lewys?' Lolita sniped.

'Okay, where is it?' the other portfolio-clutching navy woollen mix asked.

Lolita handed them a scrap of paper. 'Go past the end of the road. It's a couple of miles on a rough track. So take it easy—you don't want to need Saul again, huh?'

Dixon was suspicious. 'What's this about?'

'Just trying to do the right thing. Have someone explain that to you some time. Maybe these friends of yours.'

'They're not—' Dixon began. She took a deep breath, found some humility. 'Thank you.'

Beckman and Lolita nodded wordlessly, stood aside and let the GigantiCorp trio out of the café. The door had barely clunked into the jamb when Buck strode purposefully over. 'What are you doing?'

'You think this was an easy decision?' Lolita replied.

'You might have consulted me.'

'You made your views *very* clear.'

Buck eased in closer and lowered his voice. 'Why do you think I took her for dinner last night?'

'Because you're a good-natured guy with a soft spot for tall, slim, kick-ass brunettes. Whatever their moral compass.'

Beckman had never felt tension between the two before. Was this what disagreements on Mount Olympus were like?

Buck's teeth set on edge. He shook his head. 'Because I thought I could get through to her. Reason with her. Appeal to her good nature.'

'That gooey inside of hers is a construct. At best, it's cold, icy slush.'

The amateur staring competition lasted a few seconds, then Buck broke off, pushed past, threw open the door and set off down the street at a pace laudable for a man his size.

Beckman grabbed the door at its zenith and stepped out onto the sidewalk. Fifty yards away, Buck executed a half-decent sidestep to avoid Amaryllis as she rose from the low-slung Porsche.

'I thought only real fathers were cut out to be assholes,' he suggested.

'Unless sometimes it's the daughter,' Lolita replied.

Tyler and Amaryllis walked up. He was carrying a briefcase.

Tyler and a briefcase? Really? Next up, he'll be using a trouser press and spouting words like "synergy" and "leverage".

'Sunrise half-marathon today?' Tyler enquired with a grin.

'Watch the cafe, folks.' Lolita grabbed Beckman's hand. 'But don't break Bessie, or Buck will break you.'

With that, Beckman's hand was tugged, and he found himself jogging. Within a minute, mercifully—as Mr Oswin would concur—they caught up with Buck, Dixon and her sidekicks.

'Buck, this is important, okay?' Dixon said. 'I'll see you tonight—if you'll let me. If you even want to.'

'You don't need to go,' Buck puffed.

The suits eyed Buck with amused disbelief.

Small-town asshole, they're probably thinking.

Well, they have them in the cities too, you know.

'It's a meeting. Just a meeting. We do them every day. I know this one's not to your taste, but we can't always get what we want.'

'No,' Buck replied, 'But we can try. Sometimes once. Sometimes maybe four times.'

Dixon scanned Buck's face.

'Problem, Dixon?' Suit Number One asked.

She snapped out of it. 'No, come on.' They turned and walked away down the hill.

Buck's shoulders dropped an inch, and he faced his friends.

Lolita stepped forwards and, for the second time in two days, broke a deadlock. She put a hand on Buck's chunky upper arm. 'Sometimes, you can't stop a girl from leaving.'

'She wants what she wants,' Beckman added with a shrug.

'She's wrong,' Buck replied.

'She doesn't have the monopoly on being wrong.' Lolita took Buck's hand. 'I'm sorry.'

'And you don't have the monopoly on not giving up.' He turned and broke into a jog.

Lolita winked at Beckman. 'Looks like time to make Mr Oswin proud.'

Chapter 59

They arrived, all at a breathless quick walk, at Saul's garage.

On the forecourt, an engine fired, and a black four-seat convertible rolled away. As it did so, the electric roof retracted, revealing three occupants and their laughter.

Buck lunged forwards, but Beckman grabbed his arm and pulled him back.

Buck spun, glowered. Beckman momentarily feared for his life, or at worst his chances of having children, but Buck saw reason and softened his posture. He scanned the forecourt, trotted over to the gleaming red convertible, its hood stowed, and peered inside.

Jeez, not again. Saul's only just put the trim back.

But the keys were in the ignition: Wanda must have been due.

Buck swung open the driver's door.

'Buck!' Lolita cautioned, stopping six feet away. The response was a dismissive look. She muttered, 'Aw, screw it,' and flung open the passenger door.

Beckman was on her heels in an instant, and she scrambled into the adult-unfriendly rear bench. The 289cu engine woofed into life, and five seconds later, they were on Main Street.

'Do I bother asking what you're doing?' Lolita said.

'When I know, I'll tell you.'

The target car was out of sight, but they knew where it was heading and were more familiar with the city streets.

Five minutes later, they had it in their sights.

It swung onto Latrop.

Buck heeled the Mustang over, its tires squealing on the hot asphalt, and gunned the engine.

Beckman grabbed the door handle and hoped Lolita did likewise, as he had a sneaky feeling what would happen next.

They flashed past the German ass-wagon, gave it plenty of stopping room for its cutting-edge fancy-pants brakes to cope with, then Buck yanked hard on the handbrake and slewed the fifty-year-old Pony car across the road.

Shaken like three Polaroid pictures, the occupants watched and smelled the smoke die away across the barren vista. Beckman turned away so the others couldn't see he'd closed his eyes.

In case Saul has been a legend and got in a pre-emptive strike by cutting their brake lines.

But the Teutonic *businesswagen* came to rest with minimal drama—certainly much less than Buck's Ken Block masterclass in mechanical torture.

They'd stopped two hundred yards from the end of the road. Buck jumped out. Beckman slowly exited and let his fiancée uncoil herself from the rear pillbox. They followed Buck to his quarry.

'This better be good, Buck,' Dixon said, looking out from the pristine leather of the rear seats.

Beckman checked the mood of the other two occupants: even less tolerant.

'You... er... didn't pay for your coffee,' Buck said.

Huh?

'Pardon me?' Dixon's forehead creased.

'Or I could stand you the cost. You know, as a friend.'

In response, she dug out her purse, fiddled around, and came out with an Alexander Hamilton. 'You think I never do the right thing? Especially for... friends?'

Buck took the note. 'So, these guys need babysitting?'

'It's my deal. Was that not clear?'

He nodded. 'It not wait until Monday?'

'No. Sorry.'

'Then,' he looked towards the end of the road, 'Say hello to Adelaide.' He turned away, resignation in his face.

'What did you say?'

He turned back. 'You might catch up with Adelaide, down that way. That's all.'

Beckman's heart thumped. Admittedly not as much as during his enforced sprint down Main Street, but not dissimilar to the previous two times he'd been standing stock still on this particular stretch of road.

Pinky and Perky in the front seats didn't have a clue what Buck was blathering on about. They only cared about agenda points and signatures and digital zonal aircon.

'Why do you say that?' Dixon asked.

'Because business is not just business. And friends are… not just friends.'

She looked in their direction of travel, at Buck, Beckman, and Lolita. Lastly, at her two companions. Realisation dawned. 'You've got this, right?'

'Huh?' said the one who was a previous more-than-just-friend of Dixon's.

'It's a slam dunk. Walter's a pussycat. You can do the paperwork. Might catch some more fish besides him.' She grabbed the door handle. 'I have to get back to the hotel.'

'The hotel?' queried the other.

She stepped out, smoothed clothes down over her slim frame. 'There's a first time for everyone, boys. The undiscovered country.'

'If you think it's what's best?'

She slammed the door. 'Absolutely.'

'Come on, Brandon, let's wrap up this sucker.' Corey touched the gas pedal, the smart-aleck Stop-Start fired, and he eased the car across the road, onto the scrub margin, past the Mustang, and retook the roadway.

Then, because he'd been told he was stepping up to be a big boy now, he dropped a cog for the benefit of his audience and accelerated away.

Lolita squeezed Beckman's hand.

The car vanished.

The exhaust note of the straight-six stopped as if guillotined.

The near-silence was eerie.

'Jesus,' Dixon breathed. She was paler than usual. Less composed. More… human. The Portal did that to mere mortals, even those with hard shells.

She gazed, open-mouthed, at the thing that was impossible to see. The cicadas did their cicada thing, oblivious.

'It's true.' She moved closer to Buck. 'You just…' She glanced at The Portal again. 'Why did you do that? Warn me?'

Buck sought answers in Beckman and Lolita's faces. Then in Dixon's. Suddenly the wise old bear didn't seem so wise after all.

Then he stepped in and kissed her on the cheek. Stepped back.

Probably awaiting the Ol' Slaperoo.

'Why did you get out of the car?' he asked.

She thought for a second. Then she kissed him. Not on the cheek.

'Just another regular day in a regular town,' Beckman murmured. Lolita tugged his hand, and they walked over.

'And why did you help him?' Dixon asked.

In response, Lolita kissed Buck on the cheek. So as not to feel left out, Beckman did the same. That wrought another expression Beckman hadn't ever seen on Buck's face.

'Well, if I'd known there was competition….' Dixon chirped.

'I'm sure you know better than any of us about coming out on top,' Lolita replied.

'We offer you a ride?' Beckman suggested. Mainly because it was long past root beer time, and he'd damn well earned it.

Dixon pointed at The Portal. 'So we just…?'

'We "just" once before. It seemed to work.'

'Are they… dead?'

'Hell no,' Lolita said, chuckling. 'What are we, monsters? Hard shell, gooey inside—remember? And these two?' She cocked a thumb at the two men. 'Gooey all the way through.'

Not sure I'm one hundred percent happy with the implication, but this is neither the time nor the place.

'Could they come back?'

'We guessed not.'

'Guessed?'

'Yes. We made it back out okay, but we have a good idea why.'

'If they return, I'm out on my ass,' Dixon warned. 'Brandon especially will squeal. Reminds me of Carlton.'

Beckman pulled a sheaf of paper from his pocket. 'We might have a guarantee.'

Buck looked on curiously. 'The whoever-built-it people gave you an instruction manual?'

'Our best guess is it's a one-way valve for secrets and dishonesty,' Lolita said.

'Call me a pen-pushing, facts-and-figures, hard-ass, but there's a lot of 'maybes' and 'guesses' here,' Dixon said.

'I see the worm has done a full one-eighty,' Buck suggested.

'All I'm saying is, you wanted them to go in there for a reason. Me too, I guess.'

'If it wasn't for Mr Gooey here,' Lolita replied. 'But, yeah. It's the ultimate backwater.'

'I'd be right in thinking Carlton is in there?'

'Probably lying and cheating as we speak.'

'So you don't want him back out.'

'Hence this.' Beckman held up the paper.

Dixon reached out, and he passed it over. She unfolded it. 'Escher's "Relativity"?'

'We figured that if The Portal filters truth and lies, perception and reality, it could be short-circuited. Sealed up.'

Dixon let the paper fall to her side, recoiled a half-step. 'Permanent imprisonment.'

'That's the idea,' Lolita confirmed.

'Assuming they're still alive.'

'There's air, landscape, plants. Hell, there may even be people—we didn't hang around to find out.'

'Survivable?'

'These guys are successful business people, remember. Carlton can shoot. Hell, we even tossed a gun in there. They have transport. It's a damn sight better starting position than you get on most team-building weekenders. Who knows—they may even start a new civilisation.'

'Three guys?' Beckman wondered.

'Details, details,' Lolita replied.

Dixon eyed the three of them, then The Portal.

'Or you go in there, give them the passcode, come back out,' Buck said. 'Give Carlton that job. Get that nice car back.'

'Or go through,' Lolita shrugged. 'Stay. Break new ground. Form a conglomerate.'

'Be a lot easier for them to start that new civilisation,' Beckman murmured.

'You wouldn't get that merger done. Couldn't collect your finder's fee bonus.'

Dixon looked at Buck, turned and walked towards The Portal.

Buck took a step, but Lolita grabbed his arm and tugged him back. 'No you don't,' she said. He could have dragged her along like a child's doll, but he stopped.

Dixon reached the end of the road, maybe a metre shy of the blacktop's edge, and inspected the air with the curiosity of an apparent lunatic.

Buck clutched Lolita's hand and swallowed it in his.

Then Dixon stretched out her arm and waved the paper violently.

A crackle of blue sparks engulfed the paper, and it winked out. Dixon toppled back and clattered to the ground. Buck dashed over and scooped her up.

Beckman and Lolita followed at a trot.

Happy now, Oswin? I've barely stopped all day.

Lolita scoured the ground at the road's margin and picked up a handful of gravel. Buck and Dixon backed away, arms around each other.

She tossed the stones in a wide arc.

They all landed about six feet away.

Chapter 60

Lolita insisted Beckman drive them all back into town. She didn't need a sixth sense to appreciate his barely-bottled, kid-in-a-candy-store excitement at the prospect of meeting—from the Actual Driver's Seat this time—one of his childhood heroes.

He drove it like a Faberge egg—if Mr Faberge had ever produced V8-powered jewelled eggs, which he very much doubted.

And every spare millisecond he wasn't being careful not to wrap ex-Carlton's prized possession around some motionless part of Sunrise, he spent working out how the hell to prise it from Wanda's grasp.

He carefully nosed it into a spot near Our Buck's and rotated the key to the Off position.

'Whatever you want, it's on the house,' Buck announced from the passenger seat.

'It would be pretty churlish to turn down an invitation like that,' Beckman replied, climbing out.

Each man helped his belle un-squish themselves from the back seat and escorted them to the café. Lolita nodded at her Kinda Father and his apparent new squeeze and flashed Beckman a look of unconcealed warmth.

There has to be a hitch, doesn't there? What did we forget? Why do I think we're forgetting something important?

'I don't think we'll be on Walter's Christmas list for a long time,' he suggested.

'It's for the best. He just doesn't know it yet. EVI got along without a Big Brotherly arm around it for thirty years already. Like we did.'

'You expect us to last another thirty? Did you forget our bank manager is on a mug full of Prozac a day?'

She shot him The Eyebrow. 'Don't spoil today, Beckman. Let's have a happy spell.'

'You're right.' He kissed her. 'We're on the downslope.'

He was only half-surprised to see Tyler duly standing behind the coffee bar, tidying. He hoped the guy had had the sense to leave Bessie alone. In the intervening hour, a few customers may have been pissed off at not being able to have their coffees, but their disquiet would have been nothing compared to Buck's reaction if his beloved coffee apparatus had been damaged at the hand of a novice.

Beckman was pretty sure Tyler could function quite happily for the rest of his days with the asshole God had already provided. A second would be redundant, and its creation might scare some loyal customers away.

Tyler beckoned Buck over and slipped off the apron. Dixon patted Buck on the arm and let him go.

Amaryllis approached. She wore an apron too; it bore the word Lolita on the breast.

'Hope you don't mind.'

'It was never mine,' Lolita replied.

Tyler was conversing with Buck and pointing towards the back room, then beckoned Amaryllis over.

'Sorry, back to work.' She took off the apron, folded it neatly and handed it to its non-owner.

The Pegasus twosome disappeared into the back room—the sticky-floored, dishevelled mess where Beckman and Lolita had been forced to conceal themselves a few days previously.

The door closed.

'You think they'd at least get a hotel room,' Beckman quipped.

Lolita smacked him on the arm. 'You have a one-track mind, Beckman Spiers.'

'Not at all. At the minute, the only thing I want to get my lips around is a root beer.'

Lolita rolled her eyes at Dixon. 'Men, huh?'

'You got lucky, Lolita. Mine cheated with more than root beer.'

They went to the bar, where Buck was earnestly tapping, slapping, turning and spurting with his longtime companion.

'I think yours might cheat on you with a thirty-year-old in a moment,' Lolita said. 'He loves it when she gets all hot and steamy.'

'Don't think I don't hear every word, Lolita Milan,' Buck retorted.

The door to the back room opened. Beckman checked his watch. 'I kinda figured that about Tyler. The guy doesn't know the meaning of foreplay.'

Lolita and Dixon gave him a stereo whack on the arms.

Amaryllis approached. She was very... secretarial. 'Mr Quittle would like to see you, Miss Milan, Mr Spiers.'

Beckman snorted. '*Mr Quittle?*'

Lolita gave him The Eyebrow. So he whacked himself on the arm for good measure.

'In the back room?' Lolita's voice was edged with curious amusement.

'It's not salubrious, but we hope it'll suffice.' Amaryllis waved them, usherette-style, in the right direction.

Beckman left Dixon with, 'If we're not out in an hour, call 911.'

Amaryllis closed the door behind them.

Two weak bulbs lit the room. Four chairs, all different, were arranged around a stack of upturned apple boxes. It smelled of stale coffee, and the floor was still tacky from spilt soda dating back who-knows-how-many years.

Tyler rose and offered his hand. Nonplussed, they both shook. He waved them to chairs, and they all sat.

Maybe the back room is another portal? To a dimension where Tyler and Dixon have switched places, or everyone is permanently playing The Apprentice, only on a dime budget.

Tyler clicked open the briefcase on the makeshift table and withdrew a thin sheaf of paper.

Beckman glanced at Lolita for answers, only to find she was also seeking them from him.

Tyler laid the paper on the briefcase and turned it towards them. 'The Pegasus Corporation has decided to diversify. We're keen to explore new business ventures. To that end, we wondered whether you would be amenable to offering a stake in Milan Enterprises?'

Beckman laughed. Except it wasn't a joke.

Lolita cleared the lump in her throat. 'These are the terms?' She tapped a finger on the paper.

'Silent partnership,' Amaryllis replied.

'Why?' Beckman asked.

Ooh, look—a gift horse! Now, where's its mouth?

'Money in a safe is no use to anyone,' Tyler replied. 'Money in a stable, growing business is something else.'

'Growing,' Lolita scoffed.

'It could,' Tyler insisted. 'With the right resources.' He passed the paper for Amaryllis to hold, then turned the case around and opened it.

Lolita squeezed of Beckman's hand—borne of excitement, or to strangle the Amaryllis-unfriendly expletives in his throat?

'How much?' Lolita's voice cracked.

'Twenty-five million.' Tyler met Beckman's stupefied gaze. 'You hated me for twelve years, then repaid it by giving me your apartment, getting rid of the boss, and pretty much taking a bullet. This is not a gift. This is an investment.'

'Business is business,' Lolita muttered.

'I get it,' Beckman replied.

Tyler offered his hand. 'So, do we have a deal?'

'This is all very… formal, Tyler,' Lolita said. 'What's the catch?'

'You talked about a… Welcome Committee for potential new residents. Say we… I,' he corrected himself quickly, 'Wanted an apartment in town. As a bolt hole. Could you… put in a good word?'

Beckman assessed Amaryllis reaction to the words and the misstep: nothing bar a small smile.

Lolita eased her hand out to meet Tyler's and held it just short. 'Subject to looking over the contract, of course.'

'Of course,' Tyler said with due seriousness.

'Then, yes.' Lolita shook his hand.

Amaryllis took up the case, slid the papers inside and clicked the locks closed. Tyler stood. Beckman shook his hand. 'You're a stand-up guy.'

Tyler shrugged. 'Business is business.'

'But friends are friends,' Lolita added, popping a kiss on Tyler's cheek. Then she embraced Amaryllis.

Beckman caught Amaryllis' eye, and didn't know how to play it.

A kiss would be just too weird. Today—no, this week—no, this summer—has been off the chart crazy already.

He gave her a restrained clasp.

They exited back into the main room, where Dixon was atop a bar stool, her jacket cast across the adjacent seat in uncharacteristic abandon.

The room was otherwise empty. The welcoming neon in the door had been extinguished.

The museum piece on the wall stood at quarter after four.

Since when did Buck early close on a weekday? Was this… an intervention?

He noticed the champagne flute in Dixon's hand.

Ah. To the victors, the spoils.

Except somebody hadn't read the script.

A familiar face knocked on the door pane. Buck trudged over and allowed her in.

'Saul says you've been joyriding.'

Buck pulled the Mustang's keys from his pocket. 'You know he didn't.'

'All the same, how about asking permission?'

'I promise you, Wanda, we took good care. Saul wanted a road test check anyway. Not a scratch on it.'

'Like I care. Museum piece. Carlton loved that thing more than he did me. Be glad to see the back of it.'

Beckman's ears pricked up, but before he intervened, Wanda had the next target in her sights.

'And what the hell happened to your meeting?' she demanded of Dixon.

'We hit a….' Dixon looked round at Beckman and Lolita, who'd stopped a few paces away. '…Bump in the road. GigantiCorp withdraws its offer.'

'Withdraws?!'

'We might point out you withdrew your own offer not a day ago,' Lolita said.

'What kind of cockamamie organisation is this? Hokey-cokey with whoever is flavour of the day.'

'I couldn't, in good conscience, take the buyout forward,' Dixon said. 'Other considerations made it not… good business.'

'So,' Wanda threw up her arms, 'We're dead in the water. Back to square one.' She jabbed her thumb towards Lolita. 'Montagues and the Capulets. All due respect.'

'Sure, Wanda. Let's scrap it out.' Lolita reached out a hand towards Amaryllis, who filled it with the handle of a suitcase. Lolita hefted it flat, clicked the locks, spun it around and pulled open the lid. 'Or maybe we can come to another arrangement.'

They all enjoyed seeing Wanda's chin hit the floor. She looked at them all in turn.

Lolita flapped the lid down. 'If Walter's free nine o'clock Monday, you might want to book a few hours out.'

Wanda's eyes went from saucers to slits, then to normal. 'I guess. Fine.'

'There's goodwill you owe us. From before,' Lolita reminded her.

'Okay, okay.'

'Nine o'clock. Your offices. We'll bring donuts and greenbacks.'

'And I hope you'll cut our interim FD some slack. He's no Carlton.'

'If only you had an independent, qualified accountant on-hand,' Dixon chimed.

Wanda was taken aback. 'And why the hell would you do that?'

'Because I owe you for cancelling our meeting, and I owe Lolita for... something else. So I'll make sure it's fair all around. Who better to broker the deal?'

Wanda bit her lip. 'I guess.'

'And if it works out, who knows? I hear you have a vacancy at FD level.'

Buck, catalysed to motionlessness, reached out a hand for support and found something containing hot steam. He yowled. Beckman had never seen Buck suffer an injury at Bessie's doing, but he styled it out admirably.

'So, Monday at nine.' Wanda nodded curtly and left.

'We're not quite on braiding-each-others-hair terms yet,' Lolita said.

'Speaking of which, are you planning extra curls for tomorrow?' Buck asked, handing out flutes of champagne.

'Tomorrow?' Lolita queried.

'Saturday. The wedding.'

That'll be it. I knew there was something.

Lolita's hand came to her mouth. 'Oh God, Beckman. But we don't have anything fixed. Like, nothing.'

Beckman held up his hands. 'It doesn't have to be fancy, remember? No four courses, no rose petals, no million-dollar white dress, no orchestra.'

'But a venue would be good. And a pastor. And witnesses.'

'Count us in,' Dixon said with a shrug. 'If you'll have me.'

'Only accompanied, I'm sure,' Buck said to Lolita. 'Assuming you don't need me to walk you up the aisle anymore.'

Her disappointment was evident; rebuilding the bridge with Jack had unexpectedly denied Buck a day he'd dreamed of for years.

She laid a hand on his. 'Buck, I'm sorry.'

'It's no big deal. I can bring other things to the party. Like the rest of this booze.'

'Yeah, but a party where?' Beckman asked. After all, they could drink almost anywhere, but they couldn't get married in the middle of the street.

'Luck would have it, I had… cause to get this place approved for marriage licenses.' Buck glanced around the room, past the clock, to Dixon, whereupon he became self-conscious and flashed an awkward smile.

'Get married here?' Lolita asked.

'You said "nothing fancy".'

She embraced him. 'It's perfect.'

'So, I already fixed up some other things, pastor and whatnot. Just need your Best Man and Maid of Honour.'

She looked at Beckman. He looked at Buck. Buck looked at Lolita. Beckman looked at Lolita. They both looked at Tyler and Amaryllis.

Pennies dropped with fierce speed.

Tyler held up a warning hand. 'It's supposed to be a longtime friend, Beckman.'

'Twelve years is long enough. Maybe only twelve weeks on the "friend" part, but I'm pretty sure Saul is fixed up to be driver, and Buck has done enough. So, you're up, buddy.'

'Wow. Okay.'

'Consider it the least we can do as thanks.' Lolita patted the briefcase.

Amaryllis was a rabbit in the headlights. 'But you've lived here your whole life, Lolita. I'm…'

'In the wrong place at the wrong time.' Lolita laid a hand on her shoulder. 'Plus, I'll buy you a new dress. With your money.'

Beckman checked the clock: twenty after four. 'Shop closes at five.'

Amaryllis caught his smile. 'Oh hell, why not?'

Chapter 61

Lolita carefully brushed Amaryllis' hair. 'Beckman tells me we'd have needed to start all this yesterday if you still had that whole mess going on.'

'I can't deny it was a time strain. I should have bought shares in Pantene.'

Lolita chuckled. 'Amaryllis, you're a real one.'

'And the same to you.'

'I'm curious —the beehive—why? Although I may not be the best person to challenge someone's style.'

'On day one at Pegasus, I had it long. Malvolio told me to tie it up. I liked it long. Every day he wanted it up. And you know Malvolio—when he says "Jump", you ask, "How high?".'

'And when he says hairstyle, you say "This high"!'

They laughed.

'Were you always going to do her hair, whoever sat here?' Amaryllis stroked the arm of the dressing table chair. She was sitting at an angle to the 1950s (or at least 1950s-style) table, with its triple mirror and bowed legs.

'I doubt it. We'd be in a hotel somewhere, a few blocks down from a fancy venue.'

'Maidens ministering to your needs, as the flowing white dress hung from the wardrobe?'

'So you do dream like other women?' Lolita caught Amaryllis' reflection in the mirror and smiled.

'To not dream is to be dead inside.'

'I hear you.'

'So if you've been planning this long, even with… that other fiancé, where is the person who *should* be in this seat? Not that I'm not flattered and happy, but as I said, you grew up here. Where's the… Pink Ladies?'

'You know what, honey, the smart ones moved away— more fool them. There was never a… gang anyway. First, I was a nerd. Then I was dangerous to be around and later… I guess I intimidate women. Maybe it's the swing dresses and running my own business. Which was all aimed at Jack, but it hit plenty of targets.'

'And being so pretty.'

Lolita stopped combing, deliberately sought Amaryllis' face in the mirror. 'I don't know about that. But thanks. Probably as I speak my mind and don't suffer fools.' She resumed combing. 'Besides, you're pretty too.'

Amaryllis laughed. 'No.'

'I speak my mind.'

'Well, thank you, but not on the same scale.'

'Something is turning at least one head. Can't be a first. So—is it Maiden of Honour, or Maid of Honour?'

This time Amaryllis sought her hairdresser's face. 'First the age thing, and now my sexual history?'

'Again, I speak my mind.'

'Sometimes, I get the feeling Beckman is a brave man.'

Lolita laughed. 'So do I.'

A moment of silence. 'Lolita?'

'Yeah?'

'I don't want to come across as the old—or young, spinster—or party girl… let's say "voice of reason", but some people would say twelve weeks is not a long time.'

'It's thirteen weeks five days. But I get your drift.' Lolita stopped combing, moved around and sat on the bed to face her Maid/Maiden. 'Maybe as we're such good friends now—the kind that doesn't discuss ages or past conquests—I should be asking you for alarm bells. After all, you've known him for twelve *years*.'

'Honey, you've spent more time with him in the last thirteen weeks five days than I did behind a desk all that time. Or I damn well hope so.' Amaryllis smiled a smile that, for possibly the first time, spoke of nothing but friendship.

'So that's your blessing?'

'You don't need my blessing. You have Buck's, and that seems to be everything.'

'I have Jack's too. But he and Buck know Beckman even less than you.'

Amaryllis took Lolita's hand. 'Are you having second thoughts?'

'Call it… wondering if things are too good to be true. Whether I'm missing any important… cracks.'

'I'll say this. Women don't marry a man; they marry a project. Beckman is not the same man he was thirteen and five ago—I should know. He's not… dead inside anymore. Maybe I know a little what that feels like. So if your project's not already over, you've still done a hell of a job.'

She rubbed Amaryllis' upper arm warmly. 'He can still be an idiot sometimes.'

'I never met a man who wasn't.'

'Is that so? Lolita gave a salacious wink.

'No dice, honey.'

Lolita clicked her fingers in feigned annoyance. 'Is it us that makes them idiots? Or are they inherently kids forever?'

'You'll never change the Idiot part; just learn to love it. Like leaving the toilet seat up or noticing a younger woman's ass.'

'So you have more experience with men than me?'

'Stop fishing, Lolita, or I'll run over and tell Beckman you're too much of a nosy wisenheimer to marry.'

'The thing is, I know you well enough to be sure you wouldn't.'

They embraced.

'Come on,' Lolita said. 'Let's get me in this dress.'

Amaryllis retrieved the chosen item and helped Lolita get fixed up. 'Last night, I heard a noise outside the hotel room, and part of me hoped it was Tyler coming to visit. Is that bad?'

Lolita pulled away, half-buttoned, and turned around. 'Is it?'

'I worry I'm confusing affection with gratitude.'

'Gratitude?'

Amaryllis took Lolita's waist and turned her away to continue the buttoning. 'I see a bit of myself in Carlton.'

'Trust me, honey, you're not even in the same league.'

'All the same, one mistake and the slope only leads down. The first year I found a bounty hunter to come in for an interview with Malvolio. Then I found out what happened after. But I was caught in a lie, and I didn't know how to get out. Malvolio warned me. He said I should note well how anyone can be found—anyone with a secret. You think *I'm* strong? Not like you. I needed help. It only took twelve years.' She finished buttoning.

Lolita turned round. 'Better late than never,' she smiled. 'Like today.'

'Tyler told me he could have saved Malvolio that Monday. I didn't blame him. I was glad to get rid of the man, get out from under all that. So I owe Tyler. Always will.'

'Is that why you stayed with him? Why you saw beyond his own... less than palatable past?'

Amaryllis nodded. 'At first.'

'And now?'

The doorbell rang.

Lolita glanced at the clock. 'That's Jack. Ready?'

Chapter 62

Beckman caressed the smooth wood of the steering wheel.

'By all rights, I should be in that seat,' Tyler said.

'And if you give me my wedding gift *before* the ceremony, you think I won't drive her?'

'I had a feeling.'

'I'm not sure how I can repay you. For everything.'

'The twenty-five mill is not a gift. It's a business decision. The car? Still doesn't touch the value of your apartment.'

'Do me a favour. Consider us square, okay?' Beckman smiled. 'The Nice Guy schtick is starting to get wearing.'

'Actually, I kinda like it. I see the point of your whole honest, treating people fair, playing by the rules thing for the last twelve years.'

'Got me here, didn't it?'

Tyler slapped Beckman's thigh more than playfully, although it was meant that way. 'Enough on bragging about the soon-Mrs S. You did enough time—*we* did enough time—at the coalface to have a few years in the jacuzzi.'

'Hell, this week's been worse than twelve years.'

'So enjoy the day, Beckman, and know I'm jealous as heck,' Tyler beamed, 'Mostly about the car.'

Beckman nudged the throttle, the old iron V8 sang, and they rumbled into town.

Very little marked out that September Saturday as anything special in Sunrise, except perhaps the collective message of goodwill: the array of lights strung out across Main Street between the second storeys read "Congratulations, Lolita and Beckman.'

He got a lump in his throat but made sure Tyler wasn't aware.

Buck had put cones in the parking bays outside the café. Outside, Randall stood guard, and as the red Mustang approached, he pulled one aside, and Beckman slid gingerly in beside the kerb.

'Showtime,' Tyler said, and they hopped out.

The tables had been cleared, the chairs were in rows, and flowers had been purloined from somewhere. He recognised everyone and knew almost all their names. There were three dozen people, tops.

You never had three dozen friends in your whole life.

Maybe because you never stayed anywhere long enough. Not that it was your choice.

'Hello, Beckman.'

He froze. His stomach somersaulted, his heart did a loop-the-loop, and the rest of his organs huddled together for safety. He turned.

At least you didn't wear the uniform. That may be the deciding factor.

'Hello, dad.'

'Congratulations.'

'Afterwards, maybe. Let's not jinx it. Maybe she'll wake up and realise she's too good for me.'

'So I hear.'

'Huh?'

Someone stepped forwards. Someone exactly like Reba, only more feminine. 'Sorry, Beckman, in case I….'

'No, Reba, it's fine.' He looked at Marlon Spiers, immaculately attired in a navy suit, crew cut now longer and greying. 'You did the right thing.'

Marlon held out a folded sheet of paper.

Beckman unfolded it—a scanned photograph of Lolita, dating back about a year. She looked like her amazing self. Below it was some writing in a familiar hand; a hand more used to writing on notepads and blackboards: "Your son is marrying this woman on Saturday. She is just as incredible as she seems. Come, or don't—it's your choice."

Beckman lowered the paper. 'What else did you say to him?' he asked Reba.

'I asked him if he liked root beer.'

Marlon held up a glass. 'So even if she doesn't go through with it, it's not been a wasted trip.'

'Most of the time, dad, you're an asshole. But sometimes, you're my kind of asshole.' He smiled.

Marlon did too. 'Thanks. Son.'

A familiar paw, creator of familiar writing, landed on Beckman's shoulder. 'Pastor wants to see you.'

Buck guided him away, past a distinctly unbusinesslike Dixon, an astonishingly presentable Saul, a man-bunned Tobin, and a top-to-toe denim Clint, and into the back room.

He winced.

Hang on—Buck has a second back room?

But no. The clutter had gone, new lighting had been installed, and the floor was no longer a weak adhesive.

'Did you get any sleep last night?'

'Some,' Buck replied with a wink.

You sly old dog. But then, you earned a reward for all this.

And who's this? Chubby Checker? If not, you're in the wrong career, pal. You should be in Vegas.

Beckman met Pastor Leon Rozelle, whose voice was gravel.

He talked about Getting Married Stuff.

This is all getting very real.

Then he found himself in the main room again. People were sitting down. Buck escorted Dixon. Randall and Reba

babysat Marlon, which made Beckman feel relaxed. If
Reba had driven dad all the way from whatever base he
was currently serving on, if he spoke up during the Any
Objections part, Reba would hopefully be loyal to her
friend; shoot first, ask questions later.

*Don't be an ass, dad, just for an hour or so. That'd be some
kind of record.*

He joined Tyler front and centre.

Only now did he notice they were facing the wall where
Buck's clock habitually hung. Today it wasn't there.

In its place hung something that triggered the second,
more significant, throat lump of the day.

It was a bespoke neon, scripted "Lolita & Beckman"
with two interlocked flashing hearts.

He sought out Buck, who had spotted what Beckman
witnessed and gave a thumbs up. Beckman patted his
chest. Buck made a gesture that said, "Words—mine,
payment—Dixon" and beamed. Dixon gave a thumbs up.
Beckman was lost for an appropriate response, so went
with a thumbs up.

The pastor called him forwards. Tyler took station.
Music struck up. He didn't recognise it. He didn't care.

There were murmurs.

He turned and looked down the short makeshift aisle
towards the door.

Somebody striking was walking towards him.
Somebody very similar to what Miss Broomhead would
look like if there were such things as parallel universes.

Which there were, of course.

There was a low noise that sounded a lot like Tyler
making an exclamation Miss Broomhead wouldn't approve
of. Although this new lookalike might.

GET WITH THE PROGRAM, DUMMY!

The third lump of the day, upon seeing Lolita, was a
real chest burster.

Don't cry. Do. Not. Cry.

Dad is here.

On Lolita's arm was Jack.

Technically, the bride is generally on her father's arm, but this was Lolita, and the reverse would imply Jack was in charge. He pecked her on the cheek, eased her next to Beckman, and sat.

Amaryllis brushed past Tyler, his eyes on stalks, and sat in the front row.

The pastor began saying some Marriage Stuff. Beckman didn't hear a word of it. He was looking at what there was to see, pinching himself, trying to restrain further throat-lumps, hoping he'd remember what the pastor had told him to say earlier (even though he hadn't been listening then either), casting glances at his new friends—even Wanda, secreted in a corner—and wondering if he'd come back out of The Portal at all.

And remembering something Very Important.

Oh, snap!

He came back to reality. Vows Time was approaching.

He held up a hand. A touch nervous.

'Hold on a second,' he asked the pastor.

'Pardon?'

'Hold on a second. Please.'

Lolita gave him a wedding-appropriate version of The Eyebrow.

He flashed a weak smile. Forced himself not to look at the congregation.

He took a half-pace away from her and sank to one knee. Looked up and gently took her hand. Her face creased into a smile.

'Lolita Milan, would you do me the greatest honour in this, or any, universe, and marry me?'

She nodded firmly, beaming, voice cracking, 'I think that was the general idea. Yes.'

Out of the corner of his eye, he saw Marlon facepalm. Jack shook his head and smiled. Buck and Dixon exchanged a look of humour. Randall and Reba nodded.

He stood, desperately wanting to take Lolita in his arms and kiss her, but knowing they hadn't got to the I Now Declare, Followed By Kissing part.

Soon afterwards, it happened.

The red-letter day he thought he'd never experience.

The answer to many long years of hope, curiosity and expectation.

Amaryllis sneaked her hand into Tyler's.

She leaned in and spoke quietly, but Beckman distinctly heard, 'I'm forty-three.'

Beckman and Lolita return in

"Stow Away Zone"

in which the Sunrise trilogy concludes.

When Lolita's father dies, he leaves her a curio in his Will. It's a box, which is not to be opened unless the town faces an existential crisis.

But other people have boxes too, and they aren't prepared to wait... which may cause the very crisis itself.

Digging into the history of Sunrise uncovers a century-old mystery - a closely guarded secret which holds the key to the town's future.

Beckman and Lolita must embark on a mission to reconnect with family, rebuild a shattered friendship, and confront the most unexpected of adversaries to save the town they hold dear.

Nothing can be taken for granted – not even love.

The third book in the "Sunrise" trilogy is a humorous cozy mystery fuelled by coffee, break-ups, make-ups and a lot of sparkle.

Chris Towndrow

Chris Towndrow has been a writer since 1991, and Tow Away Zone was his most well-received book to date.

He began writing science fiction, inspired by Asimov, Iain M Banks, and numerous film and TV canons. After a brief spell creating screenplays across several genres, he branched out into playwriting and has had several productions professionally performed.

Tow Away Zone was originally conceived as a screenplay with a visual, black comedic, offbeat style, and this translated into a unique book that transcends genre.
Writing this "Sunrise" trilogy supercharged his passion for writing, and he is already looking to develop a new project in the arena of quirky black comedy.

In the meantime, he continues to write sci-fi adventures and is also broadening his repertoire of genres into historical fiction and contemporary drama.
Chris lives on the outskirts of London with his family and works as a video editor and producer.

Lightning Source UK Ltd.
Milton Keynes UK
UKHW021530031221
395027UK00009B/212